Reviews

"I am very pleased to learn that you have now published *The Emperor and the Spy*. I have learned a lot about Colonel Mashbir and his real friendship with Prince Iesato Tokugawa which was a pleasant surprise for me. Your stories about Japanese-American Military Intelligence Service have also done a great justice to so many unsung heroes."
— *Kazuo Kodama, former Japanese Ambassador to the United Nations*

"A fascinating story, a fine book."
— *Lisa Wolff, past Managing Editor of Simon & Shuster*

"The book is a page turner, one of those genuinely *'hard to put down'* novels fraught with a variety of colorful, interesting, and very informative stories weaving the protagonist's life with historical fact—a mixture of suspense, horror, humor, and romance. The historical content renders this work far more than just a fascinating read. Its life will likely be long and varied from best seller to movie or made-for-television drama to incorporation into academia and quite possibly private and government intelligence training. The cast of illustrious characters provides insight into the personalities of leaders, celebrities, even athletes who have significantly influenced our country's history and world affairs."
— *Teresa Brady*, whose father was a Purple Heart recipient in WW II

BARNES & NOBLE chose this novel to honor Veterans Day weekend with a book signing at their Oceanside, California Store.

"Just finished your book. Great read. Sidney Mashbir is a National hero."
— *Jim Desmond, Mayor of San Marcos, California*

SAN DIEGO UNION TRIBUNE feature article about the novel in their Metro and North County Editions, **by Pam Kragen**

SAN DIEGO JEWISH JOURNAL highlighted the novel with a two page review: "The Antiquarian and the Creative Writing," **by Editor-in-Chief Natalie Jacobs.**

"**Words are inadequate** to express my appreciation and awe. The importance of attempting to prevent war through personal relationships is rarely given recognition in literature. It can be every bit as exciting as glorified accounts of war and certainly a better approach."
—*Professor Claire Langham, active member of the* **East West Center,** *an organization supportive of good will between the Pacific region nations.*

The Carlsbad City Library highlighted The Emperor and the Spy, as their selection of the month, with a presentation and book signing.

JAVA (the Japanese-American Veterans Association), *an American organization, highlighted novel and website in their quarterly newsletter.*

"What a fantastic story! Individuals such as Mashbir are certainly rare, and I wish the world had more people like him."
—*Ryan Hart, San Diego High School History Teacher who lived in Japan*

"**A remarkable work of historical fiction.** I couldn't imagine why I hadn't learned about Mashbir in my history classes. Here is a virtually unknown man who valiantly tried to avert America's war with Japan. Complementing the novel is a 280-page archive of historical documents, presented on TheEmperorAndTheSpy.com website. I found myself enjoying these historical archives after reading the book. If you're a history buff, like real spy stories, or just want a great read, read this book."
—*George Eckel, Principal writer for Intuit Corp and a novelist*

"**My mother is a history expert. She taught history to high schoolers.** She read your book in a day over the weekend and is now rereading it. These are her comments:

It's a fun read, page turner;

Shows tremendous research and work; historical novels don't get better than this: intelligently written, informative, conversations enlightening, she learned a lot.

In sum, she says this is an outstanding book.

Congratulations!"

—*Dave Edick Jr., President of San Diego World Affairs Council organiza-tion* **and** *Head of the San Diego International Sister Cities Association*

"I finished reading the whole book. You did well. I enjoyed it. Too bad Colo-nel Mashbir did not get the final promotion, but I hope someone will work on the posthumous recognition. I thought your Epilogue was very appro-priate. Life is not fair, but America somehow catches up belatedly for the people who helped the country. My best wishes for your book's success."

—*Yoshi Minegishi, a founder and former-chairman of Seattle's Celebrate Asia organization. Also former executive board member of the Japan-America Society and the Seattle Symphony.*

"*The book is fast-paced yet thoroughly researched. I compare the depth and factual detail of Katz's writing with those of Wilbur Smith and Dick Francis. You'll ap-preciate the weaving of concurrent events, and the nuances only an expert in the field can convey. Like Frederick Forsyth's books, the international intrigue with imminent national security threats keep one in suspense. Katz's narrative subtly demonstrates the pivot points around which the arc of history may have been so very different. It's deliciously epic.*"

—*Rita Lim Wilby, former* **President** *of the* **Rotary chapter of La Jolla**

"The Emperor and the Spy uncovers a new important figure in American history from the turn of the century through the mid-20th Century."

—*Hilliard Harper, Commander, Retired U.S. Naval Reserve.*

THE

EMPEROR

AND THE SPY

by STAN S. KATZ

with consultation from American military historian
Charles Wyatt, ex-lieutenant, United States Navy

Horizon Productions
California
HORIZON PRODUCTIONS PUBLICATION
© Copyright Stan S. Katz, August 2015
Revised editions: January 2017; November 2019
All rights reserved.
Library of Congress Cataloging-in-Publication Data
Katz, Stan S.
The Emperor and the Spy / Stan S. Katz
Includes content on TheEmperorAndTheSpy.com website
ISBN 978-0-9903349-4-1
Printed in the United States of America
3 5 7 9 10 8 6 4 2 1
Cover design by Hsu + Associates

The Ballad of East and West

Oh, East is East, and West is West, and never the twain shall meet,

Till Earth and Sky stand presently at God's great Judgment Seat;

But there is neither East nor West, Border, nor Breed, nor Birth,

When two strong men stand face to face, though they come from

the ends of the earth!

— Rudyard Kipling

PREFACE

I was an antiquarian bookstore owner when the personal letters, secret official documents, photos, and library of an espionage agent, Colonel Sidney Forrester Mashbir, came into my possession. These materials were intriguing, but it wasn't initially clear how historically significant Mashbir's life had been. *Fourteen years later*, I stood over his tombstone at *Fort Rosecrans National Cemetery*, in San Diego, California, wishing to be in the proximity of this truly inspiring, heroic patriot, who I had studied and written about during those intervening years.

Born in 1891, Sidney grew up in *Tucson, Arizona*, where he became a *true son of the American Southwest*: surveying for the railroads, working in copper mines, bronco busting, and even doing stunt horseback riding for some of the earliest Cowboy and Indian silent movies. He came to know several of the last famous sheriffs of the *Wild West, and* developed an intimate relation with the Native American peoples of that region.

He joined the Arizona Guard at the tender age of thirteen as a bugle boy, during the time of the *U.S. Cavalry*; his long impressive military career would continue into the Atomic Age! This book reveals his exciting life and is largely based on historical research, combined with poetic novelistic license to add dramatic effect.

Several of Mashbir's early clandestine missions are presented, including chasing the bandito Pancho Villa, and later eliminating extensive enemy spy networks in the U.S., prior to, and during, World War I.

Destiny would then take him to Japan. His personal documents revealed Mashbir's unprecedented close relationship with Emperor Hirohito and other members of the Japanese Royal Family, *as well as with* other leaders of Japan. During the 1920s and 1930s, Mashbir formed a secret alliance with these Japanese in an attempt to preserve peace between their nations.

One of Mashbir's closest allies was *Prince Iyesato Tokugawa (aka Prince Tokugawa Iesato)*, who was *the heir* to the last ruling Shogun of Japan. When that 265 year old dynasty ended, Tokugawa instead took a powerful leadership role as President of Japan's Upper House of Congress for thirty years.

In his personal writings, Mashbir stated Prince Iyesato Tokugawa (1863–1940) was *"the true hidden power behind the Imperial Throne." Further research revealed that Prince Tokugawa held significant influence as mentor to the young Crown Prince Hirohito and this continued into his adult years as Emperor.*

Mashbir also stated that Prince Tokugawa was so politically influential in Japan, as well as internationally, that if he had just lived a few years longer, Japan would not have entered WWII against the Allies. I felt enthusiasm to share these new insights: Colonel Mashbir and his allies deserved to be recognized for courageously delaying and attempting to prevent war.

Regrettably, the rise of fascism and the European war would spread to Asia…When WWII pitted the U.S. and her Allies against Japan, Mashbir took a pivotal role in winning that conflict. He commanded a 4,600 member top-secret intelligence agency called ATIS (Allied Translator Interpreter Section), which is still little known about today. This organization made major contributions to the Allied victory in the Pacific, with some authorities saying they shortened the war by two years.

The Emperor and the Spy brings these characters and events to life, to be enjoyed by the general public. The book will hopefully also find its way into academic curriculum to inspire students, providing a fascinating new window to U.S.-Japan history, while fostering better intercultural understanding.

Prince Tokugawa often worked adeptly behind the political scenes during the first 40 years of the twentieth century. Among his many important accomplishments, was his guiding role as President of the Japanese Red Cross Society, in creating **Safe Zones** *in China. These demilitarized Safe Zones helped save the lives of a half million Chinese civilians, and tens of thousands of Jewish refugees fleeing the Holocaust in Europe during the years leading up to, and during, WWII.*

April 1937: the Imperial Hotel, Tokyo. *This photo was one of Sidney Mashbir's personal keepsakes. It was taken following a luncheon hosted by Prince Iyesato Tokugawa, honoring his friend and advisor, Mashbir's return visit to Japan. Prince Tokugawa is seated center with Mashbir to his left. They are accompanied by others of Prince Tokugawa's advisors. Mashbir was on a dangerous secret mission working with Prince Tokugawa in an attempt to maintain peace—Just three months after Prince Tokugawa's death in 1940, Japan signed the Tripartite Pact, a military alliance with the Axis Powers. The following year, with the attack on Pearl Harbor, war ignited between U.S. and Japan.*

Many readers of The Emperor and the Spy novel have expressed the desire to know more about Prince Iyesato Tokugawa and the period he lived. They also wanted further information about Colonel Mashbir's involvement with Japan. Based on those requests, a non-fictional sequel to the novel has been written, a biography titled: The Art of Peace.

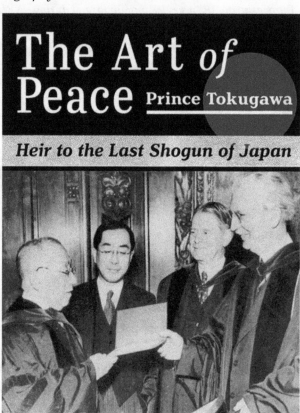

Description of the Book cover photograph:

1934: Los Angeles, California. Dr. Rufus Bernhard von Kleinsmid President of the University of Southern California (far right) and George Cochran, President of the Board of Trustees, are bestowing an **Honorary Doctor of Laws Degree** upon Prince Tokugawa, for his life-long pursuit of humanitarian and educational causes, while also encouraging respectful international relations. Iyesato's son, Iyemasa, is also present in the photo.

The Emperor and the Spy *is a saga of war and peace. This inscribed photo was* **gifted to Colonel Mashbir** *by General Douglas MacArthur. It gives a sense of the magnitude of Mashbir's contributions to winning WWII, and in re-establishing peace in its aftermath. Once the conflict ended, Mashbir used his influence to again bring together these two nations as strong Allies. He oversaw the Surrender Signing Ceremony and served as translator and liaison between General MacArthur and Emperor Hirohito during eleven secret meetings that shaped the rebuilding of Japan during the Occupation period, and far beyond. The inscription reads:*

To Mashbir
With admiration and cordial regard
from his old comrade-in-arms.
Douglas MacArthur
Tokyo – 1945

CONTENTS

PROLOGUE

In the still untamed *Arizona Territory* at the beginning of the 1900s, young Sidney Mashbir looked on excitedly as America celebrated its new role as a global power. He longed to be a soldier like Teddy Roosevelt and his Rough Riders Brigade in Cuba, or Admiral Dewey in the Philippines, who won the Spanish American War. Newspapers proudly detailed how their cruel Spanish rulers were now gone with America sending over teachers, doctors, and missionaries.

Sidney's father, Eleazer, was a professor of history and a devoted pacifist. Being a recent immigrant, he saw America as a God-sent sanctuary, where thousands like himself escaped with their lives from the violent, hatred-filled world of tyrannical Czarist Russia. He strongly supported America's message of freedom and democracy, and looked on with dismay as it moved toward an empire similar to those of Old World Europe. He explained to Sidney that things were heating up in the Orient. The Chinese were in a state of revolt, and America had been drawn into the Boxer Rebellion just so that England, France, and Germany could keep their opium concessions there. And Japan, though just coming out of the medieval ages in some ways, had rapidly become a powerful military nation that eyed Hawaii as being in her sphere of influence, only to see that independent kingdom annexed by the United States. He made it clear to Sidney that America's expansion might well bring on a confrontation with Asia, and that too much glory was given to wars, but not enough to patriots who find a way to avoid them—because once you're at war, you have to give every drop of blood in you to win it!

PART ONE

CHAPTER 1

Columbus, New Mexico March 9, 1916,

Stars burned brightly in the midnight sky, illuminating a bleak horizon stretching across miles of sand and cactus, as the small border town slept. Stampeding horses broke the silence, the sound of crushing hooves escalating until deafening, as five hundred of General Pancho Villa's revolutionaries stormed across the U.S. border. The townsfolk peered out their windows, horrified, witnessing the men with crazed eyes leading the attack, guns blazing. They were followed by a ragtag army clutching torches, transforming Columbus into a bonfire with flames starving for wood, devouring everything in reach; the air heavy with smoke and the smell of gun powder. Families huddled in their homes wondering if they'd be burned alive, others frantically ran, escaping into the desert, or sought refuge in the school house or the Hoover Hotel...The attack caught the town, as well as a detachment of U.S. Army soldiers from the 13th Calvary stationed on the outskirts, by surprise. Soldiers rushed to set up a machine gun in front of the hotel, and another on East Boundary Street, catching the attackers in a deadly crossfire. The raid lasted until dawn . . .

A broad-shouldered soldier walked amongst the aftermath of the carnage, his anger mounting as he viewed the bullet-ridden and charred bodies of Americans and Villistas strewn everywhere.

Central Chichuhua, Mexico, the following month

That same soldier entered the largest tent of the hastily assembled U.S. military installation. General John Pershing took his time sizing up the twenty-five-year-old standing at attention. Dust and sweat clung to the young soldier's well-worn uniform, and bespoke a hard ride. Pershing returned his salute without rising from his chair. "See that his mount is watered, Corporal, and leave the tent flap open," he ordered, hoping for a bit of breeze, though there was very little to be had but for the occasional dust devil that spun itself out too soon.

"So, it's *Mashbeer*, is it, Lieutenant?" The general fanned himself with the man's dossier, which had been taking up a corner of his makeshift table for the past week.

"Mash*bir*, Sir."

"Mashbir, yes. You look familiar."

"Sir, I believe that folder you're holding, if that's me, will refresh your memory."

Pershing laid the folder open and pretended to read what he had already memorized. *The man is confident,* he thought, *I'll give him that.* "You know the desert, do you?"

"Better than most. Grew up around here. I'm sure that's in my records."

"And what else is in here?"

"A couple of years back, I helped facilitate and escorted Pancho Villa to a meeting with you at Fort Bliss, Texas."

"Actually, we purged that from your records—No reason to have you connected. And at the time, I was amazed you didn't get yourself shot, Captain."

"Captain?"

"I'm afraid it's only temporary. We're pulling you out of the Arizona Guard and making you regular army. You'll need that rank so you can sit in on meetings—But don't offer advice, unless asked... How things have changed. Villa, folk hero of the Mexican revolution, was once held in such high regard in the States, banks in El Paso accepted the paper pesos he printed at face value."

Mashbir nodded.

"I know you speak Spanish," Pershing gestured to the dossier, "but it says you also speak some Russian? German? Jap? Even Apache? How'd that all come about?"

"My father emigrated from Russia and my mother's family is from Germany."

"And Apache?" Pershing's eyes widened. "You can really speak that too?"

"A fair amount—"

"I see," interrupted Pershing. "What about Japanese?"

"From our cook, Sir, but not that much."

Pershing spoke a sentence in Japanese. Mashbir responded in Japanese, and asked how Pershing knew the language.

"I was there in '05, as military attaché and neutral observer during the Russian-Japanese War…" *Spanish, Japanese, Apache, Russian, German — the man's got a gift,* thought Pershing. He closed the folder, satisfied there was no difference between the soldier who stood before him, and the one in the dossier. *Tough and smart,* he concluded. *Arrogant? Perhaps.*

"General, Sir—I can't believe you've recruited me just to sit in on meetings?" Mashbir scrutinized Pershing: in his fifties, gray-haired and distinguished with his pencil mustache, and a no-nonsense way about him.

"What do you really know about what took place in Columbus?" Pershing asked.

"I've read the papers. The place looks like a war zone."

"It certainly does . . . Thirsty? Oh, and you can stand at ease. In fact, take a seat." Pershing uncorked a decanter, blew dust out of two tin cups, and half-filled each with brandy. They downed their drinks.

Mashbir considered his words carefully. "Some speculate a Yankee arms dealer in that town failed to deliver a trainload of guns and munitions that Villa had paid for," he said, then paused.

"You think it might have been something else, Captain?"

"More likely, it's because we've been supporting his opponent, that crafty fox Carranza, and Villa wanted to get even."

"You're probably right," Pershing replied, running fingers through his slicked-back hair.

"And where do I come in, Sir?"

"I want you to once again locate Villa. But Mexico has become even more unstable these past years. You might not be as lucky as you were on your last mission."

Mashbir shrugged. "No problem, I'll be careful," he replied flippantly.

"You're pretty sure of yourself?"

"Well, General, you asked."

"All right, that's all for now. My aide will show you around." Mashbir stepped outside and encountered a tough-looking officer about his own age.

"George Patton," the captain said, thrusting out a hand.

Mashbir nodded to Patton, in his khaki uniform and broad-brimmed campaign hat. They tightly grasped and shook hands, sizing each other up. "I'm Sidney Mashbir."

The sound of something like a tornado drew Mashbir's attention. "What's that?"

"An aeroplane taking off," Patton shouted to be heard. "Something new. The Army's using them for reconnaissance."

"So, how're they working out?" Mashbir asked over the sound of the engine.

"Two crashed the first week. The rest have mainly been grounded needing repairs. What the hell do you expect with these damn whirling dust storms." They watched the plane head off into the distance, then they moved on through the uneven terrain toward Mashbir's quarters. Around them, thousands of soldiers had set up tents in any available spaces between the club-armed saguaro and the smaller hedgehog cacti, all under an intense sun. The smell of ham, beans, and the occasional treat, snake meat, cooking over kerosene stove fires, filled the air. Turkey vultures, pitch black except for their gray-edged wings and blood-red heads, glided effortlessly overhead with the thermal updrafts, waiting patiently for the desert to deliver its dead.

"So, Mashbir, I hear you're supposed to find Villa? We've been trying, but he and his men know the countryside cold and are traveling light. We're typical Army, taking everything, including the kitchen stove…Nice-looking rifle you got there. Had much chance to shoot?"

"Mostly bandits, or an occasional renegade who'd gone berserk."

"Don't know much about your Western tribes," Patton replied, "but I was at the 1912 Stockholm games where an Indian left us all behind. Son of a gun could run and jump. Name didn't sound Indian though—Jim Thorpe."

Mashbir looked him in the eye. "So you're that George Patton, the one he whupped at the Olympics. I read all about it."

"That's me," he said, holding out his suspenders. "Came in fifth in the pentathlon. Should of had the gold, but in the pistol competition you get five shots. When they pulled my target down, the middle was chewed up pretty good. Judges could only find four hits, all right in the bull's-eye. The numbskulls claimed I missed the target completely with the fifth."

"It obviously went through the center," Mashbir said.

Patton smiled, then playfully slugged Mashbir on the arm. "How about you and me getting in some shooting practice, when time permits? What do you say?"

✳ ✳ ✳ ✳

It's been ten days of scouting, and nothing to show for it. At least now I know where Villa's not, Mashbir thought, as he rode back into camp. *What's that crowd all about?* At first it didn't register. Three bullet-ridden, bloody Mexican corpses were strapped across the blistering-hot hoods of three Dodge Brothers Model 30 touring cars, tied down as trophies in the manner of deer hunters returning with their kill, with Patton strutting nearby. Other soldiers, war correspondents, and photographers gathered round, flashing photos. Coming closer, Mashbir heard Patton say, "We found one of Villa's camps. They tried to get away on horses, but we outdrove them, and bagged some of his top boys—I tell you, motorized transport is the way to go. Much as I like riding horses, their days in the army are numbered. Those banditos thought they were tough enchiladas, so that's not their blood flowing, it's *frijoles.*" The crowd gave hoots of laughter. Mashbir felt torn, wanting to put a couple more bullets into those bastards for what they'd done in Columbus, but remembering his father's words, *isn't life sacred?*

That evening at a card game, he stood on the sidelines, observing the players: Captain Patton, Colonel Jennings, two majors, and a lieutenant colonel.

Patton asked, "Hey, Mashbir, you play poker?"

"On occasion."

"Care to sit in? Six makes a better game than five."

"If these other gentlemen don't mind?"

Colonel Jennings shifted to open a space. Dragging up a chair, Sidney sat down. Before long the pot started to swell. The game was five-card draw. Jennings raised before the draw, and all but Mashbir and Patton folded. *I've got four hearts,* Mashbir thought, crossing his fingers as he was dealt his last card. Jennings also took one card and bet ten dollars more. Patton threw in his hand with disgust.

"I'll see your ten, and raise you thirty," Mashbir countered.

Jennings was startled, "Damn! It's not worth betting against your flush." He threw his cards out face up, revealing a jack high straight.

Mashbir tossed his cards toward the center of the table, and as if by accident, they flipped over showing four hearts and one diamond.

"Son of a bitch. That's a busted flush!"

"Why, so it is! I guess I didn't see it right."

The other players laughed, while Jennings gave Sidney a hard appraising stare.

The following day, there was chuckling coming out of the headquarters tent. "So, Jennings, is Mashbir as good as they say at poker?" Pershing asked. "I hear he really skinned you."

"He's one cracker-jack. You can never tell when he's bluffing or when he thinks he's got the winning hand. Then he goes for the throat. No halfway."

"It's a pity his luck hasn't extended to his mission. So far he's been unsuccessful in locating Villa." Pershing tapped his fingers on his desk.

"I'd definitely send him out again," Jennings replied. "General Funston swears by him. He's sent him on assorted special operations south of the border, including the destruction of a trainload of arms we didn't want getting into Mexico—Funston's only caution: Mashbir can be a little too independent." Jennings smiled. "When he was seventeen, just for the hell of it, he and his buddy joined up with the Bolivian Foreign Legion as mercenaries. Bolivia and Argentina were *supposedly* having a war. But when they couldn't find action there, they joined up with Mexican revolutionaries trying to overthrow the latest dictator. These men turned out to be bandits, who planned to sell Mashbir and his friend to the authorities for a reward. If they hadn't hightailed it out fast, they'd have faced a firing squad."

"Good survival skills and gutsy," Pershing replied with enthusiasm, "and clever enough to convince Villa, one of the most vicious men in Mexico, to come have a meeting with me."

"Just one thing, sir, Sidney Mashbir—what's that? Sounds Jewish?"

"Religion was left blank on his records." Pershing scratched his chin. "Maybe he doesn't want to be harassed by those officers who hate *Jew boys.*" He stared at Jennings. "And you sure as hell better not be one of them. Now, tell him I need to see him. . ."

Pershing held a newspaper, hoping he could stare Patton's grin off the front page. "Damn, look at this," he said, tossing it to Mashbir when he arrived. "That brash stunt with Villa's officers being treated like hunted animals has ignited national publicity. I've even acted pleased, saying it has enlivened our hunt for Villa. *But in reality,* this will only further enrage him, and he'll want to get even!"

His voice softened. "Captain, what I tell you now has to be kept top secret."

Mashbir nodded.

"In spite of all our troops being amassed here, this is actually a Stage show with us running around in what is supposedly sovereign Mexico, trying to capture or kill a man who claims to be the head of their government." Pershing kicked a chair over in frustration. "But for face-saving purposes I've been ordered to chase Villa for what he did, but President Wilson isn't anxious for me to launch into a full-scale battle."

"I understand, sir."

"As you well know, Wilson once encouraged me to get pretty chummy with Villa." Pershing shook his head in mirth. "We even supplied him with arms. Problem was, he couldn't get past the bloody revolutionary stage. Kept pissing off powerful people; couldn't bring the country together. Eventually, Wilson and our Mexican ambassador decided to support Carranza."

Pershing slapped his hands together hard. "But it goes beyond that. German militants know the U.S. will inevitably be coming to the aid of our European friends, in that war that's been going on these past two years. Zimmerman, their foreign minister, is trying to convince Mexico to join up with Germany and attack the U.S. If they agree, he's offered lots of weaponry and a chance for them to reclaim their so-called stolen territories: Arizona, New Mexico, California, and part of Texas. And guess what—Germany is also trying to entice Japan to come out against us."

"This is sounding worse by the minute, General."

Pershing massaged his aching neck. "We've more important priorities than fighting Mexico's legendary hero, Villa, and all the bad will that would engender. The only good thing about this mess is the training we've been getting. God knows, the army needs it! But the last thing we want is a war with Mexico, when all hell's breaking loose in Europe. *Captain, you've got to get face to face with Villa.* Explain I regret how disrespectfully his dead officers were treated. Tell him there will be no further military engagements against him if he stops interfering with our supply lines and promises not to kidnap or attack our civilians."

Pershing handed Mashbir a bottle. "Here's some tequila. Give this as gift from me, and these candies." He smiled. "They're his favorites."

CHAPTER 2

Attending cockfights in Mexico, where roosters with razors attached to their feet tore at each other's throats and eyes, Mashbir circulated among the gritty, uproarious crowd of onlookers, listening in to conversations about Villa and buying drinks for the talkative at small-town cantinas had finally paid off. From a hilltop, Mashbir peered through binoculars. *There they are, about half a mile away*, he reckoned. *I'll wait an hour past sunrise so as not to surprise them . . .*

Waving a white scarf, he cantered toward the encampment. Several men galloped toward him, surrounding him, shooting rifles into the air and yelling in Spanish.

"I have an important message for Generale Villa," Mashbir said in Spanish, while reining back his bucking horse in all the excitement. "I mean no harm, gentlemen. Don't waste your ammunition."

"Just shoot the gringo!" one shouted.

"What's the rush?" another responded. "Search him and his saddlebags. Take everything. Then tie his wrists and put him back on his horse."

They returned to their military camp, where Mashbir was dragged into a tent, where several officers sat in the shadows.

Two señoritas hovered over him, one trimming and filing his fingernails, the other snipping at his pitch-black curly hair as he ran his free hand up her skirt.

"Stop that, Pancho," the young woman protested. "How can I concentrate? I might cut you."

Villa laughed, "It would be worth it," pulling her close. He heard one of his men cough, and turned towards Mashbir. "Who is this? And *why* are you bothering me?"

"He was spying on our camp, Jefe. Claims to have a message for you. He speaks Spanish."

Villa pushed the *señoritas* away. Coming face to face with Mashbir, he spat out, "What are you doing here!"

"I've an important personal letter from General Pershing, and some gifts."

"Oh, do you?"

"Yes, Generale, they are amongst the things your men took from me. And, I wasn't spying. I came holding a flag of truce when your *brave men* captured me. Be so kind as to look through my possessions. Everything will be clear."

Without taking his eyes off his prisoner, Villa snapped his fingers and held out his hand. One of his men delivered a canvas bag containing the letter, Pershing's gifts, a gold pocket watch, and a stack of U.S. currency...Villa read the letter, then carelessly tossed it aside. "This merely says that you are Pershing's representative, nothing more." Villa grabbed a machete and brought it near Mashbir's face. "I think it only appropriate to send you back to Pershing, slaughtered and slung over a horse, like he did to my officers. What do you say to that?"

Mashbir calmly replied, "For political reasons, the general can't put down on paper his true remorse for the way your men were treated. If he could, Pershing would be drinking that tequila with you right now and apologizing." He smiled. "Do whatever you wish with me, but I don't think such petty revenge is worthy of a great leader of the Revolution, a man whom I personally heard speak of statesmanship and leading his people toward a better future."

"Oh, you quote my words back to me. You're lying! Just when and where did you hear me say those things?"

"I never lie. You don't remember me, but a couple of years back I helped arrange a meeting between you and General Pershing and served as your escort, sort of like a bodyguard. I was impressed with you as a leader then. I'm not so sure now."

Villa dropped his machete and erupted into laughter. "Well, *señor*, you certainly have *cojones*! I remember now. Perhaps *then*, we were all a little more full of ideals." He turned to one of his men. "Cut his hands free." Villa pulled the cork out of the tequila bottle with his darkened teeth and poured two glasses, which he and Mashbir downed.

"Now, I'd like to hear this proposal you carry from my former friend—Who betrayed me, and now sleeps with Carranza, that prostitute of the wealthy landowners."

Sidney exhaled, now aware that he'd been holding his breath. "First off, General Pershing knows the Mexican people must decide for themselves who their rulers are. I'm to tell you confidentially that the situation in Europe is such that American forces will not be in Mexico much longer. Meanwhile, Pershing is being pressured to retaliate against you for what happened in New Mexico—but that is not his priority."

"So he wishes to play *charade*, him pretending to hunt me, and me pretending to hide? But I hide from no one," he shouted.

"I wouldn't put it quite like that. If, for instance, you rashly attacked, he would be obliged to respond. If you don't make that first move, he'll never find you." Mashbir grinned. "And to sweeten the deal and help your Revolution, Pershing knows of an American picture company that wants to film you and your army: a *fine opportunity for millions to see you*, Generale, with your inspirational words printed on the silver screen."

"Is that really so, Gringo?"

"Absolutely. And just like you, Generale, Pershing is a man of his word."

"What do you think, Tomás?" Villa called out.

What's another gringo doing here? Mashbir thought, as a tall young man stepped from the shadows.

"Generale, I'd cooperate as long as Pershing does his part."

"All right. Go back to my old amigo and tell him. I'll keep up my end of the bargain, and he must be most careful to do the same— Besides, having Federales chasing me is enough—I don't need the Americans."

Mashbir hesitated, "And my possessions," he asked, "Particularly that gold pocket watch—It's a gift from my father."

"We're not the thieves your newspapers make us out to be." Villa handed it over. He then picked up the stack of U.S. currency, looking straight at Mashbir with a cold gleam in his eye.

"Consider that a small measure of reparation from the U.S. Army for the unfortunate deaths of your officers."

"Very well," Villa warmly replied. "And I'll keep your flag of truce as a reminder of my trip with you to Texas. I'm superstitious." Villa ate a couple of Pershing's candies and smiled. "I have the strong feeling that today's meeting was fated. My cowboy will escort you out." Tomás led Mashbir to where the horses were tethered and together they rode away from the camp.

"Thanks for your help back there, Tomás. None of my business, but what's an American doing down here?"

"Actually, my name's Tom Mix. I joined up for the excitement, though I'm starting to think this revolution business is about played out. Might be heading back to the States, if I could figure out some way to make a decent living, other than pushing cattle, that is."

Mashbir thought a moment. "A few years back, some movie folks hired me to do stunt riding in their Westerns—falling off horses and pretending I'd been shot during chases. Kinda fun. If I were you, Tomás—I mean *Tom*, I'd talk to those movie guys when they come down to film Villa's troops. Wouldn't be surprised if you hook on to something."

Once they parted, Mashbir dismounted. *That could've been a nasty end for yours truly*, he thought, as he pissed on a cactus. *Lucky thing Villa is superstitious. Pity, though, having to donate all those poker winnings. Easy come, easy go—that's what comes of gambling.*

CHAPTER 3

Hadn't six months passed without incident along the U.S.–Mexican border, So why does Pershing so urgently need to see me, Mashbir wondered... Turning from a map he'd been examining in his tent, the general inquired, "Captain, have you ever been to the west coast of Mexico, along the Gulf of California?"

"Not yet. Why do you ask, sir?"

"We've gotten reports that a large unit of foreign soldiers has landed there and are headed inland, about two hundred miles south of Nogales." He pointed to the map. "We're not sure of the exact number or what supplies and weaponry they have. We've sent two scouts. One found nothing, the other never returned." Pershing wiped sweat from his brow. "It's very important we learn what's going on. Problem is, Mexico has become more unstable than ever, with Americans even less welcome in their internal political affairs. You'll have to go as a civilian, find out what's going on, and report back quickly."

"I'll need a cover story, perhaps as a mining engineer? Those courses I took at the *University of Arizona* will come in handy," Mashbir smiled.

"I'll have the documents prepared. Leave your real papers with me. *And before you go,* I never asked the details of how you came to speak Apache?"

Mashbir sighed, "One of my military posts was adjacent to a reservation. Braves would occasionally get drunk and go crazy, shooting up nearby towns. I was assigned to track them down. It occurred to me, I didn't know much about them or their culture. Turns out, their anger stemmed from them feeling like prisoners, even though the wars were over. I did some research, and listed five hundred of their words phonetically, and distributed this small dictionary to the officers and guards staffing the reservation. Before long, it led to better

communications with the tribal leaders, which helped resolve griev-
ances—Things calmed down, and later on, a couple of these Apaches
served as scouts on some of my missions."

Pershing looked Mashbir over. "Before you were born, back in
the 1880s, I was one of those young soldiers rounding up that tribe.
Also put down one of the last Sioux uprisings in South Dakota." He
paused. "They were killing us, and we were killing them. A cruel
time I'm not proud of." He gazed off. "There was one bright spot in
Montana though, when I captured a group of *Creek* renegades who
wanted to live in open spaces. I relocated them to the wilds of Canada, instead of confining them to a reservation." Pershing's voiced
wavered. "You believe in the spirit world, Mashbir?"

"Can't rightly say, General." Mashbir scratched his head. "Probably something comes next. It's all a mystery to me." He noted Pershing's hand tremor.

"I have the occasional nightmare," Pershing blurted, "about dead
Indians—Men, women and children staring at me." He took a deep
swallow of air. "Wasn't that clever of you coming up with that Apache
dictionary."

"Thank you, sir."

Pershing's body became rigid. "One last thing. If you get into
trouble, for diplomatic reasons we'll deny having sent you. For that
reason, I'm not ordering you to go."

"I understand the risk, sir. I've no family to worry about—I can
leave at sundown."

Pershing's face drained of color.

"You all right, General?"

"Excuse me." He looked downward, his voice choked up. "Your
remark hit me hard. I lost my wife and three young daughters in a
house fire last year. Only my six-year-old son survived."

"I'm so sorry, I didn't..."

"No apologies needed, you're the one putting your life on the line."

✳ ✳ ✳ ✳

From a ridgeline, Mashbir watched, keeping the inclined sun
behind him, to avoid any reflection off his binocular lenses. He wiped

perspiration from his eyes, as he lay on a sizzling rock in the Sonoran Desert. In the canyon below, a column of men moved northward. Mounted riders led the procession, which marched in double file. They wore typical Mexican peasant garb: pajama-like bottoms, white loose tops, and sombreros. *Who were they?* He sensed the majority weren't Mexicans. At the rear were riders leading two teams of mules, each pulling a light field artillery piece. Behind them were four closed wagons, also pulled by mules, probably for supplies. He waited until the tail of the column passed around a bend and was lost to sight, leaving a cloud of rust-colored dust hanging in the still air.

Come on, come on, damnit! he thought, *I know you're back there, and I'm frying like a trout in a pan.* Finally the lone rider appeared, the rear guard that he'd been expecting. Mashbir watched the man closely surveying either side of the trail as he passed up the canyon and around the bend. With a happy sigh, Mashbir got up and climbed over the rim of the canyon to the other slope, where his burro was tethered.

Over the next couple of days he trailed their movements like a coyote, striding through barren hills and parched riverbeds, avoiding the occasional rattlesnake and taking the minimal rests required to keep going…At night, they would set up camp with sentries posted… And like clockwork, they'd set off promptly at daybreak, resuming their march at a rapid clip.

The following evening under a sliver of moon, keeping low, he approached the encampment, where lots of men, wagons, horses, tents, and assorted pieces of weaponry and gear were scattered about. As he neared, he recognized Japanese being spoken…*Well it appears those rumors Pershing mentioned about the Japan allying with Germans against us might be true.* He observed the men, some eating, others rubbing their aching feet after their long march, a few staring into the blazing campfire. A line waited to fill canteens from wooden barrels. He noted a few Mexican soldiers keeping to themselves, while in one area a couple mixed with the Japanese in playful camaraderie. Mashbir smiled, seeing the Mexicans display photo cards to the Japanese of scantily dressed saloon girls: *the universal language.*

They were mainly teenagers, he realized, not combat-trained soldiers. The officers were a different story, watching their troops with no-nonsense demeanors, allowing them a chance to vent after a challenging day.

But things were different at the far end of the encampment. Several Japanese held heavy rocks to their bare chests, as a sergeant with short-cropped hair and a small goatee spit on them and shouted, "You lazy, worthless scum. You march like slugs, not men. Have you not studied the code of Bushido?" He prodded them with a whip handle and lashed their bare shoulders and backs as they struggled to hold their rocks. One dropped his, then fell to his knees, wailing in pain. On attempting to get back to his feet, he was kicked down and taunted.

"Please," he begged, "I will do better tomorrow!"

The officer smirked, raising the whip handle, preparing to slam it against the man's head. The others froze in fear, except one, who dropped his rock and placed himself between the fallen man and the officer. "Honorable Sergeant Asimmo," he pleaded, "please don't beat him—we're doing our best."

"How dare you speak, Private Naoki!" Asimmo slammed him across the face and repeatedly kicked him until he went limp.

A real sweetheart, Mashbir thought as he crept away, keeping a tight eye on the closest guard, a dark figure outlined by the dim radiance of the campfires. He edged toward the most prominent tent, illuminated from within by a kerosene lantern. At five yards away, he could make out two figures inside. One had a short, slim silhouette and was pacing; the other, even while seated, gave the impression of a much larger man. The smaller one was doing most of the talking, and in Spanish.

"This current pace is too slow, Generale Ortega. We must be at the border within five days to reach the hills behind Tucson."

"That's not our agreement, Colonel Ennokee. It's impossible for your troops to travel that distance in less than ten. Perhaps eight days at the very least. The rugged canyons we came through are just a taste of what's ahead. However, it might just be possible, if we left the supply wagons and artillery behind."

"So be it, as long as we arrive by sunset—five days from now."

"That pace means more danger for my men, and some of their horses won't make it, requiring additional funds."

"You've already been well paid for your services."

"I must have eight hundred dollars more—it is only fair."

Mashbir watched Ennokee's shadow reach into what appeared to be a small trunk under his cot. "Here's five hundred in gold. Don't insist on any more, or you'll regret it."

"As you wish, Señor," Ortega replied, and left the tent, moving toward the outer encampment where several Mexican scouts were quartered. Mashbir followed in the darkness. "Manuel," Ortega called.

"I'm here, Generale."

"I've just left that stinking pig, Ennokee." Ortega stamped his boot. "The lunatic thinks he owns us, demanding a rapid march to the border- and the cheap son of a bitch only offers five hundred dollars for the added danger." He spit a tobacco-stained wad and considered.

"Generale, why are you now smiling?" Manuel asked.

"They'll be leaving artillery and wagons with only a small squad to watch over them. You're to leave tonight. If questioned, pretend you're reviewing tomorrow's march route. Find Jorge, and tell him to gather two dozen men, strong riders and handy with pistols. Tomorrow after midnight, return. Strike hard and swiftly; seize the supplies, especially the weapons. Leave no one alive. When these cursed foreigners return to their camp, all I want them to find is shattered remains and their dead soldiers. You understand?"

"Most certainly."

"Here, take some gold for expenses...You are to take everything back to our hideout. I'll leave these fools at the border, and then join you there. Do not fail me."

Hearing the dissension between the Mexican and the Japanese, Mashbir thought, *things are looking up.* He began sneaking back toward the illuminated tent, hoping to pick up a souvenir document from Ennokee's tent, just as the colonel stepped out. "Asimmo, come here," he heard him shout.

"Yes, sir," Asimmo replied, running and coming to attention.

"Issue ten days' food rations to each man, to be carried in their packs. All extra guns, wagons, mules, and other supplies will be left here, under the guard of eight men and a sergeant. One last thing,"

Ennokee poked Asimmo in the chest. "You must stop beating the troops to the point they are useless."

"I was only trying to instill discipline, sir. The beaten one can stay back with the camp guards."

Ennokee nodded and re-entered his tent, as Asimmo strode back to the main part of the camp.

So they're planning a mock raid across our barely patrolled border, Sidney realized. He slithered backward, but as he was about to rise, a sentry appeared. He flattened down, holding his breath. The sentry continued through darkness, stepping directly onto Mashbir's arm, losing his footing, falling, and finding himself face to face with an intruder. He let out a yell—Mashbir leaped up and began to run. On his third step he landed in a chuckhole, his ankle giving out on him. He tried to get up, but two sentries loomed over him, rifles pointed, and shouting in Japanese. They took his pistol, then marched him limping to Colonel Ennokee, who was waiting outside his tent. "What are you doing here?" Ennokee shouted in Spanish.

"I'm sorry, I don't understand," Mashbir replied.

"So you're an American," he paused, "I don't like Americans. Explain why you're sneaking around our encampment," he demanded in precise English.

"My name is Sam Miller. I work for Anaconda Mining Company. I'm surveying this region for minerals."

"Oh really…" Ennokee bombarded him with questions, hoping to see if he'd slip up, without success.

"Take him into my tent," he ordered his sentries. Once there, Ennokee smiled. "Do you have documents to prove you are who you claim to be?"

As Mashbir reached for a leather pouch hanging on his belt, the sentries on either side pinned his arms. Ennokee barked a command. The soldiers let him free and fell back a half step. Mashbir unsnapped the pouch and handed it to Ennokee, who slowly examined its contents. "Your papers are very vague."

"That's the idea, sir. I'm supposed to prospect wherever I think there might be profitable mining possibilities."

"That doesn't explain your presence in our camp, spying."

Here goes nothing, Mashbir thought. *If I can't bluff my way out of this, someone will be finding my bones out here someday.*

"Truth is, sir, I'm a complete idiot. I saw you setting up camp late this afternoon. What were Asians doing in Mexico? It sparked my curiosity. I meant you no harm, I swear it." His posture now gave the impression of outright fear, and his voice was high- pitched and strained as he said, "My company asked me to assess risks, and report on anything unusual."

"Are you alone? Where is your camp?"

"Just me and my burro, which I left about a mile north of here."

"Very well, Sergeant Asimmo and two others will escort you back. I'm doing you a great favor. You'll forget this entire night and no trace of it should ever appear in any report. Have I made myself clear?"

"One hundred percent. Thank you, sir."

Ennokee returned Mashbir's possessions, then spoke in Japanese, "Guards, take our curious visitor outside and stay with him. Sergeant Asimmo will be with you shortly."

Looking Sergeant Asimmo in the eye, Ennokee said, "Get Sergeant Hayato and another soldier, then take this man towards where he *says* his burro is. When you are far enough away from here, kill him. It must appear to be an accident. No guns or knives, perhaps a fall?"

Mashbir limped ahead as the four of them moved across the plateau. "Look, there's a cliff ahead," Hayato said in Japanese, "a perfect place to get rid of him."

This is where it gets sticky, Mashbir thought, his stomach tightening. *Damn good thing these boys don't realize I understand some of their lingo.*

"Here," Asimmo whispered, "in a few more yards."

As the first man rushed, Mashbir crouched low, his assailant tripping over him, plummeting off the side of the cliff. Mashbir tried to run, but his ankle gave way. The other two were on him in an instant, near the edge, pounding and choking him. Mashbir gouged at an eye and lashed out a kick, throwing one back.

As he came to his feet, his head exploded in pain, and felt himself hurtling forward—His attackers heard pebbles and stones dislodged as Mashbir's body rattled down to the canyon floor, and then silence.

"A tough bastard," Asimmo said, dropping a bloodstained rock.

"Almost too tough," Hayato said, rubbing a wounded eye. "Can you see him?"

He peered down the steep incline. "I think so, he's all crumpled up. And look what he left behind." Asimmo picked up the leather pouch and rummaged through it, pulling out a gold watch. He put it into his pocket, then threw the pouch over the cliff edge.

✷ ✷ ✷ ✷

Where am I, Mashbir wondered, opening one eye. He looked beneath himself to see that a saguaro cactus had broken his fall, its spines embedded into his hide. *"Damn it!" I've re-fractured the arm I'd broken taming a stallion a couple of years back. Probably cracked some ribs as well.* His vision began to clear. Glancing to the canyon floor he saw one of his attackers, his brains splattered on a rock.

The incline didn't look too bad, if only he could pull himself free in spite of the quills puncturing his hands. *Lucky to be alive,* he thought. Focusing away from the pain, he untangled himself and slid down to the canyon floor, where he lay staring up at the cliff above. The midday sun was hotter than hell. He forced a painful laugh, while betting on the odds of finding water or his burro, before he roasted. There was a shaded spot in the far distance, but elevated.

Over the next hour he pushed forward, his ribs and ankle painfully throbbing, and covered only a mile. Clawing his way up the last ledge of crumbling rock and loose stones, he pitched himself forward onto the opposite downslope, where he lay a few minutes, eyes closed, with no shelter from the sun. "What's that?" He sniffed. "Water!" He crawled to a small depression in the rocks, which contained the remnants of runoff from the last rain. He brushed aside the scummy surface and submerged his face, sucking in gulps, then began scooping with his one good arm, splashing water over himself, again and again. He moved onward to a rocky outcropping which offered blessed shade, where he slept for hours. When the frigid night arrived, he curled up, trying to avoid freezing . . .

Early the next day, he stretched his aching body to loosen up, and drank as much water as he could before the sun got high. He moved on, limping and crawling for hours, his stomach queasy, and the blisters on his hands burning. *"Push on or die,"* he kept repeating, his legs getting heavier. *Could that be a mirage in the distance,* he wondered, then lost consciousness.

Upon awakening, he was relieved to find himself on a military cot in the shade of a ragged, makeshift tent. *What's this?* He touched bandages wrapped around his head, and noted that his other wounds had been cleaned and dressed. Unsteadily, he got to his feet and looked outside; there lay the wreckage of tents and buzzards tearing at rotting bodies. Mashbir heard movement behind a mesquite bush. "Show yourself," he shouted. He tried again in Japanese. "I'm not going hurt you. I want to thank you for helping me."

A young soldier appeared, shaking.

"What happened here?"

"I, and eight other soldiers were left to guard our encampment. Late last night, just as I had gone into the surrounding brush to relieve myself, a group of Mexican bandits rode into camp, totally surprising us and firing into the tents. Whether dead or wounded, every one of my comrades was shot in the head." His hands veiled his face. "I'm a coward. I saw it all from my hiding place, but did nothing—I'm dishonored and deserve to die."

"Hold on there," Mashbir replied. "A more honorable path would be for you to help me to punish the vermin who did this." The soldier nodded in agreement.

Mashbir looked about. "It doesn't appear they left much."

"All our mules, wagons, and artillery pieces were taken. Almost everything, except for some water jugs they didn't see, and a little food and supplies."

"I've got a burro somewhere around here," Mashbir said. "He's hobbled, you know, rope looped around his two front legs. He couldn't have gone too far."

"I will look for him."

Not too long after, Mashbir sighed with relief at seeing the young soldier return, leading his burro. "Good work. What's your name?"

"Naoki."

"I'm Captain Mashbir. Thanks again for helping me. There's one more thing we need to do before we leave this cursed place. We've got to bury your comrades and pile rocks over their grave. I can't help much, but it *must* be done. I counted eight bodies. Correct?"

"Yes, that is all of them."

Mashbir took a small shovel from his burro's saddlebag. "Here, Naoki, use this." As Naoki labored, Mashbir took a sheet of paper from the burro's pouch, and wrote in big block letters in Spanish:

> *"Let this be a Warning: Here lie nine worthless foreigners who thought to do as they pleased in my country. They paid the price all outsiders will pay when they interfere with the struggle of the Mexican People! By order of Generalissimo Francisco Villa, signed by General Ortega, District Commandante."*

Mashbir sat and watched as Naoki dug a wide trench in the sandy soil, then dragged his comrades into it. Once the grave was covered with dirt and stones heaped on top, Mashbir fixed his fake proclamation onto a pointed stick, and firmly rammed it into the earth at the foot of the mound. *That ought to give Colonel Ennokee something to think about when they return, Mashbir thought.*

"Naoki, I wrote *nine* bodies, so your commander thinks you were also killed...Now please help me mount my burro, my ankle is twisted and I can't walk. You'll have to hike alongside."

As darkness descended the following day, a feverish Mashbir clung to his burro's mane, trying to remain conscious — Suddenly, a challenge rang out. "Halt! Advance, and give the password."

"Don't know today's password," he replied, barely getting out the words. "I'm Captain Mashbir. It's vital I see General Pershing at once. I have a prisoner with me, and I'm hurt." He prodded the burro forward a few yards as armed sentries emerged from the undergrowth on either side. Mashbir strained to stop coughing. "Take charge of this Japanese soldier. He's unarmed, and won't give you any trouble. We haven't had much to eat." He turned to Naoki and spoke in Japanese. "They'll give you some food and something to drink. We'll talk later."

One guard escorted Naoki, while the others led Mashbir, mounted on his burro, toward the headquarters tent. The sentry posted outside came to attention.

"I'm reporting to General Pershing directly." Mashbir slid off the burro, and would have fallen over if not for the sentries' support.

"Is that you, Mashbir?" Pershing quickly stepped out. "Good God! How badly are you hurt?"

"I'll be all right, General. I need to tell you right away what I found out." Two soldiers half-carried him into the tent and laid him down on a cot.

Over the next few minutes, Pershing listened intently. "So they mean to cross the border?"

"I don't think it's an attack, more like an exercise to see how well-defended our border is, and if they could cross undetected if they wanted to."

"We'd better not let that happen. We don't want some ranchers getting killed shooting it out with the Japanese Army." Pershing went to the tent opening and called, "Patton, come in here."

"Yes, Sir." Patton came running.

"Is that blasted telegraph working?"

"It was this afternoon, sir."

"Get off a telegram to Major Bright in Tucson. He's to mobilize the Arizona Guard. He's also to get as many of his own troops as he can down to our side of the border as soon as possible! They are not to fire across the border, but he is to make sure his forces are highly visible. Have him wire me back when they're in position. And I want copies sent to General Funston in San Antonio, also to Washington, D.C. — Make this an Immediate Priority!"

Patton snapped a salute and left at a fast trot.

Another officer entered the tent. "General, you sent for me?"

"Yes, Doc." Pershing turned toward Mashbir. "Looks like the patient has passed out. Check him over—there's an obvious head injury, and who knows what else. I want him well taken care of."

※ ※ ※ ※

Near Nogales, Mexico, overlooking the U.S. Border

Ennokee stared angrily at the distant ridgeline. "Captain Musimo, come here," he shouted.

"Yes, sir."

"Look! There's a line of horsemen patrolling the border." He handed him binoculars.

"I see a large force, and machine guns being offloaded from wagons," the captain replied.

"How can this be?" Ennokee's face was ablaze. "We were led to expect a relatively unguarded border. Someone alerted them. Bring Ortega here at once."

"What's the meaning of this, Ennokee," Ortega sputtered, as he was pushed forward by Musimo and two Japanese sergeants. "I have fulfilled my obligation!"

"Oh, you think so? You've led me to a well-guarded border which I cannot cross without a fight, and as you well know, my orders forbid me to do so."

"I can't help what those crazy Americans do. This must be some sort of exercise that has nothing to do with you."

"That is very difficult to believe, Generale. Someone must have sold them the information."

Ortega's eyes flickered between the four men facing him.

"We found him preparing to leave, sir," Musimo said in Japanese. "He came with us only by threat of force."

"Where are the other Mexicans?" Ennokee asked Musimo.

"Detained under guard. But Manuel is missing."

Ennokee's eyes narrowed as he looked at Ortega. "Your number-one man vanished during the night, and somehow the Americans have been warned." Ennokee spread his arms wide. "What do you make of this coincidence?"

Sweat soaked Ortega's shirt as he noted Ennokee and his men's malevolent expressions.

"This is all so unexpected," he replied, straining to maintain his composure, while inconspicuously slipping his hand under his coat. He withdrew a pistol and began firing, just as Captain Musimo leaped in front of Ennokee. Sergeant Asimmo raised his rifle, putting two bullets into Ortega's head and neck. The Mexican toppled backward.

"How is Musimo?" Ennokee asked, drawing near.

Asimmo knelt down. "He's dead, sir."

"I'm cursed," Ennokee declared, pounding his chest. "My mission is ruined. We must go back to collect our wagons and artillery, then return to the coast, and depart in failure—I only wish I had had the opportunity to personally torture Ortega at length."

General Pershing's encampment

Pershing and the doctor conferred as they made their way through the medical infirmary, jammed with cots lining both sides of the long tent, the pungent smell of disinfectant filling the air. "It's makeshift, General," the doctor lamented, "barely adequate for all the men suffering from dehydration and heat exhaustion. But we're doing our best."

"I can see that, Doc." They came to a closed corner of the infirmary, blocked off by screens. "So, how's he doing?" Pershing asked.

"He has a concussion and several fractures—What's strange is that a terrible throat infection has kicked in. He's coughing blood, burning with fever and delirious. We put him on a sulfa regimen and lightly sedated him…I have to make my rounds, sir. I'll be back in a little while."

Pershing entered and pulled a chair close to where Mashbir lay semiconscious. The general spoke softly. "You did real well, son, but the water hole you described that saved your life wasn't all it was cracked up to be, probably contaminated. I'm impressed you managed to get back. Got a wire from Major Bright—sure enough, something was stirring in the hills over by Nogales, but nobody tried to cross. Gunshots were heard. After they'd gone, the major sent civilian scouts over who found three bodies, Mexicans. Probably what's left of General Ortega and his boys," he said with a smirk. "That colonel had another surprise waiting for him, that so-called proclamation of yours," he grinned. "That'll slow down the love connection between the Japanese and those Mexican yahoos."

Pershing used a damp cloth to wipe the sweat off Mashbir's face. Mashbir's eyes partially opened.

"So you're coming to?" Pershing sighed with relief.

"I'm all right, sir," he replied in a weak, raspy voice.

"You know, Sidney, I never asked—your records say you joined the military when you were just a kid. Is that right?"

"Always wanted to be a soldier, ever since I made friends with a lieutenant who took me hunting and tracking. But my father hated anything having to do with guns, wanted me to be lawyer, like him."

"I was once an attorney," Pershing replied. "So how'd it work out with your father?"

"At thirteen, I ran away and joined up with the Arizona Guard. They called me a bugle boy, but because of my language skills I did translations of foreign letters and official documents." His voice faded. "My father never wanted to see me again," he paused. "And over the years my occupation has created enemies, so I distanced myself from my family for their safety, to prevent others who might try to get even with me by hurting them."

Pershing fumbled for words. "Oh, I see," he said, then forced a smile. "Well, if you'd followed in your father's footsteps, and if I'd stayed at that profession, we'd both be settled in some cushy law office now, instead of this blasted desert."

"That's not the life for me." Mashbir coughed blood into a rag. "General, I'd sure like to continue serving with you, when the U.S. gets involved in Europe."

"Slow down, son, first you need time to heal. You know, they call it *The War to End all Wars*? The Brits, the French, and their Allies—Against the Germans, each seeing who can stomach the most casualties." Pershing shook his head in frustration. "I've been given tours of the battlefronts to demonstrate just how desperately the Allies need our support. They even threw gala events, wining and dining me, all the while asking, sometimes practically begging to know *when* our men would be coming over; urging me to convince our politicians to enter the fray—It's a fight for their survival, and they're counting on us to tip the balance."

Mashbir remembered Mr. Henry Ford and his Peace Voyage to Europe, taking along 170 prominent leaders, all demanding that the U.S. not enter the war—He even tried to convince President Wilson that the sinking of the Lusitania was a setup job, not done by the Germans, when the Germans themselves admitted to having done it.

"I'd be proud to go with you, sir."

"I appreciate your offer." Pershing patted Mashbir's arm. "The Huns have had a long time to infiltrate our country. A few enemies working from the inside can do more harm than a division on the battlefield." Pershing looked Mashbir in the eye, "Your language and analysis skills will be more useful heading up an intelligence organization on our East coast, rooting out traitors on the home-front, than by you slogging through mud in France—*So you better get well, Sidney.* We're both going to be very busy. If rumors are correct, I'm likely to be the commander-in-chief of all Expeditionary Forces sent over there."

CHAPTER 4

A brief visit to Japan, ten years earlier:
The Imperial Palace, Tokyo, 1906

The five-year-old felt uncomfortable in his bulky ceremonial robes as he stared longingly out the palace window at the lush gardens below. There, children were playfully chasing one other. "Please turn around, Prince Hirohito," the court attendant pleaded as he placed a gilt-embroidered cap upon the boy's head. "Remember, Your Majesty, sit and stand straight upright—eyes forward with dignity, showing no emotion when approached by visiting dignitaries." The attendant looked about. "Now, where is that imperial staff?"

Hirohito's gaze again veered out the window. The attendant responded by closing the shutters, then placed a carved ivory staff into the boy's hand.

"I must relieve myself," Hirohito said urgently, taking off his cap and putting down the staff. Once in the outside corridor, a mischievous smile appeared. That smile vanished when he heard his father, the soon-to-be emperor, call out, "Come here, Hirohito."

Taisho, dressed in military uniform, was staring at a portrait on the wall. "Son, *why* is that painting laughing at me?"

"I do not know, Father."

Taisho walked away without a further word.

The boy shook his head in confusion, then ran to his quarters. Quickly, he changed into a pullover top and pants and was soon outside with the other boys. Picking up a smooth stone that was near the pond, he shouted, "Let's see who can throw the farthest!" They all began hurling stones over the adjacent wall.

"Now, let's see who can hit the highest windows in the palace." Hirohito dared. The boys looked to one another, but none dared do so.

"Am I not your crown prince? You must do whatever I demand!" And so the barrage began.

The office above was that of Prince Iyesato Tokugawa, the Grand Chamberlain of the Palace, who was also President of *Japan's Upper House of Congress, the House of Peers.* Tokugawa and his teenage nephew, Prince Konoe, were startled by shattering glass. They went to the broken window overlooking the gardens to see five boys throwing another volley.

Pandemonium erupted, with guards and servants shouting and running about. Tokugawa and Konoe watched the youngsters hide behind bushes, where they were quickly discovered. No one was quite sure what to do when they realized that one of the boys was the crown prince.

"Bring them up to me," Prince Tokugawa shouted from the window. An entourage of servants and guards, along with the trembling children, their heads turned downwards, soon stood before the Grand Chamberlain. "Who's responsible for this assault upon the palace?" Tokugawa demanded. The boys remained silent.

"It was probably the bad influence of the gardeners' children," a guard replied. "They should be given a sound beating," raising a hand to strike one of them.

"No. It was me, Grand Chamberlain," Hirohito declared, stepping forward. "The others only followed my orders."

Tokugawa considered the matter. "Very well, Prince Hirohito and Prince Konoe will remain. Everyone else may go." He motioned the crown prince to a chair as the others exited.

"Hirohito, I was discussing affairs of state with Prince Konoe, preparing him for his future role in government, when we were rudely interrupted. What have you to say for yourself? Why this senseless behavior?"

"I don't know, sir," Hirohito stammered.

Tokugawa softened his tone and placed a calming hand on the boy's shoulder. "There were also times in my youth when I wished to break things. Please tell me what angers you? I realize you just recently returned to the palace, but you cannot think it proper to act in such a way?"

Hirohito rubbed his eyes as he described how much he missed his prior home and his kind-hearted foster parent. "Why did he have to die?" the boy asked.

"Vice Admiral Kawamura was quite old; we all die eventually, Hirohito—that is the way. But *now* you have your parents nearby."

"I see little of my mother, and my father acts so strange."

"He's not entirely well," Tokugawa sighed, "physically healthy, but he does not always understand what is happening around him. When young, he developed brain fever. Luckily he survived. You must show him patience."

"I will try." Hirohito nodded.

"Is there anything else, my young Prince?"

"Why must I be treated so differently? I want to play like other boys. Instead, my days are filled only with instruction."

"You are not like other boys. You are destined to be Ruler of all Japan!"

"Can I leave now?" Hirohito replied curtly.

He has a strong will, Tokugawa thought. "If you wish, but I have a question. When you and your friends picked up your stones, did you notice the Koi in the pond?"

"Yes . . ."

"Do you remember what colors they were?"

"Why is that important?"

Tokugawa smiled. "The natural world is full of wonders and has much to teach us."

Hirohito closed his eyes. "I remember orange, black with white splotches, yellow, and probably other colors...But I'm not sure."

"You're most observant. Please take another look, and let me know." Then with a nod, he added, "I understand your frustration and forgive your earlier bad behavior. I am proud of you, Hirohito, for not letting those other boys take the blame. However, I would appreciate you instructing your companions that breaking windows is not the proper way to play."

"I am very sorry, Grand Chamberlain." Hirohito bowed and left.

The following day, Hirohito quietly entered and took a seat in the corner of Tokugawa's large office, cross-legged, on the matted floor. On his lap lay several sheets of paper. Rustling them drew Tokugawa's attention from his deskwork. "Hirohito, you are as silent as a hare."

"I hope I didn't surprise you."

"No, it is always a pleasure to see you."

Hirohito stood. "I never noticed how pretty Koi really are," he said, as he placed the papers upon Tokugawa's desk.

Tokugawa examined them. "You have certainly captured their colorful variety." Then, glancing at his watch, he added, "Isn't it a bit early in the day to be seeing you?"

Someone knocked. "May I enter?" a voice called out. "We're looking for the crown prince."

Tokugawa pointed behind his desk, and Hirohito quickly slipped out of sight. Tokugawa then opened his door wide. "Can I be of service?" he asked.

The perspiring man took a deep breath. "I'm one of Prince Hirohito's instructors. Have you seen him?"

"You mean he's disappeared?"

The teacher nodded.

"Well, do you see him here?"

"No. Excuse me for disturbing you, My Lord."

When he'd gone, Hirohito reappeared, grinning; Prince Tokugawa burst into laughter.

The boy announced, "My instructors are unfriendly and my lessons often boring and never ending."

"They're doing their best," Tokugawa replied. "A future ruler must be well-educated. They care about you, but it is best not to coddle you."

"Perhaps that is so...Thank you for hiding me. Tomorrow, I promise to do better at my studies."

It was mid-afternoon of the following day, when Tokugawa entered the classroom. He observed delicate brushstroke letters being drawn on parchment. "Teacher," Tokugawa said, "at what time did Crown Prince Hirohito's classes begin?"

"Just after daybreak."

"I see...I've decided to give the prince lessons on government. Henceforth, he will leave with me each afternoon. We will also visit the gardens to do his nature and biological studies."

"Certainly, Grand Chamberlain. I will advise the rest of the staff."

"Now come along, Hirohito."

Crisp autumn winds raked their faces, as Tokugawa, Konoe, and Hirohito stood near the edge of a winding river, eyes focused upward. "My *Nagoya Koryu* kite with its yellow body, black wings, and green eyes looks like a giant bee!" Hirohito exclaimed. "Look how strongly it is being pulled," he added, watching it soar.

"Yes. And my brown and orange cicada kite playfully whirls alongside yours," Tokugawa replied.

"But Konoe's kite is most impressive," Hirohito said, with a frown. "It is the shape of a giant fire-breathing dragon, flying far above ours. So high, its twine disappears."

"Yes, Hirohito and Konoe. Almost as if he were using invisible forces to direct his kite as he pleased. Like a good ruler, often guiding from a distance, with movements barely visible."

"Look there!" Hirohito pointed down the river at two groups of boys on opposite shores, taunting one another. "Their kites have frightening eyes and pointy teeth painted upon them."

"It is a game," Tokugawa said. "Those brightly colored kites are called *Hirado Oniyocho*, made especially for battle."

"Some kites are decorated with fiercesome samurai helmets," Konoe said.

"In my youth," Tokugawa said, "if a boy had a father who was samurai, his father's face was painted below the helmet."

"Look, they're diving into one another," Hirohito declared.

"Exactly," Tokugawa replied, "attempting to cut the fabric or twine of their opponents. And, if they can entangle a kite and drag it over to their side of the river, they win."

"I look forward to playing that sport," Konoe said.

"You'll be champion, I'm sure," Tokugawa smiled.

Konoe noticed the crown prince's expression and added, "And of course we'll include Hirohito."

"Why certainly," Tokugawa responded. "I look forward to it my-self!"

"Thank you." Hirohito beamed, but then turned serious. "Grand Chamberlain, I hope you will not be angry if I make a request?"

"Go right ahead."

Hirohito edged closer. "If I'm going to spend a lot of time with you, is it all right, if, on occasion, I call you Uncle?"

"It would be my *great honor*, Your Majesty."

✳ ✳ ✳ ✳

1912

The six intervening years passed rapidly, with the Crown Prince growing into young manhood. Eleven-year-old Hirohito grit his teeth as a freezing waterfall cascaded upon him, cringing at the sight of his own skin turning blue. "If you are to be strong," General Nogi shouted, while standing on a nearby rocky outcropping, "you must not even shiver."

The following day, Hirohito visited Prince Tokugawa's private estate. "Sir, I hope I am not disturbing you?" he said, entering the comfort-able and familiar bookcase-lined library. "Not at all," Tokugawa re-plied, noting the Crown Prince was dressed in samurai garb, a sword dangling at his side. "Your instructors at the Peers School have told me you're doing quite well...And how are things going at the mili-tary academy with General Nogi?"

Hirohito sighed. "He wishes to put the samurai spirit into my heart, believing war is the only glorious path, proudly displaying scars on his arms and chest from many battles, and without remorse speaks of losing two sons in heroic combat." Hirohito's eyes moist-ened.

"A future leader needs many teachers. Sometimes the lessons ap-pear to contradict, but diverse talents and insights are essential to suc-cessfully rule. The correct path will depend upon wisdom gathered over the years...The courage of the samurai is required to maintain peace, *and* for the winning of wars that are unavoidable. General Nogi is a great military leader—you will learn much from him."

"I have a question." Hirohito hesitated. "Haven't there generally been good relations between America and Japan since Commodore Perry's visit long ago?"

"Yes, Your Majesty."

"When I said that to General Nogi, he fumed with anger—Dear Uncle, you promised to one day tell me about your childhood and of Perry's visit with your father. That might help me to better understand our relationship with the West. Please make that day today?"

Tokugawa smiled. "Take a seat, make yourself comfortable young man, and I'll tell you the tale... It all started with dragons!"

"Really?"

Tokugawa's voice took a deeper tone, "It was the midsummer of 1853, the Forbidden Islands of Japan had isolated themselves for 250 years under a strong Shogunate government, ruled by my family, the Tokugawas.

"But that was to change—There had been sightings of giant foreign ships along our shores, accompanied by fearsome dragons belching black smoke, that were able to slice through ocean waves even against tempest winds and rains, unlike sailing ships. Thinking they might be evil spirits, soothsayers were consulted to obtain advice from the gods . . . Later, we discovered they were actually a squadron of steam-engine powered ships, commanded by the American Commodore Perry.

"In the past, only lowly Japanese officials would meet emissaries from other nations. Through delays and miscommunications our representatives would frustrate these emissaries, so that they left in disgust. But Perry refused to go without an official audience, stating he had a letter of friendship from President Fillmore, which he was ordered to present directly to *your grandfather*." Tokugawa smiled, "Perry mistakenly believed that power lay in your grandfather Emperor Meiji's baby hands, unaware, the shoguns held supremacy at that time.

"My father, Yoshinobu, was one of the more influential young members of the shogunate. They allowed Perry's marines ashore, who began marching back and forth in strictest discipline. Then, to their utter fearful surprise, the Americans raised their rifles and fired a volley into the sky over the heads of our nobles, who had been observing. Yoshinobu approached the commodore, and through a translator said, 'Sir, it appears you're trying to force us to open the doors to our nation, with the unspoken but obvious threat of war. And *yet* you claim to come in peace?'

"'And who might you be?' Perry asked in a booming voice, utilizing the services of his ever-present translator, a grey whiskered gentleman named Williams.

"'Just a magistrate from the north. Yoshinobu is my name,' he replied, standing his ground.

"'Well, I'll tell you what brings me here,' Perry replied, looking Yoshinobu squarely in the eye, 'American whaling ships *now* travel this part of the world and need to restock on provisions and coal. Japan has turned them away, or dealt harsh treatment to our shipwrecked sailors—accusing them of spying and throwing them into prisons. Many in *my* country are shouting, "*Invade Japan and conquer the half barbarians!*" They believe that is the only way to gain access.'

Perry shook his head. "'But I differ with them. I've studied all I could find written about Japan and its fine artistry and culture, and believe a peaceful agreement would benefit both our nations.'"

"'You're a diplomat, as well as a warrior,' Yoshinobu replied.

"'I've had enough of war. Perhaps your leaders feel the same?'

"'Why, then, do you display marching soldiers and the firing of rifles?" Yoshinobu replied, turning his gaze at Perry's men. 'Yes, Commodore, there are large cannons on your ships, but that only fosters fear. That is not the way to impress us.'

"Hirohito, you must understand, Japan was not to be rushed. My father needed to convince Perry to depart, supposedly to give us time to confer with Emperor Meiji, while actually getting the Shogunate council's permission to arrange for a more formal visit. It was hoped, and expected, that six months of waiting on the Chinese coast, with its miserable freezing wintry rains, would probably send these intruders back from where they came.

"'All right,' Perry replied, 'I'll see what I can do to impress you and your rulers when we return." The commodore beckoned two powerfully-built Black men, dressed in white sailor uniforms. One came forward, carrying an ornately embossed gold inlaid box.

"'This contains a copy of our President's letter of friendship,' Perry said. 'When I return, I'll present the original to your Emperor. And at that time, I promise to give your people a view of the future, with wonders their eyes have never beheld.'

"The Commodore and his men returned to their ships, and soon, all that could be seen were the faint lines of their vessels' upper hulls, and wisps of black smoke disappearing over the horizon."

"What happened next?" Hirohito asked, edging forward in his seat.

Tokugawa smiled. "In the interim, my father desired to learn as much as possible about these visitors. One of his loyal samurai retainers, Kaishu, informed him of a man named Manjiro, who for ten years had lived with these *barbarians*. That was the term *we both* used to describe each other. As a boy, Manjiro had been shipwrecked on a small island, and was rescued by an American whaling ship. He led an adventurous life, becoming himself the captain of a whaling ship, and later discovering gold during the California Gold Rush. But Manjiro longed to see his mother and family and returned to Japan. My father and Kaishu met with Manjiro. He described America's cities and its people—Detailing their science, history, geography, navigation, and shipbuilding.

"It was quite apparent that America was a far more technologically powerful nation. But in spite of this, many members of the Shogunate and the Daimyo lords were angered at being pressured to open Japan to the modern world, shouting that these foreign devils would destroy our traditions…For two and a half centuries under Tokugawa rule, we had lived in relative peace. Peasants working their lords' fields, artisans and merchants satisfied, even the untouchables accepted their lowly tasks—all under the strict enforcement of our Samurai overseers. Why jeopardize their powerful positions? Some strongly recommended we ambush and kill these intruders when they returned, so they'd never dare send others to our shores.

"To which Yoshinobu replied, 'These visitors are not the *Old World European Colonial invading powers*; they come from the *New World*, wishing to befriend us with mutual trade. A rash act would lead to war.

"'And if that regrettably were to be the course, would you wish to fight an opponent without understanding their strengths and weaknesses? They now offer their hand in friendship, promising alliances. If we rush, we face a dangerous enemy.'"

"So what happened, Uncle Tokugawa?" Hirohito asked eagerly. Tokugawa took a deep breath, "Let us relax and sip some tea, and then I will continue . . .

"Over the following months, my father had to remind himself that Perry's visit had not been a dream. But come early March, an even larger naval armada moved toward Yokohama, causing the entire city to go into an uproar. In all directions, mothers ran hysterically with children in arms, searching for shelter. Exaggerated rumors of invasion added horror to the already panic-stricken. Tramping warhorses, the chatter of armed warriors, and the incessant tolling bells mixed with the shrieks of the frightened populace. A city of more than a million souls multiplied the confusion. Angry Japanese officials gathered on guard boats, hoping to board and stop the arriving ships. They warned the Commodore to go no further. The Americans would have none of that, with Marines preventing their boarding with rifles.

"Fifteen cutters and longboats loaded with officers, Marines, sailors, and two full bands came ashore. In all, three hundred Americans lined up, as thousands of Japanese warriors swarmed around them, armed with swords, bows, spears, and old matchlock rifles. Gathered behind them were huge crowds of peasants watching as an American standard-bearer, waving a flag decorated with stars and stripes, marched at the lead of the procession, followed by drummers and pipers...And after them strode Commodore Perry, his blue dress uniform brocaded with gold shoulders and glimmering gold buttons upon his barrel-like chest.

"Suspicions ran high on both sides...Our visitors smiled, bowed, and extended their hands in what appeared to be an act of friendship. Yoshinobu and the other delegates copied the gesture, shaking their hands. The mood rapidly changed, and the streets of Yokohama came alive with excitement. Beggars thronged Perry and his officers, hoping to convince them to give away their gold buttons, as Japanese guards labored to push them back. Soon the American officers and Japanese delegates assembled under a large tent.

"'Look at the Commodore and his men,' Yoshinobu whispered into Kaishu's ear. 'Do you notice anything unusual?'

"'They do not appear healthy, do they?' Kaishu replied.

"'That foul weather has taken its toll. They've shown great fortitude to have lasted through it.'

"To our delegates' delight, the Americans began distributing gifts of hand mirrors, horseshoe magnets, and Colt revolvers. 'And here's French perfume for your wives,' they said.

"They also brought along an artist who displayed colorful canvases depicting fish captured in our surrounding waters. 'We're bringing these paintings back to America,' he announced, 'to display the natural wonders of Japan. We also plan to do drawings of your fine people and their customs.'"

The Commodore's men next brought forth bundles of scrolls. "'Our cartographers have been busily charting your shorelines,' Perry said. 'These drawings detail the harbors and inlets surrounding your islands, to aid future navigators to safely sail your waters. We'll leave copies for your use, if you wish.'

"All marveled at these charts, which included the Chinese coast. Up to then, Japanese were forbidden by harshest law to venture beyond a few miles from our shoreline.

"'And look,'" Perry said, 'We've included a map of the entire known world! *Here is your country*,' he said, pointing, '*and here is mine.*'

"My father examined the map. 'Is there really such a large nation?' he asked, indicating a region.'

"'That is the continent of Africa,' Perry answered, 'made up of various kingdoms and tribes. These fine sailors,' he said, looking toward two Negroes, 'trace their roots there.'

"'What took you to that distant land?' Yoshinobu asked. 'Was it also for trade?'

"Perry's expression darkened. 'Ten years ago, I was sent there by my government, not to encourage—but to stop a *certain enterprise*...I led the *African Squadron*, in an attempt to end the slave trade.'

"'So your country has no slaves?' my father inquired.

"'Regrettably, this issue still divides our nation.' Perry said bitterly. 'I still remember our bloody battles against cruel slavers, discovering their filthy, hellish cargo holes filled with humans in chains, surrounded by death.'

"'Why do you care?' Yoshinobu replied. 'Are not the mighty meant to rule?'

"Perry's face turned crimson. 'Humans are not oxen, to be whipped to work the fields. My crew see me as a strict commander, but I respect the right of all men to freely choose their life's course.'

Tokugawa and Hirohito sat in silent thought...Their somberness evaporated as Tokugawa continued. "Sailors then began unloading large crates, and to everyone's amazement, a miniature steam engine train was assembled: Bright red and white with lacquered wood paneling; the engine car a glossy black metal. Several hundred feet of iron rails were quickly spiked down...Though the train was not large enough for even a small boy to ride inside, little faces were painted on its windows to give the illusion of passengers. In spite of its size, the crowds climbed atop the passenger cars for a ride—Even the dignified Mandarin officials.

"Laughter filled the air and robes flapped in the wind, as the train whirled around the circular track at dizzying speeds. Steam drifted upward, blending with the train's high-pitched whistle. 'This is such fun,' Kaishu called out to Yoshinobu, as they rounded a bend...Perry explained that it was a gift to Japan, one-fourth the size of an actual train, which could carry many passengers *inside,* and also pull heavy loads of coal, lumber, and steel!"

"It would have been so exciting to have been there!" Hirohito exclaimed.

Tokugawa nodded in agreement. "The following day, Perry's men brought ashore strange instruments of metal and glass, and large coils of wires."

"'Yoshinobu, what would you conjecture is the purpose of this device?' Perry asked.

"Not wishing to appear the fool, my father remained silent.

"Curious crowds watched as wires were attached to the mechanism. 'We will now connect the other end of this wire to a village a half mile away,' Perry explained. '*There* it will be attached to a similar device. My crew will then use this machine to send and receive messages." Perry turned to Yoshinobu. 'Can you supply me with some Japanese who can run very fast?'

"Yoshinobu called forth several.

"Perry gave my father the honor of choosing the first message sent. Yoshinobu recited a poem: '*Abe No Nakamaro, Ama no hara, Furisake-mireba, Kasuga naru, Mikasa no yama ni, Ideshi tsuki kamo.*'

"Wells translated it for Perry and his device operator: 'The title is *Nakamaro Abe… While gazing up into the sky, My thoughts have wandered far, Methinks I see the rising moon, Above Mount Mikasa, At far-off Kasuga.*'

"'Why that particular poem?' Perry asked.

"'As a system of remembering history,' Yoshinobu replied, 'it was one of the hundred we memorized as schoolchildren. Each has a story: this one tells of two Japanese princes who traveled to China to learn its calendar, and brought this knowledge back to Japan."

"Perry nodded with approval, 'Your fine poem will be sent through that wire to the village. We'll give your runner to the count of sixty, before we begin transmitting. When he returns, he'll bring back the proof.'

"Yoshinobu shouted, 'Run,' and off the man went, as Wells began to count. At sixty, the device began chattering, the operator rapidly tapping a lever…Six minutes later a perspiring runner returned holding a sheet of paper.

"'That's amazing,' Yoshinobu said, seeing the translated words of his poem on the paper.

"Other Japanese officials came forward, desiring to send their messages, but always the text was waiting before the runner arrived.

"'Commodore Perry,' my father said, 'is there a limit to how far these wires can span?'

"'Someday,' he proudly replied, 'your grandchildren and mine, may well be speaking to each other across vast oceans!'

"Kaishu noticed Lord Yoshinobu's expression change. 'What is wrong?' he asked.

"'Look at all their wonders,' he replied. 'How can we impress these foreigners with something that is uniquely Japanese?'

"'Haven't we already given them gifts of our fine crafts and jewelry?' Kaishu said.

"'I mean *something more dramatic.*'

"Kaishu thought. 'What about sumo wrestling? I'm sure they've never seen anything like that, my lord.'

"Two days later, a dozen wrestlers strutted in front of the treaty tent, with the Americans staring in wonder at the most enormous men they'd ever seen.

"'Commodore, feel the arm muscles of Koyanagi,' Yoshinobu suggested. 'He won't mind. He's the most awesome of the combatants, *the Bully of the Capital!*'

"Perry approached cautiously; the fighter's immense size was three times his own.

"Yoshinobu smiled. 'Look Kaishu, Perry fears he is going to be eaten alive."

"Commodore,' Yoshinobu gleefully called out, 'watch how our wrestlers warm up,' as the scantily clad combatants began tossing and catching 125-pound sacks of rice as if they were mere toys. Several American sailors attempted the sport, but soon gave up in exhaustion.

"When the matches began, the Americans and Japanese mixed together, loudly cheering and betting upon their favorites, as the combatants collided, each trying to shove the other out of the circular ring... A festive time was had by all.

"Once the matches ended, Perry approached my father. 'Yoshinobu,' he said, 'wouldn't this be a good time to finalize our treaty of understanding?'

"Yoshinobu candidly explained there were many powerful Japanese who would rather fight to the death than be part of the modern world. 'Commodore,' he asked, 'do you remember describing the angry voices in America who demanded revenge against us for our past mistreatment of your sailors?' Perry nodded. My father continued, 'My question is this: If in the future we treated your shipwrecked sailors more hospitably *and* offered two ports for you to purchase supplies for your whaling ships, *Would that be enough,* without having to fully open our doors to your new ways?'

"Perry bit his knuckle in thought... 'My dear friend,' he replied,

'I admit that if your country did these things, it would avoid war. I'd return home with this limited accomplishment, but *no glory*. I can accept that. The question *you must ask* is this: If you remain isolated, your country will fall further and further behind the rest of the world, and not benefit from its marvelous advances,' his voice rose, 'and in the end, progress will be forced upon you. Would it not be better to embrace it now on your own terms and prosper?'

"At the next meeting in the Shogunate Council Chambers, Yoshinobu stood before the assemblage. 'I had a wondrous dream, a sign,' he declared. 'Japan proudly stood among the world's great nations. Its people prosperous, its heritage admired... But in order to achieve this, we must modernize quickly!' There was rumbling from some of his listeners, which he tried to ignore. 'The major challenge,' he continued, 'is how to retain our culture, while benefiting from new technology? I suggest we ask the great scholar, Sakuma Zozan, for his opinion.'

"Sakuma came forward and spoke. 'In teachings concerning morality, benevolence, righteousness, filial piety, and brotherly love, we must follow the examples of the sages. But in astronomy, geography, commerce, medicine, machinery, and construction, we should rely mainly on the West.' Sakuma was thanked for his wise guidance, but as my father exited the council chambers, a leaf of paper displaying the words *Beware Yoshinobu!* hung on the wooden door frame, pierced through by a dagger."

"What happened next, Uncle Tokugawa?" Hirohito asked.

"The calm of the following morning was shattered by the sound of splintering wood, as four samurai crashed through a door into Kaishu's home, swords drawn. 'We've been ordered to execute you and your master, Yoshinobu,' they shouted.

"'As you can see, I am unarmed," Kaishu replied, "and prepared to die...But before you take my life, or that of my master, allow me to explain why we are attempting to ally with the foreigners. After that, do as you will.' Kaishu looked at them. 'Who is your leader here?'

"'I am,' a lean, muscular man in his twenties said, stepping forward, sword raised. 'So you think you can convince us to change our minds?' he said mockingly.

"'Perhaps?' Kaishu replied. 'What is your name?'

"'Ryoma,' he answered.

"Later that afternoon, my father found Kaishu cross-legged, seated outside his home. 'Is something wrong, Kaishu?' he asked, 'You're as white as a ghost!'

"Kaishu stood. 'Today, assassins came calling; my life was held by a thread, with your death soon to follow,' he replied.

"'You killed all of them?' Yoshinobu asked.

"'No,'" Kaishu answered. 'Instead, I convinced them of your patriotism, *and said for that reason alone* you cooperated with the foreigners! I explained Japan must modernize to remain an independent nation, and not be colonized.'

"'So what came of your visitors then?' he asked.

"'They've joined our cause,' Kaishu said with a smile.

"With a light heart my father replied, 'My loyal Kaishu, diplomacy may well be in your future!'

"So under darkness of night, Yoshinobu secretly visited Perry and his translator with a request. 'Do you remember the first time we met, Commodore?' he asked, 'Your marines fired rifles into the sky over our nobles' heads during your military exercises?'

"'That was only to gain your attention and respect,' Perry replied. '*And as you commented earlier*, perhaps put some fear into you. We were only newly acquainted then. I now regret that display of force.'

"'I understand,' Yoshinobu replied, looking around to make sure no-one was in earshot. 'Commodore, many still strongly resist this treaty. They've come to see you closely, and know your humanity; there is no longer fear.'

"'What then, would you wish of me, Yoshinobu?' Perry asked.

"My father then admitted he was not a mere magistrate, but one of the leaders of the shogunate. 'Please do not look at me with ridicule when you hear my request,' he said. 'I need you to fire your mightiest cannons just before the treaty signing, to strike dread into the hearts of these rebelling lords. Aim into the nearby sea, and definitely do not hit our soil. I can *then claim* signing the treaty was a combination of the potential gains to be had, *and the fear of your weaponry*.'

"Perry bowed to my father. 'Lord Yoshinobu,' he said, 'You will be remembered as one of the leaders who opened Japan to the benefits of the modern world . . .'

"And so it came to pass: Yoshinobu, accompanied by sixteen Japanese and American delegates, gathered in front of the treaty tent the following morning, surrounded by a multitude of onlookers. Kaishu whispered to Yoshinobu, 'Will the rebelling lords interfere, I wonder?'

"'Don't worry yourself,' Yoshinobu replied, while noticing Perry glancing at his pocket watch. Suddenly, all were stunned when the ten pivot guns aboard the *U.S.S. Mississippi* erupted with a thunderous roar.

"'That's the loudest noise any of us have ever heard!' Kaishu said.'

"Yoshinobu sent a knowing nod toward Perry, which he returned✻

"The signing ceremony lasted an hour. Once it was completed, Perry put a hand on Yoshinobu's shoulder, as a father to a son, and said, '*The Treaty of Kanagawa* will be something we'll both proudly look back upon. Its preamble contains such noble words…'*There shall be a perfect, permanent, and universal peace, and a sincere and cordial amity between the United States of America on the one part, and the Empire of Japan.*'

"Yoshinobu and Kaishu watched Perry and his men trudge back to waiting barges, now overflowing with gifts and purchased souvenirs. 'Their mission has been accomplished,' Kaishu said.

"'Yes,'" Yoshinobu declared, 'the doors to *the Empire of the Sun* are now open wide!'"

CHAPTER 5

Prince Hirohito excitedly returned the following afternoon to hear the final installment of Prince Tokugawa's story. He was surprised, sensing tension, as Tokugawa plunged back into revealing his childhood memories, as if he were baring his soul: He described the early years that followed the treaty, filled with interesting and dramatic changes. Shiploads of architects, engineers, and scientists arrived on Japanese shores, reversing centuries of isolation. With them, came tourists and businessmen from around the world, exposing the populace to new, liberal ways of thinking.

Regrettably, many powerful lords refused to accept these changes and blamed Yoshinobu. So when his name was chosen as the next candidate to become the ruling shogun, these reactionaries placed him under house arrest for years!

Instead, they chose a less experienced individual, Iemochi, to become the next ruling shogun. Iemochi *again* attempted to isolate Japan, but was unable to end the political quarreling or bring economic stability. Rebellions erupted in the Southern Provinces, which for centuries had hoped to end Tokugawa rule. In desperation, Yoshinobu was released from house arrest and made the Commander of the Imperial Palace defenses, so he could protect Shogun Iemochi.

After Shogun Iemochi's death due to illness in the year 1866, Yoshinobu finally received the title he had long deserved: that of the fifteenth ruling shogun. He immediately began modernizing the army and navy, overhauling the inefficient government, and initiating public reforms. To stabilize his position, he allied with the British and the French, who eagerly supplied him with modern weapons and military advisors. And in return, those nations gained commercial advantage.

Prince Tokugawa looked at attentive Hirohito and emphasized,

"My father would have allied with the Americans, but they were entangled in the aftermath of their bloody Civil War—Sadly, Japan was similarly being torn apart, with fanatics savagely attacking foreigners, with my father and Kaishu risking their lives to protect them!

"In the year 1867, Kaishu entered Yoshinobu's castle, dressed in battle armor splattered with blood, sword in hand, with anguish in his eyes. 'My Lord,' he said, 'this violent uprising is spreading! There are men shouting, "*Restore the Emperor and Expel the Foreign Barbarians!*" *And now*, these rebelling armies wave the Imperial Banner.'

"'That can't be,' my father cried out.

"'It is true, you've been unjustly held responsible for our economic woes,' he replied. 'Emperor Meiji's advisors have convinced him *that this is the time to take back the reins of power.*'

"'My loyal Kaishu, I value your advice above all others. Regardless of threats against me, I've made reforms improving the people's lives, and yet they remain dissatisfied because things have not advanced fast enough to suit them.' His voice hardened. "Our foreign allies encourage me to fight on—even offering to assist, thereby retaining their favored status in Japan.' Yoshinobu faced Kaishu imploringly. 'What should I do?'

"'Have no fear, my Liege, I, and your armies will stand by you to the death,' Kaishu declared. 'I've studied Western military strategy and feel confident that by using new weaponry we can defend the castle in Edo indefinitely—But in my heart, I feel a civil war would be catastrophic, an enormous destruction of life and property, beyond anything imaginable. Japan would be so weakened that it would be child's play for other nations to conquer us, destroying all the things we hold sacred.'"

Pausing, Tokugawa looked into Hirohito's dark watery eyes. "My father did not hunger for the glory of being Shogun, if it would drag our country into disaster. If yielding power to your grandfather, Emperor Meiji, would unify the nation, so be it. And so he accepted his fate, relinquishing power, ending over two and a half centuries of Tokugawa rule...He confided to Kaishu that he so regretted not having a son at that time to carry on his name, nor would he now even possess a meager title to pass on to his future heirs . . .

"As Yoshinobu prepared to forever leave his castle fortress, Kaishu returned. 'Where have you been?' Yoshinobu asked. 'The Emperor's council demands I immediately go into exile.'

"Kaishu watched Yoshinobu's trembling hands clutch the throne chair one last time. 'Your life is in danger, my lord,' Kaishu replied. 'Certain pro-Tokugawa forces are angered by your refusal to fight on. To get even, Ryoma, my most capable second in command, was assassinated.' Kaishu dropped his sword.

"'I'm so sorry you've lost your close friend,' Yoshinobu replied, pounding the wall. 'Such bitter irony, that Ryoma, the young samurai who had intended to execute both of us many years ago to prevent Japan from opening its doors to the outside world, should now be murdered for supporting those very same ideals.'

"'You've heard the tragedy My Lord,' Kaishu said, 'but there is also a pleasant surprise—I have someone I'd like you to meet...*Iyesato*, come here,' he called. "I was only five years old at the time," Prince Tokugawa explained.

"'Lord Yoshinobu,' Kaishu continued, 'I've made arrangements with one of the Tokugawa families. They've offered Iyesato to be adopted.'

"Yoshinobu's dark demeanor vanished. "'Young man, come closer so I can see you,'

"'Yes sir,' I replied, feeling shy and awkward.

"Yoshinobu came down on one knee to speak face to face with me. 'Do you want to be my son and accompany us to the city of Shidzuoka, the ancestral home of the founder of *what was* our Tokugawa Dynasty?'

"And so, Hirohito, over the coming years I received a formal education and spent wonderful times with my father and Kaishu, learning Oil Painting, Archery, Hunting, and much more. Kaishu established a technical high school in Shidzuoka. There, he and I befriended a Christian missionary from America, who also taught chemistry," Tokugawa paused in thought. "Though I am a follower of Buddhism and Shintoism, over the years I've come to see the common thread that runs through all the World's great religions, and at their heart is love when they are properly practiced . . .

"One day, I was called before Yoshinobu and Kaishu, on what appeared a serious matter.

'Why are you both staring at me?' I asked. 'Have I done something wrong?'

"'No, let me explain,' my father replied. 'When I stepped down as Shogun, many who had fought against me to bring back the Emperor and expel all foreigners, found, to their dismay, that the Emperor's advisors would also open Japan's doors to the outside world as the best course for her future...This caused further revolts, which are *now* put down by the Emperor's own troops.'

"'Yes, Iyesato,'" Kaishu interjected, 'just like your father, the Emperor's officials require foreign support to stay in power. But regrettably, they sent away our long term allies, our French and British military and political advisors, who have been replaced by the Germans—Someday in the future, we will explain why we believe that is a mistake.'"

"'So is there a reason we are now discussing these political matters?' I asked.

"'You are now thirteen years old, Iyesato,' my father said. 'But someday, you will have an important leadership role in our nation.'

"Yoshinobu then described how Kaishu was nationally credited for negotiating an end to our civil war, and was becoming a powerful member of the Emperor's advisory council. He was even given the recognition of commanding the ship that journeyed to America to establish our first consulate there, and was one of its delegates."

"'Yes, Father," I replied, proudly. "All eyes are fixed on Kaishu, *while he honors you and heeds your advice!* Between the two of you, you give Japan stability—and prosperity!"

"'Thank you," he replied. "We've been considering your future, but, as my son, you are detrimentally seen as linked to the past with its old ways.'

"Kaishu stepped close. 'Dear Iyesato,' he said, grasping my hand.

'I've lost children to sickness and war. During these past years you've become like a son...Your father, and I, have decided it would be best if you are presented to, and honored by, the outside world, as the heir to the last Shogun. *But here* in Japan, I will be like a father to you, mentoring and advancing your career so as to open more opportunities—And of course, your father will always be there for you.

"They then surprised me further: I was told I was to be sent to England to attend college prep school, and during my vacations travel throughout Europe.

"'But I do not wish to leave you and our home.' I said.

"'There is only so much you can learn here,' my father's voice quivered. 'Our dynasty ended in my hands—the darkest time in my life!' his remorseful eyes looked into my heart. "'Japan must take her rightful place among the powerful nations,' he said, 'and for that to happen, she needs capable leaders! You, Iyesato, will be called upon to serve as a bridge between Ancient Japan and the modern world.'

Confused, frightened, and flustered by what they expected of me, I replied, "'If that is what you truly wish, Father and Kaishu, I'll do all I can to make you both proud, bringing back honor to the Tokugawa name.'

"'But there is one thing you must always remember!" Kaishu said emphatically. "Lord Yoshinobu and I, have seen many assassinations of our loyal supporters—So no matter how well-intentioned your actions might be, Iyesato, *you will make enemies.* You must learn to accomplish your goals from behind the scenes as much as possible.'

"As the years passed, my mentor Kaishu, though of humble samurai birth, would become the minister of our Navy and a close advisor and friend to your grandfather, Emperor Meiji..."

Iyesato smiled, "And now you've heard my tale."

Hirohito stood and bowed. "Dear Prince Tokugawa, you have devoted your life to serving our nation and the Imperial family. *Thank you so much for telling me of our history!* But one question remains: Why is General Nogi so angry at America now?"

"General Nogi led the major battles defeating the Russians seven years ago, at great sacrifice. He is still bitter over the Japanese-Russian peace treaty sponsored by the United States, which took away most of

Japan's territorial gains. There are those who wish to create a Japanese empire, just like the British: a small island nation, yet a world power."

"Doesn't that sound like a good idea?" Hirohito replied.

"Such aspirations could well bring destruction upon us," Tokugawa declared…He paused to get hold of himself, then continued, his voice softening. "Our victory in the Russian–Japanese War achieved several important goals, and we were not spiteful. Our Red Cross saved the lives of many Russian prisoners of war.

"Our main objective was to prevent Russian expansion into our region, and they now recognize our historic sphere of influence on the mainland…In addition, we obtained Russia's leases to Port Arthur on the Liaotung Peninsula and gained the southern half of Sakhalin Island…The U.S. sponsored peace treaty did, however, require *us* to return Manchuria to China."

"*All in all* it sounds like we won?" Hirohito replied.

"But at a heavy cost, Your Majesty. Eighty thousand Japanese died, and one hundred and twenty-five thousand Russians."

"But if it was resolved, why is there still anger toward America?"

Tokugawa sighed. "Public opinion has been re-ignited over the giving back of Manchuria—*Instead*, we should appreciate the treaty that President Theodore Roosevelt negotiated! If it hadn't been signed," Tokugawa's body stiffened, "Russia was prepared to regroup its forces for a major assault on our islands. With their greater resources and larger population to draw upon, who knows what might have resulted?"

Hirohito nodded. "So we were fortunate that the Americans intervened?"

"Yes," Tokugawa replied, "President Theodore Roosevelt had actually been convinced to get involved by Baron Kaneko, a former Harvard classmate of Roosevelt's, who urged him to arbitrate. A partial victory was far better than a potential total defeat. America was merely pushing apart two warring nations for their own good . . .

"And as for General Nogi," Tokugawa continued, "he is a *true* military hero, but has little interest in political solutions. He was one of the samurai who forced my father to give up his position as Shogun.

In spite of that, I respect him for assisting in the restoration of power to Emperor Meiji for the good of the country. He will teach you courage, discipline, and how to live with simplicity."

"Yes," Hirohito replied with exuberance, "he has explained that I should admire others not for their wealth, but for their good values. He advised me to study the English and Chinese languages, and to become skilled at writing Chinese *kanji* characters."

"I do as he suggests," Hirohito sighed wearily, "but I'm expected to learn so much."

Tokugawa nodded. "Dear Hirohito, do your best, but remember: No one mind can retain all the world's vast knowledge. Life is a treasure; try to keep a lighthearted spirit." He pulled a volume from a shelf." Here, young man," he said, handing it to him. "I know you're studying history, science, and philosophy. *This book* is of a lighter, more humorous nature—*The Prince and the Pauper,* by Mark Twain, a fine American author. Perhaps, we can read and translate it together, which would help with your learning of the English language. It might also give insights into your own life." Iyesato's eyes lit up. *"I challenge you to contain your laughter when you read this novel."*

Hirohito cradled the book, curiously scanning pages and looking at illustrations.

"Not to give away surprises," Tokugawa continued, "but I can tell you it is about a prince from the West who trades places with a poor commoner, to experience life in one another's shoes."

All the while as they ate lunch, Hirohito anticipated what adventures *The Prince and the Pauper* might contain.

CHAPTER 6

Returning to Sidney Mashbir

New York City, July 30, 1916

Newly arrived in the fast-paced metropolis, he felt a bit lost, missing the open skies and tranquility of the Southwest. Regrettably, it brought back dark memories from his childhood, when his family had lived there. In his free time, he immersed himself in the study of military strategy, reading such classics as the ancient Chinese book by Sun Tzu, *The Art of War*, or General Clausewitz's 1800s work, *On War*, a philosophical examination of military conflict in all its aspects. For mental diversion while walking, driving, or traveling by train, he would envision tactical situations regarding the possible attack or the defense strategy of a section of terrain he was passing through.

He did, however, find a peaceful oasis, a diner, where a sweet, young, blue-eyed waitress named Blanche would deliver an extra-large slice of pie when he came in for lunch. She was attracted to the strong, good-looking man in uniform, leaning close when serving him, allowing Sidney to smell her lavender perfume. Her attentive, honest demeanor diminished his underlying distrust of the opposite sex.

During one of their early dates, they wandered arm in arm through lower Manhattan, visiting quaint art galleries and coffee shops, strolling late into the night...Though Blanche enjoyed the city, she was a small-town girl who missed her family and their vegetable garden, back in the Midwest. They were having a beautiful evening, when suddenly, enormous explosions erupted accompanied by a storm of shattering windows that showered broken glass upon them from adjacent buildings. The city was thrown into darkness when

thousands of electric street-pole and traffic lights blacked out, resulting in automobiles colliding nearby.

"What's happening?" Blanche shrieked, watching panic-stricken
crowds running in all directions.

"Lord, if I know." Sidney replied, and shouted to those around
him, "Run for cover!" He grasped Blanche's hand, leading her to the
safety of a building entrance. It was like the Fourth of July, with thunderous fireworks exploding over New York Harbor. But instead of
sparklers and bottle rockets, these had the ear-pounding impact of a
real battle. They stayed under shelter until Mashbir noticed a policeman passing. "I'm with the military," he called out. "What's going
on?"

The policeman came over, unbuttoned his collar, and wiped sweat
off his brow. "A major munitions storage depot located on the One
Mile Pier to the Jersey City waterfront has caught fire," he explained.
"Millions of pounds of ammunition are stored in those warehouses
and freight cars. *And* the barges nearby are filled with TNT."

"Might it be the act of saboteurs?" Mashbir asked.

"No one knows. There's been deaths, and folks are being evacuated from lower Manhattan."

As the harrowing night continued, there was a communications
blackout, except for radio transmissions describing explosive reper-
cussions reaching all the way from Hoboken to Bayonne, and over
to Staten Island and Brooklyn, with windows breaking as far off as
Philadelphia. It even shook the Brooklyn Bridge and sent shrapnel
piercing the Statue of Liberty.

"How could this happen?" Mashbir wondered, while keeping
Blanche close to comfort her, as they joined the bewildered masses
streaming northward, away from the billowing smoke, flames, and
blaring noise.

Fort Hamilton, New York, a month later

"You come highly recommended, Captain Mashbir," Colonel Burnett
said. "Have a seat."

"Thank you, sir. I'm not real clear on what I'm being recommended for?" he replied, raising his palms upwards.

"To answer your question, Captain," the Colonel smiled. "General
Pershing wants you to organize the first comprehensive counter-intelligence and counter-espionage service for the Eastern Department of
the Army—Your goal is to prevent enemy organizations from gathering intelligence against *us*." Burnett poured them both cups of coffee.
"Thus far, we've muddled along with a few personnel who supposedly keep an eye on the officers and men in their branches and report
if they think something's suspicious. Then it's my job to figure out if
that *somebody* is really a spy or a traitor. And if I think yes—what to
do about it, if we can do anything! The Army's been much too blasé if
you ask me, even after that Black Tom Explosion."

"All the newspapers described it as an accident?"

"That's what they want you to think to keep folks from feeling
vulnerable. Actually, it was the largest terrorist attack in American
History. We believe it's linked to German agents. Maybe some with
ties to our own military, punishing us for sending armaments to the
British and the French. They used time-delayed incendiary devices to
set off the explosions—We won't be neutral much longer, that's for
sure."

"Why choose me? I'm from the Southwest and don't know much
about the Eastern criminal element."

"It's *because* you're not part of the Eastern Old Boys' Club that Pershing selected you." Burnett shook his head with disgust. "It's a real
shame—many of our "intelligence" personnel are incompetent, from
wealthy families who bought them their positions. And the fact you
speak German will be very helpful." Burnett grinned. "And I hear you
don't mind stepping on toes when necessary."

"Is that something you expect to happen? Shucks, it's gotten me
into a heap of trouble in the past."

Burnett nodded yes. "We need someone to go through all personnel records and find out if anybody's loyalty might be slanted. It will
require long hours and the following of suspects."

"I'll certainly do my best to make sure nothing like that attack ever happens to our nation again! But to tell the truth, I don't know how good I'd be trailing folks in the *big city*."

"Captain, just pretend the streets between the towering buildings are canyons and the lampposts are tall cacti...I've assigned you an office with rows of file cabinets jammed with personnel records to review, just to get you started."

Burnett shook Mashbir's hand.

"And, sir, there's also," Mashbir hesitated, "being newly married, I hope the missus doesn't mind not seeing too much of me."

"Well, hell, feel free to blame bad old Colonel Burnett for any and all inconveniences to the missus; it won't hurt me, and it might get you a little slack. As a married man myself, I can tell you, you're going to need all the slack you can get."

Mashbir considered how best to find traitors in their midst. He imagined himself being one of them: What positions in the military would he take?

It wasn't long before he had his first lead✻

"Mr. Offley? This is Captain Mashbir. I'm calling from Fort Hamilton."

"Go on . . ."

"There's a situation I need help with. I've honed in on a soldier whom I strongly suspect is a German sympathizer, or worse, and I don't know how to go about getting the goods on him."

There was a pause, then Offley replied, "Can you order him away from the Fort on some pretext for a minimum of twenty-four hours?"

The following day, a man in a frock coat identifying himself as Mr. Adams, presented himself at Mashbir's office. "Can I offer you some coffee?" Mashbir asked.

"Let's get right to it, if you don't mind." They walked into another building, and soon stood before a locked door. Adams opened his long coat, revealing what must have been five hundred keys hanging around his chest and midsection.

"By golly," Mashbir declared, "do you really know what locks all those open?"

"Once I've had a look at the lock in question," he replied, "I narrow it down pretty quick. Of course, some locks are so simple, you don't even need a key. A hairpin will do the trick."

Adams quickly picked the door lock, then moved methodically about the small room, careful not to disturb anything. "So his name is Paul Otto Kuno?" Adams asked.

"That's right."

"I see nothing out in the open. If we're going to find anything, it's going to be in that." He pointed to a trunk at the foot of the bed. Adams knelt down. "It has an unusual design with two different locks. Never run across this exact model. I've a feeling this isn't going to be a hairpin job."

"Mind if I sit and observe?" Mashbir asked. "I'm sure I'll learn a thing or two . . ."

Ten minutes later, the first lock opened. Another half hour passed as Adams worked the second lock, sweat beading his brow, as he spat out the occasional, "Damn it!"

Finally, Adams gave a twist, and the lock sprung open. "Tricky bastard. This son-of-a-bitch has to be turned to the left, the opposite of what normal locks do." He raised the trunk lid and studied the exact arrangement of its contents. "I'm going to hand you things, one piece at a time. I want you to lay them on the bed in the exact order I give them to you. If we don't want this bird to catch on we've searched his possessions, they'd better go back in the exact same way."

Article by article, Adams emptied the trunk. "Well, that was a bust," Mashbir commented. "Just a few novels in English, two pipes, some tobacco, and some foul-weather gear."

"Wait a minute," Adams peered closely. "See this sand-colored canvas lining?" He ran his finger over it. "Look right here at this seam."

"Looks like it's been re-stitched with an almost matching thread. Didn't we see a spool of this on the dresser? I'm amazed you found that tiny seam."

"I've had practice," he replied. "Now, let's see what he went to all this trouble to hide." Using a razor, Adams cut the stitching. "Got to be careful to pull out all the thread fragments. Look, there's a small hollow in the bottom, just big enough for this flat key." He inspected it. "Dollars to donuts this fits a safe deposit box. See these numbers imprinted on it? Given a little time, I bet we can trace it to the right bank. Meantime, before we sew her back up, let's put a substitute key in its place, so if Kuno runs his finger across, it feels the same. And even if this joker has the occasion to go into his hidey-hole," Adams gave his first smile, "this one won't open his safe deposit box. Tough luck. Now let's get this trunk repacked just right, and then re-locked."

The following week, Mashbir was summoned to Colonel Burnett's office.

"It turns out Kuno is more than a German sympathizer," Burnett said. "His safe deposit box in Norfolk, Virginia, contained a Reich pass to travel throughout Germany, and these other documents are signed by members of the German High Command. And take a look at this," he added, handing a small book to Mashbir.

Mashbir examined it. "It's related to coastal gun placements?"

"That's right, detailing the so-called *dead angles* of all the big guns in the New York and New Jersey sector. Those weapons can only be swung side to side a limited number of degrees," he said, moving his arm to illustrate. "That means that between the areas which can be covered by two adjacent guns, there's a space that's unprotected. If an enemy knows that angle, he can run a ship right in and blast you, without you being able to hit him back. And look here," he continued, pointing. "There's information on our guns' rates of fire and ammunition types. This is conclusive proof, all right."

Mashbir and two Federal agents stood at Kuno's door.

"Do you think he'll give us any trouble, Captain Mashbir?" one agent whispered.

"Never hurts to be prepared."

They smashed in the door, guns drawn, to see Kuno relaxing on the bed, reading.

"What's this all about?" he demanded, coming to his feet.

"Sergeant Kuno," Mashbir replied, shoving a document into his face, "Acting on the authority granted by the Secretary of War, I hereby discharge you from the U.S. Army."

One of the agents stepped forward. "Representing the Department of Justice, I charge you as an enemy alien in possession of materials which pose a threat to the security of the United States. You are to be interned on Governors Island."

"Now get the hell out of that American uniform," Mashbir ordered, "and into civilian clothes. You're only allowed to take personal articles, clothing and family photos."

Kuno put on civilian clothing, and as they were about to depart, the soft-spoken sergeant vanished and the German artillery officer was evident. "You do not frighten me, Gentlemen. In my country you would be executed, whereas I'll only be locked up for a couple of years." Holding up several cigars, he added, "Let us enjoy these before we go. It's pity I cannot take my silver cigar case, a gift from Crown Prince Otto of Bavaria, himself."

"I don't care if they came from Kaiser Wilhelm, himself," Mashbir replied. "We don't want your cigars! And if I happen to run into Prince Otto, I'll tell him you took good care of his gift, up until now."

✳✳✳✳

The following year, Mashbir's counter-espionage headquarters were moved to Governors Island, New York, where he had an unexpected visitor. "Excuse me, Captain," the sergeant said. "There's a colonel out here who says he has to see you on a confidential matter. Won't even tell me his name."

Mashbir quickly shoved stacks of personnel records into neat piles to straighten up his desk. "Why heck, send him in, we're not going to keep a colonel waiting."

"What can I do for you, sir?" Mashbir said, coming to his feet as his guest entered.

"You're Captain Sidney Mashbir?"

"Yes, sir. Are you to be my new commanding officer?"

"No, nothing like that." His voice dropped. "I'm Colonel Emerson. Are you sure we can't be overheard?"

Mashbir stepped to the doorway. "Sergeant, I know it's early, but now would be a good time for you to take lunch. And don't come back for a couple of hours."

The sergeant grabbed his hat and left. Mashbir locked the door. "Okay, Colonel, we're about as alone as we can get. Am I about to get court-martialed?" he asked half-jokingly.

The colonel smiled wearily. "Nothing like that…I'm aware you work under Colonel Burnett."

"Yes, sir."

"He says you're resourceful, not afraid of higher authority and can keep a secret."

"How can I be of service?"

The blood vessels on the colonel's temples were bulging and his jaws clenched. Finally he spoke. "This is very hard for me. I understand you're reviewing personnel records of the Coast Artillery. My father is assigned to that branch."

He gnawed his lower lip.

"I've noticed he's been meeting up with some suspicious characters. He, himself, was an officer in the German Army before our family came here, and has always has been German first, not American. That didn't matter when we were neutral, but now that we're at war…I'm afraid that…if the time came, he'd misuse his position."

Mashbir held up a hand. "I understand, sir. I've had challenges with my father; we haven't spoken for years. I'll do some discreet checking and have him followed. If it looks like you're right, he'll be transferred to a harmless position or retired, if necessary."

"I really appreciate this, captain. If it gets out, my career is finished. I love my father, but my country comes first."

Two inches of crisp snow were already on the ground as Mashbir, in civilian attire, paced the uptown Manhattan corner. *Looks like a lot more is coming,* he reflected, watching the heavy flakes fall in the howling wind. He laughed. "Jesus, it's cold! I thought frying in the Sonoran desert was bad, but damn if I don't think this is worse."

From across the street, a young man approached. After passing by, he stopped in a doorway just beyond, where Mashbir joined him. "Any luck, sergeant?"

He nodded. "She just went into St. Patrick's, like she's done before. I followed her and watched from several pews back as she lit a candle, then sat down and prayed. Boy, was I glad to be inside. My ears and fingers feel frozen."

"Was she carrying anything?"

"A newspaper."

"Did she have it when she left?"

"I don't think she did."

Mashbir silently considered, *So this lady regularly meets up with the colonel's father, and then visits the cathedral on Tuesdays.*

"You've done a fine job, Sergeant. Next time, I'm going with you. Meanwhile, here's some cash—four dollars and change. Go get yourself some better gloves and earmuffs."

The next Tuesday, an attractive woman entered the cathedral. Mashbir and the sergeant were already seated in a far back row of the awe-inspiring edifice. Stained-glass window panels with Biblical scenes competed for their attention…The young lady lit a candle, then took a seat. After several minutes of meditation, she came to her feet.

"Shadow her, Sergeant," Mashbir whispered. "I'll remain here." He opened a Bible and waited. A middle-aged man entered and sat close to where the young woman had been. Moments later, with a newspaper stuffed under his arm, he walked casually up the aisle toward the rear exit, with Mashbir following. *Well, here goes nothing!* Mashbir thought, hoping this wasn't a mistake, and this man was just an innocent bystander who happened to pick up an abandoned newspaper. On the steps outside, he grabbed him by the coat sleeve. The guy jutted a hand into his pocket. Mashbir shoved a gun barrel into the man's ribs, hard. "Don't force me to shoot you," he said, and withdrew the man's pistol. "I'm a captain assigned to military security. You'll accompany me to the Justice Department downtown for questioning."

Colonel Burnett had a wide smile when Mashbir arrived at his office. "Great work, Captain! The man you brought in, Klaus Reiberg, led us to a number of his associates. The F.B.I. trailed those suspects and arrested the last of them yesterday. This is undoubtedly the largest ring of spies we've encountered since the war began. Those ink markings we discovered under certain words in the newspaper, when strung together, gave a code for troop movements from New Jersey to the docks of New York on their way to France!"

"Glad to do my part, sir."

"I also appreciate your discreet handling of Colonel Emerson's father; *he's now retired*...There's a problem, however: you can't do extensive investigations of this sort over a couple of years without irritating someone, no matter how careful you are." He shrugged it off. "Anyhow, *there's some old brass and certain government agencies* who want your scalp—But we're not going to let them have it."

"I really appreciate that, sir," Sidney smiled, while running his fingers through his hair.

"Sidney, you've done a fine job of cleaning things up here, and *now* Pershing has a new assignment for you," Burnett explained. "*And, i*t will get you out of town to Upstate New York, as part of the 22nd Infantry. The General badly needs all the fighting men he can get. Regrettably, many men across America with minor health or age issues aren't able to fight, yet have the skills that could free up younger, healthier guys for the European battlefront."

Mashbir thought a moment. "You mean some might have run retail stores and could therefore manage a military supply warehouse, while others were farmers or mechanics, so they could take care of horses or maintain equipment for military transport?"

"Exactly. It's an important job," he replied. "You're to use your organizational skills to meet these men's immediate needs when they arrive. Determine their abilities, then match them to requests coming in from various units in Europe."

"When do I leave, sir?"

"Immediately. But I'm sorry to say, there'll be too many demands on you for your family to come along."

CHAPTER 7

Syracuse, New York, 1918

Crowds of the first arrivals huddled together in the open fields of the fairground and within its limited number of enclosed wooden structures. They were shivering—some making small talk, most looking lost and fragile...Mashbir surveyed it all, then walked rapidly to his tent followed by three junior officers. Inside, they sat at a table with a plywood top and crates for seats. "What's the progress on those tents, Wilcox?" Mashbir asked.

"The Quartermaster Corps says it's an impossible request, Sir. Normally that number of tents takes three to four months to deliver. I explained our emergency. They promised they'd put a rush on it and get us some in about six weeks."

"That's just dandy," Mashbir spat out. "It's November in Upstate New York. By the time they arrive, all our soldiers will be frozen to death!" He paused. "How we doing on food supply, Oliver?"

"Better there, sir. Supply has promised at least ten thousand rations by tomorrow. I'm sorry to say they couldn't offer any coffee. It's in short supply, at least in the Army system."

"How about that firewood, Dyer?"

"My crew's been working since early yesterday; so far we've got about 60 cords. But some may be a little green for burning."

"That isn't going to be enough," replied Mashbir, a furrow forming in his brow. "Guess what, I've been informed there will be close to eight thousand men coming, not five thousand, with the first large batch due tomorrow morning." He began pacing. "Okay, here's what we're going to do. I want you to get together with the other five officers in the battalion and divide up the men into eight groups. Each of you will end up in charge of a thousand." He grinned unexpectedly,

"I'm sorry I can't make you colonels to go with that responsibility," he said, "since I'm only a captain, myself."

"But how are we going to quarter them, sir?" asked one baffled officer.

Mashbir grasped his chin in thought. "I've been told there's a circus at the fairgrounds during the warmer months, which stores its gear *here* during the winter. There's a war going on, and *supposedly* I have authority to get whatever we need—So go commandeer those tents! I'll hand-print copies of a letter looking as official as I can dream up. Show the letter, and give them some sort of I.O.U. promising to pay rent. Emphasize the urgency. *Also,* contact every church in Syracuse: During the summer, they have tent revival meetings. Appeal to them; it's their Christian duty anyway."

"What if they object, sir?" Dyer asked.

"Then confiscate them, damn it," he replied, slamming his fist on the table. "And Dyer, start spreading the word we'll pay a premium price for cords of good dry firewood. Write out I.O.U.s and I'll get them approved." He turned to Oliver. "Here's eighty dollars. Go to town and get all the coffee this will buy—and remember, none of us should be planning on much sleep tomorrow night. We're going to be busy around those campfires, making sure our new recruits are drinking hot coffee and not freezing their asses off. Now get cracking. I know we can do this!"

Two days later, Mashbir was on the phone trying to control his temper. "Yes, I understand the officer in charge of the Quartermaster Corps is busy. I'm busy myself. I've got almost nine thousand men here in Upstate New York, and it's freezing. They don't have adequate tents or enough blankets or overcoats, and if they don't get them pretty damn quick, there's gonna be a disaster that will make Valley Forge look like a Fourth of July picnic." He strangled the phone. "I want you to know, I've had only five hours' total sleep in the last few days, and I'm just about out of patience." In the midst of delivering this tirade, two Army officers entered the tent, both bundled up in overcoats with captain's braid on the sleeve. They sat and waited for Mashbir to finish his call.

Just what I need, Mashbir thought, *a couple of over-age captains to wet nurse.* "Be with you gentlemen in a minute," he said.

Someone else came on the phone line. Mashbir listened with growing impatience. "Yes, sir, I fully understand, but, sir, I'm aware regulations don't authorize it, but this is a desperate situation. My men are going to get sick, and plenty of them. I know the supply depot in New York has a large number of blankets. If you could just give them a call✻"

Mashbir listened to the response. "All right, Major. Yes, sir." He slammed the phone down. "And to hell with you, Major Whiting— *Too bad I haven't been able to get in touch with Colonel Burnett,*" Mashbir said under his breath, as he picked up the phone again. "I need the long-distance operator to connect me with the Army Supply Depot, Fort Lee, New York...Hello, Supply? Get me the officer in command." A pause. "To whom am I speaking...Oh, Major Barnes, this is Colonel Burnett at the military training camp near Syracuse. I have just spoken to Major Whiting in Washington, DC. You are to put ten thousand blankets and ten thousand regulation overcoats on a train, which is to be delivered to the Syracuse, New York station by six o'clock tonight... I know it's an enormous order to fill." Mashbir's face reddened as he listened to the response. "Here's your choice," he replied, "either those blankets and coats get loaded on that train for delivery, or I'm sending my men into Syracuse to buy up every damn coat and blanket we need at retail price. Then I'm making damn sure that bill goes directly to your depot, and every superior in the Army knows about it, plus every newspaper on the East Coast and every congressman and senator for good measure, with your name leading the story...Good, then I'll have transportation waiting at the station." Mashbir hung up the phone and turned to the seated officers." I'm sorry about all that, gentlemen, just a little supply problem. What can I do for you?"

Both seated men looked at each other for a moment with a bit of disbelief, then stood and took off their overcoats, revealing the eagle insignia of full colonels on their high, stiff uniform collars.

Dang it, Sidney, you bought the farm this time. Chewing out a major, pretending to be a colonel, and God knows what else?

"I'm Colonel Kinney, this is Colonel Hirst. We're from the Inspector General's Office."

This is worse than I imagined, Mashbir thought, lowering his head. *Everything I've done since I've arrived here is contrary to the regulations, which are what the inspector general's top dogs are in charge of enforcing.*

Before Mashbir could speak, Colonel Kinney grabbed the phone and handed it to Mashbir. "Captain, get me the Inspector General's Office in Washington."

"Yes, sir," he replied, while thinking, *this is like having to dig your own grave before the firing squad does their job…*When they got someone on the line, the colonel took the handset.

"This is Colonel Kinney. I'm in Syracuse making that inspection. I've seen the situation and believe Captain Mashbir is fully justified and reasonable in all actions taken today, about which I have no doubt you will receive complaints. Now here's what I want you to do. After we finish talking, I'm going to put Mashbir back on the line. I want you to note any additional requisitions he desires, and make sure they're taken care of, as well as filling all his previous requests. And I mean immediately, not the usual foot-dragging. Is that clear?' 'Good. Now one more thing: we've been holding back a recommendation for Mashbir's promotion to Acting Major. I want that put through right now. He's to be assigned to the Inspector General's Office." Kinney handed the phone back to Mashbir, who put in a few more requests.

After Sidney hung up, he looked sheepishly at the colonel. "I appreciate all you've done, sir. For a minute, I thought I was a dead man."

"If I hadn't seen this mess for myself," Kinney replied, "it might have been a different story."

"One question, sir. Why were you both wearing *captain's* overcoats?"

"It was colder than we expected, so we borrowed them when we got here."

Mashbir took a deep breath. "Well, thanks so much. I appreciate you posting me to the Inspector General's Office. I'm honored. I know it's the most elite corps."

Kinney smiled. "I figured it's better to have you under my thumb, where at least I would have a fighting chance of keeping an eye on you..." He watched his warm breath freeze up. "By the way, *Major*, can't you at least offer us some hot coffee?"

"Sure thing. I just happen to have some of Syracuse's best."

Later, as the three men walked outside, the two colonels looked around and began to laugh. "Who'd imagine, Circus tents, by golly, circus tents!"

"Well, not all of them," replied Mashbir. "*Some* are from church revivals as well."

A month later, Mashbir and the Syracuse Chief of Police stood at the train and bus terminal, watching, as long, orderly lines of men prepared to return to their hometowns.

"You did a fine job, Major Mashbir, in organizing your men," the Chief said. "There are many city elders who appreciate how you kept things under control with that many guys running around."

"Thank you, sir. Your department was quite helpful." With a shrug, Mashbir added, "What with the war ending, those men's services are no longer needed."

"At least they can tell their families they were ready to come to their country's call." The chief pulled something out of his coat pocket. "Here's a present to remember us by," he said, handing it over.

"Why it's a leather riding crop!" Mashbir thumped it gently against his palm, and was impressed.

"That's right. It's double-leaded, like a blackjack with an extra kick. You never know when it might come in handy."

With the war over, Mashbir was once again assigned to Army intelligence at Governors Island, New York. There, he received a big surprise, a phone call from the recent commander-in-chief of the four million American Expeditionary Forces that had helped win the war. "I just wanted to touch base," General Pershing said, "and congratulate you on your promotion, Major Mashbir. Feels like a century since we last spoke. I'm well aware you hoped to see battlefront action, and I regret you didn't get a chance."

"With all your responsibilities, General, I'm amazed you even gave me a thought."

"But you *were* there in a sense. Your brief, to the point, illustrated manual on the *Art of Bayonet Fighting* came in real handy, preparing our men for what was coming their way. And I've been informed of your counter-espionage accomplishments, preventing a repetition of that Black Tom disaster."

"Your acknowledgment means a great deal to me, sir."

"Colonel Burnett told me about the birth of your daughter. How's she doing?"

Mashbir sighed. "Shirley Anne is three months old and having health issues. But our son, Forrester, who's two, is doing real well. Thanks for asking...General, please tell me more about how things went overseas?"

"It was fortunate we arrived when we did. German strength on the Western Front greatly increased after Russia's collapse. If we hadn't been there with fresh troops, the Brits, the French, and their other allies could have been completely crushed. *But* we paid a heavy price fighting against an already war-hardened enemy. Most of our officers had little practical training. In spite of that, they were heroic, with four hundred thousand American deaths and injuries, and Allied losses running into the millions—And that damn Spanish Influenza took down so many of our troops, and millions around the world." There was a long silence.

"Thank God the influenza has slowed down some and the war's over," Mashbir said. "How'd the peace signing go, Sir?"

"Can you imagine, Sidney," Pershing's voice was now elated, "when the French and British leaders joined me, we were all speechless and in tears—And after the victory, I'm proud to say, our men deported themselves well, respectfully protecting the civil liberties of all, both allied and conquered civilians alike," he paused, "There is one problem, however, the Germans, though accepting defeat, were surprised by the severe terms of the Armistice Treaty. That, combined with food shortages, has almost driven them to the point of mass depression. Some say they brought it on themselves. But I hope we're not planting the seeds of another war."

"What would you recommend?"

"We should get more involved in their rebuilding, making sure Germany moves toward a firm democratic government and stable economy. But I fear America will again blindly stick its head in the sand. Our inadequate level of preparedness for that conflict was a travesty! This is where you come in, Mashbir."

"What are you saying, sir?"

"I've a pet project you're to get involved in—you'll be hearing more about it. But for now, to end on a pleasant memory, you would have had a grand time if you'd been in Paris during the signing. Pandemonium reigned: People singing, dancing, and wearing all sorts of strange costumes. If all the ridiculous things done by normally dignified French and Americans during those days were recorded, it would scarcely be believed. *But it was Paris, and the War to End all Wars* was finally over."

CHAPTER 8

A small casket descended into the grave as Sidney and Blanche, with little Forrester in her arms, wept.

The loss of their infant daughter Shirley Anne hit Blanche hard. She threw accusations of blame and threats of divorce at Sidney. This brought back painful memories to Sidney when he was four, and his two-year-old brother, Michael, contracted scarlet fever. He'd prayed and prayed he'd survive, but to no avail…It hardened him, and after that, he didn't see much worth in waiting for invisible forces to get things done. You solved problems on your own. Sidney's mother's mind was never quite right after that tragedy, contributing to the breakup of his family. *Would history repeat itself with him and Blanche?*

Sidney's mother, Frieda, along with her parents first settled in the American Southwest in the 1860s. She loved the wild, open spaces, riding horses, and the independence given a woman on the frontier. Problem was, her father, Sidney's grandfather, was a very conservative religious man, who pressured her to relocate to New York City for an arranged marriage. The younger, free-spirited Frieda and the reserved Eleazer were a strange match. His old-fashioned ways made her feel trapped. He demanded she act like a prim and proper lady, when she'd rather be working on a ranch.

Being a recent Russian immigrant, Eleazer had limited language skills when he obtained his New York State Law License. As a result, he ended up being swindled by clients, linking him to criminal activities in which he had no involvement. Sidney watched the system beat down his father, forcing him to go through embarrassing tribunals that stripped away his license and might have put him in prison—Frieda had warned him not to be so trusting, but he hadn't respected a woman's opinion. After that, she had much less regard for him.

Hoping for a fresh start, they moved back to Arizona, where Eleazer might again practice law. But it was as if they were cursed. Eleazer soon went blind, with ten-year-old Sidney becoming his eyes in the courtroom, whispering descriptions of the mannerisms of defendants being questioned on the witness stand. He also assisted with his father's legal documents, becoming a fine technical reader in the process.

Bitter fights between his folks became a daily event. Sidney hid in his bedroom, immersed in dime-store adventure novels of the American Wild West, where lawmen chased desperados, or he escaped by reading exciting stories set in exotic foreign lands—He'd also draw pictures, all the while hoping to drown out the shouting; feeling torn apart, hearing his father call his mother *a lying tramp!* for running around with her old flames from before she married him—She denied the accusations, which Sidney knew were true. He could still see his schoolmates' mocking faces taunting him about his mother's reputation and ridiculing his father's foreign accent and strange customs, resulting in Sidney having to shut their mouths with his fists.

※※※※

The following week, Colonel Burnett noted Mashbir's weariness as he entered his office. He hesitated, "How are you doing on the home front, Sidney?"

"Getting by."

"Sorry about the passing of your daughter," Burnett looked away. "I regret having to discuss this now, but due to military downsizing and cost-cutting measures, *your rank,* like that of many other officers, will be reduced from major, back to captain."

"I understand, sir," Mashbir replied.

"The field of military intelligence is relatively new to the Army," Burnett continued. "Considering the limited resources, you've accomplished all that could be done." He heaved a heavy sigh…"There's been a power struggle going on between the military and the State Department. Looks like State won, with Congress eliminating all of our skinny budget. They plan to set up their own cryptographic codebreaking intelligence bureau, here in New York City."

"So our location is closing?"

"That's right, but it's not all bad news. General Pershing and I have arranged a unique, new assignment for you as a professor at Syracuse University."

"Really?"

Burnett explained how thirty years earlier, General Pershing had tried his hand at instructing Military Science at the University of Nebraska. It never got off the ground due to strong resistance on campus, where a military presence was not wanted. Hoping the time was now right, Pershing was ready to give it another try, and felt Mashbir was the man to head it. It would be a fully accredited degree program, the first of its kind at a public university. Because Mashbir had so impressed the city elders of Syracuse, they were allowing this to move forward. "You'll pretty much write the curriculum. We also want you to start the first *Federally authorized Reserve Officers Training Corps* unit at that university, to serve as a model for the various military branches—As you know, when the war started, there weren't enough junior grade officers. Plenty of college grads volunteered, but almost none knew the first thing about *Soldiering*. If you make a success of it, someday public universities across the nation will have their own ROTC units."

"I truly appreciate the opportunity, sir, though I had hoped to be sent overseas—to Japan, where I could improve my language skills. There are things going on there we should know about."

"That might well happen," Burnett replied enthusiastically. "Two officers are scheduled to be sent for advanced language studies in a couple of years. You might be one of them."

Mashbir saluted. "Please pass on my regards to General Pershing for his vote of confidence. I'll try not to disappoint you both."

"One last thing, Sidney," Burnett said with a smile, "Syracuse is a pleasant family town. It might be good for you and the missus to have a change of surroundings."

Entering his apartment that evening, Mashbir saw Blanche cleaning up in the kitchen, *her eyes red probably from crying,* he thought.

"Please come over here, I need to talk to you," she said.

"Be with you in just a minute, darling, after I visit Forrester." Sidney ascended the steps two at time. "That's my boy," he whispered, beaming as he looked upon his son, cuddled up with his teddy bear, both their heads peeking out from under a colorful quilt. He bent over and kissed him on the cheek. Returning downstairs, he attempted to give Blanche a hug.

"Honey, how are you doing?" She pushed him away.

"I'm angry, you've always given too much time to your job! Not enough for Forrester and me!"

"You're right, that and losing Shirley Anne is a heavy load to bear." He took a tissue and wiped her eyes.

She whimpered, "I know old folks get ill and die, and that the Lord works in mysterious ways." He gently wrapped his arms around her. "And that our baby girl is with the angels."

"Sweetheart, I know you've hated having to uproot the family for my short assignments—Well, good news, I've been offered a long-term position as a professor, in a nice town in Upstate New York."

"Really?"

✳✳✳✳

Syracuse University, early 1919

The air has a nice nip to it, Sidney thought, as he hiked the campus's rolling hills, watching students rush to classes. *Hard to believe, ten years ago that was me.*

Soon he was standing in front of a blackboard. In the chairs facing him were two men wearing crisp Army uniforms. A third was standing, looking a bit shabby in his; *probably a drinker,* Mashbir thought. "All right, gentlemen," he began, "this is a first-class university, and I intend to establish a first-class military science and ROTC program. I'm aware you were all lieutenants in the war, before budget cuts made you sergeants. You've had plenty of experience, so I invite your comments."

"This program looks pretty tough, sir," said Howell, the officer standing. "More hours than required at West Point."

"That's right," Mashbir replied. "When a student completes it, he'll really know something about Military Science and tactics. By the way, Jamison, how's that rifle team coming along?"

"The athletic department has supplied us an area for a firing range, and we've got three dozen rifles and loads of army surplus ammunition. One problem, though: Recruiting a team of twelve has been difficult. Only seven men showed up."

"Well, at least we're not at war," Mashbir replied. "I'll give this some thought. In the meantime, you're to get familiar with the coursework. We will all be teaching classes, so you'll need to advise me what areas you're best at."

Once they were gone, Sidney noticed some female students passing by his office window. An idea hit him; he grabbed his hat and was soon facing a receptionist.

"I'm Captain Mashbir. I'd like to see the Dean of Women."

"Have a seat, Captain. I'll see if she's available."

She promptly returned. "The dean will see you, sir."

Mashbir stepped into the inner office and came face to face with a large, matronly woman seated at a desk.

"What's this about, Captain?"

"I appreciate you giving me a moment of your time. I'm sure you wish to have your young ladies be involved in as many University functions as possible, including physical activities?"

"That's correct," she replied. "Unfortunately, many of the men's activities are not suitable. We can hardly have coeds playing football, baseball, or wrestling. And there's the issue of a limited budget for uniforms and equipment."

"Might I offer a suggestion?"

The dean nodded.

"Well, I recently attended a national rifle meet where one of the leading shooters was an Italian countess, along with a number of other ladies. No one could say the event was the least bit unrefined. It occurred to me, there's no reason we couldn't train female students in marksmanship, with your approval of course. Army surplus would supply .22-caliber rifles and ammunition, so it wouldn't cost the school a dime. *And* it would provide a sport for young ladies to become proficient at, while building team spirit, poise, and confidence."

She brought a pointer finger to her cheek. "I have heard of a new growing organization, the Girl Scouts, which encourages rustic outdoor skills."

He smiled. "So do I have your permission to put up notices on the bulletin boards?"

"Tell me your name again?"

"Captain Sidney Mashbir."

"Captain, my answer is yes, though I'm not sure how many ladies will be interested, or if they'll show much aptitude."

"You never know, ma'am. It might also be a useful skill for keeping their future husbands in line."

"Perhaps so," she replied with the hint of a smile.

The following week, Sergeant Jamison, accompanied by Howell, arrived at Mashbir's office. "Golly, Captain," Jamison declared. "There are a hundred girls out there. How the heck are we going to pick a team from that mob?"

"Many are really hot tomatoes," Howell commented.

Mashbir gave him a look. "Last thing we need is you throwing a pass at some student."

He stepped back. "I'm sorry, sir."

"Okay then, give each lady a slip of paper with a different number. She can write her name on it. As each one goes up to shoot, she'll hand it to me. We'll take six at a time, and have them each shoot five rounds at the target . . ."

Mashbir took a deep breath at the sight of so much feminine enthusiasm. "Ladies," he said, "I appreciate this large turnout. Unfortunately, we can only pick a team of twelve, plus two alternates. What we're looking for is a willingness to learn. If selected, you'll receive instructions and get a chance to practice three times a week, usually 4:30 p.m. after regular classes. *Remember*, try to be relaxed when you pull the trigger; that helps. And please remain until everyone's had a chance. I will then call out the numbers of those who made the team."

The field house was soon filled with the bark of Springfield training rifles. When the last group had fired, Mashbir announced, "Thank you, ladies. *We truly appreciate you trying out. All of you have potential,* however, this semester's team are numbers: 5, 17, 22, 31, 47, 51, 56, 64, 68, 75, 81, 87, 94, and 102." Those students selected jumped with delight.

"If for any reason an opening occurs," Mashbir continued, "I'll notify those I've listed as runner-ups. Those women chosen, please remain. Thank you all."

Jamison approached Mashbir and whispered, "Couldn't help noticing that many of the ones you selected were on the prettier side, not necessarily the ones who shot best."

"You weren't the only one who noticed, Jamison. There must have been sixty or seventy male students crowded in the back. I want you to post new flyer that we're holding another tryout for the men's team, Wednesday, 5:00 P.M. And make sure to mention the men's and women's team will occasionally practice together."

On his return to his office, Mashbir found a young lady waiting outside his door. He recognized her as one of the candidates who hadn't made the team, but not for want of looks. "Can I be of assistance?" he asked.

"We need to talk," she replied.

"Come in, have a seat."

As soon as she entered his office, she faced him. "What are you running, a beauty contest?" she blurted.

Without missing a beat, he responded, "Mind if I ask what you're majoring in?"

"Psychology."

"You're obviously bright and observant, so here goes—At this time," his voice took a serious tone, "women soldiers don't go into combat during war."

"What does that have to do with you picking women for their looks!"

"Did you see all those guys watching?"

She was stunned. "So all that was just to get a large turnout of guys for a rifle team?"

"To a limited degree. Remember, in the recent war, we were undersupplied with well-trained officers and infantry soldiers. Many of those young men out there might face action someday. I want them well-prepared."

Her tightly crossed arms dropped to her sides. "And here I thought you were just some stupid chauvinist! So you're predicting women might be involved with combat in the future?"

"That would be a heavy burden to bear, but it would certainly symbolize the equality of the sexes."

Appreciating his looks and brains, she drew closer. "If I can't get on the team," she said sweetly, "do you have time to give individual lessons?"

Blood was pumping to Sidney's brain and other parts. He directed attention to a framed photo of Blanche with little Forrester on her lap. "Sorry, my schedule isn't open."

"Your boy's a real cutie," she replied, taking a step back.

"Thanks. I'll tell you what, I'll put you on top of the substitute list should someone drop out. If that doesn't work, there's always next semester's team. In the meanwhile, if you do want to take a course or two in Military Science, you'd be welcome. Bet you'd do great."

Howell entered Mashbir's office several days later, grinning. "It was amazing," he declared. "Ninety-six male students showed up."

"Job well done!" Mashbir replied. "We'll put together a team that can shoot with the best of them."

"Just curious, sir…With the men's and women's team practicing together, won't the women feel depressed because they're not as good?"

Mashbir waved that idea away. "Anyone who applies himself—or herself—can be taught to shoot well. Wouldn't surprise me if they gave the men a run for their money."

Howell pointed to a table stacked high with uniforms. "I procured those from the local Army surplus, but what do we do in terms of the women's team?"

"See if you can't convince that company that got stuck with all those green Army nurse uniforms at the end of the war to give some to us, in exchange for good Public Relations. We'll have the ladies modify them themselves, making sure the skirts aren't too long. The gals these days are wearing them shorter—we don't want to be fuddy-duddy when we go to events."

Six months later, as Sidney crossed the university quad toward his office, he heard a commanding voice call out, "Good Morning, Captain Mashbir. Back from the rifle competition meet, I see," the Dean of Women said. "How did our teams do?"

"Not bad," he replied. "Our men came in second place overall, out of eleven university teams."

"That's wonderful. You've done a fine job. So who came in first?"

"Why, our women's team, of course!" he answered with a smile.

PART TWO

"Is this a B-plus or an A-minus?" Mashbir deliberated, while grading test papers, when the metallic ringing of his office phone grabbed his attention.

"Professor Mashbir, this call is from West Point, the Chief-of-Staff at the Academy, General MacArthur, wishes to speak to you."

Why is the hero of the Western Front, who led the Rainbow Division of National Guards from throughout the nation, calling me? Sidney's mouth went dry.

The phone line crackled, then came alive. "This is Douglas MacArthur, Captain. How are you doing this morning?"

"I'm doing fine, Sir."

"Let me tell you what I need: They've made me commandant of the Academy, in spite of my not having an academic background. But one thing I do know, we need to move into the twentieth century, and stop preparing for the War of 1812! Which is what they seem to be teaching around here now.

"I understand you've drafted a university course in military science at Syracuse—I'd like to discuss that with you, and have you speak to my cadets on Military Intelligence. How about coming over this Thursday morning? I'll have you met at the train station."

When a general asks, you go, Mashbir realized. "I'll be there, sir."

"We can have lunch—You'll be lecturing to the third- and fourth-year men that afternoon."

U.S. Military Academy, West Point, N.Y.

MacArthur's personal quarters are spacious, Mashbir noted, as he was led in by a butler and asked to wait. Soon a tall man in full uniform, a decade his senior, strode into the room, hand extended; following him was a petite older woman of about sixty.

"Welcome, Mashbir, this is my mother. Mother, this is Captain Mashbir, one of the young men who I hope is going to help me reform this fossilized institution, which I love with a passion!"

"My pleasure to meet you, Captain." She offered her delicate but strong hand, which Sidney shook. "I understand you're from the American Far West. I spent many years out there with my husband," she said pleasantly.

"I'm familiar with your husband's illustrious career, ma'am. In fact, where I grew up in Arizona, there were men who had proudly served under his command in that in area and in the Philippines."

"We have something in common, Captain," MacArthur interjected. "I understand you did scouting and lone wolf operations down in Mexico—I did the same thing in 1914, for General Wood, while occupying Vera Cruz against Huerta to prevent foreign arms coming into that country."

"I'm aware of that, sir—one of my adventures was chasing Villa," replied Mashbir, "while serving under General Pershing."

"Who Pershing *never* caught," MacArthur commented maliciously.

There's no love lost between these two generals, Sidney realized.

"Another of my missions there involved the Japanese."

"You must tell me all about it someday," MacArthur said with curiosity. "I was in Manchuria in 1905 at the end of the Russo-Japanese War, as an aide to my father when he was the senior U.S. observer with the Japanese. On his return to Japan he became military attaché, and we also traveled throughout the East, including Ceylon and India. You know, I like that part of the world much better than Europe. But to be fair, I can't say I saw France at its best—all trenches and mud, you know. I especially find Russian and Japanese history fascinating, though I suspect we'll have trouble out of both of them before long. By chance, have you ever heard of the author Homer Lea?"

"I'm afraid not."

"He warns Japan will be reaching out to conquer the whole Pacific. Let me get you a copy of his book."

Sidney watched him exit the room with the same quick energy that seemed to characterize all his movements.

"Douglas can be quite abrupt," his mother said. "His mind works so quickly, he gets impatient with others." Her eyes grew distant and misted slightly. "I strongly believe he's destined for greatness, in fact, even more glorious than his father, *if* that is possible."

Mashbir had heard that the soft exterior of this Southern belle concealed a will of iron, which she was not reluctant to use on her son's behalf.

Douglas returned, holding a well-thumbed volume. "Here you are," he said, handing it to Mashbir. "The author describes the weakness of Philippines' defenses against a Japanese attack. I'm very interested in those islands, since my father was the first American military governor there. As a matter-of-fact, the Philippines was my first overseas duty station, where I damn near got my head shot off a few times by rebels!"

He laughed.

"I look forward to learning more about that degree program of yours. You know, the Academy still doesn't award degrees to its graduates. *That's* something I'd like to see changed. Well, I see lunch is ready."

Late that afternoon, Mashbir and the general stood outside the now empty lecture hall.

"That was a first-rate talk, Captain. I hope you didn't mind my standing in the back."

"I was a bit nervous."

MacArthur waved off the comment. "You did fine. The field of Intelligence is fascinating. I'd like to see it taught here at the Point, as a regular subject. I intend to have officers from diverse fields come and lecture. We've got Billy Mitchell scheduled next week to talk on Air Power. There's also a young officer Patton, who's convinced armored tanks are a coming thing. I remember him from France."

"I ran into him down in Mexico, too."

MacArthur looked at Mashbir with deepened interest. "Well, here's the car to take you back to the train station. If I'm ever in a command situation where I can use your assistance, I will."

✳✳✳✳

Washington, D.C., July 1920

He'd been teaching for two years, and the hint of a new assignment aroused Mashbir's anticipation. The new Army Chief of Staff, his old commander General Pershing, stood and smiled as he entered his office.

"So good to see you again, Sidney. I applaud the fine job you've done at Syracuse. The Dean of the University told me you'd have a permanent position if you wished it?"

"Thank you, sir, but Military Intelligence is my life."

"Hopefully those programs you established can run without you."

"I believe they'll do just fine. What's next?"

Pershing described how he'd been military attaché to Tokyo in 1905 and 1906, observing battles between the Japanese and Chinese in Manchuria, as well as watching front-line action during the Russo-Japanese war.

"Now it's your turn!" he said. "I'm sixty and will be retiring in a couple of years, so I thought while I could, I'd give you a chance to spend several years in Japan improving your language abilities—while also using your Intelligence skills to keep an eye on things."

"Thank you, sir," Mashbir said, trying to hold back his exuberance. "I've enjoyed my teaching experience—but always hoped something more adventurous might come my way."

"Before you sign on, Captain, we need to discuss this further. As you know, Colonel Burnett is now our military attaché in Tokyo. We've received a most disturbing message from him. Washington had cabled him with a confidential memorandum, using Army code, informing him that you and Ed Witsell might be sent to Japan as the first officers in a language study program. On that *same afternoon*, Captain Watari of the Japanese secret service paid Burnett a visit, demanding to know, 'Who is this Major Witsell and Captain Mashbir, and why are they really coming to Japan?'

"*Somehow* he knew the contents of that coded message as soon as it was sent. Burnett advised me that anything we don't want the Japanese Secret Service reading, be sent in a diplomatic pouch."

"There's probably someone in the cable office messing around," Mashbir replied. He hesitated. "Sir, will my family be able to accompany me?"

Pershing shook his head. "There's a growing militancy there that we wish to keep an eye on, and they'll be watching you like a hawk. Your country really needs you there, but it's definitely no place for a family. Your wife and son would be left behind for a year or so, until things calm down...You'll need time to think this over."

Mashbir looked at the papers on Pershing's desk. "Are those my orders?"

The general nodded.

"I'm certain I can make this work, sir."

Pershing slid them over:

To: Captain Sidney Forrester Mashbir:
From the Secretary of War, Washington, D.C.
You are hereby relieved of your duties as Professor of Military Science at Syracuse University. You will proceed to San Francisco, California, reporting in time to embark August 7, 1920, for Japan, where you will pursue the study of the Japanese language and perform such other duties as may be assigned to you.

The following evening, back at his home in Syracuse, Mashbir ignored the food in front of him at the dinner table. Four-year-old Forrester poked him to get his attention. "Daddy, look at my bug jar—I caught a grasshopper." Sidney tousled his son's wavy blonde hair. The boy's eyes lit up. Blanche smiled, watching them play.

"Sidney, you haven't eaten a thing. Are you all right?"

"Isn't Forrester getting real big?" The boy puffed out his chest.

"Blanche, you remember how I promised we'd be settled down for a good while?" She nodded.

"Well, that period has come and gone. My next assignment is in Japan." Blanche fell silent.

"Where's Japan, Daddy?"

"Let me get the globe."

When he returned with it, he pointed and said, "Right here, son."

Forrester laughed as he gave the Earth a big spin.

"It's going to be challenging making such a long distance move," Blanche replied, her voice wavering, "but it might be an exciting opportunity to see the world."

Sidney chewed his thumbnail. *If I tell her it's dangerous, she'll do everything she can to stop me.*

"Darling, I really wish I could take you both, but the military hasn't the overseas facilities for a young family."

Blanche lit a cigarette, a new habit she'd developed when her nerves acted up. "I see. Why did they select you with a family then?"

He tried to keep eye contact. "Although I'm not fluent in Japanese, almost no one else in our department speaks it at all. I'd be a diplomatic aide, helping to keep good international relations."

She brushed back her hair and in a whisper asked, "For how long?"

"A year probably."

"A year…and if it's longer?"

"By then I'll have had time to make the necessary contacts to arrange for you and Forrester to come over. In the meanwhile, you could stay with your folks."

"Please don't lie to me. Is there anything I can say or do to convince you not to take this assignment?"

Her hands trembled. "When we lost our daughter, I almost fell apart. Can't someone else take your place?"

Tokyo Harbor, 1920

It had been a rough, stormy trans-Pacific passage. Sidney's stomach felt queasy, as he braced against the ship's railing and watched his fellow passengers disembark, moving toward Japanese passport control.

"That trip almost murdered me, Ed," Mashbir said, turning toward his military companion. "I'll never enjoy ocean travel."

Ed smiled. "One day you'll take a comfy cruise, not like this cattle transport ship, and you'll change your mind—So what's up with that fishing rod and tennis racket, and what's in that black leather case?"

"It's to create the impression I'm a carefree tourist on vacation."

As they walked down the gangplank, all the new arrivals were required to remain behind barriers until called by name. Sidney watched the security guards meticulously examine Ed's luggage and barrage him with questions. If only he could speed up the process, he'd be able to find a nice piece of solid ground to sit and relax. He saw two pretty ladies playfully chatting and approached one who appeared to be Japanese-American.

"Hello, excuse me, my name is Sidney Mashbir. What's yours, if I may ask?"

"Yukari," she replied.

"Well, Yukari, I'm sorry for interrupting your conversation." The ladies listened. "But, I've a favor to ask."

"Yes?"

"Do you see how Customs is taking all day going through my friend's luggage?" She nodded. "Well, I've had a real rough voyage," he sighed, "and I'd really like to breeze through, if I could."

"Why would they put you through that?"

He shrugged. "Guess they're more suspicious of foreigners nowadays."

"So you're not a spy, or anything like that?" she asked, looking him over and noting his greenish seasick complexion.

"Nothing could be further from the truth! All I ask is that you pretend to be my fiancée as we go through the checkpoint. Sort of a game—Then we part ways."

"But we just met, Sidney."

Sidney smiled. "Voyage romances can happen overnight and end just as quickly. Look on it as an adventure!"

Yukari and Sidney approached the checkpoint. A guard began to inspect Sidney's luggage with extraordinary care. "Excuse me, sir, but what's this all about?" Sidney demanded. "I've come to Japan on holiday with my fiancée, because I was told your country was a welcoming place to celebrate."

The inspector gave little heed to his protests as he unzipped the black leather case and withdrew two lacquered sticks and a riding crop. Holding up the two sticks, the guard asked his companion, "Are these weapons, Nunchaku, without a chain or leather attachment?"

Baffled, he tried to swing them.

Yukari flashed a smile as she reached out. The guard gave her the sticks, which she attached together.

"My fiancé plays the game of pocket billiards," she said in Japanese. "This is his cue stick," running it alluringly through her fingers, illustrating its use. She leaned the pool stick against the counter and picked up the riding crop, playfully whipping herself on the butt with its leather loop. "And *this* is for when he *pretends* I've been a naughty girl."

The guards smiled at each other knowingly and waved Yukari and Sidney through.

"You have a successful career ahead of you as an actress," Sidney remarked as they strolled on.

"My folks don't have the funds to support a struggling artist," she replied, "so I had to be more practical and become a nurse. Quite rewarding—and *acting* is occasionally required." She took hold of Sidney's arm and pleasantly asked, "Is there an encore?"

"Sorry, it's a *single* performance."

"Oh, I see." She let go of his arm.

"Really—Yukari, thanks a lot, you saved me a big hassle."

"Happy to help out, but before I go, I'd recommend you eat some ginger and drink some chamomile tea for your seasickness."

She gave him a bright smile. "Hope you have a *fun vacation*," and off she went.

When Ed finally got through inspection, he found Sidney contentedly sipping tea, seated at a food stall just outside the exit of the passport control facility. They watched the Japanese pass, some in Western attire, but most in kimonos, wearing clumping wooden clogs held by a strap through their toes. Young women carried babies wrapped on their backs, like Indian papooses. And around them, hand-pulled rickshaws, bikes, and automobiles all competed for the narrow streets.

"Welcome to Japan," Sidney said. "A blend of the old world and the new."

Ed nodded. "It certainly feels exotic." He stretched his arms out. "By the way, that was pretty slick getting the assistance of a lovely woman as your cover story."

"You know, Ed," Sidney chuckled, "a life on the stage might be my true calling."

Ed rolled his eyes. "Okay, *Douglas Fairbanks*, let's find us a taxi or rickshaw to our hotel and get settled in."

✳✳✳✳

Over the following months, Sidney found the diplomatic corps agonizingly boring; being taxied to cabinet ministries, trade boards, and embassies, merely to make an appearance with front desk receptionists to drop off his calling card showing respect—Or, being dressed up proper when the U.S. delegation needed mindless bodies to display at cocktail parties, gala events, and formal functions. *Wasn't there something more important to be expected of him and Ed*, he wondered.

It was late evening as Ed entered the dimly-lit apartment they shared, to find Sidney once again hunched over a table piled high with newspapers and books. *He's still at it*, Ed thought, *will he ever get it done?* "How's your research project coming along?" he asked.

Sidney put down his pen and opened a book. "Imagine, it says here that the current emperor is a direct descendant of Emperor Jimmu, who ruled in the year 660 B.C. And get this—it claims Jimmu was a descendant of a sun goddess named Amaterasu."

"Sounds similar to our American pioneer folk tales, like Paul Bunyan having the strength of fifty men."

"Yeah, Ed, but no one really expects to see a twenty-foot-tall lumberjack with a huge ax slung over his shoulder, do they? This goes far beyond that—more like the deities in Greek mythology who were worshipped."

"We've got politicians back home with inflated egos, but imagine what it's like to be considered a god? So, Sid, how long will your opus be?"

"Six-hundred pages or so, divided into pamphlets to make it less daunting: *Understanding Japanese History and Culture in Twelve Easy Lessons.* With a similar format to the Etiquette correspondence course I'm taking."

Ed smirked.

"Mock me now, Ed, you just wait and see. I'm a cowboy at heart," Mashbir stretched, "but I need to become a polished liaison officer who can avoid stepping on toes."

"Just don't change too much. I like the old Sidney just fine," he replied in Japanese, slapping his friend on the back.

"Your language skills are definitely improving, Ed!"

Ed smiled proudly.

"As for me, in addition to my classroom studies," Mashbir continued, "I've been learning a lot by going where the average people live and work, to better understand how they really think and feel! It's interesting how often they want to dress and act like Westerners, practicing their English on me.

"The thing is: Many of their words sound identical, but have vastly different meanings. Now I understand why the Japanese can be so patient—their language *requires* you to concentrate to get word meaning through context—or through additional discussion."

Ed nodded. "Interesting insight, Sid, ol' boy. But right now, I think you look worn out, spending too much time pushing the mental stuff. I suggest you find a physical outlet . . ."

CHAPTER 10

The Imperial Palace, Tokyo, March 1921

Crown Prince Hirohito looked fondly upon the almost sixty-year-old Prince Tokugawa, bifocaled, with sparse grayish-black hair at his temples and completely bald on top, with skin the color of ancient bronze. Tokugawa was smiling, an emotion not seen for a long while.

"Dear Uncle, are you sure this is the right thing to do?" he asked. "No heir to the throne has ever traveled outside of Japan."

"It is most definitely the appropriate thing to do! Our nation requires a worldly leader." He handed Hirohito a brochure. "Here, Your Majesty—another travel guide, should your journey take you to Egypt."

Hirohito was flustered. "But, some of my other advisors have tried to dissuade me, saying I shouldn't leave my father because of his mental condition."

"You've been a dutiful son. This is a rare opportunity to relax before you take on the duties of emperor. They can blame me or Prince Saionji for pressuring you to go."

Hirohito took a sigh of release. "I am looking forward to seeing the museums of London and Paris, but the thought of being away six months from everything I'm so familiar with frightens me."

"Don't worry yourself. The nobility of Europe will greet you with open arms. It's a royal fraternity. You've already received numerous invitations to gala events given in your honor."

Hirohito deliberated. "Is there another reason you chose this particular time for my trip?" he asked, looking his uncle in the eye.

Tokugawa smiled. "I can't get anything past you, can I?" His expression darkened. "Your liberal views have angered certain powerful individuals. For your safety it is best to leave, and come back when things have calmed down."

The following month, Hirohito was teeing off on a golf course just outside of London. His swing totally missed the ball, and he expected the other players to smirk or make some belittling remark. "Remember to keep your head down, Hirohito, as you bring back your club," the British Crown Prince suggested. "Imagine nothing exists, except you and the ball." The next swing sent it well into the fairway.

That evening in his room, Hirohito was engrossed, writing a letter:

> *Dear Uncle Tokugawa,*
>
> *This trip is the best thing I've ever done! I'm being treated graciously as their guest at Buckingham Palace. It is hard to believe I have six months to tour Europe, to do what the Americans call "letting my hair down". The British Royal Family and I comfortably laugh at each other's jokes and mistakes. For the first time in my life, I feel free to be myself!*
>
> *Last week, I accompanied King George the Fifth as he rode in his open carriage surrounded by enormous crowds of cheering subjects, anxious to see their ruler and his foreign visitor. Most exciting, and so unlike our people, who fear to look directly upon me.*
>
> *I was also given a tour of battlefields of the Great War. The royal family sincerely thanked Japan for our strong support of the Allies.*
>
> *Please deliver warm regards to my parents and the rest of the family, and I will write again soon.*
>
> *Respectfully,*
> *Hirohito*

✳✳✳✳

The following year, 1922:
A hush fell over the Japanese Congress when Prince Tokugawa came forward to speak. "It is my pleasure to address you, Honorable Lords! "During my twenty-one years as president of the House of Peers, I

believe this is one of the most important issues ever to have arisen!"
He planted both palms firmly onto the podium and leaned forward.

"I recently returned from Washington, D.C. as our representative
at the Naval Conference of Arms Limitation, where delegates from
around the world gathered. It was very encouraging; the general sentiment was that we must all learn from the recent war, and by agree-
ing mutually to limitations on the size and number of naval ships and
aircraft, as well as the caliber size of our guns, there will be a greater
chance for prolonged peace."

He waited for the words to sink in.

"Just last year, the League of Nations was founded with similar
goals for collective security, aiming to settle international disputes
through negotiations rather than military conflicts."

"Why should we have any limitations on our military?" someone
in the audience shouted out. "It's an insult to our sovereignty—and
the United States itself isn't even a member of the League!"

"A worthy question," Tokugawa replied. "President Woodrow
Wilson was actually one of the founding forces for the creation of the
League of Nations. He promised me that he would try his best to join,
but right now, many of his citizenry fear such organizations might
entangle them in foreign conflicts. They remember all too well their
losses in the European war."

Another member of the House of Peers stood. "Why are Britain
and the U.S. to have an equal number of warships, whereas Japan is
limited to sixty percent of that number?"

"A valid point, to which I have a two-part answer: First, if we
had demanded a higher ratio, or simply walked out in protest, the
whole conference would have disintegrated, with no limitations on
anyone's part."

Tokugawa's voice rose. "Do you really want a warship-building
contest against the larger nations with their enormous resources—an
Armaments Race we would certainly lose!"

He scanned the assembly members.

"Have no fear—we will be more than sufficiently armed for our
own defense, and money not spent on unnecessary battleships can

be used for schools, hospitals and new factories. These worthy goals were foremost in my mind when I signed the treaty."

A military delegation came forward; the senior general spoke, "How can you propose limiting our military when there is such instability in China, with warlords and bandits running wild!"

He pointed an accusing finger at Tokugawa. "With the collapse of Russia's Czarist regime and Bolsheviks now amassing to our north, we should instead be demanding major increases!"

Before Tokugawa could respond, Emperor Taisho, who had been sitting quietly on the dais, stood up as if he were about to address the large gathering. Grinning, he grasped a rolled proclamation scroll, and brought it to his eye in the manner of a telescope, and peered in all directions at a sea of confused faces.

"Your Majesty, what is it you wish to say?" Prince Tokugawa asked. There was no response. "Aides, take the emperor to his quarters and summon his physicians! Dear honorable fellow members, our current discussion is concluded and will be continued at our next meeting. We are now adjourned."

✳✳✳✳

The Crown Prince put down the science textbook he'd been reading when Prince Tokugawa entered the palace library.

"Hirohito, I've come to update you on your father's condition."

"How is he?"

"On the outside he is doing well enough, but mentally, it's a different story."

"That is nothing new."

Tokugawa sensed Hirohito's impatience, but pressed on. "In my humble opinion, Your Majesty, the time has come for you to take over your father's responsibilities, such as attending formal domestic gatherings and holding audiences with foreign diplomats. Emperor Taisho can no longer shoulder such tasks."

There was a long silence.

Hirohito looked at Tokugawa thoughtfully as he described his visit to Europe's battlefields from the recent war. At first, it had seemed like a game, with him posing for photographs while seated upon a cannon, with generals standing at his side.

"But seeing the demolished cities and bloody battlefields close up, where millions had died," Hirohito's hands trembled as he continued, "I came to despise the politics that allowed such things to happen!" His voice hardened, "Let my brothers take my place. I have no desire to become emperor."

Tokugawa was shaken by the announcement. "Your brothers are fine young men, but *you* are best suited. You carefully deliberate before you act. That is what is most needed by your people at this critical time."

"Let us speak candidly, dear teacher. There are many who wish me to merely strut about in ceremonial robes and pretend to rule, confined within the palace. When the British Prince visited recently, there was an uproar that I, a deity, should even mingle with mere human princes. So someone arranged for a fanatic to blow himself up in front of the palace in protest."

Hirohito gave a shrill laugh.

"Imagine what would happen if I truly exerted political power or came close to my subjects?" With the fling of his arm he added, "What difference does it really make what I do?"

Tokugawa looked at Hirohito for a long while.

"My gifted student, it has been an honor and pleasure to be by your side all these years. I do not wish to pressure you to accept this heavy responsibility. Take time to consider, but before I go, I've a question."

Hirohito nodded.

"Are you fully aware of why King George and the English people treated you so well during your visit?"

"We assisted them in the war."

"Yes, but I will now tell you some of the behind-the-scene events… In 1914, when you were much younger Hirohito—Central Europe, long a powder keg, exploded. Germany tried to enlist Japan over to their side, offering to give us the French and British colonies in the Pacific…Though Japan highly respected German scholarship and military science, and had a long tradition of sending students to German universities, and had even based the organization of Japan's army and many aspects of her government upon the German model—In spite of all this, we strongly resisted allying with them. In fact, I had hoped to totally keep Japan out of that war!" Tokugawa brought his arms outward.

"But when Britain requested our support," he said, "we honored our treaty with them, while attempting not to be overly drawn into *their* conflict," his voice deepening. "Had we instead allied with Germany, I believe we too would have experienced the massive destruction she suffered."

"But what would have happened if Germany had won?" Hirohito asked.

Tokugawa shrugged. "Some suggest they would have tried to punish us. While others point out we're on the other side of the world, and our navy was more than a match. In any event, the Allies won, and Japan played a pivotal role securing the sea lanes in the South Pacific and in the Indian Ocean, and conducted naval-launched air raids against German-held targets in China. As you may remember from your studies, these were the first air raids ever launched from ships at sea by any nation in the history of aviation!

"In addition, our cruisers and destroyers supported Allied troop transports and anti-submarine operations. They escorted hundreds of ships carrying soldiers to the front, even forces from Australia and New Zealand. Further, we rescued thousands of men from sinking Allied ships. And in spite of our past differences with Russia, because she was an ally of Britain, we supplied her with guns, ammunition, and medical materials∗"

Tokugawa took a sip of water before continuing.

"Was America fully appreciative of us joining and supporting the Allies?" Hirohito asked.

"Just seven months prior to the death of my friend President Theodore Roosevelt, Theodore felt it urgent to make a major statement as to the important role Japan had played in the Allies' victory. His statement was presented posthumously in *The New York Times* on November 19, 1919. The article was titled: *What the Japanese have stood for in the World War.* Theodore declared that, 'Japan played a part of extraordinary usefulness to the allied cause in this war for civilization. Japan's friendship should be particularly dear to the United States, and every farsighted public man in the U.S. should do his utmost to keep a cordial working agreement of sympathy between the two nations.' He also warned his fellow Americans 'Not to ever permit other nations to drive a wedge between the U.S. and Japan."

Tokugawa heaved a deep breath.

"And now with the *League of Nations,* there is hope there will never again be a world war."

"A most admirable goal." Hirohito replied, while grasping his chin in thought. "I hope you won't take offense by my question, but why, then, when Germany was defeated, did *you* not represent Japan at the Versailles peace signing? Instead, you chose Prince Saionji to go in your place."

He looked Hirohito square in the eye. "I did not wish to gloat over Germany's defeat, nor be part of the excessively harsh terms placed upon her. Now, more than ever, world leaders must encourage coexistence, not vengeance!

"Should you become emperor, it is most important to always be on guard against aggressive policies, both from our own military *and* from foreign nations who would draw Japan into their conflicts!" He paused. "I will now take my leave." With weariness he turned and walked away . . .

Hirohito felt his heart pounding as he called Tokugawa back.

"If at your age you can shoulder so much responsibility, what is my excuse? I only *pray* my decision will make a difference."

Gazing to the heavens, he declared, "My reign will have a name with significance. It will be known as *Showa!*" [Brilliant Enlightened Peace].

CHAPTER 11

The summer air was filled with the scent of pine and spruce, as two men conversed in a forest near the Russian border in western Manchuria. "I am confused, Colonel Sakoree," the Chinese man said. "Why would you pay such a large sum to have me kill your own troops?"

"I'm not here to explain my motives," Sakoree snapped. "You and your Hung Tse bandits are to do as you are told." He softened his voice. "And remember, when the attack occurs, a number of your fellow mercenaries must die at your own hands. Is that a problem?"

"Not at all," the bandit laughed. "It will be a good opportunity to prune out the most incompetent of my men."

The lush foliage resounded with croaking toads and clicking crickets. With the arrival of evening, a crescent moon shone over the military installation as Colonel Sakoree approached the head cook. "Have you done as I have requested?"

"Yes, Colonel," he replied, "I included that special spice in the men's dinner." He scooped out a spoonful of soup and tasted. "It adds a zestful flavor, but I'm not familiar with it. What is it called?"

"We'll talk later—I'm busy," he replied and left him. As the night drew on, his garrison of two hundred and fifty soldiers crawled into sleeping bags. Another hour had passed, when Sakoree walked into the darkness outside the camp to meet the waiting Hung Tse mercenaries, now accompanied by twenty Japanese soldiers dressed in ragged matching attire. "Are you ready?" he asked the bandit leader.

"Yes, Colonel, but our combined forces are barely a quarter of your garrison. Even with the element of surprise, are you sure we can accomplish this?"

"It will be far easier than you think." Sakoree turned to one of his disguised Japanese officers. "The dream of a Japanese empire requires sacrifice. *Those men*," he pointed, "*are martyrs, though they do not know it.*"

The sentries were jumped from behind and the massacre began, with most soldiers lying in a daze, shot without resistance. Sakoree ordered his second in command, "Now go with the Hung Tse and finish the job."

The dead were pulled from their tents and guns placed in their hands, as if they had put up a fight. Sakoree walked the bloody scene with the bandit chief at his side. "You've done your job well. Now for your special contribution."

The bandit whispered to some of his men, and within moments the pleading shrieks of their betrayed bandit comrades were heard as they were shot down—*Though,* a couple managed to escape into the surrounding thick forest.

"Don't let them get away," the bandit leader shouted. "The rest of you, scatter these worthless scum among the dead Japanese, and make sure it looks like they died during the battle."

※※※※

A Dojo in downtown Tokyo, 1922

The elderly sensei watched Ed charge toward Sidney, who once again clenched Ed's heavy cotton *gee* and effortlessly tossed him over his hip onto the mat.

"That-a-boy Ed!" Sidney said with a smile. "For a first visit, you're doing well. Now remember to roll and slap your arms hard on the mat, palms down, to dissipate the energy and lessen the impact."

As Ed got to his feet, rubbing a sore shoulder, the sensei said, "Be more careful rushing toward an adept opponent—He will only use your own energy against you."

"Point taken," Ed replied, running fingers through his sweat-matted hair. "Now I know where you've been spending your free time,

Sid. Those calluses on your knuckles are probably from breaking boards and doing push-ups on hard surfaces."

"Yes, karate, and I've also been learning Kendo sword fighting. But Ed, we're just playing now—*Judo* means 'the way of gentleness.' Shall we continue?"

When the session ended, Ed, Sidney, and the instructor visited a bathhouse. After steam showers, they entered a massage area where they lay in adjacent cubicles, separated by hanging sheets. "I could get used to this part of the workout, Sid," Ed called over, as a young lady worked his shoulders and back. "Thanks for the invitation."

"Anytime."

"How's the family, Sid?"

"After a year apart, it's great to be together again. Our son, Forrester, is a real charmer. Flutters those long eyelashes and the ladies go gaga✻ Pity though, the missus doesn't like living here much."

"Oh before you know it, you'll all be back in the States anyway✻ And congratulations—I hear you're now on the Board of Directors of the Pan Pacific Club's Tokyo Chapter."

"It's an island of sanity in a crazy world, " Sidney replied, "what with the Black Dragon Society with its links to organized crime gaining power in the Diet, and those rumors of Japanese troop movements into Manchuria." He took a deep breath. "I sure wish I could get the ear of Prince Tokugawa. I hear he's one of the more sensible leaders. Maybe we could work with him somehow?"

The sensei, who had been quietly listening, began coughing. "Sensei," Sidney called over, "do you know the prince?" There was silence. "*Honorable Teacher*, don't keep secrets from your prize student."

"Your sense of humor is disarming," the sensei countered.

"Enough interrogation," Ed said. "Just relax, and let these masseuses do their magic."

Dressed in formal civilian attire, Sidney and Ed left the bathhouse and strolled to the Imperial Hotel. As they entered the lobby, a Japanese gentleman greeted them.

"Welcome, Sidney-san. I see you've brought a guest."

"Ed, I'd like to introduce you to Mr. Ito, the hotel manager." The men bowed.

"Thank you, Captain," Ito said. "I hope you both enjoy the luncheon meeting."

As Ito briskly walked off, Sidney commented, "He's seventy, and I bet there are few men in their thirties who can keep up with him. Never retiring might be the secret."

Ed nodded. "Thanks for inviting me along."

"It's the least I could do after the pounding you received at the dojo. Though, I do have ulterior motives," Sidney whispered. "I'm going to sit near Prince Tokugawa during the presentation, and I'd like you to sit next to me and play along."

"Okay, mystery man, I'll wait for my cue—So what's the deal with this Pan Pacific Club anyway?"

"Their goal is to promote friendship and understanding, while encouraging commercial relations between the Pacific Rim nations. A number of presidents, prime ministers, and other dignitaries are *Honorary Presidents of this club*, including members from Canada, China, New Zealand, and our own President Coolidge. Prince Tokugawa represents Japan."

At the reception hall, a butler took Sidney and Ed's hats and coats.

"Sid, you've certainly moved up in the world," Ed declared, looking at the plush surroundings and dignified attendees.

"This is where we have our weekly gatherings. A social hour generally precedes the luncheon, followed by a presentation." Sidney spread his arms. "You see before you bankers, corporate executives, government officials, industrialists, military officers, and the occasional scientist or educator."

An anxious Japanese man and his companion confronted them. "Mr. Mashbir, when are those steam-powered shovels for my coal-mining operation going to arrive?" he demanded. Then, without waiting for an answer, he continued: "Also, I can't wait to see how that *Nelson wagon-loader* performs!" making a large scooping motion with his hand. "They claim it can do the work of *a thousand coolies!*"

"They haven't been delivered yet?" Sidney asked. "I'm sorry—I'll get in touch with the manufacturers today."

"But on a positive note," the man's companion interjected, "thank you for connecting us with that supplier of steam rollers. Our airport runway construction project is moving forward rapidly."

Once these men had gone, Ed said, "I swear, Sidney, who do you really work for? The U.S. Army or the Japanese Minister of Industry?"

"I'm just making some extra money as a consultant, advising them on the best selection of construction and agricultural equipment. They know I'm a soldier, but appreciate my technical expertise. I've even gotten full-time job offers at multiples of my Army pay—which I've turned down, because the military is my life." *And serving my country comes first,* he thought.

Without warning, at the far corner of the large conference room, an altercation broke out.

"What were you saying about this being an island of sanity?"

"Get yourself a drink, Ed. I'll catch up with you later."

Sidney approached the arguing individuals and listened in.

"British Petroleum sends too much oil to the West, but barely supplies a minimum for our needs," the Japanese minister fumed. "How is that right, when there is so much being obtained in Dutch Indonesia, *our* region of world?"

"Come to my office next week, and we'll discuss this further," the oil executive replied.

"Why bother? I've done so before with no results."

Sidney coughed, signaling his presence. "Gentlemen, might I offer a suggestion?" Both men nodded. "Commodities are generally sold to whomever pays top dollar, but that is not the issue here. Japan is willing to pay a fair price. Her need for fuel has grown to support her new technology which is supplying more food for her people."

"I understand," the petrol official replied sympathetically, "but we've already made promises to other nations."

Sidney looked the oil man in the eye. "Japan has long been a good ally of Britain and deserves at least a ten to twenty percent increase. Just have your ambassador write you a letter of commendation for keeping good international relations in the Pacific. Your company and its board of directors will get positive press exposure, and you come out as a diplomat."

The oil man smiled. "A clever idea!" Turning to the minister, he bowed. "I'll see what I can do and will get back to you soon," he said, then left.

The minister bowed to Sidney. "Thank you so much for your assistance."

"It's the least I can do—I'm one of the advisors facilitating your conversion to that new technology. Let's keep our fingers crossed it works out."

After lunch had been served, the chairman of the Pan Pacific Club stood at the front of the room and announced, "As our featured speaker, we are most privileged to have a delegation from the Soviet Republic."

Nearby, General Ennokee, accompanied by several officers, looked on with disdain as the group came to the podium. "See how the decadent Western powers gather round us," he said. "The Russians, Germans, and Americans, all sticking their noses into our political and economic affairs, while corrupting our traditions—The Black Dragon will teach them a lesson." His companions nodded.

The Russians—two men and a woman dressed identically in somber gray suits, accepted applause. The two men sat, allowing their tall, attractive female comrade with her modern short-bobbed red hair, to speak. "Thank you for your kind welcome," she said. "We are proud to report that Russia is at the height of its history. We are now more productive, manufacturing the highest-quality exports. Communism is bringing our people a better standard of living than ever before."

One of her male comrades stood. "We have heard of the challenges faced by the Japanese, in terms of food and energy, and feel we could easily fill these shortages, thereby bringing greater prosperity to your nation."

The woman turned her emerald eyes toward Prince Tokugawa. "It would simply require the signing of trade agreements. We would then be able to send advisors to your country to assist in its development."

At an adjacent table, Sidney had seated himself behind Tokugawa. He leaned over towards Ed, and in a voice meant to be overheard, he said, "Between you and me, Ed—*that alliance* would definitely lead to the downfall of the Japanese Empire!"

"Couldn't agree with you more, Sidney!" Ed replied.

The Soviet delegates glared towards them. But when Prince Tokugawa turned to face him, to Sidney's surprise, Tokugawa's expression was one of amusement.

When the Soviet presentation concluded, Prince Tokugawa came to the podium.

"As president of the Pan Pacific Club, we extend our gratitude to these distinguished delegates for their fine presentation. Their words will be carefully considered. I, and all the other members, truly hope the remainder of their visit to Japan will be a pleasant one...There is one announcement: I wish to congratulate our newest member to the board of directors, my good friend, Sidney Mashbir✳ Let us thank him for all the time and effort he's given to our organization. Please come up here, Sidney."

"We've never even spoken," Sidney whispered to Ed. There was hearty applause as he came forward and stood by the Prince, who put his broad hand on Sidney's shoulder in friendship. "This is a total surprise, sir," Sidney softly said.

Tokugawa smiled. "I heard you wished to meet me," he whispered, "and I desire the same." The Prince gave him a card. "Call my office and we'll arrange a meeting. And please remember to take along that cue stick you brought into the country two years ago."

Elsewhere in the room, Ennokee turned to his cohorts. "Who is this foreigner, and why does the Prince draw our attention to him?" Suddenly he recognized him. "How can this be? That's the man I ordered killed during that mission to Mexico, which almost destroyed my career!"

"Are you sure?" one of his companions said. "He's an engineer and businessman now, and a language student."

"He must be more than that," Ennokee snapped. "Have him followed wherever he goes."

✳✳✳✳

It was early morning at Mashbir's apartment, several days later. Forrester attentively watched as the lather on his father's face was shaved away, when they heard a knock at the front door. "Ouch," Sidney grimaced upon nicking his chin, drops of blood flowing down his neck. "Damn," he cursed below his breath. Pressing a dab of damp tissue to the cut, he proceeded to the entrance.

"You're wounded, my friend," Ed said with mock concern.

"Nothing fatal. So what brings you out so early?"

Ed noticed Forrester poking his head out from behind his father. "How are you doing young man?"

"Daddy was showing me how to shave and he cut himself."

"Mistakes happen." Ed smiled. "Now you'll know how not to do it." Then, turning to Sidney, he continued, "Something's up—a top Navy intelligence officer has wired ahead that he wants to meet you."

"Any idea why?"

Ed looked down at Forrester's inquiring face. Sidney nodded. "Son, why don't you go to your room or visit your Mama, please." Forrester looked disappointed as he reluctantly walked away.

"As for your earlier question," Ed said, "I got the impression they have an important, but possibly dangerous mission for you."

"Things have been getting a little too routine around here—I could use a bit of adventure."

When Ed left, Forrester reappeared. "So what do you think they want you to do, Daddy?"

Prince Tokugawa's Estate

The two battled game after game of Eight-ball, splitting the wins—the atmosphere congenial, but with an underlying tension. "It was so kind of you to accept my invitation, Captain Mashbir," Prince Tokugawa said.

"And most kind of you to have offered it, Your Excellency. How did you come to speak English so well?"

"As a youth, I spent five years in Britain attending Eton College, learning a distinctly new language and culture; very much like you, during your past two years in Japan."

They settled into plush armchairs and stared into a blazing fireplace. "To be totally candid, Captain, I hope you and I will become friends and allies. I admire how you've come to learn our ways and appreciate your support of our industries and agriculture. As a matter of fact, it was I who helped you acquire your first business contacts, and even assisted you in getting research books from libraries." Tokugawa smiled. "And a certain Martial Arts instructor who once trained me was persuaded to take you on as his student at my request. I, too, like the manly sports."

"Is there some way I can repay you for all you've done?"

"We're getting there, Sidney. I know you must find all this very strange, and to add to the surprise, I've been given full access to your military records."

"What?"

"Yes, with the exception of some petty negative remarks, they have admirable things to say about your bravery and competence. Yet your country is barely aware of your accomplishments, including the elimination of enemy espionage networks in your own military, before and during the recent war—Quite astounding! Had that not been done, who knows how much damage to your country's security might have occurred. Amazing how you and a rather small organization did it, obtaining confessions without torture."

Tokugawa must be on the closest of terms with my supervisors to have access to such top-secret information, Sidney thought. "Before my head swells a few sizes," he replied, "let me say that from all I've heard, you're one of the most capable and progressive leaders in Japan."

"Thank you." Tokugawa motioned Sidney to a window. "You see that bush over there?" He pointed.

"The one with someone crouching behind it?"

Tokugawa nodded. "Here in Japan, spies are everywhere; that is one of General Ennokee's men. No doubt he's been following you ever since I gave you that warm reception at the Pan Pacific Club."

The name Ennokee caught Sidney by surprise. "There was an officer by that name who ordered my execution six years ago," he said.

"Oh did he? —well now, he and his followers are some of the most dangerous men in Japan, fanatical militant members of the Black Dragon." Tokugawa sighed with exasperation. "They hate the West and its values, and see me as a fool for bridging our cultures."

"Then what was your reason for putting the spotlight on me?"

"Those men had to be made aware that you were important to me, and they had better keep their hands off." Tokugawa poured two glasses of cognac, which they sipped.

"But why would they wish me harm now?"

"Because of a mission you'll soon be asked to perform."

"Whatever I can do for you, Your Highness, I'll certainly try."

"Thank you, Sidney-san." Tokugawa gestured with his hands. "Just as I'm sure you feel about America, my heart and soul's main purpose is to serve the well-being of Japan. We are four major islands, and thousands of small ones: beautiful volcanic mountains with barely any resources. Only one seventh of our land is suitable for agriculture, and one tenth for building homes. With such limitations, there are many who see conquest and colonization as our only answer. But my hope is that international trade and industrial development can address our needs." The Prince stared at him, only the ticking pendulum wall clock filling the silence.

"Captain, I need your help to keep the peace between our peoples."

"Are you sure you're talking to the right person?"

The Prince nodded confidently. "Soon you will be offered a hazardous assignment for which you are most suited."

"It appears you have a crystal ball?"

"I wish I did! Should you decide to take this mission, I wish to meet with you once more before your departure. But before we call it a night, do you mind if I ask for some advice?"

"Not at all."

Tokugawa searched for the right words, "There is much pressure from the new Russian regime to send us a large entourage of economic advisors. What are your feelings toward Communism? Be as *blunt* as you were at the luncheon."

Sidney emptied his glass of cognac, then replied, "Initially, there's idealism to the Communist doctrine. It is all about improving the conditions of the working class. Problem is," he leaned forward, "they think they can treat everyone the same. Before long, many take advantage of the system and let the *other guy* carry the load. *The ambitious* see it's no longer worth working hard or innovating when the government ends up taking it all away. Freedoms disappear as the regime forces cooperation, with the populace becoming almost slaves of the state." Sidney paused and somberly looked at Tokugawa. "One's culture, religion, and even the sacredness of family are destroyed, replaced by the Almighty Government. It would be the antithesis of the Confucian respect of elders and ancestors, and very much against the long, proud traditions of Japan."

The following morning, Ed handed Sidney a copy of *The Tokyo Sun* newspaper, describing how the Russians' offer to send economic advisors to Japan had been refused.

"Well done, Sid—it appears your meeting with the Prince paid off. Your one conversation accomplished what our State Department probably couldn't have finessed in a year."

Central Tokyo, that evening

The large nightclub dance floor was packed mainly with college kids doing the rag and jiving to a jazz band, the music and dress largely Western. Cigarette smoke filled the air, along with lots of drinking and open flirtatiousness, with couples kissing. The university semester was over, and celebration was in full gear. Mixing with the students were young professionals and foreign visitors, all partying into the night.

General Ennokee stalked into the event with two other men, all in civilian clothing. They ascended to a balcony. "Look, Comura," Ennokee said, pointing downward. "You, as editor of the largest tabloid in Tokyo, are responsible for reporting that foreign influences are bringing destruction to our culture!" With a panoramic wave of his arm he continued, "They have no traditions. Wives and children arrogantly talk back to their husbands and parents, doing whatever they wish. Young ladies dress in flimsy attire like sluts," he clenched his fist, "Leading inevitably to a morally bankrupt society."

"Yes, it is so obvious," the editor echoed.

"I wish we could expel all these Western barbarians!"

"I understand your feelings, General, but don't we need military alliances to expand into China?"

"How can we trust the Western powers?" Ennokee snapped. "Do they not, like ourselves, want world conquest?"

The editor smirked. "Let them do the dirty work, and *as they fight amongst themselves, we grab what we want.*"

"Perhaps that is the way, Comura, though it is of little matter, for they are merely paper tigers with no discipline. At the earliest sign of defeat, their soldiers will throw down their guns and run." Ennokee laughed. "Our troops will offer up their lives in the name of the emperor and the empire, before ever thinking of surrender!" Ennokee turned to Lieutenant Asimmo. "Is there anything new you've learned about that American?"

"There are rumors that Mashbir is negotiating business deals with the Russians involving the purchase of machinery."

"Something is up—I can smell it. You and your men must continue to follow him wherever he goes." Ennokee's voice took a softer tone. "So, Lieutenant, when does the real entertainment begin?"

"I'll go outside and check on the arrangements, sir." Moments later, a mob of men in black trench coats burst in, clubbing the young partiers indiscriminately; tables were overthrown, musicians and their instruments trampled. Machine-gun fire blasted out the ceiling illumination, the room falling into almost total darkness, filled with screams and the sound of crushed bone. Ennokee and Asimmo grinned as the crowds pushed in search of exits.

Outside, they were herded into waiting police and military trucks.

When General Ennokee exited, a police chief was waiting for him.

"Look what I found," Ennokee said, handing him several plastic bags filled with white powder. "See what Westerners are doing to our young people? Their drug culture is turning them into crazed, violent animals." Ennokee looked the officer in the eye. "Now teach them a lesson for their parents' sake."

"Do not worry, General, we'll make many arrests!"

Photographers, with their cameras ready, followed the police leading the way with flashlights, into the building*

The next morning's newspapers throughout Tokyo ran this article:

JAPANESE TRADITIONAL VALUES ARE BEING UNDERMINED BY THE WEST! *Police Raid College Party! Sons and daughters of many of our Nation's Business and Political Leaders Arrested! Drugs, Promiscuity, and Corruption of Our Youth! President of the College has offered deepest apologies and promises to keep a more watchful eye in the future.*

That evening, prior to leaving his apartment, Sidney called out, "Blanche, I'm running late for an appointment—please don't bother staying up." He heard no response and found her in the bedroom, gnawing on her nails. "How are you doing, sweetheart? Where's Forrester?"

"He had an active day and went to bed early."

"You all right?"

She sprang up and pounded on his chest. "I'm so angry at you," she cried. "First, we're apart for over a year. Then ever since we've arrived in Japan, you've been so busy." She collapsed into a chair. "That I could understand. But the final straw came listening to you and Ed this morning, hearing your cavalier willingness to take on a dangerous mission. I can't stand the thought that you might die, leaving me and Forrester without a husband or father. You won't change, the military's *your life, Not mine.*"

"You're right, that was a stupid remark—I was only speaking with bravado to a fellow soldier." He held her hand. "Haven't the details yet, but I promise you, only if this mission is very important will I even consider going on it."

"If you go, I'm leaving you," she pulled her hand free, "and Forrester and I will *forever* be out of your life!"

The American Embassy

Sidney rapidly ascended the marble stairway and proceeded down the corridor. "Calm yourself," he said, then knocked. A man in his early thirties opened the door.

"Welcome, Captain Mashbir. I'm Lieutenant Commander Zacharias."

So what the heck do they want of me? Sidney wondered. "Sorry for being a bit late."

"No problem. It gave the ambassador and me extra time to discuss some serious issues."

Mashbir nodded to the American ambassador. "Nice to see you again, sir."

"Likewise, Captain," he replied.

After minimal small talk, Zacharias said, "Okay, gentlemen, let's get right down to it. Vladivostok, Russia's largest port city on the Pacific, is under siege and may well be the flashpoint for a regional war, or worse." He deferred to the ambassador, who stepped forward.

"Sidney, in response to what the Japanese have creatively called a *regrettable situation*, they've moved by our estimates 45,000 ground troops into the area. They vehemently deny such a large presence, yet assert that *any number* is an appropriate response to the massacre of one of their garrisons, which they claim was the work of Bolsheviks, supported by Chinese mercenaries."

Zacharias added, "Certain members of the Japanese High Command are using public anger over this massacre to gain political control, with those not supporting them being reviled as weaklings. The ambassador turned his steel-blue eyes on Sidney and asked, "Any of this new to you, Captain?"

"The magnitude of the troop buildup is certainly a surprise."

"We're in a quandary," Zacharias said. "Some of our people hope the local White Russian forces will regain power and kick out the communists. Others don't care whether or not Russia loses Vladivostok, but fear the Japanese won't be satisfied, and they'll begin a major campaign down the Chinese coast, all the way to Indochina, and then expanding into the interior, or north into Mongolia."

"So how do I fit in?"

"That's the tricky part," the ambassador replied. "Vladivostok is currently a puppet regime controlled by the Japanese, with an eccentric Russian president named Merkuleff, who supposedly runs the show. He contacted our embassy, saying he's willing to cooperate with us to get rid of the Japanese. Claims he can supply proof that members of the Japanese military along with some ruthless politicians in Tokyo were involved in that massacre."

"And he requested an envoy be sent," Zacharias interjected. "Someone with whom he could deal with confidentially."

"Is the State Department aware of all this?" Mashbir asked.

The ambassador shrugged. "In my opinion, Washington underestimates the threat. They're at the sidelines waiting for events to play out. Problem is, once the Japanese dig in, it will be hell to pay to turn it around." His voice deepened, "And if Russia and the Western nations get drawn in, who knows where it will end?"

"But aren't there a number of reasonable Japanese leaders?" Mashbir replied. "Prince Tokugawa, for one, has a lot influence. Can't he put a lid on this?"

The ambassador shook his head. "He's a close friend of mine. But between you and me, the Prince's life is in danger, with Japan close to a military coup."

Mashbir erupted into a coughing spasm. Zacharias tried to assist, but Mashbir held up his hand, implying he'd get it under control. "It's been a rough day," he said.

The ambassador and Zacharias now noticed just how worn out he looked.

"Sidney," Zacharias said, "I know this is a lot of information to take in. But it's like this: If there were irrefutable proof that this had been a staged massacre, then we'd have a chance to put out the fire."

"*And you're the right man for the job,*" the Ambassador said, patting him on the back.

"But you'd think the Brits or the French would have the most to lose in terms of their business interests," Mashbir replied. "And that they'd get involved?"

"That's reasonable," the ambassador replied, "but a new Fascist movement under Hitler in Germany and Mussolini in Italy is rising up in Europe; and with the recent war still fresh on everyone's mind, they'd rather ignore events in Asia and hope the problem goes away."

"This is a dangerous but critical mission," Zacharias said. "You'd travel to Vladivostok and meet with Commander Richardson, who'd update you on local developments. President Merkuleff would then hand over what he's got, and you just bring it back. With luck, we'll be successful in exposing the conspirators. Otherwise, all hell breaks loose! And China, for which we had hopes of becoming a stable democratic nation, will be torn apart by war."

Oh Lord! Mashbir took a deep, somber breath. "Okay, gentlemen, I'll give it my best."

"One last thing," Zacharias said. "Merkuleff gained control of a large quantity of armaments when the war ended, which are now in Japanese hands. If possible, we'd like you to take them out of their possession, or destroy them." He smiled. "Not your primary mission, but see what you can do."

"You'll be sent as our official embassy courier," the Ambassador said. "Take along this diplomatic pouch, it has some innocuous papers enclosed. And *here's* a little gift. I considered a rabbit's foot, but decided on something more practical."

Mashbir admired the pearl-handled, silver-plated derringer. "I appreciate the sentiment. When do I leave?"

"Very soon."

✳✳✳✳

"It's a pleasure seeing you again, Sidney," Prince Tokugawa said, while guiding him into his study. "I'd like you to meet one of my advisors, Captain Matsumoto." The two men shook hands.

"Captain Mashbir, Prince Tokugawa has informed me of your cooperation."

When the prince locked the door, his demeanor hardened as he turned to his military adviser. "Captain Matsumoto, please describe the men Captain Mashbir will be confronting."

Mashbir noted Matsumoto's posture turn rigid. "These are some of the most fervently patriotic officers in the military, whose actions are largely based on their devotion to Japan!"

"Yes, Sidney," Tokugawa said. "Many might call them fanatics—yet when younger, I too was supportive of my country's desire for an empire to match that of England—a small island nation like ourselves that nevertheless attained a vast network of colonies strewn across the globe."

"Would true patriots murder their own troops?" Sidney replied—and saw fire erupt in Tokugawa's eyes.

"I've grown wiser with the years—Look," the prince exclaimed, pointing at photos on the wall, "Here is my wife, my children, and grandchildren.

"Hear me clearly!

"I—*and the emperor*—have seen the bloody horrors of your modern trench warfare and the aerial bombings in France and Germany. We've watched revolution come to Russia, with *its* royal family butchered! These barbaric fools risk destroying the Japan that I and my forebears built and protected! I won't allow them to turn our nation into a smoldering trash heap under enemy bombardment!"

"You haughty Westerners," Matsumoto interjected, "You look at our militants with disdain, yet refuse to see how your own nations have colonized the world."

Tokugawa pointed at Mashbir. "Americans claim it was their *manifest destiny* to conquer a continent, killing native peoples by the millions or imprisoning them on reservations—cultures with thousands of years of history obliterated!"

Matsumoto stepped forward. "However, when Japan—a yellow race—wishes to gain a foothold into a weaker neighbor such as China, you call us crazed savages! Our militants are no different than your romantic conquistadors or courageous explorers and adventurers."

"I can't change the past," Mashbir replied harshly. "What exactly do you want of me?"

Tokugawa and Matsumoto stared at their visitor. Mashbir broke the silence. "Please excuse my raised voice, I've been having problems on the home front." He looked away.

"And I apologize," Tokugawa replied, "for being so accusatory in my remarks. I hope you don't mind my asking, but what is happening in your personal life?"

Sidney hesitated and looked downward. "This mission is likely to break up my family."

"And yet you go?" Tokugawa stared at him, and in a gentle voice said, *"If you can help us stop these men, Japan will owe you a great debt.* I know we've just met, but I very much respect you putting your life and family on the line." He opened a cabinet. "I have something for you," he said, bowing as he presented it.

Sidney examined the slightly curved blade as he withdrew it from its dark wooden scabbard, testing its weight and balance. "It's a wonderful gift!"

"This Samurai sword was made eighty years ago by two of our most talented craftsmen: one patiently forged and shaped the steel blade, while the other created the *tsuba.*" Tokugawa pointed to the ornate, gold-and-silver-plated handle guard. "Notice the blade is decorated on one side with my family's ancient crest, the three-petaled Paulownia blossom…" He allowed Sidney enough time to examine the delicacy of the workmanship, "And on the other side, the insignia of the Emperor, the Chrysanthemum."

Sidney bowed.

"Words are inadequate to thank you for your generosity."

"I'm fully aware of your patriotism to your country, Sidney-san— but during this mission, you are *also going as a Samurai* representing the Emperor and representing me! Our hope is that this sword will not be needed—but if it is, may it serve you well!"

❋❋❋❋

In the outskirts of Tokyo, that evening, a car drove swiftly through the black iron gates of the Sugamo prison, carrying two passengers in the backseat.

Sergeant Hayato was at the wheel, with Lieutenant Asimmo next to him. "So, Gorou," Hayato said, glancing toward his passengers, "how does it feel to be free?"

"Ahhhh," Gorou responded, taking a deep breath, "It's delightful.

And these fine clothes make me feel like a new man," he said, flexing his large shoulders.

"And you, Hibiki?"

"Prisons are miserable places," the other passenger replied in a soft, feminine voice. "And how do you like my outfit, gentlemen?"

"In spite of being a man, Hibiki, you're not half bad-looking in that dress," Hayato replied.

"Cuter than the women I've seen you go out with," Asimmo said.

"Thanks for the compliment, Lieutenant," Hibiki said. "You told us we will be traveling by train to the city of Fushiki—and from there, by ferry to Vladivostok. Why, then, are we rushing to catch a train at a depot twenty miles outside of Tokyo, instead of the Central Station?"

Asimmo answered, "We need to get into position before the train picks up a certain passenger. You'll steal what he's carrying, and we'll be nearby watching your every move."

As soon as they stepped aboard the steaming locomotive, Gorou confronted the attendant. "Here's a gift for your cooperation," he said, handing him money. "Be so kind as to allow my lovely assistant, Hibiki, to review the compartment passenger list."

"That's not allowed," the attendant replied.

Hibiki lifted a skirt hem, revealing a long knife in a sheath attached by a strap to his upper leg. The attendant almost fainted. "But, I could lose my job," he exclaimed.

"Better than losing your life," Hibiki said, withdrawing the blade.

"All right, I have a family, Please Don't hurt me." His shaking hand passed over the roster.

Gorou and Hibiki then rejoined the officers, who were seated in a private lounge car. Hibiki smiled. "We know the compartment number assigned to Captain Mashbir," he said.

"Be cautious," Lieutenant Asimmo replied, "This courier speaks Japanese and may well be a special agent."

"What do you think he carries?" Gorou asked.

"That's none of your business," Asimmo snapped.

"Perhaps he's dropping off a bribe?" Gorou said. "Or retrieving something valuable?"

"Stop these questions. You criminals are filthy trash, released simply to assist us. If you cooperate, you'll be rewarded. If you cause problems," Asimmo snarled, "you'll regret it!"

Asimmo turned to Hayato. "Go patrol the corridors, keeping an eye out for that American. When he enters his compartment, you are to stay just outside the door keeping everyone away, no matter what you hear going on inside."

Once Hayato had gone, the hulking Gorou purred, "You are wrong, Lieutenant Asimmo. Hibiki and I are not filthy trash—we are artists. Hibiki is a master thief and impersonator."

"What then, is your artistry?" Asimmo replied mockingly.

"Give me but a moment, honorable Lieutenant, to explain. First, I am not stupid—that American might be delivering or picking up something of great value. Either way, we could become wealthy by intercepting it."

"True, but he might merely be pursuing mundane business or political matters."

Sensing Gorou was about to further object, Asimmo spit in his face. "Such simpleton speculations do not make you an artist, nor clever."

"You are the wise one," Gorou replied, wiping his face with his sleeve.

Hibiki began ravenously biting his polished fingernails.

"Gorou, what's the matter with your strange friend?" Asimmo asked.

"He gets anxious easily. Perhaps he needs fresh air—I'll open the compartment window."

On the way back to his seat, Gorou pounced upon Asimmo, wrapping huge hands around his head and snapping his neck.

"Who is the fool now?" he sneered. "And as for my artistry, it is my talent for taking lives."

He spit upon Asimmo's shocked face.

The rogues cheerfully removed Asimmo's ring and wristwatch. "Look what I found in his pocket," Hibiki said, holding up a gold pocket watch.

Gorou smiled. "It will bring you good luck, I'm sure, and I can use this," he said, slipping Asimmo's pistol into his jacket pocket. "Now let's rid ourselves of this pompous ass."

"First strip him," Hibiki said. "Then when he is found, they will not know he is a soldier. And after the rats have fattened on his carcass, no one will recognize who he is."

With ease, Gorou tossed the corpse head-first out the window of the speeding train, into the darkness. "Now, let us see what this American carries."

Tokyo Central Train Station

Staring down the tracks, Mashbir wondered, *If I don't make it back, will Forrester ever receive the letter I left for him, or will Blanche just tear it up?* A train whistle distracted him from his sorrow…As it pulled in, three pairs of eyes watched him board. Entering his compartment, he found a large Japanese man and a stylishly-dressed woman already there. Mashbir did a quick about-face and was soon confronting the train attendant. "I reserved private quarters and paid in advance!"

"Yes, that is so," the attendant mumbled, "but the train is full, and those two passengers also purchased tickets. Your cabin has four bunks—you must share it." The frightened man rushed off.

On returning to his compartment, Mashbir was greeted by Gorou pointing a pistol at him. "Hibiki, carefully remove the American's gun from his holster and give it to me; then empty his baggage on this lower bunk bed," Gorou ordered.

Hibiki did as he was told.

"You travel light, Captain, considering you're going to frigid Vladivostok."

"It's just a short visit," Mashbir replied, forcing a grin.

"What an impressive sword," Hibiki said.

"A gift. I was told it might come in handy," he replied. "After all, there are the occasional bandits who hijack trains."

"Do not worry yourself with such matters," Gorou replied. "You'll be safe with us as your companions. So what is the purpose of your trip, Captain?"

"For a new acquaintance, you're certainly inquisitive."

"I'm just trying to make conversation."

Sidney put on an earnest expression.

"I'm a courier carrying materials that have little use to anyone other than the recipient—and of no value to anyone else. I swear it."

"I've heard differently," Hibiki said. "You go to meet dignitaries or businessmen in Vladivostok to either deliver or retrieve a valuable package."

"Where'd you get such a ridiculous idea?"

"Lieutenant Asimmo, one of General Ennokee's men, told me this before I broke his neck," Gorou replied, he then smiled. "Hibiki, show our guest the gold watch you found in the lieutenant's pocket."

Mashbir was surprised, recognizing watch. "So now, it's only you two on the train?" he asked.

"No, another soldier was ordered to remain in the outside corridor," Hibiki answered, as he put the watch into his pocket. He then opened Mashbir's diplomatic pouch with a key he'd found, and with confusion examined the contents.

"We have his possessions. Why not kill him?" Gorou whispered.

"We need him to explain what he carries or what he plans to retrieve."

While Hibiki pointed a gun, Gorou slapped Sidney's face twice, jarring his head sideways. "Tell us what you know," he demanded.

Enough playing around, Sidney thought. "If I were carrying something of value," he said, "what would you do with it anyway?"

Hibiki grinned. "See who's willing to pay the most—either the Americans, the Russians, or the Japanese."

"But information is like fruit," Mashbir replied. "It can rot while you search for buyers."

"So what are you offering us to save your life?" Gorou asked, bringing the pistol to Mashbir's temple.

"Gentlemen, if you work with me, you'll be well rewarded when I get back to Tokyo."

Hibiki pressed his knife to Sidney's throat. "Our faces are well known by the police. We would be back in prison within a week. What do you take us for, fools?"

"Don't do anything too hasty—there is something of great worth. Let me show you." Sidney slowly lifted a leather-wrapped rod with looped strap handle, and held it up high. "It is one of a kind; very special."

Both men lowered their weapons slightly, staring in wonder. "What is it?" Hibiki asked.

"It's a riding crop used for horses, given to me as a gift by the chief of police in the American city of Syracuse—and it's double lead loaded."

"What does this all mean?" Gorou asked.

"Let me show you how special it is." Sidney waved it back and forth as the men followed the motion with bewildered expressions. In a flash, it came down hard on Gorou's wrist holding the pistol, and with a backswing it hit Hibiki's forehead, knocking him out.

Gorou lunged at Sidney, crashing him against the wall, knocking the air out of him. He aimed a punch at his head, but Sidney dodged it; instead it fractured the wood supporting the bunk beds, with mattresses tumbling down into the tight quarters. The two men slammed into one another tripping over the clutter. Sidney landed a strike to Gorou's face with little effect.

Hibiki staggered to his feet, knife in hand, and with an arcing swing slashed Sidney's arm. Sidney leaped at Gorou, who was reaching for his pistol, and grabbed his wrist. Shots fired all directions, one hitting Hibiki in the chest; he fell in astonishment, mouth agape.

"Look what you've done," Gorou yelled. "I'm going to poke your eyes out!"

Clutching splintered lumber from the broken bed frame, Sidney rammed it into Gorou's face, tearing his cheek wide open, blood spurting. Gorou ignored the injury and came at him, flinging him hard against the wall, where he lay mangled.

"Come on, you son of a bitch," Sidney said, while sliding a hand into the top of his boot. *Get nice and close . . .*

As Gorou hovered over him, his fingers ready to plunge, Sidney fired his derringer upwards and watched Gorou's eyes flitter wildly as the bullet ricocheted within his skull, scrambling his brain.

Early the next morning, Sidney sat on the rubble, leaning against the wall of his cabin, sadly reminiscing: *Strange, somehow my father's gift found its way back to me.* He opened the secret compartment of the gold pocket watch, revealing a tiny family photo of him with his long-lost younger brother and recently-departed parents.

Someone rapped on the door. Painfully lifting himself, pistol in hand hidden in his coat pocket, Mashbir was met by the train attendant accompanied by two security guards.

From the outside corridor, Hayato observed. When they looked in through the doorway, there were the corpses of Gorou and Hibiki. The visitors gawked at the bizarre bloody mess.

"What kind of operation are you running?" Mashbir shouted. "Last night, these criminals boasted they'd killed a Japanese soldier and thrown him off the train, and then tried to murder me."

He displayed his papers. "I'm on a diplomatic mission with no time to waste!"

One of the guards reached for the documents, but the train attendant stopped him.

"Let the American go, I dealt with these cutthroats last night. We're better off with them dead."

CHAPTER **12**

A small reception committee, dressed in heavy parkas, greeted Sidney as he disembarked the small Japanese vessel that had conveyed him the last part of the trip.

"Captain Mashbir, welcome to Vladivostok. I'm Commander Richardson," one of the men said. "You chose a warm day to arrive, twelve degrees below zero, and that's *not* including the wind chill effect."

Mashbir saluted, sensing Richardson was grinning somewhere beneath his furry hood.

"Let me introduce you to Marine Captain James Moriarty, my intelligence officer. You'll be working together." The men acknowledged each other with a quick nod, then loaded onto horse-drawn droshkies and proceeded up the pier to the U.S.S. *Albany*.

As they marched up the gangplank, men under arms came to salute, as a sailor blew a whistle.

"What's going on, Commander?" Mashbir asked.

"We're honoring you—*it's part of the show*. All this is being watched, so just take it in and salute back."

Not long after, between mouthfuls of food, Mashbir described how during the last leg of his journey he'd locked his cabin door and refused to admit anyone; and went without food or water for twenty-four hours, fearing it might be tampered with. Even sealed the bottom of his cabin door to block out poison gas, and kept his porthole open at all times for fresh air, even in the freezing weather—As if that weren't bad enough, there was a constant slamming against the hull.

"I see," Commander Richardson replied, watching Mashbir ravenously finish his second serving of beef stew. "Vladivostok's harbor is completely frozen over. One of our icebreakers spent four hours smashing back and forth to cut a path for your vessel to get in."

Moriarty added, "And that slamming you experienced was large floating chunks of ice that might have broken your hull. And talking about a bruising, am I correct to assume you don't always have a swollen face?"

"Dumb luck I'm still around," Mashbir replied, opening his shirt to reveal a dried, bloodstained cloth bandage wrapped around his upper arm. "I'll probably need stitches."

"How'd that come about?" Richardson asked.

"I made friends along the way."

"There's been a lot of interest regarding your visit," Moriarty said, focusing his keen eyes on Mashbir's expression. "The Russian *and* Chinese admirals, as well as the American Consul General, appear very anxious to meet you. What's this all about?"

"Not sure myself," he replied, putting on his best poker face. "I'll probably learn a great deal from them when we meet."

"Funny thing, Mashbir," Richardson said, "I don't think they know any more than Moriarty or myself."

Captain Moriarty held the reins of the horse-drawn droshky, accompanied by Mashbir, as they trotted through the frigid, desolate streets. They passed shuttered and broken store windows, and saw crowds huddled around open fires or beggars imploring them for food. "Sidney, welcome to our fair city, Vladivostok, which in Russian means 'the Lord of the East,'" Moriarty said. "As your tour guide, our first stop will be the home of the Chinese admiral." As they rode on, Moriarty explained how the Russians gained control of this city when they defeated China in a war one half century earlier. This gave Russia its only significant Pacific port. Seeing it now, it was hard to believe this city had once been the scientific, cultural, and industrial center of the Far East, boasting impressive theaters, newspapers, and magazines." Moriarty paused.

"With the completion of the six-thousand-mile Trans-Siberian Railway linking Vladivostok to Moscow and Western Europe, it gained critical importance—However, the Communist Revolution of 1917 weakened Russian control, with living conditions deteriorating as an enormous influx of refugees fleeing the Bolsheviks arrived in the city."

Sidney nodded, taking it all in.

"Vladivostok is now up for grabs," Moriarty explained, "various nations vying for access to this valuable port, with skirmishes a frequent event." He shook his head bemusedly. "The situation was further complicated in 1918 by the occupation of the city by thousands of Czech soldiers."

"What was the Czech Army doing way over here?" Sidney asked.

"It was part of a massive retreat during the recent war to avoid being totally destroyed by the German army. They escaped on the Trans-Siberian Railway, taking along twenty carloads of munitions, with the hope of someday returning to fight. But the war ended, and the new Bolshevik regime wouldn't let them return through Russia, unless they left behind most of their weaponry." Moriarty shrugged. "So when they exited, the Japanese became the largest occupying force and immediately confiscated those Czech munitions from the weak local Russian authority."

"I was told about those weapons."

"It's kind of strange," Moriarty went on. "At first Vladivostok's populace welcomed the Japanese soldiers as their saviors, thinking they'd protect them from the Bolsheviks. To their dismay, they soon realized the Japanese had their own agenda. The harbor was blockaded and only limited supplies were allowed in." The droshky came to a halt. "We've arrived," he said, dismounting from the wagon and leading the way.

During the next hour, there was light conversation, with everything but politics being discussed. "Do either of you want another drink?" Chinese Admiral Chang asked.

"These are the most excellent Martinis I've ever had," Mashbir replied, taking another sip, "but three's enough. Thank you."

"This is my last one as well," Moriarty echoed. "Very hospitable of you to have invited us to your fine home, Admiral."

"My pleasure."

The admiral's smile vanished. "Captain Mashbir, I've a favor to ask. I realize it's not *your concern*, but it's rumored you're on some sort of diplomatic mission," he said awkwardly, "and I hoped you might assist me on a serious matter affecting my countrymen."

"What is their status here?"

"Under the Russians, the Chinese residents were always to be self-governing in their own communities," he answered. "This arrangement worked well—but ever since the massacre of that Japanese garrison was blamed on Bolsheviks assisted by Chinese mercenaries, things have changed. The Japanese now claim the right to increase their military presence. They are intimidating the Russians and Chinese into either handing over all power or instigating a fight the Japanese would certainly win."

Creases furrowed the admiral's forehead. "Last month, Russian soldiers arrested many of the most esteemed members of our Chinese community, without any credible charges against them." A pained look appeared on his face. "Some were close friends of mine." He sighed. "The Russians then handed them over to the Japanese, who placed them in prison."

"Why would the Russians be working with the Japanese?" Mashbir asked.

"It's that Merkuleff," the admiral replied. "He's an aristocrat whom the Japanese have propped up as President of the Far Eastern Republic. He's a wily one, but has no real power. This arrangement allows the Japanese to proclaim there is Russian cooperation."

"Has your consulate launched a formal protest?" Moriarty asked.

"Yes. We've notified all the embassies, including yours."

"What came of it?"

"One councilman was released, but only after he'd been beaten about the temples until he went insane." The admiral gulped his drink. "It's a form of torture they employ that leaves no bruises."

This wasn't part of the script, Mashbir thought. "Admiral, might I suggest we meet aboard the *Albany* tomorrow to further discuss this matter?"

"Thank you, Captain. I'll arrange that our consul general attends as well."

"Now, Captain Moriarty and I are off to pay our respects to the Russian admiral. Thanks again for your hospitality."

Later that afternoon, they were feeling tipsy as they left the Russian Embassy, after the several friendly vodkas their host had plied them with.

"Okay, James," Sidney said, "next stop, the American Consulate. You know, I kinda like these droshkies," he slurred. "Reminds me of horses and buggies, except for the sleds, and the passenger benches running lengthwise."

They rode silently for a while.

"Why, look at that," he remarked, nearing their destination. *Our consulate* has the Japanese Military Headquarters on the second floor, right above it."

"And look at their Rising Sun," Moriarty chuckled, "Four times the size of our American flag."

As they entered Consul General McGowan's office, Sidney noticed the fireplace ran to the floor above. *I'd bet a month's salary there's a listening device inside,* he thought; he wrote a note to that effect, which he passed to McGowan.

McGowan acknowledged it with a nod.

"Here sir, let me hand over my diplomatic pouch," Mashbir said in a clear voice. "Just the usual requests for passports and citizenship papers."

"Thanks for making the delivery, Captain."

McGowan emptied the pouch on his desk, raising an eyebrow upon seeing the splatter of dried blood on several envelopes.

As the three men ate lunch, Mashbir slipped another note to McGowan:

Something important has come up. You're invited aboard the U.S.S. Albany for lunch tomorrow at noon.

CHAPTER 13

Japanese Military Headquarters, Vladivostok

General Isobe's deep-set eyes bored into Colonel Sakoree, wondering why there was such anger in the colonel's voice as he ranted against that American courier Mashbir's suspicious meetings with the Russian and the Chinese admirals.

An aide entered. "Pardon the interruption, sir, but Colonel Sakoree has a visitor who says he must speak with him urgently."

Sakoree gave a curt bow, then rushed off to his private office.

"It's about time *you* showed up, Sergeant Hayato; Captain Mashbir arrived several days ago," Sakoree shouted. "And where is Lieutenant Asimmo and those two thugs that were to assist you in detaining him?"

Hayato looked away in shame. "Asimmo disappeared from the train and those convicts were murdered."

Sakoree put a palm to his suddenly aching forehead. "Tell me everything you know about this Captain Mashbir."

"He has many business contacts in Tokyo, and Prince Tokugawa himself has befriended him."

"Damn it! Why is he here?"

"There are rumors he wishes to make contact with anti-Bolshevik leaders."

"We must find out. Follow him."

On Sakoree's return to General Isobe's office, the general was snapping his fingers impatiently.

"General, I just received disturbing news. I've been informed

Mashbir has powerful Japanese allies, and is probably a special agent or spy working against us."

"Stop babbling. What aren't you telling me?"

"I have no secrets. Give me time and I'll uncover his true mission. But perhaps, it would be better if we just get rid of him."

Isobe slammed his fist down. "First you tell me he has highly placed allies in Japan, then you say he's up to something but don't know what. Things are tense enough with the Americans. Their expeditionary forces have just departed. Do you want thousands of Marines to return just as we are gaining power?"

"What if I could prove he's a spy—catch him red-handed? Currently, we outnumber the Americans twenty to one."

"Show me the proof, and I'll sign his death sentence."

The following day, Mashbir, Moriarty, Consul General McGowan, and Commander Richardson gathered aboard the U.S.S. *Albany*:

"It's interesting how a mutual adversary brings folks together, Commander," Mashbir said. "I've been brainstorming strategies related to the illegal arrests and mistreatment of those Chinese councilmen."

"Under international law," Richardson said, "I'm authorized to act when it comes to protecting innocent civilian lives, but I'm not sure how best to handle this."

"The trick is to accomplish the goal without turning it into a major incident," Mashbir replied. "The Chinese admiral informed me the Russians arrested them, but the Japanese were really behind it, with Merkuleff under their thumb. He believes the Japanese can't wait to begin looting Vladivostok, hoping to find hoarded gold and treasure. Chinese Hung Tse mercenaries would surely join in."

"So what's your plan?" McGowan asked.

Mashbir smiled. "What if we pretend to offer the leaders of the Chinese colony—and their families—asylum aboard our vessel, allowing them to take their most valuable possessions? That would certainly result in bad international press for the Russians and Japanese."

"Yeah, but what happens if a fight erupts?" Richardson countered.

"Remember, this is just a bluff we can back down from! Moriarty tells me he can round up fifty droshkies driven by Marines, to transport these evacuees. And as part of this charade, we raise the stakes. You see," he said, motioning with his hands, "I'm a member of the Pan Pacific Club in Tokyo; sometimes after meetings, members stick around for a game of poker. I've noticed strategically the Japanese are great game players, but in poker they tend to get too emotional when dealt a fine hand or a very poor one. Luck is a powerful force in their culture."

"And the point, Captain?" Richardson asked.

"We make them think their luck has turned sour." While his concept sank in, they heard conversation in the corridor. "Looks like the Chinese have arrived," Mashbir announced. "Now let's add them to our cast of characters."

The Chinese admiral and two others entered the stateroom. "Gentlemen, we appreciate your concern for misfortune," the admiral said. "I've invited Consul General Chin and my top aide, Ying, to attend."

"We welcome you all," Mashbir replied. "Captain Moriarty, Commander Richardson, Consul General McGowan, and I have formulated a plan to gain the release of your imprisoned countrymen by creating an illusion—with you playing a part in this gambit."

"What exactly do you mean?" the admiral replied.

"It begins with you and your consul general, meeting with President Merkuleff, demanding the release of all Chinese prisoners and the return of control of the Chinese colony."

"What if he refuses?"

"Tell him the Americans plan to assist you by evacuating the leaders of the Chinese community. And warn him you've lodged a complaint with your superiors in Peking—that all financial losses incurred here by Chinese businesses and persons will be repaid through the confiscation of Russian and Japanese assets."

"But we've done no such thing," the admiral replied.

Mashbir smiled. "It's all just for show. Then, you visit Merkuleff again and update him that provinces throughout China will soon be seizing property and cash. For good measure, tell him the world banking community is preparing to freeze assets, even the emperor's own foreign holdings, until these hostages are released." Mashbir took a deep breath and waited for their response.

"What if they don't cooperate?" Consul General Chin asked.

"That's when the live performance begins," he replied. "U.S. Marines will start an evacuation of your countrymen. But personally, I don't believe the Japanese wish to confront us over this particular matter without authorization, which takes weeks to obtain from Tokyo. We must act as though our threats are deadly serious."

After the Chinese delegation left, Mashbir turned to Richardson. "I suggest we send coded radio broadcasts using one the Japanese have broken, giving them a clear message that this is the real thing."

Richardson half-smiled, "Let's cross our fingers and hope your imaginative plan works."

"Sir, I've been doing a lot of that recently."

The next day, Mashbir was surprised to find his presence requested by Colonel Sakoree, the head of Japanese Intelligence in Vladivostok. Moriarty demanded he come along as backup when Mashbir visited Sakoree's office. As they went to this appointment, Mashbir said, "Now remember, you and I talk about everything under the sun, except military matters: Microphones will be everywhere."

On their arrival, they were met by a female receptionist, who informed them Colonel Sakoree was busy but would be with them shortly.

"What a pleasant waiting area, James," Sidney commented, as they were led into a conference room. "And look, they've graciously stocked a bar for us."

"After all the drinking we've been up to, I'll pass," James replied. The men noticed a wooden table, upon which were bundles of maps and documents, most stamped in red ink *Gokuhi*, meaning 'Top Secret.'

"What a blatant trap," Mashbir whispered. "Let's just keep looking outside the window, making casual conversation." James tugged Sidney's sleeve, directing his gaze to window curtains in an adjacent building, which were pulled slightly open, revealing binoculars.

Over the next half hour, Sakoree was regularly updated as to whether anything had been touched or taken. Finally, he ordered his guests be brought to his office.

"I'm so sorry having kept you both waiting," Sakoree said, grinning as they arrived.

"That's fine, Colonel," Mashbir replied. "You are a busy man. One must learn to be patient when waiting for busy men to grant them an audience."

"And it was nice to have some quiet time to reflect," Moriarty added.

Sakoree appeared confused by the comments. "Captain Mashbir, why exactly are you here? And, while you are at it, I'd like to hear your personal views on Japanese expansion into Asia."

"I'm so flattered you wish my opinion on such matters, but I have no interest in politics. I recommend you contact our State Department. Regrettably, our time is limited, colonel—We've an appointment with the American Consul General, who's expecting us right now aboard the *U.S.S. Albany*."

Sakoree put out his palm. "Before you go, let me give you a gift, a map showing where our two divisions are located." He began drawing. "Here, take this back to Tokyo," he said.

There are probably closer to five divisions, Mashbir thought. "I'm honored to accept this wonderful memento, but please add a personal inscription made out to me. It will then be something I will always value, from the hand of one of Japan's great officers." Mashbir gave Sakoree a pen, and he reluctantly obliged. "Colonel Sakoree, you've been so generous. Might I ask one more favor?"

Sakoree flashed a frustrated nod.

"Please send my regards to General Isobe and let him know I have a message for him from the Japanese Royal Family."

"What?" Sakoree stumbled. "Okay, tell me the message, and I will deliver it."

"Thanks for offering, but I gave my solemn oath to speak only to him."

"All right, I will let the general know."

When the Americans had gone, Sakoree exploded, "That clever bastard, I'll find out what he's up to."

Outside the headquarters, Mashbir tucked the map into his pocket. "James, one day I'll use this to prove Sakoree is a traitor assisting us," he said with a smile, then added, "With all the things that have come up during the past couple of days, I've put off my primary mission, that of visiting President Merkuleff."

They hadn't used their droshky that day, preferring mounted horses. They rode to the main public square—a silent, windswept, deserted space. "He lives nearby," Moriarty said.

"Holy Moses," Mashbir declared; surrounding them were a collection of frozen corpses on display, hanging by their necks tied to lampposts or impaled on sharp wooden stakes. "What's this all about?"

"Read the notes tied around their necks and find out."

Sidney chose one that was most likely a male—its icy covering made it hard to tell, with frozen blood, like a bib, below its neck. He translated the Russian note out loud:

"'This criminal was executed for stealing food from the marketplace. Let this be a warning to others.'"

"Pretty severe penalty for petty theft," Moriarty said. "I've seen enough. Let's get going—Merkuleff lives right over there," he directed, pointing.

Upon repeatedly banging a heavy bronze, bear-shaped knocker, a butler ushered them into a luxurious home. "Ahhhh, my American friends, I've been eagerly awaiting your visit," a slim, bald-headed man in his seventies announced.

"So, President Merkuleff," Mashbir said, "shall we get right down to business?"

"Business?" he replied, twirling his mustache. "That can wait until tomorrow—we're going to a celebration." He called, "Girls! My lovely nieces, come, don't hide yourselves—two young, handsome escorts have arrived!"

Descending the winding marble staircase came two older ladies, dressed in the traditional fashion of Dresden dolls. "Off we go," Merkuleff ordered in high spirits, herding everyone into a lavish coach pulled by two white horses.

Soon they found themselves approaching an even larger estate. Once inside, they were greeted by an orchestra playing Strauss, to which women in elaborate gowns, men with long-tailed tuxedos, and officers in medal bedecked uniforms waltzed across the ballroom.

"This is the old Russia I love," Merkuleff exclaimed. "Those damn communists have ruined it all. The Tsars knew how to throw grand parties." He looked around. "While I get myself a drink, why don't you Americans dance with my nieces, and make the other ladies jealous with curiosity, wondering who you are," he said with a wink.

As soon as he could, Sidney slipped away to get something to eat. At the buffet, a Russian general approached him, offering a jewel-encrusted medal from his chest. "Here—I received this for valor, from the Tsarina herself." He looked away. "The times are hard. Can I sell it to you?" Sidney pulled out several bills and gave them to the old Russian. "Keep your medal—you earned it."

Later that night, after they'd parted, Sidney turned to James, "That was unreal. Who would have guessed such grandeur would exist *here*, at this time?"

"And isn't Merkuleff something else?" James replied. "And his nieces. Oh God, they're old enough to be our mothers."

"Did they propose to you too?"

James laughed. "If you still have some energy left, there's another unique place I'd like you to experience."

Not long after, they were seated in the front row at a cabaret. "Welcome to the Fish Pond," James said with wink.

"Why the strange name?"

"You'll find out."

A drum roll played as a throng of half-naked women paraded onto a central stage, surrounded by a circular arrangement of dinner tables. Waitresses wandered about, offering patrons short fishing rods with foam balls attached to the end of their lines. The audience listened and watched as some women began to sing, while others did dances showcasing their skill and physical attributes.

"If a guest *appreciates* one of these ladies," James said, "he casts his line and reels her in—sometimes they catch two for the evening."

"Several of the girls don't look all that excited about being treated like halibut," Sidney replied.

"They're not professional prostitutes, mainly desperate women with no alternatives. Generally, I come for the show." A waitress offered Sidney a fishing pole. He waved her off.

"You could just keep it playful," James said.

A blonde with long hair slung over one shoulder and wearing a frilly pink slip, sat on James's lap. He put an arm around her waist and closed his eyes, taking in her fragrance. "This place is tame," he said. "Most night spots are now filled with thieves and murderers."

Sidney nodded. "Merkuleff did mention that the three cheapest things in Vladivostok were women, the taking of lives, and medals."

"That's right. For just one small gold ruble, you can have someone disposed of. For two, it's a special deal—they dig a hole in the ice, dump the corpse, and give you the victim's fur coat."

Mashbir observed a group of Japanese soldiers seated nearby. A drunken sergeant came over and jumped onto their table, and shouted in English, "We will take over all Asia. And anyone, including you Americans, who gets in the way will be crushed!" he blustered. His companions roared approval.

Moriarty tapped the girl to get off his lap and prepared to deal with the situation.

"Slow down, James—look how many there are," Sidney said, putting a grip on his arm. "Let him spout off—I'll take care of this."

"Yes, Sergeant, you are strong," Mashbir said. "Do you know Karate kicks?"

As the drunken soldier displayed his moves, Mashbir lifted the table barely an inch. The man tumbled to the ground, with his companions clamoring to pick him up.

"James," Sidney urged, "this would be a good time for a quick exit."

CHAPTER 14

With an ice pack pressed to his head, Merkuleff greeted Sidney and James at his estate the following morning. "I must have drunk *a bit* too much last night," he said with grin. "I hope you're enjoying our fair city."

"Almost like the *French Riviera*," Sidney replied, to which the Russian broke out in laughter, in spite of his aching head. "So, President, I'm ready to receive what you offered our ambassador."

"You Americans. Always in a hurry. At the party, I noticed you spoke Russian, Captain. Where are you from?"

"Born in New York City, but spent most of my life in Arizona."

"I've heard of New York, Chicago, Hollywood, but where is Arizona?"

"Near Texas and Mexico."

"That explains it!" Merkuleff threw out his arms wide. "You're that movie cowboy with the white hat, shooting bad guys and saving ladies in distress. Who else would be crazy enough to go on such a suicidal mission?" he sputtered. "I'm old with little to lose, but you're a young man."

"If that's the case," Sidney countered, "why have you shown such hesitancy in handing over those documents?"

"I've a family to think of—Find a secure location where we can meet tomorrow, and you'll get what you came for."

Moriarty replied, "There's an abandoned coach at the far western end of the railroad terminal."

"How about tomorrow evening at 7 P.M?" Sidney suggested.

Merkuleff nodded. "I'll be there."

"Before we go," Sidney said, "I've a question. At that gala event, you said you missed the good old days with the tsar?"

"Most definitely. Here we are—the last White Russian outpost." Merkuleff lit a cigarette. "Those Bolsheviks are a cold-hearted lot, and it won't be long before our world crumbles."

"I've a proposal then," Sidney said. "What if by working together we slow down the Bolsheviks?"

Merkuleff took a long drag, then crushed out his cigarette. "How might that be accomplished?"

"You know those twenty boxcar loads of Czech arms now in the hands of the Japanese?"

"Of course—they took them from me."

"What if they found their way to anti-Bolshevik forces?"

Merkuleff gave a mischievous smile.

✳✳✳✳

The first droshkies arrived at the pier, filled with Chinese civilians, their warm breath fogging the frigid morning air. "Advise them to get down carefully and proceed up the gangplank," Mashbir said to his Chinese translator. "They'll get assistance carrying their possessions, if they need it."

Moriarty approached Mashbir and Commander Richardson. "So far, so good," he said. "All across the city, Marines are waiting for the order to take on more passengers."

Their attention was drawn to a Japanese soldier on horseback galloping up the pier toward them. He dismounted and handed a note to Commander Richardson, then left. Upon reading it, the Commander displayed a wide smile. "It's from General Isobe—I'm very happy to say his note states the prisoners will be released this afternoon." Richardson gave a sigh of relief. "I was beginning to wonder where on earth I was going to house all those folks on the *Albany*, before having to send them back to their homes in few days, *if* this scheme didn't work."

A large gathering of Chinese civilians waited at the appointed rendezvous site, an isolated road on the outskirts of town. Mashbir and Moriarty were accompanied by a squad of Marines. Also present was the Chinese Consul General, and the Chinese admiral. "Look at this crowd, Sidney," Moriarty said. "Word must have gotten out to family members and friends."

The distant sound of rumbling could be heard. Soon a large covered truck escorted by several armored cars, and an open military transport filled with Japanese soldiers, arrived. The soldiers spilled out of their vehicle. The crowd parted and the two armed groups faced off. Colonel Sakoree strutted to the front, glaring at Mashbir and his companions. He ordered his soldiers to begin unloading the prisoners from the covered truck.

Some appear to have been beaten, Sidney thought. *Most look malnourished and sickly, but at least they're breathing.*

The crowd rushed to greet them.

"Thank you, Colonel Sakoree," the Chinese Consul General said. "It was most kind of you and General Isobe to release our citizens and personally return them."

With a grin, Moriarty aimed a middle finger at Sakoree.

Sakoree barked an order, and his men climbed back into their vehicles and left.

Among the crowd was Lee, a tall teenager, who ran to embrace his grandfather. *That's strange,* Lee thought, *why is that Chinese admiral and the other Chinese dignitary bowing to that American soldier and shaking his hand?* "Grandfather, please come with me," he said, and side by side they walked over. "Did this American arrange the release?" Lee asked in Chinese, pointing at Mashbir, while scrutinizing the Chinese admiral's face. The admiral hesitantly nodded. Lee translated this for his grandfather, who turned to Mashbir. "Sherr, sherr," he said, grasping Mashbir's hand firmly with both his own.

The old man whispered into Lee's ear.

"My grandfather thanks you and the others for rescuing them, and wants to know *your name*," Lee said in English, looking at Mashbir.

"Captain Sidney Mashbir, at your service."

Lee dropped to his knees. "Captain, my grandfather begs you to visit our home in the Chinese colony this afternoon."

Mashbir looked into the grandfather's bloodshot resolute eyes . . .

Sidney was soon finishing a second serving of potato dumplings and duck.

"These are true scarcities," Lee said. "My grandmother hopes you are enjoying the meal." The little lady stood nearby, bobbing her head with satisfaction, watching him eat.

"Tell her it's delicious! But if I eat any more, I'll burst."

"Grandmother says you look tired. Why don't you take a short nap in our guest room?"

Yes, I've been pushing hard, he thought. *"Thank you," he replied.*

When he awoke, Mashbir saw Lee and his grandfather in their parlor, both moving in slow, rhythmic, dance-like motions. "Come, Captain," Lee called. "We understand you don't want monetary gifts, but perhaps we can offer you a lesson in Tai chi?"

"I'll give it a try."

"First, loosen up and stretch, like this," Lee demonstrated.

Sidney rolled his shoulders, took a deep breath, and reached for the sky.

"Remember," Lee continued, "this is meant to be a rejuvenating and centering activity. If outside thoughts arise, do not resist them, let them flow through you and away."

That's easier said than done, Sidney thought.

"We will practice the *short form,* two dozen movements; the first is called *Crane Flapping Wings.*" Sidney smiled as he copied the maneuver. "Your upper body remains fluid, your legs and lower body grounded. Be here in the moment, connected to your *inner chi energy.* For martial artists, it develops a greater sense of balance…The next movement is called *Daughter on the Mountain*; step forward while reaching slightly upward with your arms curved, as if you were encircling a large ball, and then pull it toward you slowly as you move back, repeat this motion six times, first with your right foot forward, then with your left, six times as well…The one I find most relaxing is *Clouds Passing By.* I focus on one hand as it floats in front of me, like a cloud drifting across the sky. Once you reach the end of the motion, that hand lowers, and the other hand rises up and is focused upon as it repeats that motion in the other direction; back and forth, calming the soul."

After they'd completed the series, Sidney bowed to Lee. "You're a talented instructor."

His grandfather spoke, and Lee translated, "Grandfather says, if done regularly, Tai chi keeps your mind and body limber into your older years. It is part of the Tao philosophy of compassion, moderation, and humility."

"Please thank him for his wise advice."

The gentleman bowed, then bestowed upon Sidney an object. *"It is very old,"* Lee said. Sidney examined the stone carving: three inches long and one inch in diameter; its top two-thirds in the shape of intertwined dragons holding a globe between them, the lower third engraved with a mountain scene. "Please look at the bottom, Captain," Lee said with enthusiasm.

"Oh, it's an ink-imprinting stamp." Sidney gently pressed it into his palm.

"Yes. It wishes you long life, fine health, and prosperity! And, if you stamp personal letters with it, you send those sentiments to others."

"Please tell your grandfather I will treasure it. Regrettably, I need to go—I've an appointment."

Lee's grandmother came forth presenting a bag of sweet treats and gave Sidney a hug.

"Grandmother says, you are now her honorary son and has lit a candle of blessing in your name for saving her beloved husband."

CHAPTER **15**

It was early evening when Mashbir and Moriarty, accompanied by the Marines who had been at the prisoner release, assembled outside a storage depot in the countryside.

"Don't we look dandy in our raggedy disguises?" Mashbir whispered.

"Like a bunch of bandits," Moriarty replied.

"Now remember, James, once inside, you're to only say *da*—that's *'yes.'* Got it?"

"*Da,*" he replied, "and my men will keep quiet until the place is secure."

Mashbir rapped on the door hard. "Open up," he shouted in Japanese. "Colonel Sakoree is here to do an inspection."

The door opened a crack, and they slammed through, sending a couple of guards flying. The other Japanese soldiers froze at the sight of rifles aimed at them. Speaking in Russian, Sidney pointed and the Marines bound and blindfolded them, then dragged them to the rear of the building.

The rattling of horse-drawn wagons could be heard outside.

"James, it appears our friends have arrived," Mashbir said. "Let's greet them."

When the chain of wagons came to a halt, one of the drivers climbed down. "Who is in charge here?" he asked.

"I am," Mashbir replied in Russian.

"My name is Dmitri," the man said, extending a sturdy handshake.

"Glad you could make the party, Dmitri," Mashbir replied. "For tonight, my name is Mikhail. And you are to forget I—and my men—were ever here."

"Of course, Mikhail, *Spasiba*—Thank you, we appreciate your assistance!"

"Have your men gather round with mine," Mashbir said. "I'd like you to translate my directions. My Russian is a bit rusty."

"I've heard far worse," Dmitri replied, smiling.

Late into the night, Mashbir and his men, along with the anti-Bolshevik partisans, labored side by side, removing all the Czech weaponry and ammunition that the Japanese had confiscated, loading it onto their wagons and hauling it away.

The following evening, from inside a railroad car, Mashbir pulled a curtain slightly open and observed antics under the moonlight in the abandoned terminal station.

"Commander Richardson, here comes Merkuleff whirling around, sneaking looks in all directions, fearing he's been followed." They smiled as the Russian approached, dressed in a heavy coat, with a package stuffed under his arm. "Now remember, Commander, *just play along*—he's a trickster. Almost drove me nuts, promising to hand it over one minute, then changing his mind the next."

There was tapping at the side door. Mashbir slid it open. "My dear friend, thanks for being so punctual. Let me introduce you to Commander Richardson."

"I'll take this off first," he replied, removing his coat and gloves. "Have you anything to drink? I need to settle my nerves."

Mashbir poured vodka for the three of them. Merkuleff downed his glass in one gulp. "That's much better," he said, clutching his package, waiting for his hosts to broach the subject. Finally, he announced, "Are you ready to discuss my valuable documents?"

"Perhaps later," Mashbir replied. "Has either of you ever heard the opera singer Caruso?"

"I once heard him perform *Rigoletto*," Richardson replied. "Quite an amazing voice."

Mashbir turned toward Merkuleff. "Do you enjoy classical music?"

Merkuleff shook his head. "What, we're in the midst of a potential war—with tens of thousands of Japanese troops gathering—and you speak of tenors!"

"I'm sorry." Mashbir looked at him earnestly. "I'm no longer interested in those documents. It suddenly dawned on me that you resisted giving them because you doubted their authenticity and didn't want me to look foolish returning to Japan with anything that wasn't genuine."

"You really are a crazy cowboy," Merkuleff snapped. "Not a diplomat, that's for sure. First you implore me to come, then you insult me. Do you realize my just being here endangers me and my family's lives?"

"True, but the exposure of these documents might well result in the Japanese reducing their presence here, improving the situation..."

"I don't know whether to trust you." Merkuleff shook his fist. "If I had other options, I'd leave this very moment and to hell with you both!" He dumped the contents of his package onto the table and attempted to compose himself before continuing. "Three months ago my soldiers captured several Hung-Tze mercenaries frantically running through the forest. Under torture, they swore they'd been hired by the Japanese to create chaos terrorizing the local populace. But what was most astonishing," he said, clutching some letters, "*were these handwritten confessions,* detailing how a Japanese garrison had been drugged by their own officers and were slaughtered by these Chinese bandits, joined by Japanese soldiers in disguise. See for yourself," he insisted, passing a letter to Richardson. "I've attached translations. What more proof do you need?"

"Where are these prisoners now?" Mashbir asked.

"They've been disposed of."

"Are the Japanese aware of this evidence?"

He scoffed. "If they were, you and I would be dead."

Richardson offered, "Might you and your family wish sanctuary on our ship?"

Merkuleff cringed. "If I abandon my post, I'll be killed by my own people."

"Don't worry, Merkuleff," Mashbir said. "We have a plan."

Merkuleff shoved the letters forward. "Just take them and leave— and you'd better hide them well or you'll find yourself flayed alive."

Mashbir gathered the letters. "I'm leaving soon, after a meeting with General Isobe, who requested I dine with him tomorrow evening at his home. If I don't attend, he'll be suspicious."

"Isobe is quite clever—be careful."

"Is he one of the conspirators?"

"I don't think so."

Merkuleff finally relaxed, and respectfully looked Mashbir in the eye. "I've heard you were involved in the release of those Chinese prisoners, whom the Japanese had forced us to arrest. *Well done.* Also, my partisan friends send gratitude for those Czech arms. I only hope your luck continues—for all our sakes!"

CHAPTER 16

"So kind of you to accept the invitation to my humble home, Captain Mashbir," General Isobe said. Turning to his servants, he requested they bring food and drink.

Mashbir smiled.

"Prince Tokugawa did mention before my departure that you and I would have much in common, and if possible, I should visit you."

Is there truth to his words? Isobe considered. *If not, he lies so effortlessly.*

"Thank you for relaying that information. The Prince is one of our nation's most venerated leaders."

"And I am most honored to have become his friend," he replied. "Regrettably, there are those who focus on the differences between our peoples, but I truly respect the Japanese."

"Thank you, but it's strange these reports I've been receiving. Ever since your arrival, many unusual things have occurred."

"What do you mean, General?"

"A massive quantity of weapons were stolen from under our very noses."

"Really. Where do you think they are now?"

Isobe scratched his head.

"Probably on the black market. What's your guess?"

Fist to his chin, Mashbir appeared deep in thought. "When Prince Tokugawa and I discussed how the Bolsheviks had slaughtered their own royal family, the prince commented how fortuitous it would be if more weaponry could somehow fall into the hands of anti-Bolshevik partisans battling our common enemy, the Communists. Maybe that is where they went."

Isobe laughed. "You already know more about what is happening in Vladivostok than I, the Chief of Intelligence."

"It wasn't a major loss, General. Weren't those Czech munitions inferior to your own Japanese weaponry?"

"Yes, in truth they were," Isobe replied, going along with the game. "Captain, I see you're wearing a traditional Samurai sword."

"A gift from Prince Tokugawa. I've spent the past two years studying Japan's martial arts: Judo, Kendo and some Jiu Jitsu—merely a student, not a master."

"Humility is an intrinsic part of *Bushido*," said Isobe with an approving nod. "And yes, we do have things in common. It's a pleasure getting visitors from the outside world, but I hope you don't mind my asking a couple more questions?"

"Fire away."

"One of my top officers, Colonel Sakoree, claims you are an intelligence agent, but refuses to fully explain why he is so nervous about your presence. And why would a man such as yourself be sent on such a minor chore as delivering diplomatic mail, the duty of a mere courier?"

"Frankly," Mashbir replied, exuding a sense of remorse, "I'd rather not be here at all; it's a punishment for pissing off my superiors."

"Pissing off?" Isobe squinted in confusion.

"I've a hot temper. They thought sending me to this ice box would cool it down."

Isobe chuckled. "So has it?"

"Too soon to tell, General."

"An entertaining story, Captain. Speaking of travel, I haven't returned to Japan for so long, I feel like an outsider."

"When were you last there?"

"I've been stationed in Siberia for several years and haven't seen my family once. We do write often. My son wants to be a military man like his father," he said proudly. "Do you have sons?"

Mashbir's shoulders sagged and he felt a pain in his gut as the image of Forrester flashed in his mind. "General Isobe, I wish we had more time to get to know one another, but I have responsibilities early tomorrow and need to call it a night. Thanks for your hospitality."

"Please, before you go," he urged, holding up two bottles, "we must make some toasts for international goodwill. Here's whisky, your national drink, and mine, sake."

He poured Mashbir a glass of whisky, and for himself, a small cup of sake.

"All right, but to make it an international toast, let's alternate between sake and whisky."

"An interesting game." Isobe poured himself a whisky.

"Here's to your emperor." Mashbir said, "May he long reign!" They downed their drinks.

Isobe raised a cup of sake. "And here's to your President!"

After six more alternating toasts, they were now acknowledging the mayor of Yokohama and the governor of Arizona…Isobe appeared groggy as he drew close to Mashbir. "I know you have secrets; I, also, am a man of secrets," he said, his words slurring. "We can help each other—and further our careers."

"A fine offer, which I will need some time to consider."

The unsteady Isobe slapped Mashbir upon the back. "Why didn't you touch any secret documents when you visited Colonel Sakoree? Weren't you tempted?"

"What, we were being watched?" Mashbir appeared shocked. "To have done so would have been dishonorable—America and Japan are allies. Prince Tokugawa and I hope this friendship will last many lifetimes. We assume you feel likewise General." Mashbir drew Isobe close and whispered, "Tokugawa would warn you there are traitors in your midst."

Isobe jolted upright, looking Mashbir in the eye. "Japan's government is floundering," he said with a sudden flash of anger. "No one knows for sure who will be considered a traitor tomorrow. Let us share at least one important secret—Tell me about these traitors!"

"Vague rumors only, General. But if you tell me one first, I'll reveal a big important secret."

Isobe was having trouble standing. "Now you're talking. So you do have a special *hush-hush*," he said, holding a finger to his lips. "Tell me yours first, and I'll tell you two top secrets!"

"If I tell you this secret, Isobe, you swear not to share it?"

"On the honor of my ancestors. Out with it!"

"I've heard," Mashbir's voice took a mysterious tone, "that General Oi . . ." He paused to take a bite of an appetizer.

"Go on," Isobe demanded.

". . . Has been secretly cohabitating with a Russian woman for almost a year. Who knows what they might be up to?"

Isobe gasped, clutching the table for support. "Mistresses are none of my business. I want military secrets!"

"I don't have any of those kinds of secrets, but if I come across something important, I'll contact you. Now, it's your turn."

Isobe's face turned beet red, and he was about to protest—but instead, simply passed out, collapsing into a chair.

Turning to the servants, Mashbir smirked, "The general thought he could drink like a Cossack."

The ladies giggled. "Now please bring me a pot of strong coffee—quickly."

Such a waste of good whisky and sake, but I needed to get it out of my system, he thought. Leaning over the bar sink, Mashbir stuck a finger deep down his throat and threw up. Then he rinsed his mouth and slapped his face with cold water, not wanting to wander back to the U.S.S. *Albany* without his head screwed on straight. Settling into a seat, he drank several cups of black coffee.

In a dark alleyway, Colonel Sakoree was surrounded by a half-dozen soldiers. "Now remember," he said, "your goal is to bring him in for interrogation. As a last resort, kill him. I'll be waiting back at the compound."

With a slight stagger to his gait, Mashbir exited Isobe's home. Treading down a narrow winding passageway, he heard whispering; his revolver was drawn just as the men emerged from the shadows charging towards him. He aimed at the mass and in rapid succession, three men fell. Two soldiers tackled him, wrenching away his gun, while the third aimed a rifle at the tangle of bodies. One tried to hold his arms as the other choked him. Mashbir bit the man's hand and came across hard with his elbow, crushing the man's nose.

Spinning, he pounded the other in the solar plexus, knocking the wind out of him. The standing soldier delivered a solid kick to Mashbir's ribs; Mashbir ignored the pain and came to his feet while drawing out his sword. Before the soldier could aim his rifle, his arm was severed above the wrist. Blood gushing, he fell to the ground in agony as the other attacker came to his feet, withdrew his sword and plunged forward.

Mashbir deflected and slashed the man's throat, then quickly crouched as he heard a rifle cocked behind him and felt the shot graze his shoulder. Turning, he flung his sword with a flick of his wrist, its blade embedding itself deeply into the shooter's chest. It was all over now, except for the whimpering of dying men. Taking a clenched breath, Mashbir stood, bracing his wounded side as he looked at their faces. Planting a boot on the man's chest, he pulled his sword out— *Better them than me, but such a waste,* he thought.

✳✳✳✳

Lee arrived early at the harbor the following morning to say good-bye. He sat on a wooden beam at the pier's edge, wondering when Captain Mashbir would arrive. *That's suspicious,* he thought, as he watched a Japanese military officer speaking to the skipper of the docked vessel—moments later, he saw the passengers who had just come aboard, were now disembarking. Lee approached a passenger. "Why are you all leaving the ship?"

"Some technical problem or other. We were told to return tomorrow."

Mashbir was halfway down the U.S.S. *Albany's* gangplank when Lee ran up to him. After catching his breath, the teenager described the events he had seen.

"Thanks for the warning." Mashbir patted him on the shoulder. "I certainly don't want to be the only passenger; I'll wait until tomorrow and board with everyone else. Now, young man, promise you won't come near me again—it places you and your family in danger."

The following morning, Moriarty tugged hard on the reins, bringing the droshky to a halt. "Now remember, Sidney, at any sign of trouble, I'm taking you right back."

Mashbir's shoulder wound throbbed, as his hand braced against the bandage wrapped around his injured rib cage. "Time is of the essence—I have to get back. Funny," he coughed, "it even hurts to talk."

"Whatever you retrieved here, Sidney, I hope it was worth the effort."

"*It was,* and your help has been greatly appreciated, James. I hope our paths cross again."

Moriarty pulled a basket from the wagon.

"To make the first leg of your return trip more pleasant, here's a bottle of wine and a roasted hen."

Sidney proceeded up the busy walkway to the ticketing clerk. "What, you can't find my reservations?" he shouted. "I'm a special courier for the American Embassy. I don't care what others have ordered you to do. You've seen those tortured criminals in the public square hanging by their necks—you'll be in their company for this insult!"

In spite of the frosty air, sweat poured down the clerk's forehead. "I'll look again." He re-examined his clipboard. "Ah, yes, I was mistaken. Here is your key and cabin number. You have my deepest apologies."

From down the pier, Merkuleff's elegant horse-drawn carriage came racing. Mashbir watched him jump out, then run up the gangplank like a young man. "I beg you, please return those documents," he demanded.

"Slow down—you'll get a heart attack. What's the matter?"

"Colonel Sakoree suspects we are involved in some sort of plot."

"Have you admitted anything?"

"Of course not. But he's clever and will certainly find out."

"Deny everything, Merkuleff, and don't worry—Sakoree will not be around much longer."

"But, but . . ."

"*Do svidaniya,* my good friend, until we meet again," Sidney replied, then turned and left Merkuleff standing there, already formulating convincing lies to tell the Japanese.

CHAPTER 17

After an uneventful journey home, Mashbir climbed the stairs two at time, in spite of his assorted injuries. He reached his second-floor apartment, unlocking the door to darkness. "Blanche, darling, Forrester, Daddy's back!" He soon discovered all his wife and son's possessions were gone and their family's framed photographs smashed, lying on the living room floor.

The following week, Mashbir arrived at the U.S. Embassy, Tokyo.

Time to put on my mask and act all hunky-dory, Mashbir thought, before entering the office. He was surprised by applause, as the ambassador, Commander Zacharias, and Colonel Burnett came to their feet. "You performed a miracle, Captain," the ambassador declared. "We had doubts we'd ever see you again."

"Those documents have been examined," Zacharias said, "and copies sent to Prince Tokugawa and the national newspapers. That conspiracy to start a war with China has been defused, at least for now: General Isobe was ordered to arrest the mutinous men under his command, with several ending their own lives."

Burnett added, "And here in Japan, several top officers have resigned, and numerous influential politicians and businessmen linked to this matter are in custody for questioning. The proportions of this scandal are enormous. Some of the most incendiary militant newspapers have been shut down."

"And General Ennokee?" Mashbir asked.

"He's avoided being connected so far," Zacharias replied. "Hopefully, his luck will run out."

"We have a medal waiting for you, Captain," Burnett said, "and plans to have you relocated to Washington, D.C."

"You're needed there," the ambassador emphasized, "to educate our policymakers about the realities of Asia."

Mashbir reflected.

"Gentlemen, I appreciate the honors, but hope you'll accept my refusal. My continued involvement at the Tokyo Pan Pacific Club places my finger on the pulse of Japan. As for medals, they'd probably get me killed. Spies are best kept out of the limelight—Instead, I'd like to create an extensive network of paid informants within Japan to maintain the peace, or if war broke out, to supply strategic information from the inside. If it isn't established now, it will be almost impossible to organize once a conflict erupts."

Burnett coughed. "But Captain, you are aware we have a limited budget for Intelligence. And even if we had the funding, our accounting systems aren't as secure as they should be, yet they demand detailed descriptions on how and where monies are spent." He laughed. "I'm surprised we get anything done."

"If I have to," Mashbir shrugged, "I'll resign active military duty temporarily to earn a heap of money in the private sector, then join up again with that cash as funding."

"Not a bad idea," Burnett replied.

"An ambitious plan," Zacharias said. "Got a name for it?"

"It's still in the strategizing stage."

"I see," Zacharias smiled. "Well, if we can't give you medals, we can at least call it the M-Plan. It would appear to represent one of our countless military operational programs, but it would be based on your last name."

"It *does* have a nice ring to it," Mashbir replied.

As they were leaving the room, Zacharias tapped Mashbir on the shoulder. "Stay a minute—we need to talk."

"Sure."

"Sidney, your humility and service to our country is admirable, but the top brass came up through the ranks from the field of infantry. They respect guns and bullets and consider the Intelligence branch a place for misfits and losers too afraid to confront the enemy face-to-face. Without commendations and medals to back you up, you won't get your deserved promotions. Are you sure that's the path you wish to take?"

As his taxi approached the estate, Mashbir was eager to see his new friend again. Soon he was in Tokugawa's study, sipping brandy and relaxing in a comfortable chair. "I'm so glad you made it back," the prince said. "Won't you please fill me in on the details?"

When Mashbir had finished giving his account, Tokugawa smiled.

"Your mission has the makings of an exciting adventure novel."

Someone knocked.

"I'll be right there," Tokugawa called out. "Sidney-san, I've invited a guest I'd like you to meet."

Upon opening the door, a slim, young Japanese man entered wearing casual Western attire: light blue shirt, dark sports jacket, and slacks. Under his arm he held a thick book.

"Stay outside," the young man ordered his guards, "and make sure we are not disturbed." He initially eyed Mashbir with suspicious unfamiliarity, then extended his hand. "My uncle has spoken highly of you and your successful assignment."

"Excuse me, Your Majesty. I didn't recognize you." Mashbir bowed low. "Your uncle is overly generous in his description. I simply caught rebellious children with their hands in the cookie jar."

Hirohito smiled.

"No need for modesty. Your actions were courageous."

Turning to Tokugawa, Hirohito handed him the book.

"Dear Uncle, here is that new illustrated text on Ichthyology we discussed."

This elicited a blank stare from Sidney.

"It's the study of fish," Hirohito explained. "This book deals with Freshwater Biology and may prove helpful in modernizing our hatcheries."

"Oh, I see..." Sidney replied.

"Uncle Tokugawa, I hope you don't mind if Captain Mashbir and I take a stroll?"

"Certainly. It will give me a chance to review the book."

They walked the beautiful, lush gardens of Tokugawa's estate, guards trailing a far distance behind. "As you're probably aware, Captain, my Uncle is an extraordinary man; he's been a significant role model for most of my life. He highly respects you, and that is why I'm here. That conspiracy you uncovered might have led to war. I only hope it wasn't a futile effort." He stopped strolling and looked at Mashbir. "I imagine you find it difficult conversing with a future emperor, but it's just the two of us. Let's talk man to man."

"I'll try."

"You know there's constant pressure on me from both the liberals and the militants to put my blessings on their agendas, each giving persuasive arguments. Look at me," he said, arms spread wide, "I'm only twenty-two years old, and find it all quite confusing."

Mashbir nodded. "But I sense a wisdom far beyond your years, Your Majesty, and with the wise counsel of men such as Prince Tokugawa, you'll do fine."

That evening, Sidney and Prince Tokugawa dined at a rooftop restaurant. The Prince observed dark shadows under Mashbir's mournful eyes, but resisted asking questions. He remembered their conversation prior to Sidney's departure to Vladivostok and assumed things hadn't worked out well with his family.

"Just look out there," the Prince said, pointing, "the hustle and bustle of Tokyo. *Millions of people who have no idea how close they came to their world being torn apart.*"

Mashbir nodded solemnly.

"Thank you. It was a great honor meeting the Crown Prince."

"He was honored to have met you as well—He told me so afterwards. These are difficult times. There's much corruption in his cabinet and resistance to his mandates. He finds refuge in studying nature, but will mature to skillful prominence once he becomes emperor."

A long silence passed before Tokugawa continued. "Most of our forty-five thousand troops have left that region. Can you conjecture what happened next?"

"The Bolsheviks probably marched into Vladivostok."

"Right you are, machine-gunning anyone who stood in their way. So it is either brutal Russian communists or militant Japanese. Who is more worthy?"

"Who's to say, but at least there's no current threat of a major conflict."

"Very diplomatically put." Prince Tokugawa sipped his wine, before he added, "I'm enlisting Captain Matsumoto to oversee any limited troops that might return to Manchuria. He and I hope to keep the situation from getting out of hand again."

"A prudent decision, but I have a question." Sidney scratched the back of his neck. "It's strange—ever since I've returned, everywhere I go I've been the brunt of jokes: It appears everyone believes I went to Siberia searching for some Cossack leader named Semanov, a tough anti-Bolshevik, when all the while it was common knowledge he was residing in Shanghai."

The Prince's serious expression transformed into a half-smile. "I didn't wish you to be linked to the bringing back of that incriminating evidence, so I circulated that rumor."

"Your cover story probably saved my life."

"It's the least I could do, after all you've done."

CHAPTER 18

Standing in the open doorway of Mashbir's office, Zacharias silently scrutinized his friend's unshaven profile staring out a window. The workplace was cluttered with dirty coffee cups, plates, and scraps of paper scattered about. He tapped on the door.

Mashbir turned. "Hello, Zach. *You ever wonder what we're put on this Earth for?*"

"Besides wine, women and song? That's a tough question at an early hour. Let's discuss it some evening over a couple of beers."

"You know, I almost didn't make it back. It got me thinking about those who most inspire me—like General Pershing, Admiral Dewey, and now Prince Tokugawa." He paused. "During these past three years, I've made many Japanese friends and have come to truly appreciate their culture." He pursed his lips. "If I were to choose my life's purpose, it would be to prevent our two nations from ever having to fight one another—Then, it would have significance." Sidney broke into a coughing spasm, rattling his body.

"You okay, Sid?"

"It'll pass." He covered his mouth with a hand, while the other grasped the arm of his chair to brace himself.

"That's a fine goal. But right now you're going through the stress of a divorce, and your doctor says your health is breaking down." Zach stepped closer. "There's a charming seaside village called Oiso, less than one hundred kilometers from Tokyo. I've spoken to Colonel Burnett, and he hereby orders you to take some time off—whether you like it or not."

Two months later, September 1, 1923

Barely noticing the pastoral countryside fleeting by, Sidney sat in the train wondering if he'd made a mistake...Colonel Burnett had encouraged his decision to resign temporarily, saying it would give him time for his health to improve and offer an opportunity to earn enough money in the private sector to fund their spy network. His thoughts were redirected by one of the four young Japanese men seated nearby.

"Is it okay to practice English with you, sir?"

Sidney smiled at what looked like college students. "Are you gentlemen also going to Oiso?"

"Yes. Do you come here often?"

"On weekends," Mashbir replied. "I enjoy the fresh ocean air and swimming."

"It relaxing not in city, is it so?" another student asked.

"It certainly is..."

A couple of hours later, Sidney sat on a beach blanket admiring the sunlight glittering on the ocean's grayish-blue surface, barely a wave breaking its tranquility. Thatch-roofed beach cottages dotted the adjacent ridgeline✻ Further along the shoreline were a few tourists, but mainly Japanese families picnicking. Two little brothers were at the water's edge, flapping their arms while chasing seagulls and shouting, "Scraa, scraa," as if they, too, were birds. Sidney longed to know what Forrester was up to.

The water looked cool and refreshing. He stripped down to his blue-and-black striped swim trunks and got lost in the joy of the moment, swimming and floating about, seeing others happily splashing around him.

Twenty yards from shore, an enveloping undertow suddenly clutched him, pulling him down and sucking him out to sea. Sidney gasped—confused—clawing against powerful currents, fearing this was his end—and praying for just a moment's chance to take a breath before being forced down again. For what felt like an eternity, he struggled with the churning waters until at last he was able to free himself and make it back to the shore, exhausted, dragging himself onto the sand.

He'd barely recovered when the ground began to undulate spasmodically. Every time he got up, he was knocked down again...On his hands and knees he waited for the tremors to stop, his teeth chattering from the vibrations. . . During a lull, he looked out to sea. To his amazement and relief, the college students he'd met on the train, who'd also been swimming, were safe a quarter-mile offshore, scrambling about on an outcropping of rocks that hadn't been visible before. He calculated that the adjacent underwater coastline must have risen forty feet due to an earthquake. Then to his horror, on surveying the beach around him, he found no sign of all those families—they'd simply disappeared. "Oh God, no," he shouted...*While I was almost drowning, the earthquake must have heaved up the sand, burying them alive.*

All that was left were several cottages on the hillside, including his own, which were now a tangled mass of burning timbers. Feeling shock and anguish, but forcing himself to focus. He noticed the students swimming back to shore. When they arrived, they looked to him, as if he might give them guidance.

"There's not much we can do here," he said. "Follow me—we need to get to town and go house to house, extinguishing charcoal stoves or putting them into the streets, to prevent future tremors from overturning them and causing more fires."

On reaching Oiso, collapsed buildings surrounded them, with survivors walking the streets in a daze. Mashbir gave the young men further instructions and off they ran. He asked a passerby, "Where's the nearest medical facility?" Soon he stood in front of what he guessed had been an infirmary, but was now a heap of rubble. Sitting on the curb, an old lady cradled an infant.

He tapped her shoulder.

"This was my precious grandson, Tomio," she whimpered.

"I'm so sorry, Ma'am," he said, looking with pity and sadness into her pained, tear-filled eyes. "Could you tell me, though, where the injured are being taken?"

She pointed. "They go to Baron Shibusawa's villa," she replied.

The baron's estate was atop a nearby hill. Sidney found the front door wide open, with much activity inside. A gentleman in his mid-eighties, shirtsleeves rolled up, was shouting orders to servants. "Bring more tables!" Several had already been arranged in rows, some occupied with the injured. A doctor was tightening a tourniquet. Sidney stood behind him watching; sweat poured from the teenage girl's trembling body, her right leg crushed. A nurse grasped her hand, while also offering the girl a glass of brandy to sip.

There was a flash of recognition when the nurse turned. She gave Sidney a nod, then bent close to the patient's ear, speaking in Japanese, "Drink all you can."

"Things look pretty bad out there," Sidney commented in Japanese.

The doctor replied without turning, "Half the town is dead, the others injured or stunned." When he turned, he was surprised to see an American had spoken such good Japanese.

"I'm here to help in any way I can," Sidney said.

"It is fortunate I carry my emergency supplies with me, but I never expected anything of this magnitude." The doctor pointed to the sink. "Wash your hands, then rinse off my saw with alcohol and bring it to me."

Sidney and the nurse each held one of the girl's arms as the surgeon went to work. By the amputation's completion, the patient had fallen into blessed unconsciousness. The doctor appeared shaken. "I hope she makes it," he said.

The nurse spoke to Sidney. "Thanks for your assistance. It looks like our paths were meant to cross again. When last we met, I was a recent graduate from nursing school."

"Yes, Yukari—and I had just arrived in Japan. A lot has happened these past few years."

The owner of the estate, who had been directing his servants, walked over to the doctor and handed him a glass of brandy. "You've earned it," he said. Then turning to Sidney, he bowed. "My name is Eiichi Shibusawa, and yours?"

"Sidney Mashbir, sir."

So this is the man Iyesato had spoken of, who had helped him put down the rebellion, but destroyed his marriage in the process..."Oh yes, Prince

Tokugawa mentioned your name." He pointed. "That young lady you helped is one of my housemaids. Her home collapsed on her, and there are many more like her in the city—*the question is*, how do we get them here?"

"So you're willing to use your home for more of this?" Sidney looked toward the table dripping with blood.

"Yes, of course."

"Sir, give me an hour or two to recruit a team of volunteers, and we'll fill this place up."

For several days they worked nonstop: the doctor, Sidney, and Yukari, along with several other nurses and a number of civilians, bandaging, setting broken bones, and performing life-saving amputations. While outside, workers whom Sidney had organized, dug through the ruins to find those still alive . . . As time passed, Sidney and the others felt an enveloping sorrow, as the influx of patients slowed and those arriving were often too far gone to be saved.

Hoping to lift their spirits, the Baron said, "Young people, if there's one thing I've learned over my long life, it is that terrible tragedies such as we face today will pass, and the future will once again bring bright moments."

The baron noticed how Yukari and Sidney's eyes awkwardly averted whenever they spoke to one another. "You have both worked very hard and deserve a chance to rest," he said softly. "Go freshen up and relax. Others can now take over."

The upstairs guest rooms shared a bathroom, so Sidney offered Yukari the chance to wash up first. "Thank you," she said, but instead held his hand as she stood in front of the sink, staring at her waif-like reflection in the mirror, dark shadows under her lovely eyes. "I don't know how many poor souls would have been forgotten in the rubble if you had not assisted us. When you see life's fragility, you value the present all the more—Sidney, we're alive! Why do you remain so sad?"

He looked inward. "My wife recently left me and took away my precious son," he said quietly.

"I'm so sorry." She looked at him, searching for a sign it would be okay, then playfully splashed water into his face; she then led him to the shower where she removed his clothes, pausing at the sight of scarred bullet wounds and cuts on his muscular back and shoulders.

As she undressed, he leaned back gazing at her naked beauty . . . Water poured upon him, as her hands soothingly lathered away several days' worth of grime. He lovingly did the same for her; they kissed with passion and embraced, melting into one another.

Wrapping his arm around her waist, he guided her into his room.

"Look," she said, "the Baron's servants have placed two robes and two clean sets of pajamas on *your* bed."

"There's even two glasses and a bottle of wine on the nightstand." He filled the glasses.

"The Baron is a most gracious host, isn't he?"

Both smiled at one another.

They awoke to a gentle tapping on the door. A male servant's voice was heard. "Would you like breakfast in your room?"

"No, thank you," Sidney replied, while still snuggling Yukari. "It's surreal," he whispered. "One day hell, the next heaven."

"What do you plan to do now?"

"Return to Tokyo and see how my friends are doing."

She nodded. "I've done all I can here. May I go with you?"

"That's what I was hoping you'd say." Their lips met.

An hour later, Sidney came downstairs to see the Baron in one of the side rooms, now wearing traditional Japanese fighting attire: a long, brown skirt-like bottom and a light-colored, loose-fitting cotton shirt with a black kimono over it. He held two samurai swords, one long and one short, moving with agility, as if he were dancing with his weapons. Sidney waited until Shibusawa placed the swords back on their holding stand, then entered and bowed.

"Thank you so much for your hospitality, Baron."

The Baron bowed in return. "And thank you, Sidney, for all you've done." Conscious of his attire, Shibusawa smiled. "I have been Westernized, but still need to practice the old ways," he said, looking toward the swords. "It connects me to my ancestral roots." He lifted his palms upward. "I've heard you and Yukari will be leaving soon— Train service is halted, and I would offer my chauffeur to drive you back to Tokyo, but the roads are so damaged."

"That's no problem, sir. We can walk it in two or three days."

"I wish you both good fortune and hope we will meet again under more auspicious circumstances." He handed Sidney two objects. "Please deliver this letter to my young friend, Iyesato—and this book is a gift for you. It is about Confucian philosophy, and is inscribed by the author." The Baron smiled. "*It is my own humble creation.*"

Prince Tokugawa is in his sixties, Sidney reflected, *yet, he is considered a young man by this octogenarian.* "Thank you, I look forward to reading your book. May I ask how long you have known the Prince?"

"I'll let Iyesato answer that question."

Wearing backpacks filled with supplies, they began their journey. After several miles, Sidney turned to Yukari, "How is it that you ended up in Oiso?"

"The Baron is a kind and gentle soul, and is active in many humanitarian organizations. He paid the travel expenses for a number of American nurses to visit Japan, to bring their skills to his country. He made similar offers to Japanese nurses to visit the U.S. to experience American hospitals."

"He certainly handles samurai swords adeptly for a gentle soul."

Yukari smiled. "He follows strict Confucianism, yet is most tolerant. A young American woman asked for assistance in allowing her to spread the teachings of the Baha'i faith, while at the same time emphasizing it was not a political organization. Shibusawa not only supported her in Japan, but gave her introductions to leaders in Korea, so religious learning centers might be established there as well."

Could the Baha'i philosophy of universal peace and the recognition of all people as being part of one world family ever take hold? he wondered.

Yukari interrupted his reverie. "Sidney, why did you ask me to bring a notebook and pens?"

"Let's take a break," he replied, and they sat beneath a willow tree.

"Do you remember how difficult it was for the non-medical volunteers to communicate with their patients, either because of language barriers or their lack of medical knowledge?"

Yukari nodded. "Yes, especially when asking which medications they were taking or what drug allergies they might have."

"Here's what I think we can do to help." He explained that by using their combined knowledge of Japanese, and hers of medical terminology and medical care protocol, they'd create a concise Japanese-English medical guide. It would contain medical terms, accompanied by phonetic translations between Japanese and English, that could be used by both Japanese and non-Japanese speakers.

"A worthwhile project," she replied, "and it will take our minds off our sore feet during rest stops over the next hundred kilometers."

"I have a solution for that as well." He removed her shoes and socks and began massaging her feet.

"Oh, that's delightful," she said, rewarding him with a kiss on the cheek.

CHAPTER 19

Sweltering heat weighed down upon them as they trudged through the dank-smelling, rubble-strewn streets of Tokyo. "It's got to be nearby, Yukari," Sidney muttered. "Let's turn around and go back a few blocks*⬚

"Not many landmarks to go by," she replied. "Almost everything has crumbled."

"I lived there," he pointed, "in what was a building."

He swallowed hard. "My neighbors were probably crushed or burned alive." With despair the images of their faces flashed before him, "I know I shouldn't complain, but all my worldly possessions were destroyed—including two years of research on the Japanese culture for my book."

Not to mention my spy network, he thought. *I wonder if any of my agents are still alive?*

Yukari gently stroked his troubled face, and they moved on. In the distance, he found what he'd been hoping to see, the roof of the majestic Imperial Hotel. *Frank Lloyd Wright claimed his creation could stand up to the worst earthquake, and it looks like he was right.* They picked up the pace, heading toward the massive structure.

In the almost empty lobby, Mashbir thumped the front desk bell. The door behind the desk opened and a short, elderly Japanese man briskly came forward. "Sidney-san, you are alive! Everyone was worried."

"Mr. Ito, it's great to see you're okay. This is my friend, Yukari. We're very tired and hungry and have only the clothes on our backs. It's so quiet here."

"We can easily supply you with clothing. Many of our foreign visitors left in such a hurry, without taking all their possessions* I'm afraid, however, you'll have to put up with poor service. Many of our staff have not reported in; probably dead, unfortunate souls. Destruction was the worst in the poorest sections of the city, with fires spreading rapidly through those crowded quarters."

"I'm so sorry," Sidney replied. "Is there anybody here that I know?"

"I believe Major Witsell is in the lounge."

They crossed the lobby to find him seated at the bar.

"Sidney," he exclaimed, "I figured you'd show up one of these days. But your luck goes far beyond that, to be accompanied by such a lovely lady." Witsell bowed, moving his arm with a flourish as he offered them seats. Yukari blushed. Ed continued, "Let me treat you both to something to eat and drink."

"Ed, that sounds wonderful. This is my friend, Yukari. It's nice to get off our feet; we've been walking forever. And I'm glad you're treating, you're looking at my total possessions: these shorts and shirt, and a pair of worn-out sandals."

"As far as money goes," Ed said with a grin, "that's no problem— we just order what we want and mark it down on this sheet. Mr. Ito has generously offered that when things get back to normal, he'll collect from us, the U.S. Government, or somebody."

Sidney and Yukari ordered beer and sandwiches from the bartender. Just then, Captain James Moriarty entered the lounge and upon seeing Mashbir, slapped him on the back. "Look what the cat dragged in. What took you so long?"

Mashbir replied, "You wouldn't talk that way if you had to walk as far as we did. And the word is out—everybody was worried to death about yours truly."

"Not me," Moriarty said, "I told 'em you wouldn't be taken down by some dumb earthquake. Who is this?" he said, admiring Yukari.

"An American nurse. We met in Oiso."

Moriarty gave Mashbir a wink. "Leave it to Sidney to live through an earthquake and end up way ahead."

"Thank you," Yukari said, smiling.

"And thanks for the vote of confidence," Sidney said, "but that tsunami nearly swallowed me up. They say only the good die young, so our crew here should all live to a ripe old age."

"Speak for yourself, chum," Witsell said. "I for one, was doing some serious praying. Luckily this hotel only rolled and quivered, whereas most of Tokyo is pretty much wiped out. They're calling it the Great Kanto Earthquake; I hear nearly a hundred thousand have perished."

"How dreadful," Yukari cried. Sidney put an arm around her.

"Gentlemen, I don't care if it's early evening, I feel like I'm going to collapse, and I'm sure the lady feels likewise." They proceeded to the lobby, where they were met by Mr. Ito. "Any chance of finding us a couple of rooms?" Sidney asked, while gently squeezing Yukari's hand and giving her an inquiring glance. She whispered into Sidney's ear.

Sidney smiled. "Please just make that one room, Mr. Ito."

"It's already prepared, Captain."

❋❋❋❋

The Imperial Hotel, the following afternoon: "We're going to call ourselves *The Volunteer Workers American Relief Effort*," Mashbir said to the men seated around the conference table. "According to Japanese officials, this tsunami and earthquake killed more people than any other natural disaster in hundreds of years." He turned toward Burnett, standing at his side. "The colonel and I appreciate your help at this crucial time. It's up to us to spearhead this relief effort. Communications are down, and many Japanese are walking the streets in a state of shock and disbelief." He scanned the room. "We don't have official authority, but we're *not* going to let that get in the way. I've found once the Japanese see a clear direction, they snap to, dealing with the situation at hand. The stark truth is, there may be worse to come with so many injured waiting for care, especially the very young and the elderly who are most vulnerable."

He scratched his scalp. "And then there's the danger of an epidemic due to the warm temperatures and festering bodies everywhere. We need to move fast, and use every bit of ingenuity to head off that next disaster. This morning, I scouted the city looking for potential medical care centers. Each of you will be responsible for one of those facilities, supervising available resources until more help arrives."

Colonel Burnett stepped forward. "Gentlemen, our secretary will take notes, as you give your names and ranks where appropriate."

The volunteers stood and introduced themselves:

"Lieutenant McCollum, U.S. Navy."

"Captain Martin, U.S. Army."

"Lieutenant Dillingsworth, U.S. Army."

"Captain Joe Hickey, U.S. Marine Corps."

"Robert Moss, I'm a civilian, sir, as is Mr. Harper here."

"Major Edward Witsell, U.S. Army."

"Reverend Ziemans, I'm also a civilian."

"Captain W. J. Clear, U.S. Army."

"Lieutenant Tait, sir, U.S. Army."

Mashbir spoke, "This is off the record, remember—don't worry about regulations, just get things done. Do any of you have questions?" He waited. "All right then, the secretary will give you directions to your facility. We've got work to do."

Sidney visited the Japanese Military Headquarters and faced the cold, hard, impatient stare of the Minister of War.

"So what brings you here, Captain Mashbir?"

"Sir." Mashbir deliberated a moment. "I understand between fires and explosions, almost all of your fuel supplies have been destroyed. I've come as a representative of our government to offer you fuel from our ships anchored offshore. During this emergency, we wish to help in any way we can. I have some specific suggestions as well."

Mashbir noticed the minister leaned back into his chair, his posture more relaxed. "Thank you so much," the minister replied. "This is a most challenging time. Let us talk . . ."

✳✳✳✳

Immersed in death and the incessant buzzing of flies, Mashbir and his volunteers from the West, combined with Japanese soldiers assigned to him by the Minister of War, wrapped kerchiefs over their faces to lessen the stench as they searched for identification papers, then added the deceased onto the growing piles. Trucks, carts, and wheelbarrows kept bringing an endless stream of corpses . . . Finally, Mashbir gave the order: "It's time to dowse them."

Everyone moved away from the heavy fumes of burnt flesh and petroleum filling the air, but could nowhere escape the foul odor. "It's either disposing of them quickly," Mashbir explained to those around him, "or having a plague break out."

Amidst the macabre scene, an American soldier was taking photos. A Japanese man pointed at him. "The gods have wreaked destruction, and you Americans are to blame. Does it make you feel superior to see us on our knees?"

Mashbir noted that Captain Matsumoto was also angrily staring at the photographer, and he walked over to him. "It is a sorrowful day."

Matsumoto avoided Mashbir's gaze, and with bitterness replied, "What do you plan to do with those photos? It is an indignity to have our dead photographed under such depressing circumstances."

"We're not here to gloat," Mashbir said, "but to assist you at this difficult time." He strode over and grabbed the camera from the soldier and returned to Matsumoto. "These photos, unless specifically requested by my superiors, will never see the light of day." Then thinking of the ancient sword bestowed upon him by Tokugawa, Mashbir added, "I give you my word as a Samurai!"

Matsumoto stared intently at Mashbir. "Thank you for understanding," he replied, bowing deeply.

Over the next week, eighty thousand corpses in Tokyo alone were incinerated. In the midst of this horror, General Ennokee and his troops were busily rounding up any Japanese affiliated with the Communist Party. They also intimidated certain minority communities, claiming they had somehow caused this catastrophe to occur.

Lieutenant Hoshimo stood at attention before Ennokee.

"It was about time we got rid of those communist traitors," the general said with a grin.

"Yes, over three hundred have been arrested so far, sir," Hoshimo replied.

"But we have just skimmed the surface." Ennokee handed him a stack of papers. "Arrest everyone listed; those with stars near their names are to be executed on the spot."

Hoshimo was surprised as he examined the list. "You wish this done without discussion with the other chiefs of staff?"

"Have no fear. We have powerful allies. This disaster is a blessing in disguise, a chance to eliminate our enemies and blame it on the earthquake."

CHAPTER 20

Yukari swabbed disinfectant on the boy's slender arm, then carefully sutured the long jagged gash, as Sidney placed a calming hand on the fearful boy's shoulder.

"You're doing very well," he told him. The youth nodded, gritting his teeth. When she finished, Yukari washed up.

"That was some fancy stitch-work, and I should know, after all the buttons I've sewed back on and the torn britches I've patched," Sidney said, succeeding in his attempt to change Yukari's serious demeanor to a radiant smile.

"I've got something to show you." From his shoulder pack, he pulled out a pamphlet and handed it to her. "At this very moment, these are being distributed to all the Emergency Health Centers."

Yukari read the first page:

"'*This Japanese-English Medical Guide is prepared as a practical instrument with which non-Japanese-speaking medical personnel in the field may obtain case histories from non-English-speaking Japanese patients under their care. It is designed so that by using a relatively few words and phrases, medical staff may obtain important diagnostic facts in the absence of an interpreter. Japanese-speaking, non-medically-trained volunteers can also benefit from its use.*'"

Yukari stepped away from Sidney, and approached Leslie, a member of her team of American nurses, who was tending to a Japanese man who was limping and whose arm appeared broken. The nurses examined the pamphlet together…Yukari watched as Leslie utilized the pamphlet, first reading a line to herself, "'*I wish to give you medical care,*'" then pointing to the line below it for the patient to read, which had the identical meaning, but was translated to Japanese. The man smiled in acknowledgment.

Leslie read the phonetic translation on the next line: "*Anata No Kenko Jotai Wo Shiritai No Desu,*" [*I* want to inquire about your health.]

The patient's face glowed at hearing his language spoken.

Using the same principles, Leslie pointed to a long list of medical conditions written in Japanese and accompanied by English translations. This enabled her to ask in phonetic Japanese if the patient had had any of these problems in the past, or any allergies to medications. The patient was directed to point if any applied. Using the guide, she recommended he relax; then asked him to select from another list, indicating when and how he had injured himself, how much pain he was experiencing, and if there were any other symptoms or ailments. This took a few minutes, and soon, an arm sling was fabricated.

Yukari and Leslie strolled over to Sidney.

"That pamphlet really helped," Leslie exclaimed. "So much is covered in just a few pages. That man's limp goes back ten years; we could have wasted precious time trying to figure that out, or attempting to treat it. It feels like I've just gone through a mini-course in Japanese."

She was about to return the pamphlet to Yukari, but Sidney raised his hand. "No, keep it—it's yours." He took out a bunch more from his bag. "I've brought several dozen mimeograph copies with me. Would you mind working with Yukari in passing these out to the rest of the staff and explaining their use?"

Leslie edged near Sidney.

"Honey, it would be a pleasure," she said, with her Louisiana accent.

Yukari shot her a cool look, which Leslie understood.

"Why, we work together all the time," Leslie said, without missing a beat. "She's one of the sweetest and best nurses I've come to know."

Yukari smiled at her friend.

"I couldn't agree with you more," Sidney replied. "Nice meeting you, Leslie. But please excuse us, Yukari and I need to talk'…'Yukari," he said, blushing, once they had moved to a more private spot. 'I know we haven't been together long, but I may be returning to the States when things settle down here—and I want you to consider coming with me."

She looked into his eyes.

"A sweet offer. I'll think about it."

Just then, their attention was drawn to something unusual at the far end of the room: a small Japanese woman in her early twenties, wearing a fine kimono of light green adorned with yellow flowers, its delicate sleeves now smeared with blood. She was cradling a young girl in her arms, as a doctor took the child's pulse. Arousing Sidney and Yukari's curiosity, was that behind this woman stood what appeared to be a hulking bodyguard and two female attendants. Hovering near them was a woman wringing her hands, accompanied by her black and white Akita…The doctor dropped his arms and looked downward in a gesture of powerlessness; apparently, the child had died.

Tears streamed down the finely-dressed woman's face. The other woman wept, while hugging her canine companion for solace.

Sidney approached the finely-dressed woman. "Was she a relative of yours?" he asked.

"No, I'm only assisting." She gestured to the woman with the dog. "She's the child's mother; their pet discovered her buried in the rubble, but too late. She joins her dead father in the heavens."

Sidney sighed. "It is so kind of you to help. I hope you don't mind my asking your name?"

Her guard advanced; the young lady raised her hand. "It is okay." She turned to Sidney. "My name is Nagako."

So this is the future Empress, Mashbir realized.

"Congratulations on your upcoming wedding, Your Highness."

"Even an Empress cannot save an infant's life," she said bitterly.

"True, but look around you," he replied. "Do you not perceive the gratitude your subjects feel at seeing you amongst them at this challenging time?"

Nagako scanned the faces in room, young and old and in between, some lying on the ground, others seated, many standing in line waiting to be seen…She tried to project an air of confidence. "Thank you for your insight." Turning to her aides, she ordered, "Stop attending to my needs. Go console that poor mother, and ask the doctor what else you can do to help around here."

Facing Sidney, she asked, "And what is your name, sir?"

"Captain Sidney Mashbir, at your service, Your Majesty."

"It is a pleasure to have made your acquaintance. I hope we meet again." She turned to her next patient, and led her to an attending physician.

✳✳✳✳

Later that week, a black limousine was parked in front of the medical care center as Sidney exited. A familiar voice called out, "Please join me." Mashbir climbed into the back seat to face Prince Tokugawa. "Sidney-san, I need you with me when I speak with Crown Prince Hirohito. Militant fanatics are using this time of instability to wreak further havoc. What started with the arrest of Communist dissidents, has turned into a purge of any liberals who stand in their way. Journalists, lawyers, *even* judges have been arrested on trumped-up charges of sedition, with some executed on the spot!" The Prince gave a deep sigh... "Meanwhile, much of the populace remains in a state of denial, or walk the streets helplessly muttering, *"Why have the gods punished us?"* He turned to his chauffeur. "Take us to the Imperial Palace."

Upon entering Crown Prince Hirohito's chambers, they bowed.

"Dear Hirohito," Tokugawa said, "I hope you do not mind: I've brought my friend, Captain Mashbir, to join us as we discuss the current situation."

"He is most welcome. I have heard of the many arrests, and presume that is the reason for your visit. But what am I to do, if both my police and military wish to take the law into their own hands? I am but one man, and they have not sought my approval."

"You are much more than that," Tokugawa declared. *"Ruling* is a constant struggle to prevent tyranny and anarchy. It is rewarded, hopefully, by long periods of peace and stability. This is one of those times when your voice *must* be heard."

Hirohito turned to Mashbir. "Captain, what is your opinion?"

Mashbir searched for the right words.

"Your Majesty, I see this as a *coup d'état*—when arrests and even executions of civilians are decided without trial. *Your nation* is not in a state of war, but in the midst of a natural disaster. I agree with your Uncle: Your subjects need to hear your guiding voice!" he paused. "I recently met your future wife, Nagako, volunteering at one of the emergency medical centers, and observed firsthand the appreciative faces of your subjects as they beheld the future crown princess, during their time of need."

Hirohito immediately went to his desk, hunched over it, and began writing, his back aching. When finished, he stamped the Imperial seal upon the document and handed it to Tokugawa, who read it once silently, then aloud:

> *This proclamation demands that all past and future arrests require official judicial approval. Any prisoners who have been illegally detained must be released immediately. Failure to do so will result in the full anger and punishment of the Imperial Throne.*
>
> By order of Crown Prince Hirohito

Hirohito spoke. "You have guided me onto a path I had not intended to take. Tradition has long dictated that emperors are symbolic spiritual heads of state, who stay out of real-world political and military matters."

"Most Honorable Prince," Tokugawa replied, "dire times require new solutions."

Central Tokyo, that evening

Prodded on by bayonets, another load of prisoners was spilling out of military trucks into the mouth of a large, windowless, concrete structure, when Mashbir arrived with his escort: several dozen Imperial guards, a squad of U.S. Marines, and a representative of the American Embassy. He noted that the sports stadium had been turned into a fortress, with sentries posted at the entrance gates and every twenty feet or so around the periphery.

"Who's in charge here?" Mashbir demanded, approaching a Japanese soldier.

Seeing the imperial guards, the soldier replied, "I will notify Lieutenant Hoshimo of your presence."

Moments later, Hoshimo swaggered out. "Why are you all here?" he asked. "We are only protecting the empire against traitors."

Mashbir handed Hoshimo the proclamation.

"Read this, and you'll see that the future emperor himself, Crown Prince Hirohito, demands these arrests stop immediately and all prisoners be released. And, he plans a public announcement to reestablish order! It is his strong feeling that this lawlessness on the part of the military will only further destroy Japan."

"I will confer with my commanding officer and return with his response," Hoshimo said, then re-entered the stadium.

General Ennokee remained silent until he had been completely briefed. "So they wish to bring an end to our swift and efficient justice system, do they?"

"It appears so, sir."

"How many prisoners are now detained?"

"Approximately a thousand have entered; only four hundred are still breathing."

Ennokee glowed.

"Take a large detail of soldiers, and as quickly and quietly as possible dispatch half of the remaining, then release the rest."

"What about the prisoner trucks already are on their way? They plan to leave a detachment of troops to make sure there are no further arrests."

"We've made out point." Ennokee laughed. "Who will dare resist us now...Once again, are you sure they said that the Crown Prince plans to speak directly to the people?"

"Yes, that is what that American captain said."

"Our future emperor making such a presentation would be absurd. We will need the services of one of our best marksmen."

"You would have His Majesty shot?"

"Who said anything about actually hitting him?"

Lines of prisoners shivering in the cold night air trudged out of the stadium.

"This can't be all of them," Mashbir shouted, sensing something very wrong. "We demand an inspection of the stadium."

"Certainly, Captain," Hoshimo smirked. "It would be a pleasure to give you a tour."

Sidney pointed to several Imperial guards and Marines. "Commandeer those military trucks and take these released prisoners to a shelter." Then, turning toward another group, he said, "You men accompany me."

Soon they stood before mounds of corpses, some with the stench of several days' death about them. What repulsed them even more were the many others still spilling bright red blood, bayoneted, or with their throats cut to silence them.

Sidney glared at Hoshimo. "You've done your job well."

"They were a worthless lot."

Moving quickly, Mashbir landed a punch that knocked Hoshimo to the ground, his nose crushed.

"That is a present from the Crown Prince."

Several Japanese soldiers looked on as Hoshimo got up slowly, a smile on his bloodied face.

"Please thank the Crown Prince for his gift."

CHAPTER 21

As delegates hurried to appointments around them, Mashbir and Prince Tokugawa strolled the expansive wood-paneled lobby of the recently reopened Diet.

"Sidney-san, together we stopped the militants, and our congress is again in power—but those fanatics are not going down without a fight! In retaliation, my country home was firebombed, burnt to the ground. Fortunately, no one was hurt—and yes, it can be rebuilt. What is most disturbing, though, is that one of the conspirators shot at Hirohito's limousine. If he had been hurt or killed, I would have been to blame."

"How is he?"

"Terrified. His advisors refuse to let him appear in public again. They argue, and I agree, his assassination would be just what the militants need to take total control of the country."

"You've done all you can. Let's hope it works out." Mashbir sighed. "Dear friend, I'm returning to the States, and might not see you again for a long while."

"I will miss our conversations, Sidney."

"As will I."

"You're making a prudent decision. Your involvement in putting down this rebellion has been noted."

"Let's talk of lighter matters, Iyesato. What was that letter about, the one from Baron Shibusawa that I delivered to you?"

"My dear friend, Eiichi, is a renowned master of calligraphy. His beautiful letter expresses how much you helped the relief effort in Oiso, and that if you ever needed assistance from him, in any way, he would welcome it...When I was a young boy, he was an aide to my father, who had been the Shogun. He managed our household finances." Tokugawa smiled, bemused at the surprising turns a life can take, "Eiichi was a member of a Japanese delegation sent to view European societies. While touring the Paris Universal Exposition of 1867, he was completely amazed by Western industrial and economic development. He returned to Japan on fire, with many ideas to improve our economy, creating our first contemporary banks and stock exchange. Many consider him the Father of Modern Finance in Japan."

"And *you*, Iyesato, will be remembered as a *Father of Modern Japan* and its democratic representative government."

"You're most generous with your titles," Tokugawa smiled.

"Are you aware the Baron practices sword fighting like a young Samurai, even though he must be in his eighties? And he's good at it!"

Tokugawa nodded. "In his heated youth, he joined a small army which planned to kill or expel all foreigners. How ironic, now he and I are trying to bring about peaceful coexistence through cultural exchanges and trade alliances."

"Time brings wisdom, Your Highness."

"That is not always the case, Sidney," he paused, deliberating his words. "I'm sorry your spy network did not come to fruition."

"You knew?" Sidney stood in shock. "My primary goal was always to keep the peace between us."

"No apology needed; your motivations were understood. I *prefer* America keep an informed eye on our militant fanatics—It was I, who selected you as one of the directors of the Pan Pacific Club, so you'd have an insider's view of Japan."

The Prince's serious expression turned into a smile. "In truth, to understand a nation's destiny, one often gets a clearer picture by examining what is taught in its classrooms, than by listening only to the words of its politicians...Based on that principle, I'm working with Colonel Burnett to launch an essay-writing contest in all Japanese public schools and universities, focusing on one of your greatest leaders, who was both a wise Shogun and samurai, Abraham Lincoln, who fought for the equality of all peoples...Just forty-four years ago, in 1879, Lincoln's General Grant toured Japan, fourteen years after your Civil War...I was a young man when I met the then *former U.S.*

President, General Grant, at Eiichi Shibusawa's home, where he was being entertained. *And now,* we will be honoring President Lincoln's memory in Japan.

"Both, the Colonel, and I, believe Lincoln's message should be shared with the world. Those students who best describe his significance, will win the essay contest and receive bronze medallions stamped with the face of Lincoln—we plan to make it a yearly event."

"A noble idea, sir."

"Baron Shibusawa and I are also acting as co-chairmen of a committee to bring Chinese classical literature into our upper-level public schools, to develop an appreciation and respect for our neighbors' culture."

Mashbir looked at his companion with admiration. "I applaud your efforts in shaping the minds of the future."

"Thank you," the Prince's expression darkened, "but presently, my people are devoid of hope, focusing only on this disaster. I don't know what to do."

"What restores your spirits during difficult times, Your Highness?"

Tokugawa closed his eyes in thought, then answered, "First, my family…and I find listening to traditional Japanese and classical European music brings great joy. But our Imperial Theatre is in ruins! Even my own concert hall is partly destroyed. Such a pity—we were scheduled to be entertained by Jascha Heifetz, a marvelous young violinist from Russia."

"I share your love of music. Perhaps there's another location—or another way to use its healing powers…"

Sidney hadn't heard from Yukari, and no one seemed to know her whereabouts. His concern increased as the hours passed. That evening, he dialed the hotel front desk for the fifth time. "Are you sure you haven't received any messages from Nurse Yukari?"

"No, very sorry. I'll call as soon as I hear anything, no matter what hour."

Throwing on his coat, Sidney exited the hotel, thinking the cool night air might settle his nerves. After wandering the surrounding neighborhood, he turned back, hoping she'd returned while he was gone.

Nearing the hotel, he noticed something at the service delivery entrance. His fears grew as he approached, holding his breath, feeling disbelief and powerlessness as he reached down and turned over Yukari's limp body, her neck obviously snapped...*They've done this to get even with me.* He buried his face in her bosom, muffling his cries, clutching her hand.

※※※※

Sidney wanted to track down and tear off the limbs of the murderers, but there was no evidence.

Prince Tokugawa pleaded he leave while he still could, warning that powerful adversaries wanted him to suffer or he'd likely be dead himself . . .

He drank to ease the pain, while hoping he could re-enlist into active duty to take his mind off his loss; but discovered to his chagrin that that option was impossible. The reason was some obscure government regulation that neither Colonel Burnett nor Mashbir had known about when he had resigned.

Now, two pieces of luggage lay on his hotel bed. *Not much to show for three years in Japan,* he thought. He stared at an envelope sitting next to them, a parting gift from Prince Tokugawa and Baron Shibusawa, which he had promised to delay opening until safely aboard his ship returning to the States.

On entering the hotel lobby, he was greeted by the most beautiful sound he'd ever heard. It drew him to an auditorium where a slender young man with dark, curly hair played a violin on center stage, surrounded by radio recording and transmitting machines, with Prince Tokugawa standing at the side curtain.

The Prince appears entranced by the music, Sidney thought, as he situated himself in one of the far back seats.

Closing his eyes, opening himself to the music, feelings of loss welled up, though he resisted. When the performance ended, he was drained.

Tokugawa walked to center stage and bowed to the musician, then grasped a radio microphone.

"Dear people of Japan, you've just heard a performance by maestro Jascha Heifetz, broadcasting from the Imperial Hotel in Tokyo. Crown Prince Hirohito and I, Prince Tokugawa, as well as the other peace-loving leaders of this nation, hope his music has brought joy and healing to your hearts...

"Yes, this is our darkest hour, a time of destruction and despair..." His voice rose, "But we will get through this period, and move forward towards building a new, better future—Our courage is being tested, and our strong spirit will prevail."

Tokugawa put down the microphone.

Sidney hastily dried his tears on a sleeve, then stood applauding and shouting, "Bravo!"

The Prince's eyes sparkled. "Sidney-san, I feared I wouldn't get a chance to see you."

He descended from the stage.

"I hope you have some time for us to share before you leave?"

"I wish I did. Regrettably, my ship departs soon."

"Before you go, there's something I need to tell you – Crown Prince Hirohito, Nagako, and I are very aware it was you who spearheaded the American emergency relief effort for our people, including your very clever and helpful Medical Aid pamphlet.

"We also know of your involvement in that most distasteful task of eradicating thousands of rotting corpses from our streets. The Red Cross has now taken over most emergency centers, bringing in supplies and professionals to replace the volunteers you recruited. I, and my country, profoundly thank you."

Tokugawa placed a hand on Sidney's shoulder and looked into his bloodshot eyes. "Are you all right?"

"I'm doing fine."

Tokugawa smiled. "Then off you go, my young friend! I wish you a fine voyage, and don't be surprised if you receive the occasional correspondence from me."

"That would be a pleasure."

Sidney appeared lighthearted until he had fully turned...*Best not to burden him during this wonderful musical event. He looks so proud. I will truly miss him.*

Tokugawa watched him leave, thinking, *My heart shares your sorrow, Sidney-san. Your wife abandons you, taking your son. And now death steals your new love…You have my unspoken vow that those who took her life will pay dearly!*

CHAPTER **22**

Nagako's family residence, Tokyo, October 4, 1923

In the recessed corner of her dark room, Nagako sat crying. Servants entered with trepidation; one finally built up the nerve to announce, "Excuse us, but the Crown Prince has paid a surprise visit and wishes to see you."

"I'll meet him in the foyer."

Hirohito rushed to embrace her. "We need to talk—it's very important." She turned away.

"What's wrong, my love?" he asked, stroking her hair.

She looked at him with bewilderment. "So our wedding hasn't been cancelled?"

"Why would you think that? You're such an important part of my life."

Haltingly she replied, "There has been great pressure put upon my parents to cancel our marriage," she covered her face with her hands, "My father is threatening to take his own life if our family is so dishonored."

He gently pulled her towards him, "Yes, there are some in the royal court who condemn you because your family carries the color-blindness trait." He waved the thought away. "But only fools expect perfection in mortals."

His face brightened. "At this very moment, Prince Tokugawa and his entourage are on their way here, delivering Imperial gifts and a letter affirming our engagement. And as for your father, he is to be honored with the Order of the Sacred Crown."

He kissed her. "Dearest Nagako, for many years you have prepared to be the wife of an emperor! A heavy responsibility, but you persevered. We love each other. That is all that matters."

He looked into her moistened eyes. "Remember, I wish you to be a modern wife, who supports her husband, yet isn't afraid to speak her own mind."

"Then what was it that you mentioned being so important?"

Hirohito hesitated.

"Our ceremonial officials wish our wedding to be lavish, with extreme grandeur and opulence. I, however, feel a more modest one is in order, what with the enormous expense now required to rebuild the country."

"I completely agree," she said. "The people's needs come first; the rest is frivolity." He kissed her again with passion.

"Have no fear—no one will ever separate us, Nagako!"

A month before their wedding, a Japanese student attempted to assassinate the Crown Prince on his way to the Imperial Diet. The deranged young man fired a pistol, shattering a window of the Imperial carriage and injuring a chamberlain—but Hirohito was unharmed. Before being executed on the gallows, the attacker defiantly yelled, *"Long live the Communist Party of Japan!"*

✴✴✴✴

The Mayflower Hotel, Washington, D.C., June, 1926

The large reception was attended mostly by men—some in military uniform, but most wearing diplomatic evening dress, striped trousers, and formal long coats. The women were in gowns or cocktail dresses—with lots of jewelry on display. Sidney turned to Marine Major James Moriarty. "I can't get over how many people in this town have nothing better to do than to come to these stuffy events, as if they accomplished anything."

"Ease up, Sid," James replied. "For many, attending is justification for their diplomatic salaries; for others, it's an opportunity to make business contacts. And you never know when you might hit pay dirt."

"You're right, the food's not bad, and the drinks are free. Put it down to having to hustle for a living in the private sector these past few years...I know I sound bitter about not being able to get back into active duty, but at least I've got reserve status now." He sighed. "I'm not saying I haven't enjoyed launching my Research and Development firm. Problem is, instead of accumulating funds to establish my M-Plan, I've had trouble even staying out of debt."

James smiled. "Sounds like you need a woman in your life to take your mind off things."

"Haven't got the time." Adding to his frustration, was what initially appeared to be an amazing opportunity: Sidney couldn't believe his eyes when he opened Prince Tokugawa and Baron Shibusawa's parting gift: their letter offered him the chance to broker *a $100 million loan with a British-American finance firm* for the rebuilding of Tokyo after the earthquake's enormous destruction. Even a small commission would have made him a millionaire and able to fund his spy network to maintain peace between the U.S. and Japan. But his greedy financier partners cut him out of the deal, and in so doing, undermined the whole transaction." He guessed he just wasn't meant to be rich.

Sidney so missed active military service, where he felt he could make a difference helping the underdog. So, when Mussolini and his Fascists boasted of their plans to conquer Northern Africa, he obtained permission from the U.S. State Department to offer his services to the future Emperor of Ethiopia, Haile Selassie, who was said to be a direct descendant of King Solomon and the Queen of Sheba. Sidney officially proposed to single-handedly train and modernize Ethiopia's antiquated and outnumbered fighting force—whose army was no match for Mussolini's, being only one-tenth the size of Italy's; and whose barefooted cavalry were clothed in lion skins and still using spears. And as a bonus, Mashbir would advise them on improving their farming and irrigation technologies—As he waited for their response, he studied their language, Amharic.

James brought Sidney back to the moment.

"Here comes somebody very much like you: The intelligence boys inform me he's also always thinking work. I'll introduce you."

A Japanese naval officer with short-cropped hair approached. He gave Moriarty a quick half-bow, which the American seamlessly returned.

"Allow me to introduce a friend, Captain," Moriarty said. "This is Major Mashbir. Sidney, this is Captain Yamamoto, Naval Attaché."

"It's a great honor to meet you, sir," Mashbir said in Japanese.

"The pleasure is mine," Yamamoto replied. "But let us converse in your language—I need the practice."

"That's difficult to believe," Mashbir replied, "your pronunciation is the best I've heard from someone who is not a native English speaker."

"Our visitor attended Harvard University," Moriarty interjected. "It's a coincidence—Sidney was just complaining how nothing is accomplished at these affairs. I suspect you have similar feelings, Captain."

Yamamoto looked at Mashbir with heightened interest.

"I must confess, I had a specific motive in coming here tonight. I hope to meet an English journalist by the name of Bywater, who has written a most intriguing book. Do you know him?"

Mashbir nodded. "I'll be happy to introduce you, if he's still around."

"That would be greatly appreciated."

After a few more pleasantries, Yamamoto moved on to circulate the room.

Mashbir gripped Moriarty's arm. "This could be important. I'll search this side of the room, you take the other."

Making his way through the crowd, Sidney spotted Bywater trading his empty glass for another drink. "Hello, Hector, how are you?"

"Why Sidney, I'm not surprised to find you here, lurking about, picking up secret information."

Sidney waved him off, "I'm here only because I've been ordered to attend—but not misbehave."

Bywater laughed. "I'm under those same orders from my newspaper—but I, for one, intend to follow only the first stipulation!"

"Hector, there's someone who wishes to meet you."

Mashbir steered his inebriated companion across the room.

"Captain Yamamoto," Sidney said, "may I present Mr. Hector Bywater...Captain Yamamoto is Japan's Naval Attaché here in Washington."

"Pleased to make your acquaintance, Mr. Bywater. I have read your book in the Japanese translation, but I'm looking forward to reading the original English edition. Your intimate knowledge of our navy is quite impressive."

"Naval history has been my obsession since I was a boy. The Japanese Navy is of great interest to me, especially since you defeated the Russians in 1905, which I covered as a young news reporter. Your nation showed masterful strategy and achieved an amazing victory—a David and Goliath story, if ever there was one!"

Yamamoto beamed. "Yes, I also was there as a naval cadet." He held up a hand. "That is where I lost two fingers."

"It sounds like you gentlemen have a great deal to talk about," Mashbir interjected.

"Yes, indeed," replied Yamamoto, "but this crowded, noisy room is not the place to do so. I give small dinners at my apartment and would be honored if you gentlemen would join me. I'll send formal invitations of course, but shall we say this Thursday evening? I promise a tasty meal—and perhaps a game of poker afterwards."

Turning to Mashbir, he asked, "Do you play, Major?"

"I have attempted it. I expect you're a formidable opponent, Captain Yamamoto. I've heard you're a master of the game of *Shogi*."

"Ah, you seek to flatter me into mistakes. While I'm here, I prefer all things American: Poker and whisky. So I hope I'll be seeing you Thursday night then, gentlemen."

Yamamoto took his leave and walked off into the crowd.

Bywater watched him go. "Interesting chap." He lowered his voice and leaned in closer to Mashbir's ear. "Rumor has it that he's in line for Fleet Command—but there's a power struggle with the battleship boys. But he might have an edge, being an advocate of more air power in their military. Now please excuse me—I need to get this glass refilled! Can't sail on empty fuel tanks, you know." With a brisk laugh, Bywater wandered off in the direction of the bar.

James came over to Sidney and asked, "So why did Yamamoto want to meet Bywater?"

"He's interested in discussing Hector's book, *The Great Pacific War*, which predicts a surprise Japanese attack on U.S. naval bases in the Pacific."

✳✳✳✳

Yamamoto, accompanied by two other Japanese officers, as well as Bywater, Moriarty, and Mashbir, moved from the dining area into the living room, where a card table and chairs awaited. Mashbir loosened his belt.

"I must compliment you, Captain Yamamoto, I would not have expected your Japanese cook to be so skillful in preparing Maryland Crab Cakes, to say nothing of the fried chicken."

"And you'd have been correct, had it been a Japanese cook. For variety I've employed a native cook, one of your American Negroes. When I want traditional Japanese cuisine, I impose on one of the servants of my two aides here. Gentlemen, let us now proceed to the real purpose of this gathering."

His aides took their seats; Bywater settled in his unsteadily, the effect of several rapidly downed drinks.

"Shall we say dealer's choice, two-dollar ante, table stakes?"

Moriarty sat next to Mashbir and in a low voice said, "I hope you brought a stack of money—some of these pots can get up to a hundred dollars or so."

It was soon obvious that Yamamoto's aides were only present to provide numbers, being bad players and never betting against their superior. Moriarty was a cautious player, managing to stay even or win a little. Bywater bet wildly, raising on mediocre hands; he raked in the occasional pot, but overall was the steady loser. Mashbir and Yamamoto were both excellent players. A good run of cards came Sidney's way, and he played aggressively, winning three large pots in a row.

Yamamoto observed him closely.

"Major, I think no game so well exposes a man's strengths and weaknesses as Poker, particularly his military capabilities. In the Western world, war has often been compared to the game of chess. While my countrymen say the same of our game of *Go*, but I disagree. The element of luck, the skill in obtaining favorable odds—as well as the willingness to take risks, sometimes great risks—are all paramount components in both Poker and warfare. Do you agree?"

"It would be impolite to disagree with so gracious a host," Mashbir replied.

"I see a man of wisdom, as well as a bold and worthy adversary. Yours is a large, mighty nation, far better kept as our friendly ally. But if the winds of war stir, you and I will be mere puppets in the game."

"Very true, Yamamoto," Moriarty interjected. "But I caution you, whether it's a card game or combat, Sidney uses every advantage to win."

Mashbir shot an annoyed look at Moriarty. Yamamoto noticed this and smiled.

"It's all right, gentlemen, that's something else we both have in common."

When the game broke up, Yamamoto was by far the top winner, up nearly six hundred dollars, with Mashbir also ahead by a couple of hundred...Bywater was the big loser, but having consumed liberal quantities of Scotch, he didn't seem to care.

As they were leaving, Moriarty said, "I'm driving Sidney home. Can I offer you a ride as well, Hector?"

"No, thanks, my flat is just a few blocks away, and Yamamoto has kindly asked me to stay for a while longer."

Bywater was already settling into an armchair, accepting yet another drink from the ever-attentive servant.

On the way to Mashbir's home in Georgetown, Moriarty asked, "Well, was it what you expected?"

"You always learn something at a Poker game, James, if you pay attention. Yamamoto knows how to lower his opponent's guard. Before Hector leaves tonight, I'm betting he'll tell our host everything about himself and his world-class naval expertise, from nursery school up to now. I tell you, he's a dangerous adversary, very shrewd and a gambler at heart. He isn't an expansionist like some of his superiors, who dream of scooping up islands in the Pacific, but if he gets that position as commander of the fleet, I don't look forward to having to go against him someday."

The following afternoon, Mashbir was on the phone, "General Pershing, I hope I'm not disturbing you?"

"Not at all. After several hours of writing, I needed to put down my pen and take a break. Some publishers encouraged me to write my war memoirs. It's likely to take a couple of volumes to do it justice. But how can I help you?"

"Sir, I've a gut feeling another war might not be far off, but this time against Japan…My concern is our tactical response hasn't taken into account changes in Naval and Aviation technology."

"You're right. Our Battle Plan Orange is way out-of-date. Things have changed a lot these past ten years. The problem is, much of the top brass is stuck in the past—Sidney, do you think you're up to the task of revising it?"

"I'd be honored to give it a try, sir! Studying Hector Bywater's book, *The Great Pacific War*, has given me plenty of ideas."

"Remember, Sidney, you ruffled some powerful people's feathers while doing a *fine* job for me and Colonel Burnett in the past. So, even if you greatly improve Battle Plan Orange under my authority, who knows who you'll anger next by shaking things up?"

"I'll take what comes, sir."

"Okay, I'll try to get you into active duty temporarily—so, you can modernize that document for the Twentieth Century. And once you're back in, maybe they'll let you stay."

"General, hopefully this peace holds up for a long spell, but if it doesn't, at least we'll be better prepared."

"Sounds good. By the way, Mashbir, I remember your connection to Native Americans and that you speak Apache, so I thought you'd find this interesting. Several Choctaw Indians were part of our 142nd Infantry during the Great War—during a dangerous mission for our troops, they transmitted coded messages using their tribal language. The enemy didn't have the foggiest notion what was being sent. It was as if they were listening to the wind."

"Clever idea. You never know when that concept might come in handy again—I'll sign off now, sir, and I'm looking forward to reading your book."

CHAPTER 23

The Imperial Palace, June 6, 1931

Handmaidens busily packed trunks, while Empress Nagako stood watching, dark shadows under her eyes. One of her older servants asked, "Anything else, Your Majesty?"

"We're almost done here. Please bring the children and their belongings. We must leave immediately, and remember dear Shige, you've promised to follow my instructions."

That evening Hirohito returned, weary but contented, after spending his day at the Biology Research Institute. "Nagako, where are you?" he called, as he entered their personal chambers. Receiving no response, he wandered about until approached by Shige.

"Where are Nagako and the children?"

Shige flustered.

"They have moved to the home of the empress's mother."

"What. They simply left?"

"She... I mean..."

Shige prostrated herself at the emperor's feet.

"I command you, speak," he said. Then softening his voice, he added, "I don't wish to frighten you, but I need answers."

Shige stood. "Her Highness commanded me to deliver something when you returned. I pray it will help you understand." She led him into the reading room, where she pulled an embroidered book with green silk covers off a shelf.

"Thank you, Shige, you may now leave." *This must be one of Nagako's private diaries,* he thought.

He shouted to his guards outside, "I'm not to be disturbed," and settled into a chair, book in hand, but hesitating before opening it. *What could make her just disappear and take the children?*

He began to read:

July 8, 1925
Such joy for us to finally have time alone. This island in the center of Lake Inawashiro is a true paradise for our honeymoon. We're like children once again, discovering the wonders of nature, far from the prying eyes of the palace.
Hirohito is so relaxed and happy, as am I.

July 12, 1925
I challenged my beloved to a game of tennis. It turned into a comedy, us being beginners and spending most of the time retrieving the balls ourselves. We preferred that to having servants constantly at our heels. Tomorrow we go horseback-riding into the mountains. I savor every day to its fullest, knowing soon our honeymoon will be over.

December 1, 1926
It was miraculous—our lovely Princess Terunomiya came into the world today! Her radiant smile inspired us to name her Sunshine. Many court officials had hoped for a boy as a future heir to the throne, but it was not to be. My heart swells as Hirohito tenderly caresses her. I refuse to let a nursemaid and servants take over all the responsibilities of motherhood. She is my child, and I will raise and nurture her as much as possible.
As we celebrate new life, another nears its end. Though he tries to hide his feelings, Hirohito worries about his father's increasingly ill health.

December 26, 1926
Emperor Taisho passed away yesterday. I sense my dear husband is not looking forward to the responsibilities that destiny has in store for him. I will support him with all my heart.

Hirohito took a deep sigh, then continued to read.

March 23, 1927
Not a day goes by when news of more government corruption does not weigh down Hirohito's spirits. Perhaps after his coronation next year, he will be accorded the respect and fear he needs to control his cabinet.

September 2, 1927
It was a most difficult delivery, but Hirohito and I were rewarded with another precious daughter, Hisanomiya. Instead of worrying about my well-being, many simply waited with bated breath hoping for the sounding of two bells for a male heir, instead of one for a female.
If men carried a child for nine months, then gave birth themselves, I doubt they'd be so judgmental whether a boy or girl sprang forth! In England, royal princesses have come to command thrones, and ancient Japanese history speaks of female rulers.
Prince Tokugawa has been so supportive. He commemorates her birth by planting a Paulownia tree, so when she marries, the tree will be harvested and made into a dresser as a wedding gift.

January 4, 1928
Yesterday, Hirohito and I attended a celebration at which Prince Tokugawa was appointed the seventh president of the Japanese Red Cross Society. I was frightened at first when he encouraged me to give the opening address for the event, but was proud for having done it.
With great humility he accepted this position, stating the ideal of the Red Cross is service to humanity, relieving the suffering of all nations in times of disaster. He is so brave, ignoring threatening letters

accompanied by poison candies. Prince Tokugawa refuses to stand aside and let militants push Japan into war!
He is a true hero of mine and Hirohito's.

February 20, 1928
In spite of Hisanomiya having a high fever, palace officials discourage us from using modern cures and needles to administer medicines, claiming that is not the proper way for treating nobility.
We cannot accept such blind ignorance and bondage to the past and have demanded she be given up-to-date care while we pray for her with all our hearts.

March 2, 1928
Alas! Our precious six-month-old Hisanomiya is no longer with us. How do I explain this to her sister, who has come to love her so much? In spite of all our efforts, her young soul drifted away.

Hirohito's stomach tightened, seeing the dried tear drops on the page, feeling he was there with Nagako, re-experiencing the loss.

September 30, 1929
It is hard to believe when I now reread my last entry, how miserable we felt. And here, a year and a half later, we are once again joyously blessed!
Another beautiful daughter has been born, who we all believe is the reincarnation of Hisanomiya. We have named her Takanomiya. Her older sister, Terunomiya, dances with excitement at the return of her little sister's soul.
All would be wonderful—if not for the whispers that I had once again failed to bring forth a male heir.
What am I to do?

November 16, 1929
Many newspapers criticize Hirohito for pressuring his incompetent cabinet to resign. They claim the government is chosen by the people, and the emperor should not deal with the day-to-day affairs of state.

He wonders if they are not right, perhaps he should not dirty his hands? I, however, feel these newspapers are puppets of those extremists in the military, pushing us toward war. I try my best to keep Hirohito's spirits up.

<u>*May 24, 1931*</u>
Bringing forth life does not get easier at the old age of twenty-eight. There is little celebration at the arrival of Princess Yorinomiya. I feel surrounded by veiled hatred and judgment, except from my closest servants and family.
Am I a failure as a wife?
I often cry in private and try to ignore the shame.

Hirohito thought, *How foolish I am for not recognizing the great suffering she endured.* With anticipation, he read the final diary entries.

<u>*May 30, 1931*</u>
Though it pains my heart, I will not stand in the way of what is considered best for our nation.
My ladies-in-waiting have been invited by Palace officials to show special attentions to my husband. Perhaps a concubine can bring forth a male heir. I've noticed the added adornment to their hair and faces, and their more alluring kimonos. Hirohito promises I am his only true love, and if pushed to take another woman, he will abdicate the throne to one of his brothers or their sons.
My mother is of the old world and advises me that the demands on nobility are great, and I must bear them. In the past there have been barren Empresses—or those who bore only daughters—who were sent off to separate living quarters, as the Emperor took on a new life with his concubine—who would then acquire the role of Empress.
Is this to be my fate?

June 6, 1931
Today, I overheard servants whispering of a contest, from which three
of the loveliest and most desirable ladies of the royal court were to be
chosen.
Hirohito is a fine husband, father, and devoted emperor, but many
claim this lack of a male heir is a Heavenly sign that he is not fit to rule.
To strengthen his position, I will make the sacrifice and leave, freeing
him to do what he must.

With dampened eyes, Hirohito hugged the diary to his chest, moments passing in reflection. He then stood up with his face ablaze and shouted, "Enough of this madness!"

A myriad of stars glittered, as Hirohito and his entourage of guards and servants arrived at Empress Nagako's mother's home. He turned to the commander of his guards, ordering, "Stay here," then knocked on the front door and waited.

Nagako's mother opened it slightly.
    "Dear son-in-law, are you sure of what you're doing?"
    "Please let me in."
    As he entered, the children ran to him.
    "How are my beautiful swans?" he asked, as his three daughters embraced him. "You are so precious to me."
    Nagako ran off, tears flowing. Hirohito followed her to her childhood bedroom. There, surrounded by her lacquered toys and delicate dolls, they sat on her bed. He put his arm around her waist, sensing her vulnerability. "Dearest, I wish you to hear a proclamation that is going to be circulated tomorrow."

    He began to read:

    "'I, Emperor Hirohito, will no longer tolerate any suggestion that I take a
concubine or second wife, in the hope she might bear a male heir.
    It will be seen as treason to meddle in such private affairs.

Divine Providence alone decides what gender the Emperor's children are to be.

Breaching of this Proclamation will be seen as criminal and treated accordingly!'"

Looking into her eyes, Hirohito whispered, "I need you so much," and kissed her . . .

"Love of my life, all your things are packed and your servants are outside, ready to accompany us and our wonderful daughters back to *our home."*

CHAPTER 24

After taking his recently prescribed heart medication, Prince Tokugawa added a couple of aspirins for his throbbing headache. Eyes closed, he settled into a comfortable armchair in his library and proudly reflected that almost a decade had passed since his successful leadership role at the *Washington Naval Arms Limitation Conference*—a gathering supported by President Harding, in hopes of avoiding an arms race in the Pacific. It was the first international arms limitation conference in history!

When it came time to push for its renewal at the *1930 London Naval Conference*, Tokugawa requested Mashbir be part of the greeting committee for the Japanese delegates when they passed through Washington, D.C. on their way to England.

In spite of the 1930 London Naval Conference creating greater military equality between the U.S., Britain, and Japan, than the 1921-22 agreement had, that was not enough to appease the militants in Japan, who wanted no limitations. To undermine this new agreement, another incendiary incident was fabricated in Manchuria, claiming that vicious Chinese commandos had stormed a Japanese garrison near Mukden and blown up a segment of the Japanese-owned *Manchurian Railroad Line*. A bloody battle was now being waged, with twenty thousand additional Japanese troops heading toward the region.

Prince Tokugawa and Emperor Hirohito were near their wits' ends. While Tokugawa quietly worked behind the scenes to contain the conflict, the Emperor was being criticized by some, for not more openly resisting the militants. In the meanwhile, both leaders feared igniting a civil war…

Prince Tokugawa found himself once again reaching out across the Pacific to his American ally.

"Such a pleasant surprise receiving your phone call," Mashbir said.

"Forgive me, Sidney-san, for burdening you once more for advice."

"It's always a pleasure to hear from you. How can I be of assistance?"

"The emperor and I are *again* attempting to prevent a major military expansion into China. The problem is, your newspapers now proclaim war between our nations is inevitable! What is to be done?"

Mashbir deliberated, "It looks like *we* need to come up with some creative ways to change American public opinion..."

Several days later, Prince Tokugawa was seated at a table in the Imperial Palace sipping plum wine in the company of Emperor Hirohito, Empress Nagako, the gray-haired but robust General Shirakawa, and a newly-arrived American diplomat named Joseph Grew. Tokugawa turned toward the tall, distinguished Joseph Grew. "We so appreciate your attending our gathering and look forward to you soon becoming U.S. ambassador...We are aware of the fine job you've done in other nations in that capacity—But you are new to the ways of Japan."

Grew smiled. "I'm anxious to learn more about your culture, and thank you for the warm welcome you've given me, Prince Tokugawa. President Hoover sends you and the rest of the royal family his regards."

With confidence, Tokugawa replied, "I hope you don't mind if I call you Joseph. Please forward our best wishes to him as well, and emphasize we wholeheartedly desire stability in Asia. The Emperor and I plan to reverse the military expansion into China, but need your involvement to improve public sentiments between *our* two countries."

Tokugawa deferred to Hirohito.

"Future Ambassador," the Emperor said, "we have a two-part plan: *First,* my younger brother, Prince Takamatsu, and his new bride are on a goodwill tour of Europe, America, and Canada. When they arrive in the United States, we hope you'll arrange as much positive press coverage as possible."

"So, I'm to be your public relations agent?" Grew grinned. "I'll certainly do my best."

Tokugawa turned to Shirakawa.

"Dear General, you're aware of how highly esteemed you are in the eyes of the Emperor and Empress."

"Thank you for the kind words...I am only their humble servant. How can I be of service?"

"General," the Emperor replied, "the second part of our plan requires you to take command of the forces in Shanghai, and bring this mounting violence to an end before it's too late."

"Is there truly no-one else who you can ask to do this?"

Nagako answered, "You are most capable for this act of loyalty to the will of the Emperor in his desire to maintain peace."

"Divine Emperor, Empress, and Honorable Prince Tokugawa, I will be candid," Shirakawa replied, standing rigidly. "There are many other generals who want nothing more than for war to erupt. If I do as you ask, my only consolation will be that I died in your service."

"Dear friend, old age has its advantages," Tokugawa said wryly. "There's little that can be taken away, which will not soon be gone in its own natural course."

Shirakawa bowed, and then declared, "When do I leave?"

✳✳✳✳

"Welcome to San Francisco!" Mashbir announced, as Prince and Princess Takamatsu and their entourage entered the elegant hotel lobby. "Your uncle, Prince Tokugawa, and Emperor Hirohito requested I assist in planning your itinerary. I've arranged for my good friend Commander Zacharias to travel with you during your two-month tour of the States."

"Thank you," Prince Takamatsu replied, "and I convey my brother and Tokugawa's warm regards to you."

"You're in for some excitement," Mashbir continued. "After

you've checked in and made yourself comfortable, our first stop is the historic Presidio."

There, the royal couple was greeted by a reception of Japanese and non-Japanese men and women from San Francisco's high society, wearing top hats and fur wraps, waiting excitedly to show off their fair city. But first, standing beside Major General Craig, the Takamatsus received the highest honors of four ruffles and flourishes with drums and bugles and a twenty-one-gun salute. This was followed by the playing of the Japanese National Anthem, as they watched the 30th Infantry march on parade. Their lush park-like surroundings made it hard to believe the Presidio had been a military base since 1776... With the forest as a backdrop, the gathering posed for a newspaper press photo for worldwide distribution. Mashbir deftly moved out of the frame, orchestrating things as usual from behind the scenes. A few days later, they excitedly traveled south to Hollywood, and got the chance to see how studios produced silent and talking movies.

The Prince and Princess also explored the East Coast. In Philadelphia, they visited Independence Hall, where they were told the story of the fifty-six patriots who risked their lives in defiance of the British King and read the Declaration of Independence, announcing these patriots' intention to found a new American nation. They also touched the Liberty Bell, the iconic symbol of freedom...Then on to Boston, where they strolled Harvard's campus, and visited the nearby stately home of the poet Henry Wadsworth Longfellow.

In Upstate New York, cadets proudly marched on display at West Point Military Academy in their honor. The following day, journalists swarmed Prince Takamatsu and his beautiful wife, Kikuko, on their arrival in New York City.

"What are your plans in the Big Apple?" a reporter shouted.

"We wish to see the things that make America great, and meet with your prominent leaders," the Prince replied.

The Princess smiled beguilingly.

"We're very excited to go to the top of your newly-completed Empire State Building," she said. "We also look forward to visiting your Bronx Zoo, the Brooklyn Botanical Gardens, and Central Park!"

Preceded by strutting cavalry horsemen, New York City's dapper, song-writing Mayor Jimmy Walker, accompanied the royal couple's motorcade down Fifth Avenue for a ticker-tape parade attended by fifty-thousand cheering onlookers; the event had been partially arranged by the billionaire financier, J.P. Morgan, who just happened to be a cousin of Ambassador Grew.

The imperial couple then traveled to Washington, D.C., where President Herbert Hoover himself personally greeted them at Union Station and then escorted them, walking down Pennsylvania Avenue, as soldiers lining the boulevard held back the large crowds.

The following evening in the Capital, two thousand guests of Japanese Ambassador Debuchi and his wife, gathered in the enormous reception hall of the Mayflower Hotel.

"As your host, it is my honor to welcome Prince and Princess Takamatsu," Ambassador Debuchi announced. "Let us make a toast," raising a champagne glass. "May their visit to America enhance mutual understanding and appreciation between our two great nations."

Mashbir, accompanied by a vivacious woman in her mid-twenties, as well as the Japanese foreign minister, all tapped each other's' glasses then sipped their drinks. Mashbir gently took hold of the young woman's hand.

"What a sweet coincidence," remarked the minister with a smile, "that you, Sidney and Irene, are also recently married! And I notice *your* family is growing," he added, glancing at the expectant mother. "Congratulations!"

Irene blushed, turning her pretty brown eyes toward the minister. "Thank you, Minister. I would never have thought when my mother and I arrived from Russia two years ago, that I would meet Sidney, who not only speaks my native tongue, but has been very patient while teaching me English—We're so happy!" She placed her hand on her stomach, and Sidney gently put his hand over hers.

Wishing to redirect the conversation, Sidney said, "Prince Takamatsu certainly looks sharp in his white naval uniform."

"He's a lieutenant," the minister replied, "but deservedly destined for much higher rank."

"Isn't Princess Kikuko Takamatsu, Prince Iyesato Tokugawa's great niece?" Irene asked.

"That is correct. Her great-grandfather, Shogun Yoshinobu, was Iyesato's father."

"I've heard," Sidney hesitated, "that Prince Takamatsu and his older brother the Emperor are at odds on occasion."

"Such is the world of siblings," the minister replied with a shrug. "Prince Takamatsu believes his brother should more strongly resist military expansion, while certain of the emperor's military advisors feel quite differently."

"Poor Emperor," Irene said, "he's being pressured on all sides."

The minister lowered his voice. "It's not clear who's responsible, but there have been assassination threats made against the royal couple during their stay in Boston."

Irene shuddered.

"Yes, I know," Sidney replied. "They've doubled their police guard. It looks like someone doesn't want them to succeed in their good-will tour."

The minister nodded, then something caught his eye.

"Do either of you recognize that fellow over there? He looks so familiar."

Irene squinted her eyes.

"Oh, that's Charlie Chaplin, I believe."

They strolled over and saw Chaplin radiating a mischievous smile as a well-dressed Japanese man whispered in his ear. In exaggerated fashion, Chaplin held shrimp over his upturned face and gulped one after another...They overheard the well-dressed Japanese man speak in a scolding tone, "This is a diplomatic event, Charles. Won't you show some decorum?"

"You're no fun, Kono," Chaplin replied. "Don't worry so much—go mingle around the party."

Chaplin turned, and when he again faced his companion, two up-turned shrimps protruded from the corners of his mouth, as if they were a curled mustache. With a playful wave of his hand, he shooed his frustrated companion away.

Sidney, Irene, and the minister broke out in laughter. Chaplin turned toward them and in a clipped British accent said, "Oh, have you come to help me with the prawns? Dig in. They're first rate."

"Thanks for the offer, Mr. Chaplin," the foreign minister replied, "but my primary desire is to obtain an autograph for myself and one for the prime minister back in Tokyo—he's quite a fan of yours."

"It would be my pleasure!"

Taking the pen and memo pad the minister offered, Chaplin created two caricature sketches: each had a bowler hat above bushy eyebrows and a mustache, with pouting lips beneath. His inscription read:

> Here's to my delightful fans, from the Islands of Japan.
> Best regards, Charles Chaplin

He presented these mementos with a flourish.

"Most generous of you," the minister exclaimed, admiring the whimsical creation...Chaplin explained he had long been a Japano-phile and that Kabuki theatre had influenced his artistry. Hearing about this diplomatic event, he just had to attend, and managed to finesse an invitation.

"Mr. Chaplin, should you ever visit Japan, I'm sure Prime Minister Inukai would be greatly honored to have you as his house guest."

"*Really*? I have long desired to visit your country—and would certainly do so with such a generous invitation!"

The minister bowed.

"I'll begin working out the details at once."

"Thank you so much. And how about you," Chaplin said, turning to the Mashbirs. "Are you, perchance, also fans?"

"Most certainly," Irene replied, as Sidney proffered a pad and pen. "Please make ours out to Sidney and Irene," and with a smile she added, "and could you draw a heart around it?"

When Chaplin finished, Sidney said, "Here's my business card. Should you visit Japan, I've some contacts there as well—By the way, I hope you don't mind my asking, but who was that Japanese man you were bantering with?"

"Oh, you mean Kono. He's is quite a character. Ran away from his old-fashioned family and an arranged marriage back in Japan. His well-to-do parents cut him off financially, so when he came to California, he settled for a job as my houseboy and driver. He's been with me fifteen years and has become my business confidante and friend."

"I see," said the minister, "but we couldn't help noticing Kono appeared annoyed with you."

"He's always reprimanding me for my poor manners. I can't help myself—it's a holdover from my half-starving days in the slums of London." Chaplin smiled. "Though, one pleasant benefit of being in the Movie Industry is that people expect you to act eccentric!"

CHAPTER 25

Japan, May 15, 1932

Ken faced his elderly father, Prime Minister Tsuyoshi Inukai. "Our guest, Mr. Chaplin, and I, will be leaving soon," Ken said. "Are you sure you don't wish to come along?"

"I'm a bit tired and plan to relax with a good book. If I want conversation, I'll invite Kono to describe his colorful life back in California."

"Okay, Father, as you wish."

Soon they were in the back seat of a chauffeured car driving off. "Charles, how do you explain your popularity," Ken asked, "even in countries with very different cultures?"

Chaplin smiled. "I'm a spoof of every man with a bit more license. I've played a tramp, a gentleman, a poet, a dreamer, *always* searching for romance and adventure. Though my character might have you believe he's a scientist, a musician, a duke, or a polo player, yet he is not above picking up a cigarette butt, or mischievously robbing candy from a baby. They see a person they can relate to, and at the same time feel sorry for, coping with life's predicaments and eventually triumphing—even if only in a small way."

They arrived at the busy arena entrance, and while purchasing tickets, Ken whispered to one of the staff.

Moments later, they were ushered within eight rows of ringside, where two ponderous Sumo wrestlers, clad only in loincloths, faced one another from opposite sides. In the center stood a kimono-clad announcer, waving a colorful fan to gain the attention of the crowd as he bellowed into a megaphone. Chaplin's ears perked up when he heard what sounded like his name mentioned, accompanied by a spotlight directed at him.

Chaplin turned to Ken. "So what's going on here, my friend?"

"They want you onstage to say hello before the match begins," Ken replied. "I can't imagine how they knew you were here."

Chaplin shook his head in mock disapproval.

"Okay, Ken, but at least escort me."

As they moved down the aisle, Chaplin asked Ken to borrow a hat and cane from members of the audience, then spryly climbed up into the ring, bowing in all directions as he doffed his hat and twirled his cane. As the announcer again spoke into his megaphone, Chaplin snuck behind him. Whenever the man turned, Chaplin stayed just out of view. When the moment was right, Chaplin grabbed the megaphone and began to mimic the announcer's mannerisms, pretending to introduce the combatants, eliciting uproarious laughter.

Chaplin then jumped behind one of the sumo wrestlers, slyly peeking from behind the mountain-sized fighter. Getting into the game, the announcer pretended to chase Chaplin around the ring to retrieve his megaphone. Feigning fear, Chaplin crawled between the stout legs of the other wrestler as he scrambled to exit the ring.

A standing ovation was given to Chaplin as he waddled back to his seat, twirling his cane.

Ken patted him on the back.

"Those wrestlers will have a hard time following up your act."

Chaplin wiped his sweaty forehead with a kerchief.

"So that was what you were arranging with your whispers when we arrived at the gate. I'm lucky I got out of there alive!"

Back at Ken and his father's home, a group of young Japanese naval officers and cadets, most barely past the age of twenty, gathered at the entrance. It had been nine years since Sidney had broken Lieutenant Hoshimo's nose: the welt on his face, combined with his misshapen nose, almost produced a comical appearance, if not for his savage, piercing eyes. He was now a captain commanding an assault.

"Use your rifle butts and ram the door," he ordered. Upon their entry, the frail prime minister stood up from his study chair and shouted, "How dare you break into my home!"

Hoshimo without hesitation fired point blank into his chest. "Now kill the rest of the family and servants," he ordered. "If you find Chaplin, kill him also."

Gunshots and screaming were soon heard from all directions.

One cadet returned.

"Captain, please follow me. We have a prisoner who is not part of the family, nor is he staff; we don't know what you might want to do with him."

Hoshimo followed the cadet to an upstairs guestroom to find Kono huddled inside a closet with two soldiers pointing rifles at him. A newspaper on a nearby table caught Hoshimo's eye. He compared the cover to the man in the closet.

"Is this you in the photograph with the prime minister and Mr. Chaplin?"

Kono was shaking as he nodded yes.

"What is your name?"

"Kono. I'm Mr. Chaplin's driver and assistant in California, and when he travels," he answered in a dazed voice.

Hoshimo aimed a pistol at Kono's head.

"Follow me."

They went downstairs, where Kono almost collapsed when he looked upon his host lying in a pool of blood.

"Why are you not with Mr. Chaplin tonight?" Hoshimo asked. "Is he hiding nearby? Don't lie to me."

Kono's teeth chattered. "He went out for the evening, I swear it."

"Killing you both would teach the Western world a lesson. *Especially the Americans*, to stay out of Japanese affairs. Our late prime minister was foolishly developing close ties with them."

"But sir," Kono replied, "Mr. Chaplin is British, not American. Yes, America would mourn him, but what would you really gain? I, however, in my capacity as aide to Chaplin, might be helpful to your cause. We once even met the American President. I'll forever be indebted if you let me live."

"Give me your wallet."

Hoshimo searched its contents and shoved a photo into Kono's face. "Here's your family. When I contact you for assistance in the future, you'd better cooperate, or I'll slaughter them all, and then kill you and Chaplin as well. Do you understand?"

Kono's gaze was riveted to the minister's sprawled body. He nodded.

"And remember, our conversation is to remain secret. Now go escape out the back entrance, and when you're found, claim you heard the shooting and ran off."

Back at the sports arena, it was the start of the third match. The wrestlers prepared for their first collision, when the lights went out. A hush passed over the audience, as they patiently waited for them to be turned on again. Several minutes passed; the announcer mounted the darkened stage carrying a lantern. "Stay calm. You are in no danger," he said in Japanese through his megaphone, "but listen carefully. I've been informed the prime minister was assassinated, and the electrical power to the city has been cut. Leave your seats slowly, then go back to your homes to await further updates."

Chaplin turned to Ken, wishing him to translate.

"Charles," he stammered, "my father has been murdered, probably part of a coup d'état."

Chaplin supported his unsteady companion, as they moved toward the exit doors and out into the night.

✳✳✳✳

Two months later

Several generals led the long procession into the Imperial Hall, followed by servants burdened with stacks of paper. One servant, however, held only a small ebony and pearl inlaid wooden box. All bowed to the Emperor.

"Your Majesty," General Ennokee said, "behold the voice of the people, *Three hundred thousand signatures gathered,* begging you to show clemency. You, yourself, spent years at the military academy, and should understand these young soldiers' fervent patriotism. Truly, they felt they were doing your will by eliminating those standing in the way of Japan bringing all Asia under our rule, as part of our co-prosperity plan."

Hirohito shouted, "How dare you connect me to such a heinous crime! And you have the temerity to request they go free with no punishment?"

"Of course not, Your Majesty."

Ennokee beckoned the servant carrying the box, who presented it to the Emperor. Upon opening it, he felt utter disgust. There, neatly arranged, were eleven severed fingers. Hirohito almost threw up.

"So you see, most enlightened Emperor, there has been justice," Ennokee said. "Without their pinky fingers, they can no longer properly handle a sword, a pistol, or a rifle. Isn't that enough?

"Haven't our people spoken in their defense?" he asked, pointing at the stacks of petitions. "Will you not listen to their pleas?"

I feel so alone, Hirohito thought, then declared, "This is mild punishment for the cold blooded murder of a prime minister, his family, and his staff. I will heed your request this time only. But if another act such as this occurs, a more appropriate punishment will be meted out. Now leave me."

❋❋❋❋

Later that year, Hirohito and Nagako stood on the palace roof, transfixed by the swirl of white doves circling the sky. "Sometimes, I wish I were one of them," he said, "free of earthly responsibilities to this insane human world." His heart ached, recalling recent events: They'd had been in fine spirits after leaving a celebration at the Tokugawa estate. Their carriage was returning to the palace, followed by several other carriages conveying the ministers of the imperial household, when suddenly, from out of the bushes, a man in peasant garb ran toward them and threw an object beneath one of the ministers' carriages. It rolled past the intended target and exploded, killing the horses. Guards ran at the assassin and bayoneted him, as all of the passengers stared out their carriage windows, shaken and speechless.

But at least things were getting better in China, he and Nagako thought, with *General Shirakawa enforcing a cease-fire. Sadly, that was not to last. Those hopes were dashed, when General Matsumoto informed them that in Shanghai, during an address given by the consul general, a bomb was thrown into the gathering, injuring Admiral Nomura and Commander Ueda, and killing General Shirakawa...And now, certain officers were again stirring up trouble in China, leading maneuvers over deserted battlefields and shouting Banzai, as their troops pretended to be in battle, firing their rifles at nothing.*

It was well past midnight that evening, when Nagako was awakened. "No, don't!" Hirohito shouted, flailing his arms.

"Wake up!" Nagako pleaded. "It's just a nightmare."

Hirohito rubbed his eyes, while looking around.

"Oh, Nagako, we were again in our carriage when a fanatic rushed toward us with an explosive." His voice became almost inaudible, *"but this time, you died."*

"Look, I'm all right," she said, stroking his hair.

Hirohito went to his bedroom desk, his face strained as his pen hovered over a sheet of paper.

"Please come back to sleep—you need your rest."

"I must write a poem of peace, like my ancestors have before me, to convince them that is the way." He struggled, then crumbled the paper. "Oh, it's no use! Poems cannot stop bullets and bombs."

"My dearest," Nagako replied, "let's pay a visit to Prince Tokugawa. It has been a while since we've seen him. He'll raise our spirits."

The following afternoon, with bright smiles, Nagako and Hirohito carried packages of Tokugawa's favorite treats. Tokugawa's aides allowed them to enter unannounced. As they came into his study, their smiles evaporated. They faced a rare sight: Tokugawa was weeping, staring at open photo albums strewn on the table before him. "Dear Uncle, what is the matter?" Hirohito asked.

"Oh, children, so good to see you…I've been thinking about my old friend, Baron Dr. Takuma Dan," he said, pointing to a photo of the two of them standing proudly together…He described how Dan had studied International economics and worked hard to build their nation, respectful of both Japanese and Western ways. And, as past owner of *Mitsui Gomel Kaisha Conglomerate*, he had led Mitsui Bank to enormous success, with income exceeding all the tax revenues of every city in Japan combined. But despite his high position, Dan was kind and generous.

"At his funeral," Tokugawa spoke in a strained voice, "his son confided that the day before his father was killed, his father had met with the League of Nations Commission in an attempt to arrive at a peaceful solution in China, *and that is why*, a naive twenty-one-year-old was manipulated to assassinate him."

Tokugawa raised a clenched fist.

"Many police are now under the militants' thumb, falsely accusing a humble Buddhist priest and his followers of the murder, and spreading rumors that this death squad has targeted any politician, banker, or industrialist who refuses to support a war economy," he sighed. "And I have the honor of being included on that death list."

Hirohito and Nagako hovered near him.

"Please, Iyesato, you must leave the country," Nagako implored.

"But I'm needed here, to hold things together," he replied. "It is not clear who killed General Shirakawa, perhaps those who wish Japan out of Korea. Either way, our capital is in a state of siege, with soldiers surrounding the Diet and intimidating lawmakers who dare criticize military policies. Any who speak out, find their homes destroyed with dynamite."

"Dear Uncle," Hirohito said, "many years ago you encouraged me to travel abroad when things became too heated. I now urge you as your nephew, and also Command you as your Emperor, to take leave—perhaps, you'll learn something overseas that will help us in these desperate times."

Washington, D.C., 1933

Camera flashes exploded as news reporters and photographers gathered round. "So, Prince, what brings you back to the States?" one reporter called out.

Tokugawa, distinguished-looking in his black trench coat and black felt Classic Dome hat with its slightly upturned brim, casually replied, "Travel broadens one's perspectives."

"Will the assassination of Takuma Dan lead to a major run on your Japanese banks?"

Before the question could be answered, another reporter shouted, "How close is Japan to facing total anarchy?"

Holding up a hand to slow the questions, Tokugawa replied, "Yes, the times are hard in Japan, like everywhere else, due to the economic depression—But your country and mine can work together to get through this dark period."

"So this isn't just a vacation?"

Tokugawa allowed a half-smile.

"My itinerary includes meetings with both Rotary International and with the International Red Cross for joint goodwill projects. I'm also working with American universities to create international student exchanges, to encourage better intercultural understanding. And on a personal note, I plan to visit our eldest son, Iemasa, and my granddaughter, who is named Hope. I must admit, I'm proud of the fine job my son has done as Consul General in Australia, and currently as our first Minister to Canada."

A reporter yelled, "Now that you have a new ambassador in Japan, Joseph Grew, how about giving us the inside story regarding the old one? We've heard your Foreign Minister Yoshizawa fondly describe Ambassador Forbes as neither credulous nor crotchety, nor is he troubled by nightmares or suspicions."

"A colorful description indeed," Tokugawa replied. "Ambassador Forbes is a worthy compeer of George Washington and has done great things during his service in Japan."

The same reporter asked, "We've heard before his departure, Ambassador Forbes met with the Son of Heaven in an unusually long audience."

"Yes, they came to a great mutual understanding. Ambassador Forbes told us that nothing has occurred—nor **will** anything occur—to menace the good feelings between the U.S. and Japan."

"What are your thoughts about the new ambassador?"

"Joseph Grew is a fine diplomat. We have already held banquets in Tokyo in recognition of his arrival."

"Isn't he a cousin-by-marriage of the financier J. P. Morgan?"

Tokugawa smiled. "So much the better to have the ear of the wealthy and powerful of your nation."

"You make everything sound fine and dandy, but we've heard Secretary of State Stimson has absolutely refused to recognize Japan's puppet régime in Manchuria—and your Foreign Office responded that the U.S. cannot rob the Japanese of the fruits of their victory by withholding recognition of Japanese sovereignty."

Tokugawa bowed. "I thank you for your keen interest and insightful questions, but these matters are far beyond the scope of my simple visit to your great nation. Thank you."

Chicago, 1933

Gliding along the aerial cable-car, a hundred feet high, Tokugawa and Mashbir sat side by side.

"So kind of you to meet me, Sidney."

"Your visit is a pleasant surprise, Prince Tokugawa—"

The tour guide's voice broke in:

"Ladies and Gentlemen, welcome to the Chicago World's Fair. We're calling it *A Century of Progress Exposition*, commemorating the hundred-year anniversary of our city, and serving as a testimonial to mankind's architectural and technological accomplishments.

"Our motto is, 'Science Discovers, Industry Applies, and Man Conforms!' We offer a glimpse into the future, while honoring the achievements of the past. During our two-year run, we expect to host fifty million visitors…We're now passing over two man-made lagoons. Notice the many multicolored exhibit structures below, resulting in our exposition being called *The Rainbow City*.

"Speaking of the latest technology—imagine, the first lights turned on at our event, were activated by *solar light rays* sent by the star *Arcturus*. Those sun rays were collected and transformed into electrical energy, which triggered the lighting for the fairgrounds... *Arcturus* was chosen, as her solar rays, traveling at the amazing speed of light, 186,000 miles per second, started their journey to Earth forty years earlier, during our previous Chicago World's Fair, to reach us now. . . To give you an idea how vast our universe is, they traveled **sixteen hundred billion miles!**"

The audience was hushed in amazement.

"Makes one wonder, Sidney," Tokugawa said, "if perhaps someday we'll be harnessing our own Sun's energy as a substitute for our limited oil supplies?"

"That would be a day for celebration."

The announcer then described how the creators of this exposition had been very lucky. A $10-million bond to fund the event was issued on October 28, 1929; the following day, the stock market crashed, and that money would not have been available.

"Okay folks, we're nearing our unloading dock," he said. "Hope you enjoy your day at the World's Fair."

"Look there," Sidney said, "let's start with the General Motors exhibit!"

"*Welcome to the future of car design!*" a recorded presentation announced as they were swept in on a conveyor belt sidewalk.

"*The building you've entered is an eighth-of-a-mile long and divides into two vast display rooms. Our main feature is an assembly plant where one thousand visitors at any one time can witness a car's actual creation... Raw materials enter one door, and by the time visitors exit, those components have been turned into finished automobiles. Buyers can choose the options as they enter, follow the progress along the assembly line, and actually drive off with their car.*"

"How cleverly efficient," Tokugawa commented.

They next visited the Chinese Pavilion, where they admired a representation of a seven-story temple carved out of a single block of jade weighing 18,000 pounds, which had taken ten years and a small army of men to create.

"An exquisite piece of art," Tokugawa said, "and an admirable display of patience." He shrugged. "Militants back in Japan pressured me to boycott this exhibition, but how can we be at odds with a people who can create such beauty?"

They exited, looking for the next attraction.

"This wonderful event does a fine job of diverting your people's minds," Tokugawa commented. "I'm well aware of America's farm foreclosures and factory shutdowns—Not to mention the bank failures and soaring unemployment."

"Yes, both our President, and you, Prince Tokugawa, have a tough job ahead of you dealing with this damn Depression. Roosevelt's trying to stabilize farm prices, and he's testing job creation programs to rebuild the nation's confidence. So, how's Japan coping?"

"Just getting by. Your journalists call me a wealthy tycoon, but my estate is in shambles," he said with a shrug. "I've resisted spending on maintenance—there's too many needy charities, such as orphanages, requiring my donations. Cosmetic repairs can wait for better days."

Entering the Moroccan Village exhibit, they were surrounded by costumed desert nomads, dancing girls, and shops overflowing with rugs, engraved metalwork, pottery, and the scent of exotic foods.

"How about a bit of local cuisine?" the Prince asked.

They dined upon a hand-tooled, circular copper table, while sitting on colorful leather-covered, stuffed cushions.

"This couscous dish is delicious," Sidney declared. "A blend of curry spices with vegetables, nuts, and raisins, mixed with chunks of lamb."

Iyesato nodded. "Quite delightful. I feel rejuvenated." He looked at his companion, "Let's get caught up, Sidney. What have you been *up to*, as you Americans so delightfully put it?"

"As you're aware, I attend the occasional diplomatic event, but mainly I've been busy in the private industrial sector. A few years ago, I patented a device I'm proud of—it mixes and measures concrete by weight, rather than volume. It's more predictable, less wasteful, and gives a much stronger result. If it weren't for slow-moving government bureaucracy, my system would have been used for the Hoover Dam." He shrugged with annoyance. "Though, it did get utilized in Cumberland, Maryland, for a dam which delivers water to that city."

"Impressive. It's a pleasure to hear your enthusiasm for invention."

"Thank you. And how are my friends, the Emperor and Empress? It must be difficult for them to see all the suffering during these challenging times."

"In spite of the dreadful economy and heated politics, they've handled their official responsibilities quite well. As for family life, they're happily raising three lovely daughters."

"Please send them my warmest regards."

"I certainly will—Sidney-san, you mentioned that you had remarried?"

This evoked a smile. "I'm a lucky man, we have a three-year-old son, Donald."

"It is a pleasure to hear of your good fortune. Shall we move on?"

"Look," Tokugawa pointed, "Egypt's Valley of the Kings has come to America." They approached the bright orange-colored structure, surrounded by massive red and green columns and towering life-like imperial statues. "The actual Pharaohs and their pyramids date back thousands of years. At my age, Sidney, you wonder if anything you've created will last."

Sidney intently focused his gaze at him, "Not all monuments are of marble. Some are the wisdom passed down from one generation to the next. Your teachings will live on through the many you've mentored and befriended."

"Perhaps."

Not far off, a crowd stared skyward.

"Look, that's the Graf Zeppelin—it's gotta be eight-hundred feet long!" a bystander shouted.

Tokugawa cast a quick glance upward. "Hmm, so Germany's new chancellor Hitler and his propaganda minister Goebbels wish to steal the show?"

"If only I had a slingshot right now," Sidney replied, gritting his teeth.

Tokugawa chuckled.

"Did you know that Goebbels, in a moment of candor stated, he was amazed the U.S. hadn't attacked Germany the day Hitler forcefully took power—what with Hitler's obvious hunger for world domination?"

"That fascist blimp shouldn't be allowed in our country!" someone said.

"Germany isn't our enemy—there's a lot we can learn from them," another countered.

"You know, Sidney," Tokugawa said, "I've kept an eye on extremists in Japan for decades. I recommend you do likewise in America. Now, let's visit my nation's pavilion, which emphasizes Japan's ancient arts . . . "

Sidney admired the classical tiered architecture, the green shingled roof and surrounding verdant gardens...Tokugawa guided him in. "This first exhibit displays silk creation, starting with lowly silkworm cocoons and ending with these lovely kimonos."

"The old ways have much beauty, Your Highness."

"Yet it appears, we're being driven into the future as fast as our car throttle can take us. Progress: a mixed blessing."

Tokugawa hardened. "While your industries produce cars by the millions and design better home appliances, industrialists in Japan and Germany are be pressured to expand their production of aircraft carriers, submarines, and guns."

"Dear Iyesato, you have something on your mind. Shall we sit for a while?"

Two graceful ladies dressed as geishas greeted them in the Tea Garden and led them to a table. A long silence passed, with Tokugawa watching the shifting surface reflections in his teacup.

"Sidney, do you know why the U.S. wants to keep Japan out of China?"

"To maintain stability in the region."

"That's part of it—Two years ago my wife and I visited Cuba while it was in the midst of a Communist insurrection, attempting to create a foothold in the Western hemisphere, thus presenting a threat to America." The Prince took a long sip of his tea, then continued, "Batista, whom some called a benevolent dictator, gained power by crushing those Communists with the support of U.S. business and political interests; even your organized crime mobsters, Meyer Lansky and Lucky Luciano, lent a hand."

Mashbir wondered how this refined man from a distant island nation, still remote in many ways from the Western world, knew so much. "What does this have to do with China?" he asked.

"If Japan takes over Manchuria, this would lead to China's fledgling democracy to crumble. Russia would then jump at the opportunity to spread Communism there—America sees this Red Threat as most ominous, wishing to prevent it at any cost."

"Interesting analysis."

Tokugawa continued, "And, if Japan expands into China, encroaching on Russia's border, Japan and Russia might soon be at war, crippling one another. The great irony is," he sighed, "even though America distrusts Russia, they wish to stay on her good terms, so she doesn't actively join with the fascists in Europe.

The day is coming," his voice rose, "when a strong Russian ally, even though Communist in nature, will be needed✻ During the last war, Russia sustained major casualties to defeat Germany, and there may well be a repeat performance."

"And what do the Russian leaders want?"

Tokugawa silent recalled events from earlier years.

"Sidney, it was you who first opened my eyes to the shortcomings of Communism a decade ago. Stalin is clever and brutal. He wants five years to prepare his country for war. But in the meantime, he negotiates non-aggression pacts with Japan and Germany, while at the same time manipulating the West, by secretly offering to ally with them—if they promise generous territorial spoils of war when this conflict erupts."

Tokugawa spread his arms wide. "Look around you—all these beautiful buildings filled with Fine Art and the marvels of Science," he paused, "Sidney-san, I truly fear a global war will plunge us back into the Dark Ages!"

Mashbir noticed the Prince's age-weathered hands shaking, and he replied softly, "My dear friend, each of us will do what we can to prevent this, and I pray your fears do not materialize—But for now, let's enjoy our day at the fair and delay our serious discussions until tomorrow."

"I bow to your wisdom—Where do you suggest we go next?"

A young lady passed wearing an advertising sandwich board sign.

"I've got a couple of ideas," Sidney replied. "How about us visiting *The Homes of the Future Exhibit*, and after that, I've heard this fair has a burlesque-type show with a lovely young lady by the name of Sally Rand, who does quite an alluring Fan Dance."

"Do lead on," Tokugawa said with enthusiasm.

CHAPTER 26

Imperial Hospital, December 23, 1933

High-pitched crying filled the air as Prince Tokugawa entered the room. He held Nagako's hand as she lay in bed, while nurses busily tended to the newborn, wrapping the child in blankets and putting a bottle to its mouth.

Nagako whispered to Tokugawa, "They think it's wrong, but I so wish to nurse the infant myself."

Tokugawa turned to the staff.

"Please give the empress her child and leave them alone, until she calls for you."

They promptly exited.

"You've always been so supportive Dear Uncle Tokugawa." Nagako began crying. "Could you please tell Hirohito the news?"

On seeing Tokugawa's serious expression as he walked into the Imperial chambers, Hirohito collapsed into a chair. "So it's not to be."

"You're right..." Tokugawa replied. "No longer will you endure the barbs of fools who see you as an unfit ruler, simply because you do not have a male heir!"

Hirohito pondered the Prince's comment for a moment, then jumped to his feet. "What, really?!?" he exclaimed.

Tokugawa smiled. "I have even seen his full young manliness myself."

"Are they all right? I must go to them immediately!"

"They are doing fine, Hirohito; the 125th successor to the throne has been born, a Heavenly sign that peace may well endure. Let us celebrate!"

✳✳✳✳

Industrial Exhibition, 1934, Pittsburgh, Pennsylvania

As Sidney strolled the many display areas housed within the vast convention hall, a poster caught his eye. *Look at that,* he thought, *Goodrich Company has developed a flexible hose that transports oil from offshore tanker ships. Floats suspend the hose on the water's surface, instead of using a rigid pipeline requiring an expensive pier to support it. Amazing, only eight inches in diameter, and yet it can move three million gallons in just ten hours!*

The exhibitor in the next booth held up a small object.

"Come on over," he called. "Bet you never thought much about metal caps for cans, bottles, or jars when you use their contents? *But we think about them a lot*: Our business is improving the tinplate industry for consumers everywhere, based on research at our steel plant at Wheeling, West Virginia."

"You're right," Sidney replied, "there's a world of things we take for granted," and he never knew when or where something relevant to his Research and Development firm might present itself.

The Corning Glass Company exhibit was his next stop. Its timeline chart detailed its long history in Corning, New York, from its founding in 1879, when it supplied Thomas Edison with his first lamp bulbs. *And now* it boasted the largest telescope mirror in the world and Pyrex bulbs used in medical X-ray machines that could detect broken bones right through patients' skin! Someone in the crowd tapped Sidney's shoulder.

"Oh, Dr. Briggs! How nice to see you."

"Hi, Sidney. I couldn't help noticing that you look like a kid in toy store."

"That's me when it comes to technological innovation," he replied. "So, Doc, how's your research coming along?"

"What with this lousy economy, I've been forced to lay off some talented Radio Aeronautical scientists, and they're having one heck of a time finding another job. It's strange though—they're getting plenty of offers from abroad, especially Germany and Japan. Sure wish there were a way to keep them here."

※※※※

Navy Bureau of Aeronautics, Washington, D.C.

Sidney stood rigidly at attention in front of a tall, distinguished man in his mid-fifties. *So this is Admiral King, the man President Franklin Roosevelt described as being so tough, he cuts his toenails with torpedo net clippers and shaves with a blowtorch!*

"Take a seat, Colonel Mashbir," King said, "Commander Zacharias speaks highly of you. I value his opinion."

"Thank you, sir. Kind of you to fit me into your schedule."

"Actually, I'm glad you contacted me. Those scientists you described over the phone are just the kind of men our military needs to develop the best Aeronautical Guidance and Navigation systems. It's a travesty we almost lost them."

"I'll go tell them the good news, sir—"

"Wait a minute, there's other things to discuss. Though, we've never met, I've done research—and we've something in common."

"And what is that, sir?"

"The belief that war with Japan may not be too far off." King pointed at him. "Colonel, do you think we're ready?"

Mashbir resisted laughing. "Neither militarily nor industrially, sir."

"That's exactly how I feel," King replied, running fingers through his silver-gray hair. "Your name came up a while back; I appreciate your fine work on the Battle Plan Orange, updating it with the latest technology and air power considerations."

King looked him straight in the eye.

"Some of my colleagues didn't particularly like how dramatically you revised it. They're comfortable and don't want things to change, but who cares what the hell they think—Colonel, I have several million dollars to spend on research, but I'm not allowed to hire one civilian worker. On the other hand, I can award contracts to private outside corporations. That's where you come in. Your business and engineering credentials make you the right man for the job."

"What job?"

"Congratulations!" King extended his hand, which Sidney felt obliged to shake without knowing why. "It's your patriotic duty to kick-start a new company specializing in the unique technological needs of our military. Improving what we have or spurring invention where there's a need; thereby connecting our military to the industries that can manufacture these items. The only difference is, your private firm is going to be *top secret*."

"Let me get this straight, sir—*funding* is really no issue?"

King smiled. "Scores of government contracts will be directed your way. So—what are you going to name your new company?"

Mashbir appreciated the admiral's no-nonsense-get-it-done style. "How about *The Washington Institute of Technology*, so it appears to be an educational organization?"

"That'll work just fine."

Downtown Washington, D.C., six months later

The small lobby of the two-story hotel was run-down, almost grimy, with no magazines to peruse, to help pass the time. "Sidney," Irene said, "Are you sure this is the right place?" "One-hundred-percent, sweetheart. They're only a few minutes late."

Just then, Colonel Kenji Matsumoto and his wife came into view descending the staircase, their elegant evening attire greatly contrasting their surroundings. Sidney observed Jinne's subtle limp and the thicker sole of her right silver dress shoe, designed to compensate. In spite of this, she moved smoothly.

"Hello, Jinne, I'm Irene—So nice meet you. Sidney has told me how much he enjoyed getting to know your husband while in Japan… And, I must say, you look lovely in that lavender dress!"

"Thank you, I hope it is suitable? Diplomatic gatherings are difficult for me. In my country, wives are expected to say little or nothing—that is, if they are permitted even to attend."

"You'll do fine," Irene replied.

They exited the hotel, just as three American sailors staggered out of a nearby cocktail lounge and saw them. One yelled, "Hey, you lousy Japs. Go back to where you came from!"

Jinne shuddered, but Kenji appeared ready to deal with the situation. Sidney spoke softly to him. "I know you could easily take care of these young punks, but you're our guests. Please let me handle this."

Kenji nodded, drawing his wife near.

With a few swift steps, Sidney confronted the one who had yelled, and held an open wallet up to his face. "In case you're too drunk to read this," he said, "I'll tell you what it says: Though I'm not in uniform, I'm a Lieutenant-Colonel and those are my personal guests. That gentleman is a diplomatic attaché, but he's also a Martial Arts expert who would have kicked all your asses if I hadn't held him back. So unless you want to spend a couple of months in the brig, you'd better apologize!"

The loudmouthed sailor was pissed, but after a couple of shoves from his buddies he called out, "Sorry," and they stumbled away.

"That was most regrettable," Sidney said on his return. "I apologize for their rude behavior."

"Oh, think nothing of it." Kenji forced a smile. "Thank you, it would not look good if the new Japanese envoy was on the front page of your newspapers brawling with drunken sailors."

Mashbir replied, "I also have challenges controlling my temper. If unchecked, my picture would be on the 'Most Wanted' list at the post office, just like Al Capone."

They all broke into laughter, then strolled to the Mashbirs' automobile. "I hope you don't mind my asking," Sidney said as he pulled away from the curb, "but how did you select your hotel?"

Jinne looked to her husband before responding, "It was the only one available."

"Then you must be our guests until a more suitable location comes up," Irene said.

Sidney noticed that Kenji looked embarrassed.

"That's American hospitality. It would be our honor. I'm sure you'd do the same for us."

"We are in your debt," Kenji replied stiffly.

A massive, white marble obelisk highlighted by spotlights appeared in the distance.

"That is your Washington Monument," Kenji exclaimed. "I have seen photos...It is most interesting Americans name their capitol after one man, George Washington. Do you, yourself, admire him so much, Sidney?"

Mashbir nodded. "He's probably the only man who could have held our young nation together during the Revolutionary War. Many wanted him to become our King. Instead, he built a democracy that has lasted a hundred and fifty years."

Kenji thought a moment, then replied, "Shoguns once unified our nation and drove out foreigners who would have ruled us. Prince Tokugawa's father, Yoshinobu, and his father's samurai retainer, Kaishu, peacefully relinquished power to the Emperor Meiji, rather than see Japan torn apart in civil war...Although, Prince Tokugawa is far from six foot tall and there are no portraits of him as there are of George Washington mounted upon white steeds: nonetheless, he has continued his father's legacy, holding our nation together for decades, more like your Abraham Lincoln." There was a long silence.

"You men, always talking politics," Irene interjected with a smile. "How about we all visit the National Arboretum tomorrow? I hear it has a wonderful gardenia collection."

The ladies looked to their husbands, who nodded affirmatively.

"Do you have children?" Jinne asked Irene.

"We've a young son, Donald, who can be a bit mischievous at times." Irene smiled. "Do you and Kenji have children?"

She looked away. "We've patiently waited; perhaps adoption will be the path."

"That's a fine option...And as our house guests, I'm sure you'll enjoy meeting and playing with Donald."

Jinne brightened up. "Oh, look at that large park," she said.

"It's a golf course," Irene replied.

Jinne glanced at Kenji. "My dear husband wishes to learn, but has never attempted it."

"I'm a bit of a duffer myself," Sidney said. "It would be my pleasure to invite him along."

There was a sparkle in Kenji's serious eyes. "Thank you, I look forward to it."

As the two couples entered the Mayflower Hotel's marble-columned ballroom, they were greeted by harp music, which softened the multitude of conversations going on. Turning to Jinne and Kenji, Sidney said, "Looks like another lovely event thrown by your embassy. It would probably be a good idea for you two to circulate. We can meet up later in the evening."

Something caught Sidney's eye. "Oh no, there's Reichmann," he said to Irene, "probably talking the Japanese Foreign Minister's ear off again." They strolled toward the minister, who was dressed in the standard diplomatic attire—a diagonal white silk band adorned with gold insignia across his chest. Next to him, crammed into a tuxedo, was a tall, hulking man gesturing with his hands as he spoke.

"Dear minister, I'm soon to be relocated to Japan. Certainly, it would be very beneficial for Japan and Germany to strengthen their relations, exchanging advisors to better bind our two great nations together."

Mashbir had been staring intently at them as he approached.

"What's this I hear, Herr Reichmann," he said with a smirk, "you're generously offering to *bind up* the Japanese? Reminds me of my experiences in Arizona, where one lassoes a steer for branding—before taking him to slaughter!"

"If it isn't our witty businessman, Mashbir." Reichmann fumed. "So kind of you to tell of your exploits. We, however, are at a diplomatic event where your crude cowboy stories are out of place."

He turned to the minister.

"Let us talk further on these matters when we will not be disturbed," he said, and stomped off.

The Minister smiled.

"Hello, Colonel and Mrs. Mashbir. So nice to see you again. Your husband is an island of unique sensibilities in an ocean of meaningless chatter."

"I'm honored," Sidney replied, then turned to Irene with a look she'd seen before.

"Oh, there's the Ambassador's wife, Madame Debuchi," she said, pointing. "Haven't seen her in ages! Is it okay if I give you gentlemen time to converse?"

Once she'd gone, the Minister asked, "So, Sidney, how did you know what Reichmann had been saying?"

"Take a guess?"

"You were a fair distance away..." The minister thought, laughed, then silently mouthed the words: *So you can read lips?*

Mashbir smiled as he nodded in the affirmative.

"Sidney, you're full of surprises! Now, if I may, I'd like a private word with you."

They strolled out onto the balcony, where they were greeted by the Capitol's sparkling incandescent lights against a black sky.

"So how can I be of assistance, Minister?"

The minister fiddled with his mustache.

"Here we are at a diplomatic event thrown by our embassy, and mainly mid-level American representatives attend, with *you* being one of the few who can even speak our language. Do you not find this strange?"

"It's not an insult—there's a wide ocean between our nations. Few Americans have been exposed to your language."

"That may be so, yet recently I've tried to meet officials from your government, and my requests have largely been ignored."

"I'm sorry to hear you're getting the cold shoulder. What's on your mind?"

"Promoting bilateral business ventures to economically help both our nations. As well as a token increase in U.S. immigration quotas for Japanese, to better present the message that we're true allies— and not the Yellow Peril portrayed by certain American newspapers. Even your popular science fiction series, *Buck Rogers*, depicts Asians as cruel warriors ready to conquer America...And in California, Japanese-Americans are singled out, and are not even allowed to purchase farmland—only lease it!"

The minister's voice rose.

"*Fortune Business Magazine* describes us as *monkeys*, merely copying other nations' inventions, and complains that Japan is not playing by the rules because we're charging less for our goods."

The minister clutched the balcony railing.

"In reality, our people work in highly technical industries for a fraction of the salary of yours or Europe's. It is *you* who must adapt to a global marketplace! Be candid, Colonel, what do you think of my requests?"

"This is a diplomatic event, sir—Honesty couldn't get past the entrance."

The minister laughed.

"One would not think that, if they had heard your bluntness with Herr Reichmann."

"*Touché!*" Sidney moved his wrist as if fencing. His tone then turned serious: "You're right, Minister, there is racism and jealousy involved. And what I'm hearing around the Capital, is it's not our concern that Japan is growing faster than its resources can support. Why should we be the answer to other nations' internal problems by accepting immigrants, who will compete with our own citizens for hard-to-find jobs? The U.S. is not alone, nations around the world have drastically cut immigration, at least until their economies improve."

"True, America isn't obligated to solve our problems," the Minister declared. "And we understand your desire to protect the Philippines—but why warn *us* against controlling Manchuria, a relatively sparsely populated area with vast untouched resources, when your own nation's Open Door Policy resulted in a large portion of China being divided up between a half-dozen Western powers. And historically, did not the murderous Mongol hordes twice attempt to cross the Sea of Japan to conquer us? If not for the blessed Kamikaze winds destroying their fleets, they might have succeeded."

The minister struggled to contain his emotions.

"Right now, as we speak, insurgent Communist forces in China are encouraging Russia to join with her and attack Japan. Instead of calling us predators, your country should encourage our expansion as a means of preventing the spread of Communism. Japan was your strong ally in the last war, and could once again assist the Western democracies in defeating the Fascists."

Mashbir loosened his tie. "I understand, sir—But China perceives the past hundred years of colonialism as *a century of humiliation* which they wish to finally end. You asked for candor. All right: U.S. analysts feel China, with her vast populace of two hundred and fifty million, would be best served by democracy, but is drawn to Communism as her only means of freeing herself of outside domination!

"But I do recognize Japan's dilemma. During my father's day, a half-dozen children might be born to a family, and only one survive to adulthood. Modern medicine and a better supply of food changed that for the better. *But now,* many countries find themselves in a constant struggle to supply jobs, housing, health care, and education; and when they can't meet their expanding needs, they repress the voices of their dissatisfied citizens to stay in power—Or they start coveting the resources of neighboring nations, inevitably leading to war."

"You remind me of that British Reverend Thomas Malthus, who gave similar warnings in the late 1700s," the minister replied. "Humanity didn't listen then, nor is it ready now. Instead, Darwin's theory of *the Survival of the Fittest* seems to apply. In a mere sixty years, Japan has transformed from a feudal society to an advanced modern state, who many believe, because of its disciplined spirit, could conquer all of Asia!" His voice softened. "Though, Japan would in great likelihood settle for just Manchuria."

"Colonial empires are vanishing," Sidney countered. "Gandhi is slowly, but surely, pressuring Britain out of India—and through nonviolent means no less. As for the Philippines, they're only under U.S. mandate for ten more years before becoming a sovereign nation." He raised his palms. "Japanese militants wish to conquer an empire, when much of the world moves in the opposite direction."

"Are you blind?" the Minister replied. "Brutal regimes are currently rising up, with dreams of empires of a magnitude unseen in history. I wish it were not so, but do not delude yourself—Japan is being lured to join them."

Sidney was shaken by the intensity of his companion's words and demeanor. "I promise you, Minister. I'll contact our State Department and see if my small voice can make a difference."

The minister took a deep breath and then bowed.

"I'm sorry, it is most kind of you to so patiently listen to my frustration. Shall we return to the festivities?"

Upon re-entering the ballroom, the minister commented, "Our island of discussion is about to be invaded."

Sidney looked in the direction indicated, as the Army Chief of Staff continued his advance, nodding at people as he passed— but not once pausing.

"Good evening, Minister. Everything well with you, I trust?"

"Most well, General MacArthur. Do you know Sidney Mashbir?"

A puzzled look appeared. "Haven't we met before?" MacArthur asked.

"Yes, sir, you were kind enough to once have me over to West Point to give a talk."

The Minister sensed an awkwardness on the part of his companions. "If you'll excuse me, gentlemen," he said, "Please don't let me get in the way of your conversation. It's a pleasure seeing you both," and he graciously smiled and left.

The general thought a moment, "Yes, you gave that lecture on the Art of Intelligence-Gathering. We're making some progress, but this damn Congress wants to cut appropriations in half. You still in the Army, Mashbir?"

"I'm a Lieutenant-Colonel in the Intelligence branch of your Army Reserve, but mainly I run *The Washington Institute of Technology.*" A flicker of recognition flashed in the General's eyes. "Our team does some interesting Research and Development for the military."

"I'd like to talk to you more about that. Call my office tomorrow and set it up."

MacArthur suddenly appeared startled. "Oh no! There's Mrs. Biddle heading our way—She's one of the Philadelphia Main Line

Biddles. And if she traps me, she'll keep me for hours, so she can brag to her friends how she told me what's wrong with the army, the economy, and *everything else*. You're on your own, Mashbir."

Spinning smartly, while giving a pleasant nod to the advancing woman, MacArthur vanished through the exit door.

With a polite smile pasted on, Sidney turned to greet the formidable Mrs. Biddle. She smoothly sailed up in spite of her large girth and launched right in. "That was General MacArthur. How unfortunate that he left. I was hoping to have just a tiny word or two with him," she said, staring longingly at the door through which he had made his hasty retreat.

"I'm sorry, Ma'am, the general was called away on a matter of military importance," he said, lying for what he hoped was a good cause.

She looked directly at him.

"I'm Mrs. Cornelia Biddle."

"I am honored to meet you. My name is Sidney Mashbir."

"What a charming name, Sidney. Our family has almost always had someone with that name. You undoubtedly know of my great uncle, Algernon Sidney Biddle. He was the most prominent jurist in the country." Mashbir resigned himself to the ordeal of being instructed in Biddle history.

In the far corner of the ballroom, a collection of bronze and ceramic vases were on display. Irene, accompanied mainly by other women, listened to Madame Katsuji Debuchi, a slim, elegant woman in her fifties…"My husband the Ambassador, and I, are very pleased you could attend this event. As a surprise, we've organized a little demonstration of Japanese flower-arranging." With a snap of her fingers, hotel bellhops entered, laden with colorful flowers and bundles of small branches. "This artistry dates back a thousand years, when Buddhist priests beautified Temple altars, attempting to capture life's progression through the subtle spectacle of small twigs evolving into branches and buds gradually blossoming into flowers. The fully open flower represents male energy; the bud, that of the female. The top of the leaf is masculine, the underside the feminine—I hope you don't see this gender selection as anything more than a means of attaining visual balance. As a matter-of-fact, flower-arranging and the appreciation of Nature are honored elements of Bushido training and the Samurai spirit. They represent a state of calm and gratitude, because in the Buddhist religion, life is of supreme importance✳ The West views the world as man-centered, whereas the East tends to be more nature-centered."

A gentleman in the group asked, "Madame Debuchi, do certain flower varieties have significance?"

"Very much so. For instance, this Lotus stands for purity, the Iris for patriotism, the Plum for courage, and the Pine for long life. The Imperial flower, the Chrysanthemum, stands for immortality…And now, you will all get a chance to trim and shape flowers and branches to a height and form that best fits your particular vase and sensibilities."

With zeal, they began.

Madame Debuchi slowly strolled among her focused students, nodding approvingly. She stopped when she reached Mrs. Mashbir. "So wonderful to see you again, Irene." She studied her arrangement. "You're doing very well."

"Thank you. It's so generous of you to offer us this opportunity."

"My pleasure. And before I forget, Prince Tokugawa sends you and Sidney his regards."

"Please send him our best wishes as well."

"I certainly will. Being close to nature is one of Prince Tokugawa's favorite pastimes. He and I have organized upcoming tours for the *Garden Club of America* so its members can visit Japan's most renowned gardens. We also plan to arrange tours for Japanese to experience your country's lovely gardens. The Prince is certain that tourism between our nations can boost both our economies and lead to an appreciation of one another's cultures."

"I'd love to visit Japan and go on that tour!"

Madame Debuchi smiled, then described how Prince Tokugawa, as president of the *America-Japan Society*, was bringing an exhibit to the Boston Museum of Fine Art, in recognition of the three-hundredth anniversary celebration of the founding of Harvard University. That exhibit would include treasures from the Imperial Palace Collection, giving Americans an insight into the poetic soul of Japanese Art.

"A delightful idea!" Irene replied.

Something across the room caught her attention.

"Please excuse me, Madame Debuchi, I have something to attend to—perhaps we can get together next week for lunch?"

Irene swiftly strode over to Sidney and grasped his arm.

"Oh, Darling, we haven't danced once all night!" and off they went, leaving Cornelia Biddle to survey the ballroom for her next victim.

As they waltzed, Sidney whispered in her ear, "You saved me from certain death."…"I was jealous," Irene replied mischievously. "I saw you rolling your eyes at that woman."

"No—*that* was me losing consciousness from extreme boredom!"

CHAPTER 27

Washington, D.C.

Mashbir sensed an underlying tension as MacArthur led him to a seat in his living room and sat opposite him. "Colonel, I appreciate your coming to my residence for this meeting. I mentioned to my mother I'd run in to you. Pinky fondly remembers your visit. You two discussed my father's career in the Southwest."

"Please give her my regards. And I still have that copy of Homer Lea's book that you loaned me at the time."

"Keep it! It's a gift. If anything, those warnings about Japan taking over the Philippines are more pressing today than when he wrote it." MacArthur leaned back into his chair. "All right: First, tell me everything you know about the state of our military intelligence. Take your time—as long as it's not more than ten minutes."

"Don't worry, sir—ten *seconds* is more than enough. There's not much of it, and what there is, *generally stinks.*"

MacArthur's eyes opened wide.

"That good, eh?"

"I'm afraid that's my considered opinion. The Navy is better off than the Army because Commander Zacharias is in charge, and he's as good as they come! The basic problem is twofold: Lack of trained personnel and Money. We don't even have a crypto/code analysis bureau since the State Department killed the Black Chamber in 1928. Yes, we intercept all kinds of stuff—but less than a dozen people in the Army can understand Japanese well enough to evaluate it."

MacArthur began pacing.

"You're right about a lack of funds; can't pry nearly enough out of this Congress, especially during these challenging economic times.

And I should know—I was the one assigned to evict that mob from Congress's doorstep a couple of years back. You never saw such a ragtag bunch. *Veteran's Bonus March,* indeed. I bet far more than half of them never even saw military service. Agitators, communists, and rabble-rousers, that's what they were. Some fools in Congress actually encouraged them to come and complain about inadequate veterans' benefits!"

MacArthur's eyes rolled upward.

"Then Congress gets scared out of what few wits they have and pressures the president into using the army to break them up—and I'm ordered to treat it like an insurrection! My aide, Major Eisenhower, strongly advised me to have nothing to do with it—just let some junior officer handle it. I simply couldn't let someone else take the heat. If it had to be done, it was my job. I like Ike, don't misunderstand, but sometimes I think he'd make a better politician than a soldier. Patton's the other extreme. He was all for charging right into that mob with those tanks he's so fond of, *if it became necessary.* So I authorized *only* four tanks, just for show, and pushed them back without firing a shot."

He tapped a pencil on the table.

"We did, however, have to gently poke a couple of them with bayonets"—he used the sharpened pencil to illustrate. "Very few got hurt, and a nasty situation got cleaned up in a matter of days. *Now,* some people are trying to crucify me for it!"

MacArthur snapped the pencil in half.

"That slimy bastard, Drew Pearson, is writing all kinds of lies about the atrocities committed under my authority. My attorney assures me I have a solid case for Libel and Character Defamation. I'm going to sue the living Hell out of him and that rag of a newspaper he works for."

Sidney noted that MacArthur, who had a reputation for never losing his temper, was very close to doing so now.

"Back to the issue of money," MacArthur said. "I'll tell you just how bad it was. In 1921 the entire U.S. Army had a total of seventeen operational tanks. Seventeen! When one broke down there was no replacement, not for the next ten years. If a part couldn't be fixed or jury-rigged, Patton ordered it from Sears-Roebuck, paying out of his own pocket!" He calmed himself. "Anyway, I've heard some good things about your *Washington Institute of Technology*. Its role could be vital when we get into another war, which I believe is highly likely. Though funding is tight, I'm going to slant some Army contracts your company's way."

"That's fine, General, but I've never been in it for the money."

"That's admirable." MacArthur's voice now lowered. "There's another matter I'd like to discuss, of a personal nature. Can I offer you something to drink?"

"Maybe later, sir."

"It's very important what you hear stays between us."

Sidney nodded.

MacArthur scratched his head with agitation.

"When I was in Manila in the late twenties after my divorce, I met a young woman named Isabel Cooper. Her father was a Scotsman, her mother Filipino. I was lonely, and she was incredibly beautiful. You can guess the rest."

His chest deflated. "When I came to Washington as Chief of Staff, she remained in Manila. I couldn't bear the thought of not having her with me."

He reached into a drawer and pulled out a photograph. Sidney found himself looking at an extremely attractive woman, her green eyes staring into the camera with a provocative smile. It was signed, "To Douglas, All My Love." Sidney offered the portrait back.

"No, you keep it—I don't want to ever see her again! When I first brought Isabel over, I put her up in a luxury apartment. Bought her all kinds of expensive clothing and jewelry. Instead of being appreciative, she complained about being trapped, so I provided a chauffeured limousine."

MacArthur threw his arms upward.

"All she did was cruise every nightclub in town, then wheedled money out of me and took off for Havana, where she blew the whole wad gambling and buying drinks for every lowlife in Cuba."

MacArthur poured a full glass of whisky, drank it in two swallows, then sat the empty glass down hard.

"The night I found out she'd returned, I went to her apartment building, and there she was walking arm in arm down the corridor with some young bastard, both drunk as skunks. I found out later he works at the State Department. I was wearing civvies, of course, so I don't think he recognized me when I knocked him out cold."

He refilled his glass, but resisted drinking it.

"Isabel went crazy, cursing me worse than I'd ever heard."

Sidney guessed *MacArthur, being fifty-four, probably didn't like seeing his lady with a much younger man.*

"I told her that her rent was paid through the end of the month, threw my keys on the carpet and left." MacArthur shuddered. "Haven't seen her since, although I've heard enough about her, God knows, she's gone out with half the diplomatic corps, married or not—Stories of wild carryings on! Douglas massaged his stiff, painful neck with his hand, took a deep breath, and then continued:

"It appears, Pearson got hold of Isabel and is threatening me that if we go ahead with my lawsuit, he'll play the whole story about my supposed sex life in that rag of a newspaper of his—and every other paper in the country will pick it up as well. I can't have that!"

For the second time, Sidney was aware he was seeing the legendarily unflappable MacArthur very close to losing control.

"I've sent Eisenhower to find out where they've hidden Isabel, but no luck." He looked Mashbir in the eye. "I know you've done a lot of intelligence work—I've a big favor to ask: I want you to negotiate with Pearson. I'm willing to drop the lawsuit if he stops printing those damn personal attacks against me—*and* assists us in getting Isabel to leave the area and never return. Nor is *she* to sell her story to anyone else."

In a small restaurant in downtown Washington, D.C., Sidney sat in a booth at the rear. A tall man in civilian clothing strode toward him, a broad smile creasing his face. "Colonel Mashbir, I'm Major Eisenhower."

"Glad to make your acquaintance, Major. Let's get the food ordering out of the way: Then, I'd appreciate your briefing me."

The waiter took Mashbir's order, then turned to Eisenhower.

"I'll have just a salad," he said. "I need to watch every bite while I'm on desk duty—I put on weight too easily."

That's the truth, Sidney thought. Ike's paunch, coupled with his receding hairline made him look more like a businessman than a career army officer.

"I played football when I was younger," Eisenhower confided. "Could eat almost everything and still be in shape." They chatted about that sport, for which Ike had great enthusiasm. Once done eating, Eisenhower said, "Now back to the current problem: I followed Pearson as best I could, mainly to a bunch of nightclubs, then back to his house. I couldn't get a smell of Isabel, though."

"Let's hope I have better luck," Mashbir replied. "A question: since the general was divorced when this was going on, and he's still single, why doesn't he just tell these guys to stick it in their ear? Most people might be amused, but I think by and large they'd understand."

"Douglas is an excellent commander," Eisenhower replied, then leaned forward and whispered, "But just between us, in spite of him being strong-willed, he's still scared to death that his mother over in Fort Myers will find out."

"You're kidding me."

"The all-powerful Pinky rules that household, always has; she even ordered Pershing around when he was a junior officer! She's been pushing her son's career for the past thirty years."

"Okay, Major, I'll see what I can do to keep her son out of trouble," Sidney said, while thinking, *How dare they attempt to ruin the reputation of a national hero!*

Several days later, Mashbir was on the phone with MacArthur.

"What have you got to report?"

"Isabel's staying at Pearson's brother's apartment, over in Maryland."

"Great work! What do we do next?"

"It will take a good deal of money, and in cash, I'm afraid."

"I can go up to $20,000, no more."

"Sir," there was a long pause, "what if she takes the money and promises to keep quiet, but refuses to leave town?"

"Leave that to me. Good luck—and a warning: Don't let her dazzle you—she's capable of almost anything."

The next evening, Mashbir was in rural Maryland.

Several rings on the apartment doorbell brought a middle-aged gentleman, who opened it slightly.

"Mr. Pearson, I believe," Mashbir said, placing his foot in the opening. "I have business with you and Miss Cooper."

"I have no idea what you're talking about. Now move your foot if you don't want it slammed on."

"I wouldn't do that. I represent General MacArthur, and he's trying to keep it friendly."

"Who is it, Noel?" a feminine voice called from within. "What do they want?"

"*The game is up, Pearson.* This is your only chance to hear what we're offering."

Pearson moved aside; Sidney entered and saw Isabel standing by a fireplace, one hand on the mantel, the other on her hip—a posed effect, but a very effective one. She was even lovelier in person than her portrait.

"Good evening, Miss Cooper, my name is Mashbir. I represent General MacArthur, and I have an interesting proposition for you."

He sat on a couch, placing his briefcase on a coffee table, with Pearson reluctantly sitting in a chair opposite him. Isabel slinked toward Sidney, sitting down—quite close—with her dark, sheath-type dress slit high up, seemingly careless of how much shapely leg it showed.

"I enjoy hearing propositions from handsome men," Isabel purred, reaching across and over Sidney for her silver cigarette case. Sidney was well aware she had let her breast brush his arm as she did so. She held up a cigarette, obviously waiting for him to light it. He took the accompanying lighter and as he brought it up, she cupped his hand in hers guiding the flame, her jasmine perfume filling his senses.

"Thank you so much," she said sweetly.

Sidney opened the briefcase and handed them each a folder. They spent several minutes carefully examining the paperwork; then with venom, Isabel jumped to her feet, throwing the folder on the coffee table.

"Is this a joke? This piece of shit says I'm to move away a thousand miles and never come back! You have a better chance of becoming President than getting my signature on this ridiculous document!"

Pearson chimed in: "And these other terms are also totally out of the question. You say MacArthur will drop the suit against us? He damn well better—it's without merit. And as for not printing anything bad about the illustrious general, there is a little matter of freedom of the press."

"Let's not be too hasty," Sidney replied. "I have a few things to show you." He opened the briefcase and deliberately placed stacks of currency on the table. He then offered additional documents to Pearson.

"These are copies of the rental receipts for this place that you paid for, showing both your name and Miss Cooper's. If this ever goes to a court, it will be obvious you suborned her as a witness. As for you, Miss Cooper, here's ten thousand dollars, yours free and clear. A woman of your obvious charm and beauty should have no problem establishing herself with such a sum elsewhere in the country."

"Ten thousand? Ha!"

She snatched a wineglass resting on the mantel and threw it into the fireplace, smashing it to bits.

"That's for your old general and his measly offer! He thought he could keep me locked up like a bird. I'm young—I need freedom, to live, to love!"

"Consider this carefully, Miss Cooper. This is a one-time offer. If I walk out without your signature, I won't be back."

Mashbir pointed at the now sweating Pearson. "And don't count on him and his brother. As soon as this lawsuit is over, they won't need you anymore, that's for sure."

He began returning the bundles of cash into the briefcase.

Isabel watched, greed shining out of her emerald eyes. By the time Mashbir got to the last pile, she spoke in a softer tone. "Not that I would consider such a meager proposal, but tell me, Mashbir, why should I take this, when I could get more by telling my story to the newspapers and still remain in Washington, where the power is? I love men who wield influence—it's more intoxicating than liquor."

With confidence Mashbir stared at her.

"You shouldn't be so certain newspapers will be eager to print your story and pay you well for it. Look at Mr. Pearson—he's terrified. Ask him if his brother really wants to take on the most respected military figure in America, a genuine hero. Instead, there might be a more interesting story about a blackmailing, gold-digging woman who started out as a dancer in Shanghai, if that's what they call it there."

Isabel took three quick steps while bringing her hand up from her side and slapped him hard. Sidney grabbed her wrists to prevent an encore.

"Isabel!" Pearson shot to his feet. "No more of this nonsense!"

She calmed, and Sidney loosened his grip. She sulked away, then turned like an animal at bay, pointing a crimson fingernail at Pearson and practically spitting, "So, this is how it is. You used me to save your precious brother's skin. And now, you don't even defend me against this insulting liar!"

Pearson turned his back on her accusations.

"All right, Mr. Mashbir," she said, "I don't for a moment believe that is the total amount Douglas is willing to pay. You haven't held back when it came to saying nasty things about me. Now tell me how much you can *really pay*?"

Sidney slowly reached into his pocket, removing another packet of bills, all hundreds.

"Miss Cooper, here's the other five thousand dollars, I was wrong not to tell you earlier."

"Now empty all your pockets, just to be sure there aren't any other delightful surprises."

Out came his keys, a few coins, and a handkerchief. He opened his wallet, revealing only a ten and a few ones.

"This is my own money."

She gave a poisonous smile.

"As for your spiteful remark...Ha! You just gave me fifteen thousand dollars! You can keep your pocket change. You may need it—that's the price of a common downtown Washington, D.C. streetwalker."

Mashbir ignored the comment.

"Looks like your little scheme has fallen apart," he said to Pearson. "How about you signing these documents? I'll even take your assurances as a guarantee of your brother's acceptance."

Pearson, his forehead blood vessels bulging, watched Isabel counting the cash. "I can't answer for my brother."

"Damn it!" Isabel shouted. "Do as he says, or I'll testify how you forced me to cooperate in slandering dear Douglas."

"Okay, I'll phone him from the other room," he said, and disappeared.

Sidney wrote on the back of a card and handed it to Isabel. "You said you like being in the company of powerful men. This is the private number of Tim Pendegrast. Should you consider relocating to Kansas City, he's a very influential man to know. He, and his father, Big Tom Pendegrast, just about run the state of Missouri. Recently, they were able to get an obscure county judge elected to the U.S. Senate, a guy named Harry Truman."

"Perhaps I will," she said, stroking her chin.

Pearson returned.

"My brother says he'll only consent if he gets to write in his column that MacArthur is dropping the suit and that absolutely no money was paid to him for doing so."

"Okay, I'll write that into your copy and sign it."

As Mashbir drove away, he thought, *I still know how to run a bluff; good early training in poker pays off again.*

He grinned, thinking about the extra $5,000 he'd hidden in his car's glove compartment, to be returned to MacArthur...*As for my slapped cheek, I could have blocked it, but wanted her to vent and think she was in charge...According to Isabel, I had a better chance of becoming President than getting her signature. Perhaps, I should reconsider my career options?*

CHAPTER 28

A small airfield in rural Maryland, June 1934

Mashbir, accompanied by Admiral King and several other high-ranking naval officers stared upward in anticipation.

The pilot's voice came from the radio transmitter: "Okay, altitude one thousand feet, time to see if this gizmo is all it's cracked up to be. I've turned on the auto-navigation, and I am now taping dark crepe paper over the cockpit's windows."

Why'd he have to use the words "cracked up," Mashbir thought, stuffing his hands in his pockets and crossing fingers, as the small plane gradually descended. Within ten minutes it came to a smooth landing. Applause rang out from all the spectators.

Admiral King turned to Sidney.

"I didn't believe you could pull it off; this is a first of its kind. You and your team have just changed the world! We've got to get that *Blind Landing Auto-Navigation Sonar Device* into production fast, so every military aircraft can land more safely regardless of miserable weather and zero visibility." King considered a moment. "Though, it would be a strategic military advantage to limit access to this new technology, something this important will certainly find its way to our private passenger airlines, *and* to other nations."

College Park, Maryland, later that afternoon

Phone in hand, and waiting, Sidney sat, admiring the placard on his desk:

Sidney F. Mashbir, President, Washington Institute of Technology

"Hello, Frank, please pass on the great news to our team: the blind landing tests went extremely well! Admiral King and the Navy are one hundred percent behind us. It's been an impressive week, what with that, and our discovery of how our soldiers' standard-issue helmets were mistakenly painted with a material that shines under infrared light, allowing enemy planes to easily spot our ground troops. Glad it's being corrected. We'll talk later, keep up the good work."

Mashbir's secretary spoke over the intercom: "Sir, there's a Mr. Moe Berg to see you. He won't say what it's about. I'm not sure if he knows."

"That's fine, just send him in."

A tall, well-dressed man in his early thirties with short slicked-back hair, entered and looked around curiously. Sidney stood and extended a hand.

"Sidney Mashbir, so glad to meet you, Mr. Berg...Say, you've got quite a grip there!"

"Sorry about that. It's my pleasure to make your acquaintance, but I'm not quite sure what's going on. My manager only told me a car would come by my hotel and pick me up. Until I saw the two armed Navy guys at the entrance gate, I thought I'd been traded again, but this doesn't look much like a baseball establishment."

Berg hummed, waiting for a response, then continued, "There has been talk about me being traded, though we did win the pennant last year; too bad things aren't going well this season."

"Actually, Mr. Berg, you're at the *Washington Institute of Technology*, though your visit does have something to do with baseball. I understand you and a couple of other players spent time in Japan after the '32 season?"

"That's right. Mr. Yakamoto, the head of their amateur baseball association, asked me if I'd come over and give their players instruction. I got Ted Lyons, who had been my teammate on the White Sox, to come along, as well as Lefty O'Doul. That way we could cover pitching, batting, *and* catching."

Out of the blue, Mashbir launched a stream of Japanese at his visitor. Without blinking, Berg replied in Japanese, "Yes, I did have a fine trip traveling through Japan. And yes, though I already knew the language, getting a chance to speak it every day improved my ability."

Mashbir grinned. "Sorry I sprung that on you. I was told you spoke Japanese, but didn't know just how well. That leads me to my next question. It has been suggested an All-Star Team of Major League players might tour Japan after this season is over. Are you interested?"

"Sure there's been some talk about me going because I know the language and could communicate with foreign newspapers and such. But I'm just a second-string catcher. Rumor has it that the Yankees will send Babe Ruth and Lou Gehrig, and probably a bunch of stars from other teams."

"That sounds about right," Sidney nodded. "Mr. Berg, I've heard you have law degree?"

"Never used it much, always wanted to be a ball player. And you can call me Moe."

"We appear to have things in common, Moe. My dad pressured me to be a lawyer; instead I went the military route."

Sidney rolled his shoulders to loosen up.

"I can assure you this All Star Tour *will* happen, and if you want to be on that tour after hearing me out, you'll get your chance."

Mashbir walked to a window, turning his back to his visitor. "I lived in Japan," he said, "and have many good friends there, some in the royal family. I highly respect these people and their culture, but in the past ten years the moderate elements have largely lost control. The country is now virtually ruled by the military. And with Japan's withdrawal from the League of Nations, and its expanding presence in Manchuria, I believe war may well be inevitable." He turned to face Berg. "I hate the thought," he said emphatically, "But if it is to be, the better prepared we are, the more American lives will be saved. I need to know how you feel about what I've just told you. I've asked around, and have complete confidence in your discretion. Though, I must caution you that everything that is discussed here today must be treated as top secret."

Berg nodded. "I'd say your evaluation's pretty accurate. When I was in Japan two years ago it was obvious that the military, supported by newspapers, were whipping up feelings against the U.S. Just about every day there was another front-page anti-American article."

Berg looked at Mashbir with confusion. "But what is it that you think I can do?"

"You'd be a spy, gathering information, while also doing some goodwill diplomacy as your baseball team tours the country. You'd take notes of where you see troops training, what ports are set up for warships, and where new factories are located: Things like that. We could really use photographs, if you can manage; you'd appear to be a camera-happy American tourist. If caught, probably the worst thing they'd do is to confiscate the camera and film. I'm not saying there's no risk, but because you're associated with the Major League All-Stars, you can get away with more than if we sent an agent posing as a tourist."

Berg's coal-black eyes bore through Sidney.

A long silence passed before Sidney spoke again, his voice strained. "Let me clarify my earlier statement, Mr. Berg. What I'm asking you to do is very dangerous. But your country needs you."

"So you want to know where their strategic military targets are. I've never done anything like this. I hope no guns are involved, they make me queasy."

Berg heaved a deep sigh. "Okay, Mr. Mashbir, I'll do my best."

Mashbir shook his hand again. "Your country appreciates your support, and please call me Sidney. By the way, how is it you speak Japanese so well?"

"Guess I have a knack for languages. I can also get by in German, French, Italian, Hebrew, Russian, and a smattering of others; I'm working on Chinese currently. For me, dialects are what you might call an obsession."

He relaxed for the first time since entering Sidney's office. "Languages reveal so much about World history and Philosophy. For instance, take the word *diplomacy* that you used earlier: Its root is derived from the Greeks two thousand years ago. It originally meant a folded letter or document, which was sealed with its contents hidden. During the late eighteenth century, an English philosopher described diplomacy as 'an ambassador, who is an honest man sent abroad to lie for the good of his country...Though my favorite definition by far is by a contemporary writer, who said, 'Diplomacy is to do and say the nastiest thing, in the nicest way!'"

Moe shrugged. "Excuse my cynicism—I actually applaud those diplomats who work for Peace and Understanding."

Later that day, Mashbir was on the phone.

"I'd like to speak to Commander Zacharias...*Zach*, I just interviewed Moe Berg; he's our man all right. He'll need a small movie camera⁕ His Japanese is very good, and he's as sharp as they come, a terrific intellect. Make sure that gentleman doesn't get away from you when his baseball days are over—he'll make a top-notch Intelligence agent!"

CHAPTER 29

Tokyo, November, 1934

The sixty-five-thousand Japanese spectators packing the Meiji Shrine Stadium respectfully listened as Prince Tokugawa stood at home plate, speaking into a microphone, addressing them.

The American All-Star players were lined up along the third-base line, with the Tokyo home team players along the first-base line. At the extreme end of the American line, Jimmy Foxx was listening with a puzzled expression on his broad, square face. He turned his head toward Berg. "Hey, Moe, what's this guy saying, anyhow?"

"Prince Tokugawa says he's been a devoted fan of baseball for decades, since attending games in America back in 1910. He knows there've been difficulties between our nations, but since we both love baseball, he hopes this tour, which he helped arrange, will act as a bridge bringing our nations closer together."

Moe listened some more.

"He goes on to say how much better to compete on the friendly playing-field, rather than on a battlefield. When he's done, you watch: He'll give the translation. I've heard his English is impeccable—far better than some people standing along this baseline, I would wager."

Moe gently elbowed the player on his other side.

"*I hoid dat!*" Babe Ruth said, annoyed. "But is dat de straight skinny dat guy at da hotel was saying? Dat de Jap who organized dis trip got stabbed?"

"I'm afraid so," Moe replied. "I myself have received threats of being shot, stabbed, or blown apart."

Ruth surveyed the vast stadium with its throngs waiting for the game to begin.

"Nuttin' against you, Moe, you know I like you, but would you mind goin' down to de otha end of de line?"

"Relax, Babe," Moe replied, giving his best deadpan stare. "That's why I've been crowding up close to you all this time. Not even the most militant fanatical maniac would dare harm the great Babe Ruth!" He now smiled, "But you may not be as safe when it comes to their seventeen-year-old pitcher from the Tokyo Giants, Eiji Sawamura. I hear he's amazingly talented."

St. Luke's International Hospital, Tokyo, a few days later

A tall man entered the lobby and approached the admissions desk. Though Caucasian, he wore a flowing kimono, and carried a large bouquet of flowers.

Facing the receptionist, he bowed politely, and addressed her in perfect Japanese. "A thousands pardons, I'm seeking the room of Mrs. Lyons, the daughter of my friends, Ambassador and Mrs. Grew. I understand she and her newborn baby are receiving visitors." Lifting the flowers, he added, "I wish to give her these, and pay my respects."

The receptionist surveyed him with considerable curiosity. "They are in room 714."

"Thank you," Moe Berg replied, then confidently strode toward the elevator, passing several Japanese security personnel. Getting off on the seventh floor, he turned left and walked briskly down the corridor past room 714 without stopping. At the end of the hall was a door marked with Japanese characters meaning "Fire Exit."

Glancing over his shoulder to make sure no one was watching, Moe slipped inside, then climbed the stairs to the top floor and spotted what he was hoping for: iron rungs set in the wall of the stairwell. The characters on the trapdoor above said 'Roof Access.'

He emerged to a magnificent view of downtown Tokyo and the harbor. From inside his kimono, he withdrew the movie camera strapped to his chest and slowly panned 360 degrees. When finished, he concealed the camera, climbed back down to the Seventh Floor and

quickly dropped off the flowers at Mrs. Lyons's room, before exiting
the hospital.

College Park, Maryland, four months later

Mashbir was at his desk when his secretary announced, "Mr. Berg
has returned."

"Why, send him right in."

"Moe, so glad to see you. I was getting a little worried!"

"I took my time returning by way of Vladivostok, and from there
took the Trans-Siberian Railway to Moscow, where I stayed for a week
before going on to Berlin. That's sure a terrible place now; by chance,
the day I arrived in Berlin, Hitler was sworn in as chancellor. In his
speech, he used a seemingly innocent term, *Lebensraum*, 'living space,'
as his country's destiny. No doubt it's just another way of saying territorial expansion, but what happens to the people in those adjacent
countries?"

Moe placed a circular metal case on the desk.

"Here are those pictures you asked for. Hope they're never needed."

"All we can do is be prepared."

Sidney put the film canister in his safe before continuing.

"Now tell me about your travels. I bet you heard a dozen different languages on that Trans-Siberian trip. How long did it take, two
weeks?"

"Actually, nine days, and you're right about languages. There
were more like twenty, counting local dialects. I took notes, and also
shot footage of the people and countryside. Too bad I couldn't record
sound. Sure wish I had one of those new wire recorder devices, then
I'd be able to play back those languages when I returned."

"Tell you what, Moe, you deserve a lot more than that. I'll get you
one before you leave for Florida Spring Training, for your future travels."

Mashbir patted him on the shoulder.

"So how do you feel about playing for Boston?"

"Boston? I've been traded again?" Moe shook his head.

"I thought you'd heard. Joe Cronin was traded to the Boston Red Sox over the winter to be their new manager. The first thing he did was trade for you."

"Well, that's good. Anyway, I'll probably spend most of my time on the bench catching up on my newspaper reading. Not much baseball coverage in the countries I've been recently."

※※※※

Newark, New Jersey, 1935

Small family-owned stores lined the avenue: delicatessens, grocers, shoe stores, and barber shops—a typical American downtown. Sidney strolled for a time, window-shopping, before slipping into a phone booth.

"Irene, darling, just arrived. I'll be back tomorrow by five P.M. for sure. I've heard the rumors, but have to see for myself."

"Promise me you'll be cautious…" she replied.

He approached a three-story brownstone building; outside was a gathering of men, along with a few women and youngsters. He walked past them and through the entrance into a spacious foyer adorned with large posters of Hitler, surrounded by swastika banners and American flags hanging side by side. A jovial crowd hovered around tables laden with food, or sat in folding chairs scattered about, busily eating, drinking, and talking. It felt like a picnic✳

From behind a serving table, a stout fellow called, "Hey mister! For just two bits you can have Knockwurst, Sauerkraut and Potato Pancakes!"

"Sounds good," Sidney replied.

As the jovial man served a heaping plate, he asked, "Would you like me to throw in a mug of beer, for free? I brew it myself. It's a good thing that damned Prohibition ended. How can a man eat tasty German food without a beer?"

"Can't argue with you there," Sidney chuckled.

The man handed him a frothy mug.

"Haven't seen you before."

"I'm from Syracuse, looking for a job—an electrician by trade...I heard about your meeting and thought it would be interesting."

The man nodded. "Yeah, tell me about it!—Nowadays, it's hard to find a job. Talk to me later, maybe I can assist you. You might meet others here tonight who can also help. There'll be regulars, and some new faces. We want to establish many local chapters. But you go eat," he said, waving him off. "We can talk later."

Sidney planted himself in a chair and ate quietly, observing. A robust man with blond hair, blue eyes, and a Nordic complexion sat nearby, holding a plate of food on his lap. He smiled at Sidney and said, "Pretty good, huh?"

"Delicious."

The man extended a hand speckled with white paint and plaster. "Don't worry, it's dry. I'm a builder. My name is Frederic."

"I'm Robert, glad to make your acquaintance."

"You been here before, Robert?"

"My first time."

"Same for me. I came for that film they're showing about Germany. I'm originally from there, but what's happening now is disturbing. Here in America is a good place to raise a family. Do you have children, Robert?"

Sidney nodded. "Two boys, a little one and a teenager. Don't see the older one much; lives with my first wife."

"Oh, I see," Frederic replied with empathy. "I have a son and a daughter. My son just became a Boy Scout."

"You must be proud."

A light switch was flipped on and off; the gathering entered the adjacent auditorium, with Sidney situating himself on a side aisle for an easy exit...The front platform had a microphone stand and a large projection screen pulled down. He looked all around, noting the diversity of people attending: young and old, well-dressed and not so well-dressed, most looking like regular working-class. The American National Anthem was played on a piano as a man walked onto center stage. Everyone stood in respect.

When the music ended, the speaker announced, "We're so honored you could attend our celebration for the New Germany. We've had some recent changes—our organization is no longer to be called the *National Socialist Party.* Henceforth, it will be known as *The German-American Bund,* meaning an 'Alliance' or a 'Federation,' whose belief is that the Aryan race is superior in intellect and physical qualities compared to the colored breeds." He saluted the flag.

"The U.S. economy is dismal," he said. "We can learn from Germany's success! The Treaty of Versailles vengefully pushed her into an economic depression—her money valueless, with unemployment and despair...Families starving."

He raised a fist. "Hitler has brought jobs and health care, and sends the children to wonderful forested youth camps." He looked around at his audience. "Germany is the birthplace of many of you, or of your parents and grandparents. As German-Americans, your loyalty is linked to these two great nations."

He saluted and called out, "Heil, Hitler!...How fortunate we are to have him at the helm, protecting Germany from a rising tide of Russian Communism, and those many *Jews* who support that godless form of dictatorship. We in America must also be ever vigilant!"

The room darkened as he continued: "We're about to view the film *The Triumph of the Will,* where we will accompany the Führer to one of his great rallies in the medieval city of Nuremburg, which connects Germany's Gothic past to its glorious Nazi future!"

The subtitled documentary began.

Sidney intently watched as thousands of impassioned onlookers gathered outside Hitler's hotel, shouting, "We want our Führer!"

Camera close-ups of the crowd made sure to highlight attractive young ladies anxious for Hitler to appear❋

When he strode out onto his balcony, many became hysterical with excitement or fell into a state of awe, as if seeing a famous movie star, or the Messiah himself.

The scene then transformed into quick clips of youth groups, joyfully listening to the words of their leader. This was followed by S.S. troops, goose-stepping in parade . . .

One of the most powerful of the film's scenes occurred in a huge auditorium decorated with hundreds of banners, complete with classical organ music and dramatic stage lighting, creating a cathedral atmosphere of mystical pageantry. There, Hitler made a dramatic entrance, accompanied by ministers Goebbels, Hess, Himmler, and Goering, marching down the central passage to the front, as thousands of hands raised in the Nazi salute.

Once on center stage, the audience hung onto his every word, as Hitler shouted, *"The German Third Reich will last a thousand years!"*

The cinematography was hypnotic. Creative camera angles and editing made Hitler appear ten times his normal size, like a marble statue of a Roman emperor, as he exclaimed, *"The National Party will be unchangeable in its doctrine, hard as steel in its organization, supple and adaptable in its tactics. It will be like a new religious order!"*

By the time the lights came back on, Sidney had a painful headache. *That's one hell of an amazing propaganda film,* he thought. *Must be a million participants involved in that performance.*

From several rows in front of Sidney, Frederic stood.

"I'm ashamed," he shouted, grasping the crucifix on his neck chain. "I already have a religion and I don't need Herr Hitler's racist version. I've been told by my relatives in Germany that the film we just watched was made to replace an earlier one, because in that prior film, Ernst Rohm, Hitler's commander of the *Brownshirts* militia, had been highlighted. Rohm later dared to call Hitler, 'that ridiculous corporal.' And, for that, Hitler ordered Rohm and many of his officers executed, and all copies of that film destroyed. In reality, most of Hitler's staff are afraid of his lunacy, but are too cowardly to act!"

"Oh, shit," Sidney said under his breath, as several men in the audience, fists clenched, moved toward Frederic. *I promised the missus to stay out of trouble, but...*He started to lift himself out of his chair. The gentleman seated to Sidney's right, whispered, "Don't blow your cover helping your new friend; it will all work itself out."

"What?" Sidney replied, focusing on the tall, lean fellow for the first time. "Who are you?"

"I've been watching you since you arrived, and guessed you're U. S. military or a Federal agent." Sidney's body tightened. "Relax, I'm with British Intelligence. We're keeping an eye on the political climate in the states...My name's David."

The Master of Ceremonies called out to the audience, "Leave him alone—Let the fool say his piece before he leaves!"

Frederic continued, "We've just seen German youths in uniforms similar to the Boy Scouts, but unlike the Boy Scouts of America, who teach personal responsibility, community service, reverence for God, and *tolerance* for other religions—these Hitler Youth groups teach hatred! They even give them consecrated daggers to defeat their enemies! *Ja, yes,* Hitler has improved Germany's economy. But you wait and see, he'll lead that proud nation to its ruin!"

Frederic walked out, with a dozen or so others following.

The Master of Ceremonies gave an ingratiating smile.

"We're better off without them. Someday they'll see the error of their ways. But for now, please, everyone stand up and repeat after me: *The New Germany has risen from the ashes, moving forward toward a glorious future.*"

※※※※

Washington, D.C.

Irene and Sidney sat on a park bench watching their little son, Donald, repeatedly climb up the slide. At the bottom, a small girl with pigtails pretended to catch him, but always let him slide by, both giggling; nearby, other children chased one another around the playground, lost in laughter.

"Sweetheart, aren't they cute?" Irene said, and got no response. She squeezed his hand. "Sidney, you haven't said much about your trip."

"Oh yes, kids are wonderful." He held her hand.

"As for my trip…" he rattled his head, "Some folks can be so gullible, I can't fathom their notion of a Master Race; where does that leave the rest of humanity?"

She looked into his eyes. "But isn't it better that you know what's happening. Earlier today, I heard you making hotel arrangements. Is that trip connected to the one you just returned from?"

"It's the other side of the coin…"

Madison Square Garden, New York City

Sidney noticed the heavy solemnity of the crowd entering the massive arena.
A couple of guys passing by approached him. "There a game tonight
at the Garden?" one asked.

Sidney pointed to an announcement pasted on the building.

"Oh, I see...," he said to his companion, "Hey, it says here that
American Jews are discussing the problems that European Jews are
having. What difference does it make to them what happens over
there?"

His companion replied, "Don't we have enough of our own problems? Maybe *they* ain't feeling the economic squeeze of these hard
times. Why don't those kikes mind their own business!"

There's no shortage of idiots, Sidney thought. He then entered the
stadium and found a seat.

Up front on a platform, a man with a neatly-trimmed, mottled,
grey-and-black beard, stepped forward. Behind him was a long table, where the other participants sat. In a resonant voice, the man
began: "We thank you for attending. We must not hide from world
events. Knowledgeable representatives from various national Jewish
organizations are on our panel."

The first panelist to stand was a slim, bi-focaled gentleman who
approached the lectern.

"I'll start my presentation by giving you a short summary of recent events in Germany. Hitler ordered his Storm Troopers to burn
down their own congress building, the *Reichstag,* and then made himself Chancellor. These lying Fascists redirected the blame for the fire
towards communists and Jews, using newspapers, radio, and pamphlets to spread hatred, hysteria, and fear. We must increase world
awareness, and pressure this new regime to stop their obscene behavior, or they'll face a national boycott of German goods!" Many in the
crowd applauded.

The moderator invited the next speaker forward.

The man carried a stuffed folder. Shooting an irritated glance at
the prior spokesman, he declared, "If you expect protests and boy-

cotts to succeed, you are deluded. That will only strengthen their resolve, and they'll punish Jews with greater intensity."

He withdrew a stack of papers. "These letters are from prominent German-Jewish families, begging us to avoid any anti-German activities. They understand the difficulties which would arise." He took a deep breath…"Instead, we must give our national Jewish organizations time to find diplomatic and economic ways to resolve this problem. German Jews have a long history there, going back hundreds of years. The German people and their heritage are admirable: Once their economy improves, all will be well."

He pointed at the audience. "Some suggest Jews should leave Germany, now that Britain's mandate over Palestine and their Prime Minister Balfour's Declaration states they will not stand in the way of a Jewish state." His voice rose. "But I, and *many* others strongly feel that during this unstable time, that would be a disaster. Other Jews around the world might also be forced out of the nations in which they are currently well-established, and they would instead find themselves expelled to Israel against their will! We must show patience, and you'll see that behind-the-scenes negotiations will win in the end."

The next presenter, wearing a U.S. military uniform, came forward and stared at the last speaker.

"So you're worried about the imminent creation of a Jewish state!" He laughed. "You're out of touch with reality. There's a rising tide of nationalism in the Middle East; they control the oil, and no American or British administration wants to piss them off by giving the Jews control of even a tiny piece of that region. *God Almighty!*" He slammed the lectern.

"*Our people* have been persecuted and dispersed for two-thousand years! Isn't it time *we* had a homeland. Yes, Jews and Muslims honor the same patriarch father, Abraham, and are descendants of stepbrothers, Isaac and Ishmael. Therefore, instead of fighting, they should be treating each other with dignity and bringing each other prosperity!"

He shrugged.

"Maybe someday, but for *now*, let's focus on what's happening in Germany—and in our own country."

Raising a fist high, he said, "This is the only thing those fascist bastards understand. I represent Jewish-American veterans who fought and defeated the Huns in the Great War. The Nazis will never back down; diplomacy will not work. It's time to strike, and strike hard! As we speak, infiltrators right here in America are establishing themselves. We must protest, boycott, and do *whatever* it takes to bring these bullies down!"

The prior speaker stood.

"Enough of your loud-mouthing. You risk the lives of millions of Jews in Germany with your bravado. We need time before going off on a rampage."

"Gentlemen, gentlemen," the moderator said, "Everyone's opinion should be heard."

He turned to the next speaker. A man in his seventies with bright blue eyes, wearing a yarmulke, came forward.

"I'm a rabbi, so it's natural to hope for the best in humanity. There are merits in the words of all who have spoken. They express heartfelt compassion. I suggest we start with diplomacy and see where it takes us."

The veteran stood. "You don't understand, Rabbi, we'll lose the momentum of this mass meeting to act! Committees move at a snail's pace. You appease these thugs, they'll blackmail you for more later!"

The panelists erupted into private debates, as the audience watched in bewilderment.

The Rabbi raised his voice. "Enough. You're all on the same side!—A good strategy isn't going to be obtained at this first meeting. I recommend we issue a general protest against Hitler's actions and send it to our new presidential administration; but no more than that, at this time. Hopefully, we come together again in the near future and vote on various other options...

"In the meantime, let us pray that where there is darkness, let there be light; where there is hatred, let there be peace and understanding. And please remember, we're part of a larger community, and should assist those in need. That is our tradition, and may our own cause be supported, God willing!"

Talk about being between a rock and hard place, Sidney thought, as he joined the crowds heading for the exits.

Nearby, a couple was speaking loudly. The woman said, "Samuel, you were raised in Germany. I know you feel affection for that country, but it's changed. My cousin lives there; his son was beaten for refusing to salute *Heil Hitler.*"

"But Sophie, that's the work of a few hoodlums. You saw those letters from German Jews urging us not to get involved?"

"They were probably written with guns to their heads!"

✳✳✳✳

Berlin, Germany

The black-robed, white-turbaned Grand Mufti of Jerusalem sat opposite Hitler, both scrutinizing each other, with their translators and ministers nearby; a small child sat cross-legged on a rug near the mufti's feet.

"So kind of you to accept my invitation, Your Excellency," Hitler said.

"I've long wished to meet you," the mufti replied. "I hope you don't mind, I've brought along my brother's son, Yasser. He's a very clever five-year-old and will be no bother, I'm certain."

Why the hell did he bring his nephew? Hitler thought, but replied, "He's most welcome. So how are things going, my friend?"

"In the name of Merciful Almighty God, and with the aid of your weapon shipments, our common enemies, the British and French, are being pushed out of their colonies in the Middle East."

Hitler smiled. "I'm happy to be of assistance."

"But *Führer,* if we're to continue working together, I need a guarantee."

The Mufti's piercing eyes bore down upon him. "Zionism is on the rise, pushing for a Jewish state. This must never happen! If you wish a strong alliance with the Arab world and access to our oil resources, you must prevent the immigration of Jews to Palestine."

Hitler tightly interlocked his fingers in thought.

"I'll need a few moments to confer with my advisors."

Once in private, Hitler looked to Goebbels. "What do you think about his request?"

Goebbels grinned. "There may be a way to play this to our advantage. Certain American government representatives have recently offered that if we improved our treatment of the Jews, financial benefits in the way of foreign trade, even loans, would come our way." He laughed. "Imagine, many of those loans probably coming from the wealthy Jews themselves."

"It's a trap!" Hitler shouted.

"I don't think so," Goebbels calmly replied. "Their new president is dealing with an economic disaster and doesn't want a costly foreign war. It's more likely powerful American Jews think by paying us off, the problem will go away…We had hoped to push our cause in America through Bund organizations, but that might backfire, by inciting anti-German protests. Instead, if we *temporarily* soften our approach, this will slow Zionist efforts."

His eyes glowed as he nibbled on his thumbnail, considering the possibilities. "Let's publish a series of news articles flattering the economic skills of Jews—but meanwhile, our military grows ever stronger. And the time is not far off when we will not have to answer to anyone!"

"But what of our agents in America?"

"What a delightful game we're playing!" Goebbels grinned, "We'll have them start a new movement without the swastika, and give it a patriotic name. How does the *America First Movement* sound? Whose primary goal will be promoting isolationism. After all, European affairs are really not their concern."

Hitler returned flushed with enthusiasm.

"I make a vow to you, Grand Mufti. We will do all we can so that not a single European Jew steps foot in the Holy Land. And in repayment, you must do all you can to move the hearts and minds of the Arab world to see us, the Nazis, as their liberators, so they will fight alongside us."

The Mufti smiled.

"Let my voice be broadcast from Germany's radio stations, and I will declare a *fatwa* throughout the Middle East, a holy war against the British and their allies."

The Mufti pulled a booklet from his robe pocket.

"Here's a present: *The Protocols of the Elders of Zion*. We use it to foment hatred toward the Jews."

"A good idea," Hitler replied. "I've read it, though it's unclear who truly authored it—between you and me, I'd guess it's a hoax or forgery."

"Its authenticity is irrelevant! Like your *Mein Kampf*, it is a powerful tool for shaping public opinion," the mufti replied with enthusiasm. "Your German word *Judenrein* describes a Europe free of Jews. This concept will be expanded," he said, spreading his arms, "to include Jews throughout the Middle East, who will be expelled, or if necessary, eliminated."

Hitler firmly shook the mufti's hand and smiled at Yasser. "Young man, you will learn much from your uncle."

The boy nodded with pride.

As they exited, the mufti whispered to Yasser, *"Hitler is the Führer of the West—Someday, I will be known as the Führer of the Arab world!"*

CHAPTER 30

Japanese Imperial Palace, February 1936

Hirohito placed the needle gently on the spinning record, then reclined on a couch as the Chippendale Victrola played delicate piano pieces by Liszt. When the record had run its course, he withdrew to the dining room, where he was met by Nagako.

Halfway through their meal, the War Minister rushed into the room. "Forgive my intrusion, Your Majesty, there's been another rebellion! They targeted our Prime Minister and two former Prime Ministers. Prime Minister Keisuke Okada survived, but former Prime Minister and Lord Keeper of the Privy Seal Makoto Saito and current Finance Minister Korekiyo Takahasi were both assassinated," he hesitated. "They've also seriously injured Grand Chamberlain Kantaro Suzuki."

"This can't be, they are some of my closest friends and allies," Hirohito shouted angrily, stunned.

The minister continued, "They've burned down the *Tokyo Sun* and several other newspapers supportive of your policies. With this instability, mobs have gathered around banks, anxiously demanding the withdrawal of their money with the police unable to keep order."

"Dear Wife, madness and treason is upon us again."

"Perhaps your voice should be firmly heard," Nagako replied.

"The last time I spoke out against the militants, I was portrayed as a despot for interfering in worldly matters."

The minister interjected, "Your Majesty, you don't understand, I've been pressured to ask you to make a statement in support of these rebels' actions."

"These savages must be stopped!" The Emperor grabbed a sheet of parchment and with a trembling hand wrote several lines, then stamped the Imperial Seal upon it.

"Here is my response, a Decree demanding this riot end immediately for the sake of the country. All those who disobey will be shot!"

On the grounds of a Shinto temple the following month, weeping women and taciturn men in black robes surrounded a tranquil lake, as candle floats with their flickering flames drifted under the moonlight in remembrance of the departed souls.

"It was not an easy decision to make," Nagako said, squeezing Hirohito's hand, as they watched from a distance. "Their families understand it was done with a heavy heart, and that you are honoring them with our presence."

"This is the first time I've sentenced men to their death," Hirohito replied, barely able to get the words out. "But a strong message had to be given. I only wish I could behead those generals who instigated this, instead of these seventeen young officers bearing the punishment."

"Let us hope and pray that your action will prevent future rebellions."

✳✳✳✳

The life of the Imperial Family gradually returned to calm. The three princesses enjoyed assembling puzzles with their little brother, Akihito. They stopped when Princess Terunomiya, the eldest, recited a poem:

> *The rains of spring,*
> *Which hang to the branches,*
> *Of the green willow,*
> *Look like pearls upon a string . . .*

"That was written a thousand years ago by Lady Ise," Terunomiya told her siblings. "And, Look, here is one about an Emperor called *The Mikado's Bow:*

"When the day is come,
He takes his bow,
And fondles it with pride,
When the day is done,
He lays it on his side,
Hark to the twanging of the string!
This is the bow of our great Lord and King!
He rides forth to the chase at break of day,
At evening he once again rides away."

Akihito listened joyously. Terunomiya gave him a hug, then strolled to the kitchen.

"Mother, where is Father?"

"In his sanctuary, the marine laboratory. Terunomiya, please assist me with preparing dinner."

"Mother, **you** have a passion for cooking—but may I please help you another time?"—and off she ran. Soon she was standing on tip-toes at her father's tall laboratory counter.

"Father, may I look?"

"Certainly my dear, let me slide a new specimen into the micro-scope viewer."

He slowly turned the fine-focus adjustment as his daughter, now standing on a footstool, looked through the eyepiece.

"Tell me when you see a clear image."

"Now, now! What is it I'm looking at?"

"What do you think it is?"

"A giant, shimmering net."

"You describe it well; it is a thin section from the dorsal fin of a salmon, magnified two-hundred-fold."

"Oh," she replied with zeal. "Can we look at other specimens?"

"Of course! This next slide is a developing Koi fish embryo. It is composed of hundreds of cells, but a mere two weeks ago, it was only a single fertilized egg cell!"

"How wonderful!" She hesitated. "Father, I wish I could become a scientist."

Hirohito sighed.

"Destiny has chosen our paths, both yours and mine."

"It doesn't seem fair. Why shouldn't girls become scientists? And you know, Father," her voice wavered as she moved close to him for comfort, and so he would not see her eyes tearing: "I'm only ten years old—and already a husband has been chosen for me. One that I haven't even met!"

"Those are our ancestral ways."

"Yes, I know; that is why even though I'm much older than Akihito, I walk behind him. But in my heart, I feel that is wrong. Oh, Father, you look sad. I hope I did not hurt your feelings with my questions?"

"No, it is because Akihito will soon leave our home to be raised and educated at the Peers School."

"We can't let that happen!" She bolted away and was soon being escorted by her servants to Prince Tokugawa's estate. "Dear Great Uncle, we need your help," she pleaded.

"Calm yourself, my pretty butterfly, and explain*"

That evening, voices raged. "Enough!" the Lord Steward shouted. "The Crown Prince is three years old: It is time for his formal education as future heir to the throne."

"I also respect tradition." Tokugawa stood his ground. "Do you even know where this practice began?"

"No—but I'm sure *you'll* educate me," the Steward replied, through lips pulled tight by a frown.

"It goes back a thousand years, when women in the Imperial Harem plotted against each other, so their own sons might rule rather than the sons of the other Imperial wives. If the Emperor's favorite became pregnant, others might attempt to frighten her, or set traps to cause accidents and miscarriages. For this reason, the Crown Prince was removed for his safety from the Palace. We now live in different times."

"I disagree," the Lord Steward replied, jutting his jaw out. "Our Emperor was raised this way, and so will his son!"

The following day, Hirohito thanked Tokugawa for his efforts, and apologized for his heated encounter with the Lord Steward; Hirohito emphasized Tokugawa should do no more, explaining that his ill mother, the Empress Dowager, had made a request which he could not refuse, that Akihito be raised outside of the Imperial household. Nagako would never disobey her mother-in-law's wishes, and in truth, she, herself, accepted this tradition as one of the heavy responsibilities of nobility.

"Then I will make you an offer, Hirohito," Prince Tokugawa replied. "I'm certain Akihito will do very well, but if you wish, I'll visit him on a weekly basis keeping him fully aware of his family's activities. I will also convey messages back and forth between you both. In this way, you will be connected."

Tokugawa smiled. "Perhaps Akihito and I might go on adventures, like you and I did thirty years ago, when *you* were five years old." He chuckled. "Oh, where have the years gone?"

Hirohito embraced him. "You have always been the one who is there for me!"

CHAPTER 31

Washington, D.C., 1936

At a local pub, Sidney pulled darts out of the board hung against the wall. "Zach, why did you let me beat you three games in a row, when you usually whop me?"

Zach smiled. "I hoped a winning streak and a couple of beers would make what I'm going to tell you a bit easier."

They sat at a table away from the crowd. "Just as I promised, Sid, I researched where your M-Plan recommendations might have ended up, but couldn't find them anywhere in Naval *or* Army Intelligence records."

Sidney's jaw dropped. "You mean I resigned, sacrificing my military career for nothing?"

Zach gulped his beer. "No, I eventually found them, gathering dust these past thirteen years along with your other reports left with our military attaché in Japan."

"That can't be. Both the Army and Navy encouraged me to deliver that document!" Sidney stared hard at Zach, his voice overwrought. "I need your help to push this through!"

Zach remained silent, his eyes downcast, listening.

"Do I have to beg you? I've already begun making arrangements on my own. My friend Robert Moss is willing to partner up with me on a Japanese business venture, giving me an excuse to visit Japan on a regular basis."

"Does Robert know what you're really up to?"

"I thought it best not to tell him."

"All right, Sid. Let's arrange a meeting between you, Admiral King, and Captain Puleston, the man I answer to, he's Head of Navy

Intelligence. If he hears from Admiral King about your accomplishments, you'd gain his confidence—and just maybe he'll support your plan."

Several days later, Zach noted Sidney's ongoing frustration.

"I don't get Zach, Admiral King was pleasant at the meeting, but avoided any discussion of the M-Plan?"

"I never did ask you," Zach replied. "How do you manage to get along so well with King? Yes, he has vast experience on submarines, battleships, and with aviation, but he's considered demanding, stubborn, and rude by some."

"It's probably because we agree on the imminent danger of War."

"That's probably it." Zach nodded. "But don't underestimate the support you've given him. You've streamlined the *Federal Bureau of Standards*, permitting private businesses to produce equipment faster, of better quality, and at lower prices."

Zach moved his hands as he spoke, "You've created something like a *Military-**Industrial** Complex* by recruiting fifty large corporations to design and manufacture whatever you thought would aid our military-preparedness, whether weaponry or Aviation Electronics, or just figuring out how to improve our garden-variety of cables and spark plugs.

"*Hundreds* of patents have come out of your *Washington Institute of Technology*—for which King has been the *one* receiving plenty of accolades—And yes, if war erupts, we'll be much more ready...But you know, King made Rear Admiral in '33, and it looks like Vice Admiral will be coming his way soon."

Sidney fumbled for words. "But, Zach, King's a great strategist: He sees a good idea and jumps on it. Where are you going with all this?"

Zach scratched his head. "I'd guess good ol' Admiral King doesn't want you to go on your mission. When you leave, he loses his top man in Research and Development."

"Then why'd he even show up for the meeting?"

Zach smiled without replying.

"Don't play guessing games with me!"

"Cool down! He doesn't want to piss you off, like I just did. He shows up, then makes a lame excuse about not being able to talk openly about your M-Plan with the *Head of Naval Intelligence?*—You mean to tell me there's a security risk there?" Zach hesitated, "Do you really want my opinion?"

Sidney nodded.

"Okay, Number One, King fears you could get killed on this mission. Number Two, you might not be able to accomplish it anyway, Number Three, if you did accomplish it, it might not last when war broke out. And lastly, Number Four, in his mind, you're far more valuable in your current position."

"He could have just said his schedule was too busy."

"That's where the master strategist comes in: King wanted to appease you while getting a chance to meet Captain Puleston—but he kept it social, without pushing your project."

Sidney slammed his fist down.

"First, you swell my head a couple of sizes describing all the good work I've been doing. Then, you shrink it like a *Headhunter*, revealing how I totally missed what was going on. *Zach, I'm going on this mission, one way or another!*"

"Well, there's good news in that case." Zach grinned. "Captain Puleston noticed that King wasn't too keen about your venture, but *he* wants to finance it *himself*, out of the Navy's budget. But he can't openly acknowledge that you have his backing."

"I appreciate the offer," Sidney replied sullenly. "But it's the same old problem—Get money through regular channels, and everyone knows about it. It's got to come from private funding. I've recently received some money from several of my patents, and all of it is going towards M-Plan setup costs. And who knows, maybe after that I'll be able to persuade some wealthy patriots to help out?"

CHAPTER **32**

Germany Embassy, Tokyo, 1936

With elaborate flourish, Herr Reichmann bowed to Prince Taka-matsu, who was dressed in his white Naval Squadron Commander's uniform. "Most Noble Prince, I'm honored by your visit."

"How could I refuse your six invitations?"

Reichmann blushed. "I wished only to meet face-to-face when be-stowing a very special invitation to you from **the highest echelons**," he paused dramatically, "to visit our country in order to attend the greatest Olympic Games *of all times!*"

"A generous offer," the prince replied halfheartedly, as his hulking companion edged uncomfortably close.

"*Der Führer Himself* sends his sincerest regards, wishing to meet and have you at his side during this important event. Perhaps, you are not aware that members of your military are currently working together with my countrymen in drafting an Anti-Comintern Pact, so we can move forward as allies to confront the Russians' and their Worldwide Communist Threat!"

He smiled. "And of course you're aware that we applaud your expansion into Manchuria and the necessity to create the state of Man-chukuo, even though those fools in the *League of Nations* reject it."

Takamatsu avoided his companion's piercing eyes as he replied, "My dear Herr Reichmann, I fear that perhaps you are using the term *ally* too freely. This Pact you speak of is only a non-military under-standing between our nations, nothing more at this point." He loos-ened his collar. "And I will let you know in the near future if I will be able to attend your event. Good day, and do send my deep thanks to your Herr Hitler for his most kind invitation!" The Prince turned abruptly, and left.

✳✳✳✳

Takamatsu entered Tokugawa's study. "Dear Uncle and Dear Brother, I thank you for meeting with me."

"What concerns you?" Hirohito asked.

"I've been given a tempting offer but wish your counsel and approval. Herr Reichmann invited me to the Olympic Games in Berlin. He's anxious to have me meet his leaders and witness his country's military strength."

Hirohito nodded deferentially to Tokugawa, so he might speak first.

"Takamatsu, you show great wisdom asking advice on this delicate matter. It is proper for you to explore and understand the *outside world*. I, myself, have been offered the position of President of the Olympics Committee for the upcoming 1940 games!" Tokugawa smiled. "I can't wait to welcome visitors from around the world, so as to encourage a better appreciation of Japan."

He put his hand on Takamatsu's shoulder. "If my schedule permitted, I would travel with you to the Berlin Games, but will instead settle for hearing of your experiences when you return. Should you decide to go, I recommend you arrive a week early so your hosts will be less prepared: The stage setting will not be as polished and *hidden* truths more likely revealed."

Takamatsu turned to Hirohito. "And what is your opinion?"

"By all means, go!"

✳✳✳✳

On Takamatsu's return, he gave the following account to Prince Tokugawa and his brother: "My unexpected early arrival indeed created a stir, especially when I made it unmistakably clear that I wished to tour Berlin for several days accompanied *only by my own aides and translators*. My hosts—after many attempts to dissuade me, agreed. Everywhere I went, hands were held high with salutes of *Heil Hitler*. And in public spaces, signs that had spouted hate were being painted over or removed, creating the image of a far friendlier, more inviting nation for the many international visitors who were soon to arrive.

"I witnessed the *Brown Shirts*, the Reich's para-military police thugs breaking into homes and businesses: pulling out their occupants—men, women, and even children—and loading them like livestock into trucks!" He gave a look of disgust.

"While at a restaurant, I met a social worker named Adele, who bravely agreed to talk with me privately. She explained how most Civil Liberties in the nation had been taken away three years earlier—and shockingly, she told me of a small town near Munich, known as Dachau, contained a prison where the so-called 'enemies of the state' were sent: Liberals, Socialists, and Communists, but especially Jews... They also target those *they label* sexual deviants.

"The Nazis boast that they are in fact *improving the nation's genetics* by performing forced sterilizations on handicapped persons, and on Gypsies and Negroes, whom they see as subhuman."

Tokugawa tried to contain himself by grasping the arms of his chair, as Takamatsu continued, "Can you imagine, school children are instructed to spy on their parents, and report to their teachers if they hear anything critical about Nazi policies...*No group* is immune! There were even massive arrests of Christian Jehovah's Witnesses, when they refused to cooperate."

"Thank you, dear brother, for describing your tour of the city and what is happening in that nation. It is all quite disheartening—But the Olympics, what were the games like?"

Takamatsu's eyes opened wide. "Even that was insane, the pre-game entertainment presented thousands of troops practicing military drills in the sports stadium, with young boys displaying their skill at throwing mock hand grenades* It's hard to believe, but soldiers in full uniform dove from high platforms into a swimming pool." He threw out his arms in astonishment. "The Olympics have historically brought nations together in friendly athletic competition, but this felt more like war games."

"If it wasn't so serious a matter," Tokugawa commented, "I'd be laughing."

Takamatsu remarked, "The Nazis use the term *master race* for their white Aryan heritage, claiming physical and mental superiority. I found *this* most strange, in that Dr. Goebbels, who heads their Public Enlightenment and Propaganda Agency, is himself five feet tall, weighing barely a hundred pounds, and limps with a clubfoot."

"Really?" Hirohito replied.

"Yes, and he has the temerity to offer the Japanese the title of *honorary Aryans*, should we become their allies, as if being a yellow-skinned Asian were a weakness. Or a disease!"

Takamatsu wrung his hands angrily.

"Adding to these double standards, Hitler congratulated the white Finnish athletes who won the Gold, Silver, and Bronze medals for the shot put, but, *on the same day*, he left before congratulating the American Negroes who won the Gold and Silver medals for the high jump."

Hirohito stepped closer to his brother. "Did you challenge anything they said?"

"When I did, they smirked and admitted that Racism served their purposes...Hitler's staff is an odd mix, with Goebbels one of the only ones with a college education—but, his Doctoral Degree is based on a Thesis he wrote on Eighteenth-century Romantic Drama." Takamatsu's voice rose. "And listen to this: Goebbels was a bitter, unsuccessful novelist before entering government! It appears that Reality and Fantasy have currently lost their distinction in that nation."

"Yes, it is most disturbing, but on a bright note, perhaps," Tokugawa said, "you must have witnessed some exciting athletic events."

"Certainly, I enjoyed seeing Jesse Owens, another American Negro who deflated their puffed-up Aryan-Supremacy, when he won Gold medals in *both* the 100- and 200-meter races! The most challenging competition was yet to come, the long jump, when Owens went against the German, Luz Long. For five rounds, they tied at the amazing distance of twenty-five feet, ten-and-a-half inches. The final jump gave Owens the Gold medal, with Luz receiving the Silver.

"Despite the bigotry of that nation's leaders, most Germans cheered when these two men, black and white, who had learned to value each other through spirited competition and good-natured rivalry, embraced one another, and then walked arm in arm as friends. So yes, the games were thrilling—but my patience was wearing thin, having to hear their national anthem every day: *Deutschland, Deutschland, Uber Alles,* "Germany, Germany, Above All Others."

"With pasted smiles, Hitler and his ministers hoped to gain my friendship by flattering the invincibility of the Japanese Warrior Spirit. But I felt like prey, encircled by a pack of animals. *At all costs, we must avoid any alliance.* They sensed my reticence; my translator overheard them planning to invite our brother, Prince Chichibu, to visit, hoping he would be more receptive."

Prince Tokugawa turned to Hirohito, who appeared lost in thought. "Takamatsu did extremely well. It is good to know the values of those who wish to become your friends."

Hirohito lifted a somber face. "These rabid wolves are already at our door, with no intention of leaving."

CHAPTER 33

Georgetown, Washington D. C.

After a delicious weekend barbeque dinner with the Matsumo-
tos at the Mashbirs' home, Irene led Jinne to her workshop, displaying her latest hobby to her new friend. On a wooden stand was the
emerging image of a young girl's face, shaped from rust-colored clay.
She displayed the magazine illustration that inspired the sculpture,
along with the various carving instruments she'd used. With enthusiasm and patience, she gave Jinne a new block of clay to work with
and illustrated the use of carving tools and finger shaping technique
so she could begin to move forward on her own creation.

Kenji and Sidney sat in the outside patio, sipping coffee and
watching the sunset. A sense of solemnity filled the air, which Sidney
could not understand.

"It's so quiet without Donald around," Kenji said.

"He's playing at a friend's home, a few doors down."

Kenji nodded. "Sidney-san, I've something to tell you," his voice
lowered, "I haven't even told Jinne yet. We'll be leaving soon."

"I had so hoped you'd stay another year," Sidney replied sadly.
"I'll miss our weekly golf games and family outings."

Kenji smiled. "If the rumors are accurate, there'll be a promotion.
Then after a short assignment in Japan, I'm bound for China, as Chief
of Staff of the Garrison."

Kenji's voice hardened.

"Sidney, you know a great deal about concrete construction. Is
there anything that can dissolve it?"

That's a strange question, Sidney thought. "Well yes, if things like sugar or sawdust are added to the mix before it's set. Otherwise, nothing—to *my* knowledge."

"The Russians are so foolish," Kenji blurted. "They've built a triple row of concrete bunkers, each a thousand meters apart that extend the full border with Manchuria. But, if we need to get past this barrier and can't dissolve them, we'll simply drive our tanks right up to their openings and toss in phosphorus grenades—It would be difficult for even the hardy Russians to live at temperatures of 2300 degrees!"

"Why are you telling me this, Kenji? You appear to welcome confrontation."

"There is arrogance—but in truth, I answer to others who demand territorial expansion." Kenji's tone softened. "Sidney, what I tell you now is between us?"

"You've got my word."

"The League of Nations was powerless to stop Mussolini and his fascists' conquest of Ethiopia, and has even accepted it—If it's okay for Europeans to invade their weaker neighbors, why should Japan stand by the sidelines? Our military strength in China is increasing rapidly—By summer," he looked away, "you and I might well find ourselves on opposing sides."

"I hope that doesn't happen," Mashbir replied sorrowfully. "But I'll offer you an insight. Our military isn't anxious—nor ready, in my opinion—to get involved in such a conflict—But, in the long run, it will rise to the occasion, and who knows how large this bloody mess could get."

Sidney looked earnestly at him. "At least we've both done our best to head it off—and remember, you'll always be my good friend. Let's cross our fingers—and hope!"

When the ladies returned, Irene declared, "You gentlemen look so serious. Let's have some dessert, followed by a game of Bridge."

Several weeks later, with a heaviness of spirit, Sidney read the handwritten letter for a third time:

Dear Sidney, October 13, 1936

I am writing this note in the mid-Atlantic Ocean aboard the steam liner Norddeutscher Lloyd Bremen. We are enjoying some leisurely time after our hasty preparation for departure.

We are so grateful to you and Irene for the family-like affection you rendered to us. My wife regrets very much her inability to call you and your better half again before departure. I tell her that our thoughts are lingering with yours. Our every memory in associating with you is a very pleasant one. My wife joins me heartily in expressing best regards to you and all.

With love, newly promoted,
Major General Kenji Matsumoto

I'll save this letter, Sidney thought, tucking it away with his most valued personal papers and photos.

✳✳✳✳

The following year at the Mashbir residence:

"What are you thinking about, Sidney?" Irene asked. "You're staring off into space."

Japan is like dry tinder waiting for a match, he thought. *I wish I'd taken those acting courses in college.* Giving his sweetest smile, he replied, "Darling, I'll be gone for a while, I'm booking passage to Yokohama, on business. My friend Robert Moss believes there's a fortune to be made selling concrete to the Japanese."

Irene gave him a skeptical look, "That's reckless. There could be war at any moment and you know it!"

Sidney fumbled. "Alright, I'm sorry for trying to deceive you. You've heard about my M-Plan, how it gets vital intelligence information into and out of Japan? Well, if it's not established now, soon it will be impossible."

"Don't you already have a successful Engineering firm doing a great deal for the Armed Services. Isn't that enough?"

He leaned forward. "Irene, you have no idea how important this is to our country. It might even prevent war. How can I not attempt it?"

She thought a long while, then surprised him with a kiss.

"I love both you and my new country," she said with passion. "So if you wish to appear merely a businessman visiting Japan, while also vacationing, then a wife and a seven-year-old son coming along will greatly enhance that image, *and* your likelihood of returning alive."

"But, but," he trembled, "I've already lost someone dear to me, who I endangered by becoming too close to, while working in Japan— I can't do that again!"

"I won't take no for an answer!"

Pacific Ocean, February, 1937

The huge ship *Tatsuta Maru* was an impressive part of the Nippon Yusen Kaisha Cruise Line, with its three levels of cabins above the main deck and two below. One of the ship's recreational leaders was teaching Donald and several other young passengers how to play shuffleboard, while Irene and Sidney reclined on deck lounge chairs, looking out to the gently rolling sea.

"So far this vacation has been delightful, but I have a question," she whispered. "You warned me our room might be bugged—so why did you choose a Japanese liner?"

"I wanted there to be no hint of undercover activity. I'm broadcasting to anyone interested that I'm visiting one of my favorite places, Japan, with nothing to hide. This way, I'll also get a chance to brush up on my Japanese with the passengers and crew."

Irene's voice tightened. "About Donald—the other day, when he and some of his new friends got into mischief, you were too hard on him."

"What? Their playing with matches almost started a fire!"

"He might have just been watching the others, and kids do make mistakes."

"*You're* too soft on him," he replied, his voice rising.

"We're on vacation, Darling. Why don't you just have a Martini and calm down."

He rolled his eyes. "Okay, I'll try to be gentler. I've had a lot on my mind." He paused. "I need to get back to our room for a little while. Do you want to come along?"

In the cabin, Irene silently watched Sidney crumple and dog-ear a couple of letters he'd been carrying. He brushed a clear liquid on the edges, followed by fanning and blowing them dry; then, back into their envelopes they went and into the pocket of a suit hanging in the closet. Once outside their room again, she whispered, "What was that all about?"

"In case anyone messes with our stuff, those letters reinforce that I'm only on a business trip. And, if tampered with, I'll know by putting them under a U.V. light."

"So you want them to be found." She smiled. "If it weren't dangerous, spying could be pure fun."

Tropical breezes and lovely young ladies in hula skirts awaited them when their cruise ship docked at Honolulu. Irene strolled down the gangplank, one arm looped around Sidney's arm, her other holding Donald's hand. Colorful and fragrant leis were placed around their necks, with Donald giggling as one of the girls tousled his curly red hair.

"Aloha! Welcome to our island paradise. We hope you have a wonderful time during your stopover."

"Thank you," Irene said. "Aren't these flowers lovely, Donald?"

"And the Hawaiian girls are very pretty, too," he replied, looking to his father, who gave an approving nod.

Irene pursed her lips. "Once we've checked into our hotel, I want to get my hair done."

"Sure, sweetheart. Donald and I will explore the town while you're making yourself even more gorgeous."

When father and son returned to the salon, Irene was under a dryer, her perm finishing its cycle. In adjacent chairs, women were in varying stages of being beautified. Sitting in the reception area, Sidney couldn't help overhearing a conversation between a young stylist and an older woman having her hair dyed.

"It must be difficult being married to a commander, with all his responsibilities. Does he find time for you and him to go out and enjoy each other?"

The client shrugged. "He does work long hours, and often brings assignments home."

"At least he isn't planning any long trips away, soon, is he?"

"No, the fleet is pretty much settled for a while..."

As the family strolled from the salon, Donald exclaimed, "Mom, you look great!"—and Sidney gave an admiring whistle.

"You're both so sweet," Irene said, blushing.

"One thing, though," Sidney said, "while we were waiting for you, I overheard some conversations—"

Irene interrupted. "I know where you're going; the salon owner, Frau Friedel, is a sweet, grandmotherly type. She and her daughter, Ruth, give special discounted rates and great service to the wives of many high-ranking military officers. What with Pearl Harbor nearby, half of the mid-level officers' wives frequent their establishment as well. Sidney, I also heard conversations centered on ship schedules and movements of troops, all interlaced with friendly conversation."

"That sounds very suspicious," Donald interjected.

They both looked at their son with surprise.

The next day, Mashbir visited Captain Henshaw at Army Headquarters, Oahu, Hawaii. "First off, Mashbir," Henshaw said, "you're an outsider and you don't understand Hawaiian society."

"I agree," Sidney graciously replied, "but how well do you know the Kuhns?"

"They run with the upper circles. Moved from Germany a couple years back. I've heard their daughter, Ruth, was romantically involved with a high-ranking official there. The father, Bernard, is a retired doctor with a large inheritance. So you see, I'm not sleeping at my job."

"Have you seen anything unusual?"

"Not really—though Bernard and their seven year old son often visit battleships when tours are given. The kid looks sharp in his naval-style clothing, just like a little sailor. A bright boy, asks lots of questions."

Henshaw flung his arms outward as he jutted his jaw forward. "Are you trying to tell me that cute child and his doctor-father are part of a spy ring? You must be nuts!"

Their son is as old as mine, Mashbir thought, *and if he's a spy, he's the youngest I've ever heard of.*

"Please, just promise me, Captain, you'll at least keep an eye on them?"

"Easier said than done. That beauty parlor is a real hit with military wives, as you know. How do you stop women from gossiping? Those places are like confessionals, but I'll see what I can do . . . "

Yokohama Harbor, the following week: The six hundred passengers disembarked the cruise ship. To the Mashbirs' surprise and delight, Kenji and Jinne were waiting for them at the end of the pier.

"Dear friends," Kenji said, "such a great pleasure to see you again. I left my division, which was on practice maneuvers in Sendai, to spend some time with you."

"That's wonderful!" Irene replied. "How did you know we were coming? You must have heard from our mutual friends?"

"No, it was common knowledge at the Pan Pacific Club." Kenji noticed the confused look on Irene's face and asked, "Sidney, you must have called or telegraphed ahead, did you not?"

"Yes, before we left San Francisco."

"Good, then!" Kenji said. "Where are you staying?"

Sidney coughed. "We just received bad news. Neither the Imperial Hotel in Tokyo nor the Grand Hotel in Yokohama have rooms."

"I will not stand for that," Kenji said. "Let me see what I can do."

"You're so kind," Irene said.

"Oh, it is nothing," he replied. "And guess what? You are all going to dinner with us this evening as our guests."

Jinne turned to Donald and gave him a hug. "It's so good to see you again. We will spend much time together over the coming days. We've obtained tickets to Kabuki Theater, with its exciting expressive costumes and masks. Would you like to go?"

The boy bobbed his head eagerly.

"And here's a gift: a book on *Origami*, the Art of breathing life into paper by *folding* it," Kenji said. "Look, it shows you how to create a turtle, a swan, and a butterfly!"

Donald looked at Jinne and Kenji. "Thank you so much!" he said, and threw them each a kiss.

An hour later, the Mashbirs were checking in at the Grand Hotel. The front desk clerk bowed.

"It is my honor to have you as our guests. Here are the keys to one of our best rooms; a gift from your friend, General Matsumoto."

As they walked to their room, Irene softly asked, "Sidney, did you really call from San Francisco to let the members of the Pan Pacific Club know we were coming?"

"Just a white lie to keep things friendly. I tested those letters; lots of strangers' fingerprints all over them. Welcome to the new Japan."

Over the next few days, the Mashbir and Matsumoto families strolled the lively streets of Yokohama, including the Benten-dori Shopping District, surrounded by vendors hawking succulent skewers of shrimp and fish, and selling bamboo flutes and trinkets. "It's amazing how Yokohama has rebuilt since the earthquake," Sidney said. "And even Tokyo, I've heard, now has so many modern buildings and broad streets brightly illuminated by neon and incandescent lights, that it matches New York City's Theatre District on Broadway!"

Kenji and Jinne smiled with pride.

A gentleman called from a shop doorway, "Would you like a group photograph, to remember your good times together?"

"Sounds like fun," Donald said. "Can we, please?"

Mr. Enami, the photographer, was soon arranging the group: "Young man, please move to the center; ladies are behind him, and on either side of the boy. Esteemed gentlemen, please stand adjacent to your lovely wives."

He cloaked himself beneath a black cloth and peered through his lens.

"Stand perfectly still, smile, and hold it. My dry-plate method won't take very long…"

They cheerfully exited the studio, photos in hand, and continued their way down the main boulevard.

"What are we doing tomorrow?" Donald asked.

"This is our last day all together," Sidney replied. "We'll be in To-kyo for the next few weeks, and Kenji will be returning to military duty tomorrow." The boy looked disappointed.

"Yes, Donald," Kenji said. "So let us appreciate the present moment even more."

Donald nodded, his spirit brightened.

"Sidney," Kenji said, "I need a private word with you." Once they'd moved off a distance, he said, "All looks safe, calm, and stable, but it is not so. Please be very careful, my brother."

"Thanks for the advice."

Kenji looked into Sidney's eyes.

"During the earthquake, Sidney-san, you vowed as a Samurai not to publicly release those nightmarish photographs of my people. You kept your word."

"Yes, and together we worked to prevent a plague."

He grasped Kenji's hand. "May our friendship hold strong through the times ahead."

They returned to see Jinne stroking Donald's hair. "I'll miss you so much," she said.

Donald forced a smiled, revealing several missing baby teeth. "And I will miss you…I love you Aunt Jinne and Uncle Kenji."

Imperial Hotel, Tokyo, the following day

With luggage piled high, the family waited to check in.

Donald tapped his father's arm and pointed. "Look, Daddy, why is your name on that poster?"

There on the lobby bulletin board was an announcement:

> *The physicist Dr. Niels Bohr, and Sidney F. Mash-*
> *bir, past director of the Tokyo Pan Pacific Club, will be*
> *guests of honor at a Pan-Pacific luncheon to be held to-*
> *morrow afternoon at 1 P.M. in the banquet room.*

Sidney looked bewildered. "Donald, you're quite observant."
Irene was looking at her son with pride, when the hotel manager, Mr.
Ito, appeared.

"Mashbir, my friend, you're here with your family—how wonderful! We've anticipated your visit and reserved a fine room. You are our
special guest after many years away. There will be no charge for your
first week. I know earlier you were told there was no room reserved
for you, but that was only a mistake: They misspelled your name."

With good spirits he said, "Follow me," as bellhops brought along
their luggage.

Once in their room, Irene and Sidney laughed over their good
fortune, while Donald jumped on his bed like a trampoline.

"Who is Dr. Niels Bohr?" Irene asked.

"He's a highly respected physicist; I look forward to hearing his
presentation."

"I hope it isn't as confusing as my high-school science courses."

"At least now you won't be tested on it," Sidney said with a smirk.

"Stop showing off—science is second nature for an engineer!"
She playfully poked her husband, then turned to Donald, "We'll be
leaving you with one of the hotel staff and will return in a couple of
hours."

As they entered the Imperial Hotel's Banquet Room, Sidney's past
friends and colleagues warmly greeted him and Irene...When the approximately two hundred attendees had finished their lunch, Baron
Tadashiro Inouye, president of the organization, spoke. "Ladies and
gentleman, it is my pleasure to welcome our honored guests. Many
of you already know Sidney Mashbir as one of the founders of our

Tokyo Pan Pacific Club, back in the early 1920s." The baron turned to Sidney, who was seated next to him, and shook his hand. "It's wonderful to see you again, my friend."

Sidney stood.

"My sentiment as well, Baron Inouye. And I thank you all for keeping the club alive!" He bowed to his audience. "I've been away from Japan fourteen long years; it's about time I returned. I'm here both for business and to celebrate our wedding anniversary—a second honeymoon, so to speak. My wife, Irene,"—he directed his gaze toward her—"and I look forward to rekindling old friendships, and making new ones. In a week from now, I'll be contacting some of you for assistance in researching possible locations for a cement mixing plant, which utilizes my new, improved methods for stronger concrete...*By then*, the honeymoon will be over, and business will begin."

He threw Irene a kiss and signaled her to rise.

"This is my beloved wife."

She stood, smiled, and nodded respectfully in all directions, but took Sidney's advice to say nothing and keep her eyes and ears open.

Baron Inouye continued, "Esteemed guests, it just struck me: here I am a Japanese professor of Metallurgy, introducing an American engineer, followed by our guest speaker, a Danish physicist. Perhaps, *science* will become the universal language bridging nations?"

He turned toward the speaker.

"It is my pleasure to introduce Dr. Niels Bohr! Let me speak briefly of his accomplishments: He received a Nobel Prize in 1922 for his research, and now travels the world lecturing about the wonders of the atom. In Copenhagen, he heads the Institute for Atomic Studies, bringing together the greatest minds in the field of theoretical physics."

The baron bowed to Dr. Bohr, who came to the lectern.

"I'm privileged to speak before such a distinguished gathering. And don't worry, it will only take ten minutes to describe my twenty years of research," he said, smiling.

Irene turned to Sidney, feigning a yawn while squeezing his knee playfully under the table. He gave her a mock look of disapproval.

Dr. Bohr, with enthusiasm explained that everything in the entire world was composed of approximately one hundred different elements. And that each of these elements was made up of minute atoms unique to that element. He then stated that he was the first physicist to describe the basic microscopic structure of these atoms.

He emphasized that only a limited few elements were radioactive and unstable, pointing to a diagram behind him, which he called a *Periodic Element Chart.* "When the universe was formed," he stated, "an enormous amount of energy went into the creation of these elements. The goal of my research is to bombard the atomic core of these unstable radioactive elements so they violently explode, their fragments colliding with other atoms nearby, with them also exploding—repeating itself over and over again, until it results in a billion-fold chain reaction, unleashing the enormous energy that they contained, to power huge ships, generate electricity for cities, and serve a myriad of other uses—Thus making life better for humanity."

Dr. Bohr looked at his watch. "Hmm, under ten minutes, as I promised. Are there any questions?"

Sidney turned to Irene and whispered, "What he's *also* talking about is an all-powerful weapon."

"Who funds your research?" an attendee asked.

"Obtaining funding isn't easy. It's a joke in our lab: You see, our main support comes from a foundation set up by the Carlsberg Brewery of Denmark. So remember," he smiled, raising his glass, "when you drink Carlsberg beer, you're supporting scientific research."

The audience broke into laughter.

Another attendee spoke, "Thank you for the presentation, but on a personal note, is it true you once wanted to be a professional soccer player?"

"I wasn't good enough," Bohr replied. "Though my brother made the 1908 Danish Olympic team. If I'd been a better player, the current state of physics might have been delayed a dozen years, but others would have certainly come up with similar theories." After several additional questions, the luncheon came to an end.

Sidney turned to Irene, "I'd like to speak to Dr. Bohr. Please wait for me in the reception area." She walked leisurely down the hallway and settled into a seat in the hotel lobby, near two men, who had their backs toward her.

"General Anami, you see how impressive his credentials are?" one of the men said. "The best scientists will follow him wherever he goes. If you could only convince him to bring his research team to Japan, your country would become a leader in Atomic Energy."

"I've already spoken to him," Anami replied. "He's hesitant, says he needs time to consider. I never asked you—how did you get him to accept our invitation?"

"I pulled strings for his friends and family in Germany, so they could escape to Denmark. With the current situation, he would never work directly for us, because his mother is Jewish—So it was decided, if Germany can't have his expertise, our future ally Japan should receive it."

"That is most appreciated," Anami said.

Irene quietly tiptoed away, blending into a gathering at the far corner of the room.

Elsewhere, Sidney and Dr. Bohr were in the midst of a conversation.

"Doctor, you describe the enormous energy being released. Are you sure you'll be able to contain the process once it begins?"

"A good question. Yes, the results might well surprise us. At first, only a limited amount of fuel will be used. We'll be cautious until we have some precedents to go by."

"Is there a chance it might first be turned to destructive uses, before it goes the path of benefiting mankind?"

Wiping his forehead with a handkerchief, Bohr replied, "As with all new technologies, politicians make decisions—and scientists hope for the best."

Irene came near and heard Bohr's remark.

"Excuse me, Sidney, might you introduce me to your new acquaintance?"

"Why certainly—this is my wife, Irene."

Dr. Bohr turned to her. "My pleasure," he said.

"Science wasn't my favorite subject, but your presentation was very interesting," Irene said sweetly. "I'm just curious, though—are you returning to Denmark soon?"

Where's she going with this, Sidney wondered.

"I've heard," she continued, "that you're considering relocating your research facilities to Japan?"

There was a flash of surprise on Bohr's face.

"I haven't decided yet. How did you know about that offer?"

"Someone made a comment during lunch. Are you visiting Japan by yourself?"

"Yes, my wife and sons are back in Copenhagen."

"Sidney and I are traveling with our seven-year-old, Donald."

We certainly don't want this brilliant researcher bringing this technology to Japan, Sidney thought, *considering we might soon be facing off against her.* "Dr. Bohr," he said, "I've heard things are quit unstable in your neighboring country, Germany."

"I'm well aware."

"Do those Nazi fanatics have allies?" Sidney asked.

"There are ties to Mussolini in Italy and to Franco in Spain."

Sidney stared at him. "There are also rumors that the militants in Japan and Germany may soon be joining forces as well."

Bohr broke into a bout of loud coughing.

Reichmann turned to see him with the Mashbirs—and noted the distressed look on Bohr's face.

Irene offered Bohr a glass of water.

"Enough depressing talk," she said, waiting for Bohr to compose himself before she continued. "Perhaps for fun, we can get together for dinner tomorrow. I've always wanted to learn what life is like in Denmark."

Looking toward Sidney, she added, "My husband promises to keep the conversation more convivial."

As Dr. Bohr moved toward the exit, Reichmann stepped forward quickly to intercept him.

"My friend, you did an excellent job describing your research."

"Herr Reichmann, I truly appreciate all you've done for me, but

I'm having second thoughts about relocating to Japan. Please convey my thanks to General Anami for his generous offer, and let him know I'll get back to him if I change my mind."

Sidney pulled Irene aside to a quiet spot and asked, "How did you know he was considering moving his research facilities?"

She smiled. "You suggested I keep my eyes and ears open."

"Very well done for an amateur."

"Amateur!" She affectionately bumped her hip into his. "What were you saying earlier about this being our second honeymoon?"

They left holding hands.

That evening, Reichmann, General Anami, and several of their aides gathered in the private back room of a restaurant. "Gentleman," Reichmann began, "a goal I've worked long and hard for has just been stolen from me!" He directed his gaze at Anami. "And from you, General!"

"What do you mean? Has Dr. Bohr rejected our offer?"

"I'm afraid so," Reichmann replied. "That engineer-businessman Mashbir is likely responsible. Years ago, I dealt with his arrogance when I was stationed in Washington, D.C."

One of General Anami's aides, Colonel Hashimoto, came forward. "He was once in the military and has close ties with the Prime Minister and other high-ranking Japanese."

Reichmann grasped his triple chin.

"We must eliminate him."

Is Herr Reichmann lying? General Anami considered. *Perhaps he wishes to take Bohr back to Germany instead, and killing Mashbir is a cover-up?*

Anami replied stiffly: "Based on Mashbir's connections, if we kill him there may be serious consequences."

"Regardless, we must find out why he is really here."

✳✳✳✳

"This sushi roll with eel tastes delicious!" Bohr loosened his belt a notch. "It was kind of you," he said, as he looked toward Sidney and Irene, "to invite me. There are few Japanese restaurants in Denmark." With a napkin he wiped his lips.

"If I remember correctly, Sidney, you're researching sites for a cement factory?"

"Yes, as well as observing where Japan's political climate is going."

"I sensed you were more than a businessman, based on your comments yesterday: I'm well aware that my research is a Pandora's Box. I've already assisted many German physicists so they could relocate to Denmark, out of the reach of the Nazis. But it's only a matter of time before that country starts devouring her neighbors."

"If you wished to relocate, America would open its doors."

"I appreciate the offer," Bohr replied frostily. "But what makes you think America should be trusted with so much power?"

"Just how powerful is it?" Irene asked.

Bohr heaved a deep sigh. "It releases the forces that created the universe! My *great fear* is that it could destroy humanity. Such knowledge should be shared; otherwise a single country might hang this weapon over the heads of all others."

Sidney leaned forward. "But, if too many countries possess it, what with violent *coups d'état* regime changes and international rivalries, it would be worse than giving loaded guns or sticks of dynamite to children and hoping for the best." He waited for his comment to sink in. "And considering the current instability, I don't understand why you remain in Denmark?" he asked.

Bohr shrugged his shoulders. "I've a working relationship with the Nazis. They're kept aware of my research—and they allow my Jewish friends and their friends to leave Germany for my country, Denmark.

"I'm very proud of the Danes; they've done all they can to shelter Jews. And if things turn bad in Denmark, it would be advantageous for me to be on good terms with the Nazis in order to negotiate for the eight thousand Danes of Jewish descent."

He's a brave man walking a tightrope, Sidney realized.

"I assume you hold back as much of your research as you can?"

"Of course."

"As for your earlier question why America should be entrusted with this new technology?" Sidney smiled. "I'll admit it: I'm prejudiced. Democracy is not a perfect system, but its ideals never change—to be a beacon of justice."

"You're quite a patriot!"

Sidney nodded. "Yes, I am! Now please excuse me, Niels, I just remembered I need to make a phone call."

After he left, Irene commented: "I know my husband has strong feelings. That's what I love about him. His life's purpose, above all else, is to realize America's potential to preserve peace, or, if that effort fails, to maintain our country's preparedness in the event of a war against aggressor nations."

"A tall order."

"But you're like him, Niels—trying to make sense of a violent world."

"He's a lucky man to have such an understanding wife."

She smiled. "And *your* wife is most fortunate to have such a compassionate husband."

"What does Sidney actually do back in your country?"

"He runs a research company that designs, oh, all sorts of things—improved gas masks in the event of germ or chemical warfare—Advanced electronic components for Aviation—both civilian and military."

"I imagine military contracts are quite lucrative?"

Irene laughed. "Sidney is full of contradictions! Very analytical on military and technical matters, and yet idealistic and sometimes naïve and over-trusting on a personal level. It's been a constant struggle to keep his company *solvent*, while playing totally by the rules. We manage—but he could have made a fortune, and that's fine by me."

CHAPTER 34

On a back street in Tokyo, at the end of an ill-lit alley, a tall man in a trench coat, his short-cropped hair covered by a cap, eyed the rear entrance of a building and slipped quietly inside. There, he was greeted by the oily smell of fish and the clatter of conveyor belts moving canned tuna. He took a long stare at his host, then smiled.

"Lieutenant Colonel William James, Military Attaché, at your service," he said, taking off his coat and hat.

"Nice to see you again, Bill," Mashbir replied. "Let's go to a quiet office to talk."

"You chose a unique setting." Bill held his nose. "I barely recognized you in that factory uniform, and your eyes look almost Asian."

"I'm being followed, and needed a disguise and an out-of-the-way location. I'm friends with the owner here."

"What brings you back to Japan?"

"Under the guise of finding a site for a new cement factory, I'm visiting every industrial complex, memorizing the locations of military factories and warehouses...Up to now, I've avoided our embassy and any contact with officers of the U.S. Army or Navy."

Mashbir then described his M-Plan with its network of informants who would be paid to observe the internal politics of Japan. They'd also scout out and monitor industries that were gearing up for war, while watching harbor and port activity for troop movements.

This strategic information could be transmitted into and out of the country through coded messages in magazine articles and advertisements, by using international business trade publications that operate during times of war and peace. Sidney emphasized, "My primary goal is to prevent war by assisting my Japanese allies in their struggle against their militants, while also sabotaging any alliance between them and the Nazis. But, if war does regrettably break out, this intelligence-gathering system will better prepare America to win it. I need your help Bill in setting it up and keeping it going once I leave."

"I'll do all I can," Bill replied. "But things are likely to blow at any time."

"I understand, and strongly recommend that you use lower-level go-betweens to distance you from the operation."

Mashbir opened a duffel bag.

"Included here are miniature radio transmitters of a totally new design, not detectable by ordinary means. And these are code books, and a list of publications and contacts."

He presented several stacks of currency.

"This should be enough to fund it for a long spell, and more will be coming...We'll also need to create a red herring: Pay off a couple of workers at the Japanese Embassy who will of course inform on us. In the meantime, our real organization does the job."

Around noon the following day, Sidney left the Imperial Hotel, with two men across the street ready to follow him. The prior day he'd somehow given them the slip, but they weren't going to let that happen again. Suddenly, there was a crashing sound and someone shouting. An old woman pointed, directing police officers toward the two men. "They broke that store window!" she said with sincerity.

"That's a lie!" the men protested, as the police dragged them away.

Moments later, Mashbir slid into the backseat of a black sedan with tinted windows.

"Don't just sit there, get moving!" Prince Tokugawa ordered his driver, then smiled. "This cat-and-mouse game is exciting," he declared—and then handed a decorative box to Sidney:

"It's a gift," said the Prince.

The contents made Sidney aware that he had not till that moment noticed the Prince was not wearing his usual Western attire, but instead black ceremonial robes.

"What a beautiful kimono. Thank you!"

Their car soon pulled up in front of a small inn.

"I've asked them to allow you to use one of their rooms to change your clothing. Sidney, I know you're an American, and proud of it, but in your soul there is a part that is also Japanese. It would be helpful if you wore your gift to our gathering."

He soon found himself wearing a true work of art. The decorated kimono was dark brown with a hint of blue. It had a picture-book theme with ornate covers and illustrations inside that revealed traditional Japanese scenes of pavilions, trees, and foliage—with mountains and a steep-roofed temple in the distance—all enveloped by beautiful skies with vaporous clouds.

Once back at the limo, Sidney turned in a graceful circle to display his gift from Prince Tokugawa, who remained seated inside.

"It is quite becoming," Tokugawa beamed.

Sidney reentered the car, and off they drove.

"It's made from Tsumugi silk from handspun thread," explained Tokugawa. "I had also considered a fearsome tiger, a dragon, or a hawk design, but felt that you are at heart a scholar, and not solely a warrior...So I chose the theme of books and art."

"I will always treasure it."

They traveled then in silence toward the Imperial Palace.

Meanwhile, in Hirohito's reception chamber, there was shouting — Prince Konoe and Emperor Hirohito faced one another.

"I'm sorry to raise my voice, but enough, Hirohito, I mean Your Majesty!" Konoe said through clenched teeth. "I wish I could, but I am not able to do what you request!"

Hirohito countered: "We need your help now more than ever."

"It will be a waste of time," Konoe replied.

When Prince Tokugawa and Sidney entered the chamber, Sidney bowed to the Emperor and Konoe.

"It is a great honor to see you both again," he said.

Hirohito calmed himself, then smiled.

"When first we met, Sidney-san, I was a young Crown Prince excitedly giving you a tour of my fish collection, while hiding from the outside world. And here I am *now*, an emperor with the responsibilities of a nation on my shoulders."

Gazing upon Konoe's distraught face, Tokugawa understood. "Dear Konoe, might you and I speak privately before we all lunch together?"

They left Mashbir and Hirohito to chat, as they went to an adjacent room, where Tokugawa inquired, "Konoe, do you remember the stories I told you and Hirohito when you were young men?"

With frustration, Konoe replied, "What is it you wish me to have gained that fits the current crazy world we live in?"

Tokugawa patiently stared at him.

Konoe felt trapped.

"I apologize for my lack of respect, Uncle. This situation is very difficult."

"I understand, and I appreciate your listening to what I have to say: First, when a leader in his heart knows what is best, he does not let others stop him. Second, when dealing with what appear to be impossible domestic issues, you must form alliances with outside nations."

Tokugawa smiled.

"Hirohito and I feel you are most capable, and indeed the natural choice to become the next Prime Minister. With you in that position, we would have a better chance to prevent war."

"But I'm only one man!"

"There are many others who agree with our position. On the surface, you'll cooperate with the militants. But secretly, you'll be working with our Western allies to neutralize the actions of these fanatics. Otherwise, Japan is on a course towards self-destruction."

"This is not a game and I'm not as good an actor as you might suppose."

"Don't underestimate yourself; I saw your great potential when you were young. You must at least attempt this venture."

Konoe bowed.

"For no one other than you and the emperor, would I even consider such a course. I will abide by your wisdom and hope for the best."

"I respect your courage."

Sidney noticed Konoe's despondent look when they returned. To his surprise, Empress Nagako entered soon after, accompanied by servants laden with food and drink and three musicians.

"Dear Nagako, perfect timing!" Tokugawa exclaimed.

As the gathering enjoyed their meal, musicians performed on classical Japanese instruments. Sidney particularly appreciated the beautiful *Koto*, a six-foot-long, thirteen-stringed zither made of golden Paulownia wood and inlaid with ebony and tortoise shell. As it was plucked by one of the musicians, another stroked a three-stringed lute, while the last played a wooden flute.

Once the meal was over, Tokugawa gestured that they should relocate to the library, where Sidney perused the shelves: *A window to the heart and mind can be seen in one's book selections*, he reflected. The topics included history, politics, and religion; travel guides, adventure novels, and science texts, along with metaphysics, philosophy, and a large section on Marine Biology.

They sat in armchairs in a circular arrangement.

Mashbir seated himself last, allowing the others to organize in whatever positions they felt appropriate. He scanned the serious faces and sensed uncertainty. The last time he'd seen Crown Prince Hirohito, he was the age of a college student, slim built, with a full head of black hair. Now, his face had broadened, with worry lines around his eyes, and with his metal-rimmed glasses, he looked more like an accountant.

Perhaps they wish me to break the ice, he thought.

"Emperor, I see your interest in fish has continued. You've quite an extensive library."

"In another life, I would have been a Marine Biologist," Hirohito shrugged, then turned to Nagako.

"My wife is present, because she often advises me in matters of state."

The Empress expressed how she and her husband well remembered Mashbir's assistance many years ago, in putting down a rebellion that could have led to war. They also appreciatively recalled

Mashbir's leadership role during the earthquake relief effort. She turned to Prince Tokugawa.

"And our Dear Uncle speaks highly of your modernization of our farm technology to better feed our people."

"You're too kind with your praise, Your Majesty."

Nagako shook her head. "You deserve it. We now hope you might again work with us in these troubled times."

She rose and moved toward Sidney, took his callused hand with her delicate fingers and placed a small kiss upon the top of his hand before returning to her seat adjacent to her husband.

Mashbir blushed, and searched for words.

"*Thank you* for bringing me into your confidence and allowing me to hear of how we might again work together to maintain goodwill between our nations."

Holding up a crystal goblet filled with sweet liquor, Hirohito toasted, "Here's to Sidney Mashbir, a man who bridges East and West!"

A long silence followed, broken by Prince Tokugawa, who spoke remorsefully. "We were so close to having Japan chosen for the 1940 Olympics, an opportunity to proudly display our culture to the world—and I would have presided over that wonderful event. But these violent fools dashed my dream!"

His hands trembled, and he held back tears.

"Dear Uncle," Hirohito said, "I promise you we'll bring the following one to Japan."

"Perhaps it will be so," Tokugawa replied, looking away wistfully.

The Emperor again lifted his goblet and stepped toward Tokugawa.

"Here's to you, Dear Iyesato. You have been more than an *Uncle*, more than a *Mentor*, like a *Father*, filling a great void in my life." Both men's eyes moistened.

All followed suit, raising their glasses to honor Tokugawa, then downing their drinks. After a pause, their focus redirected toward Sidney, who asked, "So how might I be of assistance?"

Prince Tokugawa began, "I'm well aware that General Watari has already spoken to you Sidney-san, describing events here spinning out of control. Normally, we would have an Admiral or Army General and/or two Aides-de-Camps, one from the Army and one from the Navy present during our discussion today. But these are uncertain times, with unclear allegiances, so we wished to keep our discussion as private as possible. This past year we faced another potential *coup d'état*. Next time, there will be no stopping them."

"Yes," Mashbir replied, "General Watari warned me he had overheard preparations for a major Japanese invasion of China. There was also discussion as to whether to have a surprise assault against America, using bombs. Some extremists even contemplated germ warfare involving Anthrax, Cholera, and other contagious diseases, requiring the release of hundreds of air balloons carrying these deadly agents to drift with the winds to your country—But they decided against it, fearing there would be similar retaliation." He hesitated, then added, "Another recommendation was the destruction of the Panama Canal, to disrupt the flow of supplies and military support between the East and West coasts of our nation."

Mashbir's stomach tightened.

Prince Tokugawa studied Sidney. "I advised General Watari to inform you of these matters—You, above all people I've met from your country, understand Japan. With your assistance, we can influence your top military officers and politicians to aid us."

"But Prince, I'm still a relatively low-ranking reserve officer and don't get all that much attention when I speak."

Tokugawa continued, "Sidney-san, Japan is in *kurai tanima*—a dark valley—with nowhere to turn and no one truly listening. The United States wishes us to resolve our internal problems without their support; which I frankly do not believe is possible. Your country's attention is directed at the inevitable war in Europe, not the one coming from Asia!"… He shook his head with bitterness. "What was effective for Fascists in Germany, is now being taught to our militants. Any books in our country challenging military expansion are censored, while hateful Nazi writings become best-sellers, poisoning the soul of Japan!"

Konoe added, "And there are new laws limiting free speech and assembly. Propagandists use newspapers and radio to promote a veritable Holy war between the White and Yellow Races and the expulsion of all Western powers. These militants *claim* Japan is liberating her Asian neighbors, but they will instead replace them as their new masters." There was a pause.

Nagako leaned forward, anxiously wringing her hands. "Schoolchildren are brainwashed by distorted textbooks and trained to march on school playgrounds with wooden rifles hung over their shoulders in preparation for war."

"It is mass suicidal hysteria," Hirohito said. "We wish we could speak openly, but our opposition grows stronger daily."

Tokugawa softened his voice, trying to calm everyone's emotions: "I feel certain this major assault against China will be launched this summer. If they are not stopped there, the Philippines will be next. If that happens, the U.S. will certainly be drawn in."

Tokugawa put his hand to his chest, flinching in pain. All hovered around him.

"Are you all right?" Sidney asked.

"My health is far from good," he replied.

Here is the one man that holds this country together, Sidney thought. *Who can fill his shoes?*

"You must immediately seek medical specialists," he urged.

"I've already secretly done so, or I would not be here today. But enough of my condition!"

He turned to Konoe.

"I'm proud to announce, Prince Konoe will soon become Prime Minister."

Konoe stood and in a controlled, dignified fashion said, "Colonel, *our goal* is to work with your country to maintain our long, peaceful relationship of mutual respect and prosperity. I have been complimented on my diplomatic skills and will do my utmost to get along with the Japanese militarists, giving the illusion of moving toward war, *but secretly* cooperating with your country to undermine their efforts."

"So in essence," Tokugawa interjected, "Colonel Mashbir, we want you to advise your superiors that conflict will temporarily expand in China—But Prince Konoe will contain it. We are hopeful that your people will work with us."

"I'll do my very best to convey your message," Mashbir replied, "But I urge you to directly contact as many others in my government as you can."

The Emperor walked over to Mashbir.

"And for that, my friend, we all thank you. Let us hope and pray for the best."

Hirohito's serious demeanor changed, as he added, "And, I must say, Sidney, you look quite stylish in your kimono," which brought smiles to all.

CHAPTER 35

The long nails of Reichmann's left hand clawed at the wooden arm of his chair. "Frau Kuhn," he roared into the phone receiver, "Where have been! I've been waiting to hear from you!"

"How pleasant to again hear your powerful voice, Herr Reichmann. Always so impatient. Not good for your health, you know. Here in Honolulu, things move at a slower pace," she paused, then added, "And yes! I've done as you requested."

"Give me the details, damn it!"

She laughed. "It's quite ironic that I should be ordering our agents in America to spread incriminating rumors to government and military agencies, against a man who was recently warning officials in Hawaii *that I and my sweet family were spies!* Can you imagine?

"We've gained access to many of Mashbir's records, and guess what? There are hints of his active involvement in uprooting our own spy networks in America, before and during the last war."

"Really? Well it's time to pay him back."

With a conspiratorial tone, Reichmann spoke to General Anami. "My sources tell me that Mashbir's an undercover agent, but in spite of his high-level contacts in Japan, he hasn't much standing or influence in his own country."

Anami straightened his eyeglasses. "It illustrates how little the West understands the ways of Japan. Since his arrival, my men have been arrested on trumped-up charges, and money is being paid for Intelligence information. He sticks his nose everywhere, scouting for a factory site while obviously spying."

"He thinks we're sleeping fools," Reichmann replied, "as he hides behind the royal family!"

"What do you suggest?"

"We destroy whatever Intelligence network he's created and teach him a lesson he won't forget."

"My resources are at your disposal."

✳✳✳✳

The Imperial Hotel's dining room ceiling was forty-feet high, illuminated by colorful stained-glass fixtures, with a great deal of natural morning also streaming in. Geometrically decorated panels adorned the walls; broad stone columns gave support. It was filled with tourists and businessmen enjoying breakfast.

A waiter approached Irene and Donald with their menus.

"Where is Mienshi?" Irene asked him.

"He is very busy in kitchen. My name is Gunji; I am your waiter today."

"I don't wish to offend you, but could you please let Mienshi know that Mrs. Mashbir and her son would greatly appreciate his service? You see, we're leaving Japan soon, and he's been our waiter during our entire stay and has become a friend."

Back in the kitchen, Gunji put a butcher knife to Mienshi's throat and led him into the stockroom.

"If you signal them in any way, I'll murder you and your family," he said, pulling up his shirtsleeve to reveal a muscular forearm with the insignia of the Black Dragon.

"I'll, I'll do as you say," Mienshi replied.

Gunji emptied a vial of clear liquid into two glasses of water.

"Go serve them this health tonic and take their breakfast order as usual."

At their table, Mienshi feigned a smile.

"I hope we didn't cause inconvenience by asking for you?" Irene said.

"No problem." He placed one glass in front of Donald, but as he did so for Irene, his shaking hand lost its grip, her glass shattering on the travertine tile floor.

The manager rushed over.

"Clean up this mess!" he shouted.

With sweat running down his forehead, Mienshi grabbed Donald's glass and returned to the kitchen, where Gunji was nowhere to be seen. Mienshi hurried back to their table, ready to mop and sweep up.

Donald noticed Mienshi's nervousness.

"Don't feel too bad—we all make mistakes," Donald said.

When the manager was out of earshot, Mienshi looked intently at them. "Dear most honorable Irene and Donald, the food here is not so fresh anymore; manager buys old produce to save money. I recommend you try another restaurant."

Sensing something wrong, Irene took Donald's hand and left.

During the return-voyage stopover in Honolulu, passengers moved through customs promptly—that is, until the Mashbir family reached the waiting officials—who appeared to be anticipating their arrival.

"Sidney Mashbir, will you, your wife, and son seat yourselves down," an official said, pointing to a wall lined with chairs. "We need to search your baggage."

Sidney nodded agreeably. "Okay. I do have purchases from Japan, and in order to avoid customs delays, I've prepared a typed inventory. The articles are tagged and a receipt is attached to each item."

Irene noticed the officials gave little attention to anything her husband had said. The family watched as their possessions were examined with extreme care, not once, but three times. *Something extraordinary is going on,* Sidney realized. "I demand to see the chief customs inspector," he said.

This resulted in their luggage being taken into a private inspection room, and the hours passed.

It was near midnight when Irene and Sidney, with sleeping Donald in his arms, checked in at their hotel. After tucking the little guy into bed, Irene turned to her husband. "They're treating you as if you're a foreign spy or a smuggler."

"I'm under suspicion for something, that's for sure."

At the same moment, both declared, "What a day!" bringing laughter and hugs as they went to bed, expecting tomorrow to be better.

Sidney gave a big yawn as he picked up the hotel room phone early the next morning.

"Mr. Mashbir, this is Officer Gregory, Chief Customs Inspector. I need to speak to you."

"What about?"

"Those possessions you brought into the country yesterday. I'm downstairs."

Sidney's voice rose, "*We waited ten hours yesterday* to get out of your station. You'll just have to wait a couple of hours for us to eat and dress," he said, and hung up.

"Try not to antagonize the man," Irene advised. Sidney reluctantly nodded.

Exactly two hours later there was a knock at their door. Sidney opened it, extending his hand with a tight smile.

"Hello. Good to meet you, sir." They shook hands. "How can we be of service?" he asked, shooting a glance toward Irene, acknowledging her advice.

"About yesterday—my men were just doing a thorough job. I've got a suggestion: To avoid further difficulties, I recommend you come to my office to have the things you acquired in Japan bonded for the remainder of your trip to the States."

"I'll get right on it. Anything else?"

"Just you take care now," the inspector said, in what Sidney felt was a menacing tone.

As soon as the official was gone, Sidney turned to his wife and son, who had been listening.

"I'll be back in an hour or two."

"Please control your temper," Irene said, with Donald nodding in agreement.

Four hours later, Sidney's strained expression transformed into a smile as he returned to the hotel lobby and beheld Donald and Irene blissfully reading magazines under whirling fans, sipping tropical drinks. "Can you get me one of those, but with a punch to it?" he called out to a waiter.

"Hello Darling," Irene said. "Have that drink first, then let's talk."

He sat in a rattan chair and gulped down his drink.

"It's crazy—those guys at customs went through my stuff another three times before bonding it."

"At least that's out of the way," she said, taking his hand. "What shall we do with the rest of this beautiful day? Maybe a bus tour of the island...?"

To his surprise, upon their return at the end of day, Sidney discovered a card in his hotel mail slot requesting an official meeting the following afternoon. *When is this charade going to end,* he wondered.

He dragged himself to the office of Colonel Thornton, the Intelligence agent assigned to the G-2 Hawaiian Department.

As soon as Sidney entered, and without so much as a hello, Thornton dug in. "Take a seat," he ordered, pointing to a chair. "I want to know everything you've seen, done, and who you've been with since you left the States. Don't leave out a single detail, or else!"

Sidney replied calmly, remembering his promise.

"You've no right to ask about my personal visit to the Orient. I've committed no crime, nor been charged with any. If you can tell me what this is all about, I'd be better able to cooperate."

"Okay, I'm following up on a telegram from Tokyo, stating you have some kind of valuable intelligence about the Far East. Is that so?"

I have to be very selective who I open up to, or I put Prince Konoe's life in danger, not to mention jeopardizing my M-Plan.

"Your sources are incorrect—I don't have any such information."

"So that's the way you want to play it! Just get out of my sight."

Thornton was soon dictating a letter to his secretary:

> *"The questioning of reserve officer Sidney Mashbir has just been completed. The suspect was totally uncooperative. He did let slip that he possessed significant information from the Far East which he refuses to share with G-2 Army Intelligence. I recommend he be carefully observed and prevented from having access to any security information. I also advise he be put on any and all lists of persons who pose a risk to national security. Signed, Colonel Thornton."*

"Now send this out, ASAP."

CHAPTER 36

The Mashbirs were spending a week in Los Angeles, before taking a Pan Am flight back home to Washington, D.C. The sound of laughter and splashing water filled the air, while warm Southern California sunlight shined down upon father and son, as they stepped out of the bustling hotel swimming pool.

Sidney grabbed a couple of towels, handing one to Donald. They sat under a colorful beach umbrella sipping soda pops, while Sidney proudly inspected his muscular young son. *That's strange,* he thought, seeing sweat bead down the boy's forehead, even in the shade. *Perhaps he's under the weather?* He put a hand on Donald's forehead.

"Irene, come over here," he called. "Donald's got a high fever."

She checked his brow and neck lymph nodes. "He's burning up!"

They rushed to L.A. General Hospital, checked him in and waited until a physician came out to meet them.

"Hello, I'm Dr. Cooper. You were right to bring Donald here immediately. We've given him medication and a cool bath to lower his temperature. There's weakness of limbs and some difficulty breathing."

"What could it be?" Sidney asked.

"We'll talk this evening after we've completed lab tests. You both get some rest in the meanwhile."

On their return, the doctor met them in the Contagious Illness Ward reception area. "I didn't want to worry you earlier," he said, while looking sadly downward, "but our specialists, Dr. Cobb and Dr. Moore, feel certain your son has Infantile Paralysis, also known as Poliomyelitis. Most forms of this disease don't actually cause paralysis, but five percent have that potential. Unfortunately, Donald appears to be part of that five percent."

"What can we do?" Irene asked, tears flowing.

"Not much right now. He needs lots of bed rest, and we'll monitor his respiration. It will take months to see where the chips lay in terms of his prognosis."

"He's always been so healthy. How could he catch this?" Sidney almost demanded.

The doctor took a breath, then rubbed his weary face. "I know it's hard to accept, but there's been an epidemic from travelers returning from Africa, the Middle East, and the Philippines. This past year alone, L.A. General has treated twenty thousand cases. That's fifty new ones a day, and no one's sure when it's going to end."

"Are there medications that can fight it?" Irene asked.

"There are experimental serums derived from the blood of horses, and others from the ground-up spines of monkeys infected with the illness. None have proven effective, and some actually caused harm," he sighed. "Now remember, take care of yourselves. Donald will need all your support. He's in good hands. I'll see you tomorrow."

After the doctor left, Sidney spoke to Irene in a choked-up voice. "My older son, Forrester, doesn't even want to see me, and now our son, Donald, is very ill...Things are falling apart, and I'm to blame; I should never have taken you both with me on that trip."

She looked into his shadow-encircled eyes, as her fingertips gently brushed the side of his face. "It's not your fault, my love."

L.A. General Hospital, three weeks later

"Mom, Dad, I wish we could all go home," Donald declared, while covered under a heavy blanket in bed.

"Your strength will return—you'll see," his father replied. "We'll be back in a minute son." Sidney and Irene stepped just outside the room.

"I don't see much positive change," Irene whispered. "He just lies there as helpless as ever."

"I swear, I don't know what to do," he replied.

A young nurse arrived. "Hope I'm not intruding. I need to take some readings on your son."

"Alright," Irene replied, drying her eyes. "Can we please stay?"

"Oh, that will be fine."

Sidney observed her going through various procedures.

She appears conscientious, but something's wrong—It's her expression after she took off the blanket and looked at Donald's legs.

"Ma'am, we're at our wits' end. Our boy hasn't walked for almost a month, ever since they put on those wraps."

After making sure no one was in earshot, the nurse explained she'd just graduated from nursing school. In the past, she said, that was the standard treatment. But during the last week of her semester, an instructor by the name of Elizabeth Kenny visited her school with a new protocol *she'd* created that involved massage, exercise, and covering the affected limbs with hot, moist compresses to reduce muscle spasms and the accompanying pain. She also stressed the importance of Psychotherapy in the treatment, insisting that children be strongly encouraged to move their paralyzed limbs. This new approach was contrary to accepted medical practice, which involved splints and casts to immobilize limbs, combined with prolonged bed rest.

"Does the traditional system generally work?" Irene asked.

"Sometimes it does, but many patients end up with atrophy and loss of flexibility in their already weakened limbs—However, this new system is considered experimental."

Moments later, Sidney was at the hospital front desk, requesting Dr. Cooper be paged.

Ten days later, Donald moved at a snail's pace, as Irene and Sidney accompanied him down the hospital corridor, each supporting one of his arms. "You keep this up, son, and you'll be running before long," his father encouraged.

"And when we're done, you'll have some ice cream," his mother promised.

"Can it be chocolate?"

As Donald savored his dessert, his parents and Dr. Cooper spoke privately.

"What do you think, Doc?" Sidney asked.

"So far, so good. We're trying that new technique with others, but even with the best care, there's still a fair chance he'll continue to have mobility issues."

Irene gave him a hug. "We so appreciate you trying out this approach," she said.

"I'm just a doctor, not a god. I learn something new every day."

A week later, Donald sat in wheelchair, whizzing around the park-like grounds of a convalescent home, laughing, as his father playfully steered.

"Sidney, I'd like to speak to you privately," Irene called out.

He left Donald under the shade of a tree and strolled over.

"Darling," she said, "I know you've been attempting to conduct business over the phone, but you have lots of projects waiting for you in D.C. I suggest you fly back by yourself. This place is working out fine. I'll rent a cottage nearby, and we'll stay until Donald's gotten stronger."

He hugged her.

"I'm going to miss you both so much, and I pray it won't be for too long!"

CHAPTER 37

As soon as the taxi delivered him to his residence, Sidney left his luggage in the entrance foyer and hustled to his garage; pumping the car's gas pedal and crossing his fingers as he turned the ignition key...On returning home from the post office, he carried a basket piled high with over two months' worth of mail, which he dumped on the kitchen table. Three groupings, he figured: the junk, the can-wait-till-later, and the important stuff. One letter appeared official, which he opened:

> *Colonel Sidney Mashbir, you are to report within fourteen days for a physical examination, so as to be reinstated as a Lieutenant Colonel, Military Intelligence Reserve.*

His jaw dropped. "Damn, it's dated over a month ago!"

Mashbir was soon facing a receptionist, as he leaned hard against the front counter of the military medical facility. "You're telling me I've lost my reserve status? There's no way I could have gotten here earlier. I've been active or reserve military for over twenty years."

The receptionist slid a form across the counter. "Sorry, but without formal approval from headquarters, we can't give you a physical at this time. Fill out this reconsideration request, and I'll pass it on."

"How long does that take?"

"It varies."

This can't be, Mashbir thought, as he dialed from the lobby's wall phone. "I want to speak to Commander Zacharias. I'm Sidney Mashbir, a colleague of his."

"I'm sorry, sir," the secretary replied. "Commander Zacharias is no longer in this department."

"Can you give me a number where he can be reached?"

"I'm not allowed to do that, sir."

"Then who's sitting at his desk now?"

"Commander Arthur McCollum."

It's getting worse by the minute, Mashbir thought.

"May I talk to Commander McCollum?"

He didn't have to wait long.

"What are you calling about, Mashbir?"

"Arthur," he replied, using an upscale tone, "it looks like whenever Zach takes off, they can confidently assign you to fill his position. I'm only trying to get in touch with him."

"I don't know what the Hell you did, but I'm not authorized to tell you anything!"

"Didn't Zach explain that he and Captain Puleston encouraged my recent trip to Japan?"

"Puleston's out. He's been replaced by Admiral Holmes, and I don't know anything about your visit to Japan."

He hung up.

That evening in Baltimore, Maryland, Unger, a solidly-built, middle-aged man focused on his reflection in a mirror as he pressed a mustache into place and waited for the glue to dry...He then again scrutinized a photo taped to the mirror, as he brushed gray coloring on the temples of his now neatly combed reddish-brown hair, instead of its usual tousled black...An hour later, he rang the doorbell of a Tudor-style home. An eye peered through the peephole, he heard a sliding deadbolt, and a man opened the door and said, "Good to see you again. Please sign in."

Unger leaned over the entry ledger, concentrating as he obliged. He ladled a cup of warm cider from a large pot simmering in the kitchen, the rich smell of apple and cinnamon sticks filling the air. He briefly mingled among the gathering, then filled his plate with assorted appetizers, and seated himself on a couch next to a woman wearing a wide-brimmed, black felt hat with protruding feathers, and began to eat.

"Why, this is the third week in a row I've seen you here." She extended her hand. "My name's Emma, and yours?"

"Sidney Mashbir."

"Pleasure to meet you, Mr. Mashbir. Rumor has it, our speaker tonight is a high-level official."

"How interesting." They spoke for a while as Unger studied the attendees, conversing, sitting in armchairs and couches, a crackling fireplace giving the room a warm crimson glow. Up front, stood a frail-looking man wearing bifocals, his unexpectedly strong voice bringing all to attention.

"Welcome to the Soviet-American Friendship Society, a patriotic international brotherhood. If there's anything this economic depression has proven," he said, slapping his hand on a table, "it is that no longer can the reins of power be limited to just a few selfish millionaires! We, the workers, must liberate humanity from exploitation. Our sympathizers in America now number in the thousands, but soon there will be millions!"

There was enthusiastic applause.

"We're fortunate," the speaker continued, "tonight we're going to be given a clear view of the future by someone highly placed in our federal government."

He turned to a man whose black bushy eyebrows framed a no-nonsense stare.

"My name's Henry Wallace," he announced. "I can assure you war is coming—and that an alliance with Soviet Russia will be crucial to America's victory."

"But isn't Stalin a brutal dictator?" someone asked.

Wallace smiled indulgently.

"His purges have mainly targeted the International Fascist Alliance who are trying to undermine his regime. If we're going to defeat Hitler and Mussolini, it will take the combined strength of the United States and Russia! Europe's too weak to do so on her own. Just look at Spain's democracy which collapsed last year, *and America did nothing*."

His voice took on a clandestine quality. "It can't be openly admitted, but officials high in our own government are planning to send vast convoys of food, Jeeps, and other military equipment to Russia. Their Port of Murmansk has been chosen for these shipments, as it is ice free most of the year."

A sly grin appeared on Unger's face; *Herr Reichmann will pay a nice bonus for that information,* he thought. *All it will take is a few German submarines to shut down that port.*

Wallace continued, "I know a number of you also work in government agencies. I invite you to share information you might have access to which can help our Russian friends. I'll make sure it gets to those who can use it. It's your patriotic duty!"

During the group's next weekly meeting, G-men smashed in the front door with a battering ram, and poured in. A throng of indignant men and women were dragged out in handcuffs and taken to waiting paddy wagons. An agent exited with the sign-in ledger under his arm. "Well, Adams," he said to a fellow agent, "that tip paid off. A major ring of Bolshevik infiltrators has been eliminated."

"Too bad we don't know who the informant was, Martinez," Adams replied.

"He sounded frightened—only gave the time and location."

✳✳✳✳

With disgust, Sidney was in the midst of re-reading the letter from the Army for the third time, stating they weren't going to let him back in, when he heard his doorbell ring. Two men in dark gray suits and hats were at his doorstep. One held up an I.D. folder. "We're from the F.B.I. You're Sidney Mashbir?" He nodded yes. "Well, I'm Agent Martinez, and this is Agent Adams. We'd like a bit of your time."

"What's this about?" Mashbir replied, keeping the door slightly ajar.

"It would be more comfortable for all concerned if you invited us in," replied Adams.

Over the next twenty minutes, the questions became increasingly hostile.

"Okay, that's it!" Mashbir shouted. "I've told you everything you need to know about my politics, religion, and love of country. This conversation is over!"

"Do you mind if we have a quick look around?" Adams asked.

Mashbir glared. "Only if you have a search warrant!"

"We can certainly get that," Martinez countered. "We're trying to handle this in an informal manner, which requires your cooperation. Since that's not the case, I must ask you to sign this form, stating you refused to give permission for a search of your premises."

Mashbir signed and thrust it back.

"Excuse us for a moment," Adams said. "I need to confer with my colleague."

They left and sat in their car, with Sidney observing them through his front window.

"You know, Adams, I did research; this guy's father was from Russia and so is his wife. His military records state he was born in South Carolina, but his birth certificate says New York City and gives another date. He's hiding something. What do you think?"

"Let's see if his signature matches the one in the ledger from that commie gathering," he said, comparing it to the document Mashbir had just signed.

"They look very similar," Adams said. "And the description from those birds we pulled in fits him close enough. He's our boy—arrogant, thinks he can brazen it out. Let's lean on him a little more."

The agents knocked on the door; Sidney came to the entrance with no intention of letting them in again.

"You'd best get off my property, and I mean right now. F.B.I. or no F.B.I., you're trespassing! Far as I know, nobody's done away with the Constitution just yet."

Martinez moved forward.

Adams placed a restraining hand on his partner's arm.

"We're leaving, but this matter is far from over. I'd be careful about

using that tone with federal law enforcement officers if I were you,"
he said, and they drove off.

It was well past midnight, when Unger cruised that same neighborhood in his shiny black sedan, parking in the alleyway behind
Mashbirs' home. Carrying a bundle of papers tied up with twine, he
walked around to the front of the house, where he put down his package. He then mischievously wedged a nail under one of the rear tires
of Mashbir's car which was parked in the driveway, and removed one
of the windshield wipers.

He then smirked, as he dumped his package into the street side
trash can...*If the Feds are doing a thorough job, this ought to provide some
interesting reading. Wait till they find these Daily Worker newspapers and
pamphlets from communist front organizations being thrown out in Mashbir's trash, as if he's trying to get rid of evidence.*

During the coming days, Mashbir heard clicking listening-device
sounds while making phone calls from his home, and his mail showed
signs of tampering. He saw agents canvassing nearby homes, doing
research on him. *Damn, just what I need,* he thought. *Now my neighbors
will be suspicious!* He slammed a fist into the wall; his unkempt hair
and unshaved face gave him the appearance of a desperado. A ringing phone grabbed his attention. "Who is it!" he asked.

"Excuse me, I must have dialed the wrong—"

"No, no, Irene, sorry for the harsh response. How are you and
Donald?"

"He's getting better little by little. We miss you. But how are you
managing?"

"To be honest, federal agents are driving me nuts. I'm being followed, and this phone is probably wire-tapped."

There was a long silence. "We've all been under a lot of pressure.
We'll be returning in a week or two and things will work out. Take
care of yourself."

"I can't wait to see you both. Please don't mention my problems to
Donald; he's got enough challenges of his own."

The few days later, Mashbir thought he was feeling pretty miserable already, when a telegram arrived from Colonel James, the military attaché back in Japan, telling him his M-Plan had been uncovered and all his recruited agents killed—and their equipment and code materials destroyed. James wasn't sure, but speculated that someone on their own side might have been involved?

It felt like an anvil had dropped on Sidney's head.

Dressed in pajamas, with his window shades drawn to block out the afternoon sunshine, Sidney slept, oblivious to the knocking that grew louder, accompanied by a ringing doorbell. The outside tapping on his bedroom window finally aroused him. He unlatched the front entrance deadbolt. Irene met him with a look of remorse mixed with anger.

"Sidney, my key doesn't open the door."

"I put in a new lock."

He tried to hug her. She resisted, frowning as she surveyed their home and the several empty liquor bottles scattered about.

"I'm sorry about the mess—"

She held up her hand to stop him.

"You know we've barely heard from you?"

"Didn't want to burden you." He dug his nails into his face, his voice strained. "I've been blackballed out of the military, my M-Plan's dead, G-2 and the Feds think I'm a *commie* or some sort of double agent. And our poor son Donald is…" He began to cry.

She hugged him. "You'd think Zacharias or Admiral King could help?"

He shook his head violently. "Zach is unavailable on some kind of secret mission, and Admiral King contacted J. Edgar Hoover himself, telling him about my work with the Washington Institute. Hoover shut him down, saying the Navy had no business interfering in Federal investigations of potential communists. Some sneaky bastards are trying to destroy me," he said, his voice rising.

Irene spoke softly. "Then I recommend you keep your head low and act like that animal who pretends to be dead—or these powerful people will keep attacking you."

"You mean *play possum*?"

"And live to fight another day. Now please wait here while I get Donald from the taxi."

Wearing metal leg supports, Donald entered. "Watch this, Dad!" he shouted, and haltingly walked the long stretch to his father. They embraced. "It's wonderful having you back and doing so well! You must have grown a couple of inches!"

Donald kissed him on the cheek.

"I really love you, Dad!"

Several months later, Washington, D.C., December 1937

High impacts resonated within the four-walled enclosure; there was lots of elbowing and pushing as both men tried to make their shots, sweat drenching their clothing.

"Is this a game of squash, or are you trying to kill or just maim me?" Zach asked.

"Where have you been?" Sidney replied. "I needed you to cover my ass. I've been hounded by the Feds and Military Intelligence as if I were Public Enemy Number One!"

Zach put down his racket and wiped his face with a towel.

"Well, I wasn't vacationing in the Greek Isles, and would have gotten back to you if I'd known. But don't worry, your problems will work themselves out."

They exited the court and sat on a bench.

"Sidney, I need your advice, that's why I contacted you as soon as I got back—*and* I guess, I missed your ugly mug," he added with a grin. His expression darkened as he continued, "What's your take on the recent sinking of the U.S.S. Panay?"

Mashbir bit the side of his lower lip while thinking.

"The fact that Japanese planes—with no provocation dive-bombed American and British ships in China, killing lots of civilians, leaves no doubt that they're hell-bent on overrunning all East Asia. Even if it means war with the West."

Zach sighed. "Thank God we've gotten appropriations for four new aircraft carriers, but it will take three years before they're operational. Meanwhile, the Japanese have seven aircraft carriers and are building more. Our latest Naval study on fleet readiness reveals that the Japanese have the best and close to the largest navy in the world. The Brits thought they did, but they put too much reliance on the almighty battleship, and are ignoring air power. And most U.S. admirals are stuck in the same rut."

Sidney's head started pounding as Zach detailed how the Japanese also had the best submarines and torpedoes, and their fighter planes were the most advanced in the world, with some of the best pilots, especially the naval ones.

Zach looked Sidney in the eye. "Both of us believe it's likely we'll have to fight Japan in an all-out war, but if it were tomorrow, I think we'd get our butts whipped."

Once back at his office, Mashbir put down his drafting instruments on the design table and picked up the ringing phone. "Hello, who is it?"

"Sidney-san?"

"Prince Tokugawa, is that you?"

"Yes, indeed!"

In spite of a weak voice, Mashbir noted exuberance in his reply. "It's wonderful to hear from you! How are you doing my dear friend?"

"Using an American colloquialism: *Don't ask.*"

The now seventy-four-year-old Prince Tokugawa turned somber. "Actually, I was recently again admitted to a hospital, suffering chest pains." He paused. "At that time, I was visiting my son and his family in Canada, when all hell broke loose in Nanking; the ground fell from beneath me— "I'm bitterly ashamed of the terrible violence. For years I've attempted to prevent our military presence there, while at the same time *trying to minimize casualties.* I did this by working through the Red Cross to create Safe Zones in cities like Shanghai for Chinese civilians caught in the crossfire, as well as for European refugees, including *your* people, escaping Nazi brutality."

"*My people?*"

"You are Jewish, are you not?"

"I've wrestled with religion," he replied.

"*Sidney,* we're also working on a declaration in our congress that would serve as the official authorization for the fair and humanitarian treatment to given to Jewish refugees residing in Japanese controlled regions. It will be called the Diet Declaration of 1938."

Something inside Mashbir resonated, hearing the benevolence Tokugawa had shown. "Dear Iyesato," he said, "*My people* and I thank you for your kindness." Though seven thousand miles apart, they felt the warmth between them.

Tokugawa continued.

"The Emperor and I were trying to defuse hostilities when the sinking of the U.S.S. *Panay* and those two British oil tankers added fuel to the fire. My good friend, you understand there are two Japans—one war-crazed militarists, the other a civilian government struggling to maintain peace. If your country over-responds, our government will topple."

A wheezing in the Prince's voice was noticeable. "We must prevent the *Panay* from becoming a battle cry! I need your advice on how best to make restitution."

Mashbir pondered. "I've got an idea," he replied, "But it requires a fair amount of work on *your* part."

"Go on."

"You might consider having schoolchildren and ordinary citizens gather money door-to-door to compensate the families of those killed or injured."

"Yes, I see it! We'll admit the attack was a mistake and write letters of regret to those suffering families; I'll also convince my colleagues to contribute to this worthy fund."

"There's one possible drawback, Your Highness. What if my government sees it as blood money and refuses your reparations?"

"Hopefully, you have an answer to your own question?"

"I'd suggest first going the unofficial route—directly to the American and British news media, expressing the heartfelt remorse of the Japanese people."

"You are one of my best advisors, Sidney-san!"

"I only offered you the shadow of a plan, and would be most satisfied to have one-half your energy and determination."

U.S. Embassy, Tokyo

Dressed elegantly in a three-piece suit, aided by a bronze-handled walking stick, Prince Tokugawa entered Ambassador Grew's office. He noticed Grew's awkwardness at his surprise visit, bringing on a stammer which Grew generally kept under control. "Welcome, Prince Tokugawa. How can I be of service?"

"I've come to extend deepest apologies to your government for recent events in China."

"Your condolences are most welcome."

"Thank you, but my visit goes beyond condolences," Tokugawa replied. "I felt great shame when I was informed of the violent cruelty in Nanking and Shanghai at the hands of Japanese soldiers who had lost their moral compass—probably the result of seeing the many deaths of their fellow comrades while fighting Chinese forces: Though of course, I realize my nation had instigated the conflict." Tokugawa sat and caught his breath…"Something has to be done to remedy this state of affairs," he declared.

"This is a complicated situation, Your Highness." Grew gestured with his arms thrown upwards, giving the message that he didn't know what to do.

"Dear Ambassador, I want you to be aware I've been using my influence as President of the Japanese Red Cross, while allying with the President of the Chinese Red Cross. We are working with a courageous French Jesuit priest named Jacquinot, who is acting as an intermediary between their nations' militaries, who refuse to speak to one another directly…

"Our goal has been the creation of *demilitarized Safe Zones*, where hundreds of thousands of Chinese civilians—men, women, and children, along with European refugees—can escape to, as we attempt to end or at least contain this conflict."

"*Safe Zones*, quite a benevolent gesture in the midst of the horrors of war," Grew replied, toying with his mustache. "I've never heard of that concept before. So my friend, how can I be of assistance?"

"For forty years, through good times, and some that were most challenging, I, as a humble representative of Japan, have worked with a half-dozen of your presidents in promoting amity between our nations."

Tokugawa smiled. "And now, *you and I*, will work together to prevent a few lunatics from misdirecting the fate of nations."

Grew eyed the prince inquisitively. "That's not going to be an easy task; the Panay Incident mirrors events that led to the battle cry, *"Remember the Maine!"* back in 1898—the spark that ignited the Spanish-American War."

"I'm well aware, but is that how *you* feel, Ambassador?"

Tokugawa gave him a cool stare.

"Of course not! When I first arrived here I was an outsider—ignorant of, and uncomfortable with your culture. Your friendship and support these past six years has opened my eyes to a great appreciation of Japan. I don't want war, and only wish I knew how best to avoid it."

"There is a way, Honorable Ambassador. Your wife, Alice, is a proud descendant of the great Commodore Perry, and I am a proud descendant of the Shoguns who welcomed him, and who negotiated a peace treaty that has lasted many decades. Just as it was for our ancestors, it is now *our obligation* to find a way for our nations to remain cordial. As I have already strongly and openly expressed, I wish China to remain stable and sovereign."

"What then, do you suggest *we* do?"

"Thank you, Joseph! That is what I wished to hear."

Iyesato placed a newspaper on Grew's desk.

"This is tomorrow's headline, which will appear in Japan, America, and Britain."

Grew read it aloud:

"'Prince Tokugawa of Japan forms Alliance with U.S. Ambassador Joseph Grew to compensate the families of those injured or killed during the Panay Incident.'"

"So you foresaw the future, did you?" Grew said, with a wry smile.

Tokugawa maintained a somber face. "Ambassador, I had little doubt of your compassion and wisdom in assisting me to resolve this matter."

Over the next several months, Tokugawa worked with Ambassador Grew and Cordell Hull, the Head of the State Department, moving through a complicated maze of negotiations. Grew graciously sent a letter to the Japanese donors, acknowledging their contributions and informing them of the establishment of a Japan–America Trust, whose mission statement was as follows:

> *Our hope is that the Japan-America Trust, which received its original impulse from the feeling of sympathy with which the news of the Panay incident was met in Japan, will become an important foundation in the maintenance of friendship between our peoples, symbolizing the generous feeling that has been manifested.*

Once tensions had been defused, General Anami visited, bowing low. "Prince Tokugawa, I must congratulate you on forestalling hostilities with the West. But how long can you prevent the inevitable?"

"For as long as I draw breath, General," Tokugawa replied, straightening his posture.

"Respectfully, I ask again. Can you not see how strong Japan is militarily, and that the moment is now right for conquest?"

"I have spoken!"

"Then I thank you for your time and patience." Anami left.

Just outside Tokugawa's estate, Anami returned to Reichmann, who had remained seated in his vehicle. Reichmann observed Anami's flushed face and guessed the outcome.

"When will you get rid of that old fool? He's been a thorn in our side for years."

"You'll never understand our ways!" Anami shouted. "That old fool, as you call him, is one of the patriarchs of our nation. He intimately knew my father, even my grandfather. I only wish he could be swayed to our side, but his health is failing and it is only a matter of time—once he's gone, *that will be when* we strike **with an iron fist!**"

CHAPTER 38

Office of Naval Intelligence, Washington, D.C., March 1938

Zacharias scrutinized his longtime friend seated in front of him: forty-seven years old, though he looked younger with a distinguished sprinkling of grey in his pencil-thin mustache. "Sid, I was asked to find someone who knows the Japanese mind intimately and has connections there. Naturally, I thought of you."

"So some bureaucrat finally wants to ask me what the Japanese are going to do next?" he replied dryly. "They don't know themselves; their leadership is changing all the time. And what difference does my opinion make anyway?"

Zach smiled. "That bureaucrat you're talking about is the President of these United States, and we're due at his place at eight-thirty tomorrow night. Can't tell anyone, not even our wives."

"You gotta be kidding—Roosevelt?" He searched Zach's eyes. "What's this really about?"

"That's for F.D.R. to know, and for us to find out. We drive to the back entrance of the White House grounds and they'll take us in. There's even a password…"

Secret Service Agents stood on either side of them, as they waited in the corridor outside the Oval Office, with two young Marine sentries on guard in front of the door. Mashbir was perspiring. He whispered to Zach, "This is unreal: For the past six months no one would even give me the time of day."

The door opened, and a thin man, conservatively dressed in a black suit, white shirt, and olive-green tie, emerged. "Commander Zacharias?"

"Yes, sir," Zach gestured. "And this is Sidney Mashbir, until recently, Lieutenant Colonel, Army Reserve."

"I'm Harry Hopkins. Please follow me, gentlemen."

Mashbir recognized Hopkins from magazine photos.

So this is Roosevelt's chief political advisor, who almost single-handedly is directing most of the major federal job creation projects.

With a nod from Hopkins, the Marines stepped aside, and one of the Secret Service agents opened the door.

Hopkins led them in, where, seated behind his desk, was Franklin Delano Roosevelt.

From the waist up, he gave the appearance of a vigorous man in his fifties, radiating his famous smile as he spoke. "Come on in. Please take those chairs nearest you, and drag another one over here, Harry."

Hopkins placed his chair alongside the desk, so he and the President were facing their visitors. "This is Commander Zacharias, and this is," he hesitated, "Lieutenant Colonel Mashbir."

"Welcome. I appreciate you putting up with the melodramatic way you were smuggled in. It's of utmost importance you tell no one of this conference. I've reviewed your records and have had people I trust make discreet inquiries, so I'm confident I can rely on both of you."

FDR pushed a pack of cigarettes towards them. "Smoke, if you like." The men declined. Roosevelt fit a cigarette into a long black holder, as Hopkins lit one of his own, and immediately broke into a racking cough, which he managed to suppress.

Roosevelt leaned forward. "You're here because I need help of a very specialized kind."

"Anything we can do, we certainly will," Zacharias replied.

FDR smiled. "Good. I'm aware both of you are as well informed on Japanese political affairs as anyone in my cabinet. But in addition, you're both fluent in their language."

He slowly inhaled from his cigarette holder—then let it out.

"Extremely grave circumstances exist between our nations since the sinking of the *Panay* and those additional reported atrocities from

Nanking. We've formally protested in the strongest terms through diplomatic channels, but to no avail. My advisors tell me things will probably get worse, and no one can stop it. Well, I hope maybe one man can, and that man is Emperor Hirohito. He's both official head of state and supreme commander of their armed forces. My uncle, Teddy, was a good friend to the Japanese. And I know, if I could only speak directly to the Emperor, we might avoid armed conflict. Since direct access is not possible at this time, I wish to write him a personal letter, man to man, appealing to his sense of responsibility to his people. If war comes, it will mean terrible suffering for everyone.

"What do you think about this idea, gentlemen?"

Both men appeared stunned. Mashbir recovered first, realizing the President was *really* waiting for a response and answered, "It's brilliant, sir. If it worked out it could avoid the very thing we're all dreading, an all-out war in the Pacific."

"Good," Roosevelt replied with enthusiasm. "Harry and I will get something out within the next day or so. Mashbir, you're to read it carefully and provide as close a Japanese translation as possible, stressing this is a head of state–to–head of state personal appeal."

Sidney gulped. "Certainly, sir, I only hope I can do it justice. I've met the Emperor on several occasions. The first time was fifteen years ago, when he was a young man in his early twenties; our last meeting was around a year ago, but much has changed since then—I also became a friend and advisor to his Uncle, Prince Iyesato Tokugawa."

"Really! Prince Tokugawa was a friend our family. My uncle Teddy, and I, would regularly invite him to dine with us and discuss political events, whenever he visited our nation. He's fine statesman, who's getting up in years…Well then, Mashbir, based on your contacts, you, better than most, will know the right phrasing that might convince the Emperor." He smiled, "Now, if you'll excuse me, I need to get back to a reception in the East Room, where I was supposed to be all this time."

Roosevelt rolled his wheelchair from behind the desk, exposing withered legs supported by metal braces. He shook the hands of his visitors. "Pleasure to have met you both."

As Sidney watched the most powerful man in the world exit, he couldn't help thinking of his own son. *By God, FDR hasn't let polio stop him. I hope Donald can learn from that example and not let anything hold him back either!*

While driving away, Sidney said, "Well, Zach, not in a million years would I have imagined meeting the President. One question: If I'm on everyone's blacklist and can't even get back into the reserves, why is Roosevelt going on and on about my fine credentials?"

"You gotta understand, his man Hopkins used to be a Socialist in the twenties, and many consider him and Roosevelt Communists at heart. His critics can't relate to having the government being the major employer, rather than private enterprise, even though their public work programs have gotten millions of unemployed guys off the dole, *instead of* receiving government support for doing nothing!"

"So you're saying FDR may or may not believe my records are correct?"

Zach laughed. "I'm saying, even if you were a double agent, who better to get communications to the other side?"

"But FDR was so friendly."

"He's a master politician."

"Well, Zach, I hope *you* trust me."

"One hundred percent!" he replied, punching Sidney in the arm. "With one exception—when we're playing squash, that is."

Office of Naval Intelligence, Washington, D.C., several months later

Coat and tie off, chair tilted back, feet resting on his desk, Zach seemed to be staring at nothing in particular when a secretary popped her head around the door and announced, "Mr. Mashbir has arrived, sir."

In an exaggerated Texas accent, Zach said, "Howdy, Partner, take a seat and set a spell!"

"I notice you aren't working yourself to death," Sidney replied.

"That's because they don't let *Navy Captains* do so—that's for the lower ranks."

Sidney's eyes opened wide, swiveling his head toward the rack where his friend's uniform was hanging with four broad gold stripes on the sleeve. "My God, it's true!" He snapped to attention, giving a crisp salute. "Lieutenant Colonel Mashbir, late of the Army Reserve, humbly awaiting your orders, sir."

"My first is you stop acting like an idiot and tell me what brings you here to the halls of wisdom. It's been a long while since you've graced us with your presence."

Mashbir sighed. "I'm fed up trying to get reinstated at the War Department. How about using some of that new-found rank and influence to help me?"

"I'd be glad to, except the Army doesn't cotton to Navy types messing in their business. And, I may not be around this crazy town much longer. Rumor has it that I'm headed for the bounding main, my boy. It's about time—I'm sick of Washington's power games and turf wars. Fresh sea breezes are just what I'm craving."

"Congratulations on the promotion—I never asked if you heard back about that letter we drafted for Roosevelt."

"Nothing yet," Zach said, brushing his hair back. "But I do have something to show you that came in from Naval Intelligence, Honolulu. Thought you'd find it interesting, since it was your inquiry that started the whole thing."

Zach retrieved a manila folder and tossed it over.

"Why, this is about that numbskull, Captain Henshaw! Did he ever get around to investigating the Kuhns' beauty parlor?"

"You could put it that way, I suppose," Zach replied slyly.

Mashbir continued reading. "What! Henshaw investigated the family and ended up getting engaged to their daughter, Ruth?"

"Bigger than life. The happy couple is being seen at all the best places in Honolulu."

"Jesus, Zach! I'm one hundred percent sure that family is all spies, probably working for the Japanese and the Germans!"

"You're right, but at least now we've got our eye on them. I'll tell you a little secret: we're feeding them all kinds of misinformation through female operatives going in for beauty treatments. So it's all working out for the best."

✳✳✳✳

Military High Command Headquarters, Tokyo, August 1938

Major General Matsumoto, General Anami, the Vice-Minister of War, and the Commander of the Air Force surveyed maps scattered across a large table.

Anami laughed. "That naïve American president thinks he can just send a sweet letter and a war that has been years in the planning will magically not happen."

The air commander held up a fist.

"They are merely a paper tiger when it comes to the Pacific!"

"What letter is it that you speak of, General Anami?" asked Matsumoto.

"One *supposedly* sent by Roosevelt, pleading to the Emperor. My spy in the diplomatic office stole it, and I've kept it a secret."

The following day at the palace, Nagako watched her weary husband in his study, surrounded by official documents needing review. "Dearest," she said, "you've been working such long hours. You deserve some pleasant diversion."

He rubbed his bloodshot eyes. "What do you suggest?"

"I've heard of a fine musical trio who also teach at the Imperial Music Academy who might perform for us."

"A wonderful idea, please arrange it."

Nagako smiled. "I've already done so."

Upon exiting, Nagako encountered Matsumoto, pacing in the corridor. "Oh, General, so nice to see you," she said. "Are you here to speak to the Emperor?" Before he could answer, she added, "He's been working so hard. I hope you don't have anything too serious to discuss?"

"Nothing of importance, it can wait for another day."

With that, Matsumoto bowed and left.

That Friday evening, the Emperor, the Empress, and their three daughters sat mesmerized, listening to Stravinsky's *Petrushka*, as Leo Sirota's fingers danced across the piano's keys, accompanied by a violinist and cellist. During an intermission, Princesses Terunomiya, Takanomiya, and Yorinomiya, aged thirteen, nine, and seven, excitedly approached the musicians. "We wish to tell you how marvelous your music is," Terunomiya said, "and that we have friends who enjoy being your students at the Academy."

Sirota bowed gallantly. "Thank you for your kind words."

Takanomiya's eyes twinkled as she asked, "If we obtained our parents' permission, might you give us piano lessons at the palace?"

"It would be my pleasure."

Hirohito and Nagako approached. Sirota prepared to bow, but to his surprise the Emperor offered a handshake instead.

"Your music has lightened my spirits."

"It is my honor. Your daughters are charming young ladies."

"Do you have children?" Nagako asked.

"A daughter, Beate. A bit older than yours. She studies at the American School."

"Is she a talented musician like her father?" Hirohito asked.

"Her greatest gift is language. She speaks Russian, French, German, English, and Japanese."

"Quite a talented young lady," Hirohito declared.

"But dance is her passion. As a matter of fact, her school group will be performing this week." The princesses had been listening. Little Yorinomiya whispered into her father's ear.

Two days later in the Palace Reception Hall, a dozen young ladies in long, flowing, lilac colored dresses, with blue sashes draped around their slender waists, danced in a modern interpretive style...These were the daughters of foreign diplomats and businessmen living in Japan, accompanied by several Japanese students. The performers leapt and spun across the stage, then reassembled in group formation—some stretching upward, others crouched or lying on the ground nearby, supporting themselves with one arm, while their other arm reached dramatically skyward; as the contemporary music of Sirota's band filled the air. Hirohito and Nagako glowed, seeing their daughters sway in their seats, as if they, too, were dancing.

When the performance ended, the imperial family and the other attendees gave a standing ovation. The Empress and her daughters walked over to a girl with black curly locks.

"Hello, Beate," Nagako said in English. "You and your father were most kind to arrange this performance. How long have you been taking dance lessons?"

"Two years."

In Japanese, Princess Takanomiya said, "Beate, your father mentioned you speak our language. Is that true?" Princess Terunomiya added, "He said you also spoke several others?"

"Foreign languages are fun to learn," Beate replied in Japanese. "It is dancing that I find most challenging."

Takanomiya shook her head. "No, your dancing was delightful!" she declared, her sisters nodding in agreement.

"Thanks for the compliment. Come, let me introduce you to my dance instructors and the other performers," she said, and off they went.

CHAPTER 39

Washington, D.C., October 1938

Nursing a gin and tonic, Sidney sat at a cocktail lounge, not far from the Capitol. Zach trudged through the front door, pausing to let his eyes acclimate to the dim lighting. As he moved toward Sid's booth, he called for the waiter's attention. "Double Scotch, water on the side." He sank into the bench opposite his buddy, leaning his head back against the cushion, eyes closed and saying nothing.

"Hello, Zach. Yes, I'm doing fine, thanks for asking."

"If you want pleasant conversation, you'll handle both sides. I'm exhausted—nearly dead, if you want the unvarnished truth."

Dropping the bantering style, Sidney said, "I know this Munich crisis has been rough on you."

Zach yawned. "Haven't slept for Lord knows how long; one military or congressional hearing after another to consider the unfolding events. What time is it, anyway?"

"Five-thirty P.M."

"Let's see, that makes fifty hours straight since I've slept—What a goddamn week! I'm too old for this crap!"

"You're younger than I am."

Zach cracked a smile without opening his eyes. "You're too old for it, too."

"Your Double Scotch has arrived," Sidney announced. "Want to drink it, or take it by injection?"

Zach opened his eyes, leaned forward, and drank half in one swallow. "Ah, that's a little better." He sighed. "How come you let that waiter get away? Order me another."

"It's really that bad?" Sidney looked at his friend in alarm. "I've never known you to finish more than one Scotch, let alone two doubles."

"Well, old friend," Zach lifted his glass and drained it. "Welcome to a nightmare scenario, complete with yours truly as Scotch drinker par excellence, as the old world goes to hell in a hand basket."

Mashbir shook the ice in his glass…"Surely, you're not going to let a pompous fool like British Prime Minister Chamberlain drive you to drink, though I understand your feelings. Hitler rattled his saber, and they handed him a chunk of Czechoslovakia," he smirked, "based on the promise he wouldn't ask for anything else."

"Yeah, for how long?" Zach gnawed his thumb nail. "Chamberlain and his stupid slogan, *'Peace in Our Time,'* he sputtered. "His appeasement policy delays war for eight to ten months, a year, tops. Will the Brits be more ready then? I doubt it. And now all Eastern Europe has lost faith in the Western allies."

Sidney shrugged. "You have to admit, Germany's military strength is very intimidating: Strange, though, Russia offered an alliance with Britain and France should Hitler attack them, but was refused."

"Maybe they hope Russia will slug it out with Hitler, without them having to get involved." Zach smiled. "You, of all people, remember 1922: fascist regimes rising in Europe, and the Japs ready to overrun Manchuria and perhaps all China. Then what happened? A dumb Army captain named Mashbir bluffed the Japs to clear out, and the whole thing went away. That's all *this* was, Hitler running a gigantic bluff." Zach flopped his arms down. "I'm crawling into a taxi and heading home—probably sleep for a solid week, I swear."

"Forget the taxi, I'll drive you: Maybe on the way we'll think up a scheme to halt the craziness brewing in Europe."

During the following year, 1939, Mashbir watched events move rapidly toward war. In March, just six months after the *Munich Pact* had given Hitler a section of Czechoslovakia, he broke his promise, conquering the remainder of that nation. In May, the *Pact of Steel* was signed—a military alliance between Germany and Italy, which was originally intended to include Japan; however, Japan wanted the pact aimed at her potential adversary, Russia. While Italy and Germany's priority was targeting Britain and France, this resulted in Japan's refusal to sign.

In August, Russia, having watched the Western Allies idly stand by as Hitler pushed his weight around, decided she also wanted territorial expansion, and signed a non-aggression pact with Germany... Within five weeks, Hitler and Stalin split Poland between them, thus igniting war in Europe.

Mashbir guessed these events were linked to the admiral's urgent request to see him. *The usually imposing Admiral King looks weary and older than his sixty years,* he thought, as he entered his office.

"Thanks for coming on such short notice," King said, handing him a two-page document. "This was recently forwarded to me. Because I respect your opinion and your scientific background, I'd like your feedback."

When he'd finished reading, Sidney appeared grim and lost in thought.

"So, what's your take on it?" King asked.

"You've verified this letter to Roosevelt was actually written by Albert Einstein?" Mashbir asked. King nodded. "Well then, it describes something I've thought a lot about these past couple of years, ever since I met the physicist Niels Bohr, who foretold that the release of energy from radioactive metals could produce an almost unthinkable explosive force—a weapon beyond anything previously known."

King looked Sidney in the eye.

"I've been in uniform since the Spanish-American War, with weapons getting ever more powerful over the years, but if what Einstein says comes to pass, we're in big trouble. Sidney, I realize you're neither in active or reserve status currently, but I'd appreciate your advice."

Sidney slowly reread the letter.

"This explains Hitler's early conquest of Czechoslovakia, one of the few locations known to possess uranium ore, along with Canada and the Belgian Congo. Einstein warns FDR that Nazi research actively aims to create such weapons; and he offers reasonable suggestions to counter it, such as increasing funding to our research programs and securing as much radioactive ore as possible, thereby limiting its access to enemy foreign powers. But equally important: We need scientists who know how to turn theory into a reality."

"Where do we find them?"

"Most are in Europe, though some have already fled to our country."

King clenched a fist. "How would we go about getting those European scientists, now that war *over there* has started?"

"Admiral, a few years back I met a gentlemen named Moe Berg who did a little undercover work for us in Japan."

"Yeah, he's a baseball catcher—I've seen him play."

"Terrifically bright, speaks a bunch of languages. If he were approached in the right way, appealing to his patriotism, he'd be very useful. He's something of a celebrity and could recruit them under the cover of advancing his language studies. His status allows him to blend into social and scientific gatherings. We'll need to move fast, while America is still neutral."

"Good idea, I'll set that in motion. But one thing irritates me to no end: with all the armed services having their own intelligence bureaus, as well as what the FBI and the State Department are doing, why did we still need to have a concerned foreign scientist tip us off to what's going on?"

"Turf wars have long complicated the sharing of intelligence," Sidney replied. "With military and government agencies guarding information as if it was the last turkey drumstick at a boarding home!"

King laughed. "Then that's got to change."

"Well, Admiral, what we need is a *centralized intelligence agency* responsible for all overseas operations, and *you're the person* who could get something like that started."

"Maybe so," King smiled, "especially if those rumors that I'm to be promoted to the *Head of all Chiefs of Staff* comes true."

"Let me congratulate you in advance; and I suggest this organization runs separate from the military branches."

"Thanks for the advice, and when that time comes, Sidney, I'll turn to you and your buddy Zacharias to create the guidelines for setting it up."

King sheepishly averted his eyes as he added, "You'll finally get a chance to incorporate your M-Plan ideas into it."

"I'm looking forward to that day." Sidney began whistling.

King appeared confused. "Why are you whistling 'London Bridge is Falling Down'?"

"Has anyone shown this letter to British Intelligence? Seems they'd be a bit concerned if they were aware the Nazis might soon be able to blow London off the map."

King nodded. "I'll get on it ASAP. This will certainly light a fire under the Brits!" He laughed. "Maybe they'll find a way get rid of that madman Hitler before we get sucked into their war."

British Consulate, Washington, D.C.

As Mashbir sat, examining a dossier, a British-accented voice commented, "And so our paths cross again; the last time was when a fight almost erupted at that Bund gathering," the man smiled. "It was most kind of you to advise Admiral King to rush over a copy of that letter to us."

"My pleasure," Sidney replied, putting down the folder and taking a sip of brandy. "David, you fellows at British Intelligence, M-16, move pretty fast."

David smiled. "As you can see, Johann Georg Elser is a thirty-six years old carpenter, who's also done mechanical work at a watch factory—a devout Protestant—even plays the organ for his church choir."

Sidney studied Johann's photography as David continued.

"In the past he's had a limited affiliation with the Communist Party. Gutsy fellow, once refused to salute Heil Hitler in public!"

"What motivates this German to risk his life?" Sidney asked. "He appears more a simple workingman than an assassin."

David lit a cigarette. "Terrible habit—can I offer you one?"

"No thank you."

He inhaled, placed his cigarette at rest into an ashtray, then settled into a chair. "Now where were we?"

"You were about to tell me why Johann is willing to face almost certain death."

"It all started with a teenager named Herschel Grynszpan a Jew of Polish citizenship, living in Germany prior to his escape to France. Do you remember that international conference in the French city of Evian-les-Bains last year, where thirty-two countries including yours and mine, gathered to discuss how to best handle the Nazis' abuse of Jews?"

"Yes, where nothing was accomplished."

David nodded. "That's right; for nine days, one delegate after another expressed sympathy, but not one country from Europe, or North or South America agreed to accept any refugees." He forced a smile. "They couldn't even get a resolution approved condemning Hitler's behavior. Only the little island nation of the Dominican Republic offered to take some, but with no definite details given."

"Where are you going with this?" Sidney asked.

"I was there as one of the advisors for my government." David avoided Sidney's gaze. "My superiors spoke to your representatives prior to the meeting and came to an understanding: If Britain promised not to pressure America to take in more immigrants, the U.S. would not push Britain to further open the doors of Palestine as a homeland for Jewish refugees." David's eyes dulled. "It's not a pleasant memory…He continued, "When the conference ended, a woman named Golda Meir, the Jewish observer from Palestine, confronted our delegation and declared: *The world appears to be divided into two parts, Those places where Jews cannot live, and those where they cannot enter! There is only one thing I hope to see before I die, and that is that my people should not need expressions of sympathy ever again!'"*

"I don't envy you having to be part of that."

Sidney poured himself another brandy as David took another drag on his cigarette.

"One can understand," David continued, "many leaders are in great fear of the German war machine, while *others* encourage Hitler's actions."

"But at least there have been many individual acts of courage,"

Sidney replied. "Thousands of brave souls throughout Europe, such as in Holland, France, Poland, Denmark, and Germany itself, who have put their lives on the line aiding their Jewish friends and neighbors⁕ And in the Middle East, Turkey has remained neutral, protecting her Jewish citizens; even retrieving those living in France: and also has allowed two hundred Jewish-European professors to immigrate and teach in her universities...

"And in Morocco, that nation resisted pressure to hand over 260,000 of their Jewish citizens to the Nazis."

"Impressive," David said. "I see you've been carefully following these events."

"That's right, and in Asia," Sidney continued, "a Japanese diplomat, Chiune Sugihara, serving in the Lithuanian Consulate General, stuck his neck out, signing thousands of Japanese visas allowing desperate Jewish refugees to escape from Lithuania to Asia before the Nazis arrived." He paused and reflected, "Similarly, thousands of Austrian Jews were saved by the Chinese Consul-General in Vienna, Ho Feng-Shan, who issued visas against the orders of his superior, the Chinese Ambassador in Berlin."

"*All that is so*," David replied, "but regrettably, on an international basis, little has been done, making Hitler all the more brazen. Three months after the Evian Conference, he ordered ten thousand Jewish Polish citizens living in Germany to be forcefully returned to Poland, leaving behind all their possessions. Problem was, the Polish government no longer recognized them as citizens. They were sent back and forth like unwanted garbage, with little food and no shelter. Finally, Poland gave in, placing them in miserable expatriate camps."

David fell silent.

"So how does this teenager, Herschel Grynszpan, fit in with Johann's willingness to kill Hitler?"

"Herschel's family were among those put into those Polish expatriate camps. Out of anger, he purchased a pistol and talked his way into the German Embassy in Paris. There, he put a bullet into the stomach of one of their staff, creating a Nazi uproar. How dare a mere boy assassinate a diplomatic officer!—So two days later, on the evening of November 9, 1938—less than a year ago, our man Elser was in a crowd listening to Hitler rant against Herschel and all Jews. The boy's act of rebellion gave the perfect excuse for a massive orchestrated assault across the Reich."

"I'm well aware," Sidney replied, recalling that that night and into the next day became known as *Kristallnacht*, or *'The Night of Broken Glass'*, with police standing by as mob violence, storm troopers, the SS, and Hitler Youth groups rampaged homes and businesses, attacking and murdering Jews throughout the country—the horror spreading into Austria and other regions controlled by the Nazis. Hundreds of synagogues were burned to the ground as fire departments merely stood nearby, there only to make sure the flames didn't spread to adjacent properties owned by non-Jews." Sidney rubbed his tired face with both hands. "There wasn't much of the international outcry you'd expect."

"The bloody bastards cleverly stifled it," David replied. "The Nazis made mass arrests, dragging the eldest sons from the homes of the most influential Jewish families and imprisoning them, thus keeping those families fearful, quiet, and cooperative. They even had the audacity to blame the Jews for the riots and forced them to pay reparations."

"So Johann Elser was touched by all this?" Sidney asked, staring at his photo.

David nodded. "It appears Elser had developed a friendship with a Rabbi and a Cantor, for whom he'd done carpentry work at their temple. He enjoyed listening to the Cantor's fine voice singing prayers, reminding him of his own organ performances for church choirs."

David loosened his collar and took a long breathe . . . "During *Kristallnacht*, Johann helplessly watched as this Rabbi and Cantor along with their congregation who had refused to abandon their synagogue with its holy ark and sacred books, were burned alive, their shrieks filling the air."

David crushed out his cigarette while scrutinizing Sidney's distraught, flushed face and clenched fists, guessing he was struggling to contain his anger and loathing.

There was a long silence, which Sidney broke.

"How did Johann come to your attention?"

"He described his abhorrence in letters to his relatives in England, who informed us."

"How will he pull it off?"

"A month from now, in commemoration of the one-year anniversary of *Kristallnacht*, Hitler plans a celebration, and Johann will deliver our gift."

Sidney's expression morphed into a smile.

"If you don't mind my asking," David said, looking him in the eye. "Now that war's been declared by Britain, France, Australia, New Zealand, and Canada—how long before you Yanks get into the fray? We could certainly use your assistance."

Sidney began shifting his footing and moving his arms like a boxer preparing for a fight. "If I had my way, we'd have been in it years ago! Before the Nazis armed to their current levels."

He let his arms drop and spoke in a serious tone: "I remember serving under General Pershing prior to America's entrance into *the last war*. He spoke of being wined, dined, and practically pleaded to by the British and French to bring American forces over during the early years of that war." He paused.

"To emphasize the urgency, Pershing was given tours of the European battlefronts, all the while knowing inside that the U.S. was not ready. American industries needed time to retool for military supplies and weaponry...It took several years before we arrived, and I'm sorry to say, it's a similar situation today: So I'd guess you're on your own for at least a couple more years."

"You certainly don't mince your words, my friend."

A month later, Mashbir read *The New York Times* with bitter disappointment. Due to bad weather, Hitler cancelled a scheduled flight and was forced to shorten his *Kristallnacht* commemoration speech to a mere thirteen minutes to catch a train back to Berlin. Otherwise, he'd have been blown to bits! Eight people died, and sixty-three were injured in the blast.

Damn it, Sidney thought, *that lucky son-of-a-bitch lunatic got away. Wish I could tear out his heart myself. And what's worse, now he'll have his guard up...The article says poor Johann managed to reach the Swiss border, but was stopped—He's probably being tortured right now.*

CHAPTER 40

Chicago, March 1940

Thousands of enthusiastic spectators filled the amphitheater, with banners and American flags everywhere. Irene turned to Sidney. "This has all the excitement of a presidential candidate convention," she said. "But I still don't understand why you thought it so important to travel all this way to listen to things I'm sure you don't even believe in."

He nodded. "I wanted to see for myself if these guys are pushing the same fascist Bund agenda. At least now I don't see any swastikas. And besides, the featured speaker is Charles Lindbergh himself!"

The first hour passed with assorted prominent speakers voicing their views while attendants strolled the aisles handing out small envelopes.

"Welcome, folks," they said. "This event is free, but for those who wish to make a contribution to support our cause, please use these envelopes. They can be dropped off at the exit gates at the end of the program."

Sidney noticed the envelopes requested name, address, and phone number: *A perfect way of gathering a mailing list for future events and soliciting contributions,* he thought.

A gray-haired gentleman with a thick mustache, who was missing most of his right arm, walked to center stage. Behind him hung a large portrait of George Washington.

"We wholeheartedly thank you all for attending," he said. "As you've heard so far, it's important we discuss the European war that's been going on for these past seven months...I fought in the last European war, and this is all I have to show for it." He held up his stump of an arm. "And you have my *guarantee*," his voice hardened, "this current war will be even bloodier, and it will last for years and years!"

His tone now became amiable. "If your neighbor needs help, it's your duty to pitch in. But this conflict is far away and none of our business...Today, we're most fortunate to have a true American hero give *his* opinion. Let's welcome Colonel Charles Lindbergh!"

Stars and Stripes Forever played as the massive crowd stood to applaud the boyish-appearing figure who came forward. Lindbergh grasped the podium with both hands, leaning forward, scanning his audience, patiently waiting for the supportive uproar to settle down...

"I'm under no illusion," Lindbergh said with a smirk, "that I could be considered a polished speaker. I leave that to Roosevelt with his *cozy*, carefully rehearsed fireside chats."

This brought laughter and some snickering.

"Many remember my father as the congressman who spoke out strongly against America being dragged into that last European disaster. Time has proven him right! The supposed shining hope that came out of that war was the League of Nations, and our country didn't even become a member of that powerless organization, *and rightly so*. We don't want to be at the beck and call of international groups, because they don't have our well-being as their primary objective.

"Some call what's going on in Europe a *phony war*, because as of yet, there's been little actual fighting." His voice ascended. "I promise you, that won't last much longer! This is a clash between two empires—the new German and the old established British one. And God forbid one drop of American blood be shed fighting their quarrels!"

The crowd wildly applauded. Lindbergh waited, then raised his hand for silence.

"I resigned my commission with the armed forces, rather than remain silent. Modern aerial warfare will make this conflict horrific beyond imagination. We well remember the massive loss of life and property resulting from *the War to End All Wars*, or so they claimed it would be. I tell you, this will be ten times worse, with casualties not in the hundreds of thousands, but in the millions!"

He straightened his posture.

"I've been accused—not openly, but by rumor and innuendo, of being pro-German. Those accusations were made by our current administration to discredit me. Yes, I toured Germany to evaluate their aviation facilities, including the military ones. I also visited those in England and France. What they aren't telling you is that my tour was undertaken at the request of this same Washington administration."

He spread his arms wide.

"I am neither pro-German nor pro-English. I am an American *one hundred percent*. Nor am I a pacifist; peace is good, yes, but not at any price. If this country is attacked, I will be in the first rank to defend it. The fact that we are safely isolated by two vast oceans makes that highly unlikely."

Lindbergh looked around.

"When our forefathers forged this great nation, what did they say about foreign wars?"

He pointed to the portrait behind him.

"In his farewell address, President Washington sternly warned against foreign entanglements. And Jefferson, when drawn into the War of 1812, wrote bitterly against those who pushed him into that conflict. And later, when President Monroe formulated the doctrine that bears his name, he warned European powers against meddling in the affairs of *our* hemisphere; and it would be folly on our part to interfere in Europe's ever-recurring quarrels!"

His voice softened. "And so, I appeal to you: Tell your friends, your neighbors, everyone you know, to oppose our involvement. I believe this with all my heart, that our primary duty is to *America first!*"

"That's quite a persuasive speech," Irene commented.

"He's got a point," Sidney replied. "But Lindy and his *America First* friends would like to think they live on Mars, and this war can't touch them. But they're wrong. It can, and it will!"

Germany, May 1940

Field-Marshal Jaeger observed his opponent, a lieutenant, move his queen diagonally four spaces forward. *How aggressively he plays so early in the game, hoping for a quick checkmate. Perhaps I can use that against him.*

The conference room door burst open and both men sprung to their feet, saluting, "Heil Hitler!"

"We need to talk, Jaeger!" Hitler swept the pieces off the board and ordered the lieutenant to leave. A wooden pointer was slapped into the field-marshal's palm.

"Now update me on our progress."

"*Mein Führer*, things are going well," he asserted, pointing to a map on the adjacent wall. "Look! Denmark is under our thumb, and Norway will not last much longer; then we march into Belgium, Luxembourg, and the Netherlands. And once we begin bombing Paris, the French will quickly cease resistance."

Hitler paced. "But I'm very concerned about Russia."

"Don't worry yourself. Splitting Poland was a marvelous idea, creating a brotherly bond between us," Jaeger replied. "Stalin now feels secure in attacking Finland, and our spies have heard he plans to expand into the Baltic States." He smiled. "With that information, we could convince the Balkans to become *our* allies, seeing us as their savior."

"Not a bad idea." Hitler suddenly slammed his fist down. "But that clever bastard Stalin meets with Churchill and Roosevelt, playing us all against each other...And it won't be long before the Americans rise up against us!"

Jaeger lit a cigarette..."If only we could get Japan to join us. We've been in contact with certain of her generals who hunger to pounce upon the Philippines. That would so entangle the Americans, they'd be much less able to lend their support in Europe."

"Then we must make that happen!" Hitler shouted.

Jaeger smiled. "And the Japanese wouldn't stop there; they'd expand further into China and perhaps Russia."

"It would be delightful to see Stalin's expression as they breathed down his neck!" Hitler said gleefully. "But would Russia turn on us if we became allies with the Japanese?"

"Unlikely, they currently have a non-aggression pact with that nation. Mother Russia will patiently watch our expansion in Europe *and* Japan's growing presence in Asia, all the while knowing she will eventually be sandwiched between her growing enemies. That will eventually push Stalin over to the Allies." He waved off the idea. "But don't worry, *Mein Führer*— Stalin is not so revered by his countrymen as you are in Germany." He hesitated. "When we attack, I advocate a gentler touch—many Russians might actually come over to our side."

"Ahaa...Imagine his worthless, ignorant, peasant masses turning against him," Hitler sneered. "Good idea, but only if it does not slow our advance."

The German Consulate in Tokyo, two days later

Reichmann held the phone receiver a safe distance from his ear. A harsh voice emanated:

"You must convince the Japanese High Command and the emperor's ministers they need only look at Germany's rapid conquests to know we're unstoppable. Inform them that our Non-Aggression Pact with Russia is just temporary. We have four million troops ready to invade her, which will free up Japan's forces guarding the Russian-Manchurian border."

The voice turned syrupy sweet. "It is important to play the Japanese's fear against them. Let them know we also covet China's resources. But if Japan joins us, *we will leave Asia to the Japanese* and cease our current support of China's industry and military. And **emphasize** that an alliance between Germany and Japan will so intimidate the Americans, they'll no longer stand in the way of Japanese control of Manchuria and her expansion beyond. *If they hesitate*, they lose the opportunity to gain the empire they've long desired."

"But sir, certain powerful Japanese leaders stand in the way."

"Get rid of them!"

The phone went dead.

Washington, D.C., the following month, June 5, 1940

The smell of melting butter and cinnamon filled the kitchen, as Sidney and Donald waited hungrily.

"Do you gentlemen want strawberries or blueberries with your French toast?" Irene asked.

"Mom, can we have both?"

"That sounds good to me," Sidney concurred.

Breakfast was interrupted by a Western Union delivery boy, ringing their bell and waiting at their doorstep with his bicycle at the curb.

What's this about? Sidney wondered. He returned to the kitchen and opened the telegram:

> *Dear Colonel Mashbir:*
>
> *We haven't spoken for several years. It wasn't easy getting this message to you. Japan has been shut off from the outside world. It is with a broken heart that I inform you Prince Tokugawa is dead; the doctors say from pneumonia. One of his last requests was that I should convey his regards. You might not have been aware, but you were one of his most trusted advisors and a close friend.*
>
> *My husband is in deep mourning over his uncle's death, but in spite of that, certain generals are pressuring him more than ever to support their goal of bringing all Asia under Japanese rule. There is scheming and deceit in their words, claiming Japan must display her military might so that the West won't dare attack our country. Hirohito is overwhelmed and doesn't know what to believe. Our family struggles to raise his spirits.*
>
> *Please wish us strength for the days ahead.*
>
> *Sincerely, Nagako*

With a stunned look on his face, Sidney's coffee cup slipped from his fingers, crashing to the floor. "Are you okay?" Irene asked.

"Prince Tokugawa is dead."

"I'm so sorry," she softly replied.

It was a rare sight…Tears in Sidney's eyes, as he put his hand upon Donald's shoulder. "Son, I went without a father most of my life, and well, I came to love that man—Iyesato had such strength, yet could be gentle and understanding: a *noble Statesman*, who almost single-handedly led the forces preventing Japan's entry into a global war."

And now that he's gone, he thought, *all hell will break loose.*

"I hope you'll both excuse me, I need to be by myself for a while."

Once in the sanctuary of his office, he removed his clarinet from its blue-velvet lined case and played several soulful melodies.

Three months later, September 27, 1940, newspaper headlines around the world announced:

JAPAN SIGNS TRIPARTITE PACT: **Germany, Italy, and now Japan, Join Together as Axis Powers!**

CHAPTER 41

Hollywood, California, October 1940

A black sedan pulled up to the mansion's front gate. Into the inter-com, one of the four passengers shouted, "We're from the F.B.I., we need to speak to Mr. Chaplin."

The gate opened, and they proceeded along the driveway through the expansive terraced grounds, accented by shrubs, stone pathways, and waterfalls.

"It's a Japanese garden, and all the staff appears to be Japanese as well," one commented, pointing at several gardeners pruning bushes, while another waxed a car.

At the residence entrance, the doorman who greeted them was also Japanese.

"He's waiting for you in his study," he said. "Please follow me."

As soon as they faced Chaplin, one agent asked, "How many Japs you got working around here?"

"Seventeen, sir. I'm very fond of the Japanese people and their culture—so courteous, for the most part! They maintain the tranquil-ity that surrounds us."

"Seems kinda strange," the agent remarked. "We're looking for Kono—he was in your employ, right? Do you know where we can find him?"

Chaplin was startled. "Why do you want him?"

"Just answer the question."

"He hasn't worked for me for two years, though he is the one who first introduced me to Japanese traditions many years ago."

"Well, we have a warrant for his arrest…"

✳✳✳✳

Sidney picked up his office phone to hear a somehow familiar voice.

"Colonel Sidney Mashbir?"

"Yes, that's me, but I'm no longer in the military. Who is this?"

"Charles Chaplin; we once met. You gave me your card."

"Oh, of course! Why, hello, Mr. Chaplin. What can I do for you?"

"My good friend Kono has been arrested, accused of being a spy for cooperating with Japanese naval officers. It can't be true—he's a loyal American."

Sidney rekindled his memory of the debonair Kono at that diplomatic party.

"So you haven't noticed any strange behavior on his part?"

"He once mysteriously hinted about something related to our visit to Japan, during which time our host, the Prime Minister, was assassinated."

Chaplin paused, and then continued with a sudden rush of emotion: "Look, Mr. Mashbir—I foolishly denied knowing his whereabouts to the F.B.I., but they found him and want to either keep him prison or deport him! Is there anything you can do? You mentioned you had connections in the U.S. and Japan."

"I presume you spoke in support of Kono's character?"

"They didn't give it much weight. Some call me a Communist because of my film *Modern Times*, you know—because it showed automation displacing flesh-and-blood workers. But that film, like **all** my films, was largely meant to be comical entertainment for Heaven's sake. I'm no Communist!

"I've driven myself hard to achieve my economic success, but have sympathy for the underdog!"

Sidney remembered reading Chaplin's personal history; *His mother institutionalized when he was seven, a father who drank himself into an early grave by the time Charles was twelve...To think that out of such darkness, a great comedian was born!*

Chaplin went on.

"I appreciate Democracy and Capitalism! They've given me the chance to lead a life beyond my wildest dreams. *My goal* is to make sure they maintain their humanistic treatment of people...I firmly believe that if we're to remain strong, we must accept, not silence, comic barbs."

"You could be on a pulpit, Mr. Chaplin."

"That's what films are."

Sidney cleared his throat.

"All right, I'll look into it. No promises. I'm making a business trip to Los Angeles next week; perhaps we can meet face-to-face. Give me your contact information. You'll be hearing from me soon."

✳✳✳✳

A winding road cut through sage-covered hillsides accented by an occasional cactus, as the white limo sped from Laguna Beach, California, toward San Simeon. Chaplin turned to Mrs. Mashbir, "Irene, I'm so glad you and your husband accepted my invitation—a token of appreciation for his assistance." He smiled. "And I hope you've been enjoying your stay at my friend's cottage in Laguna?"

"It's wonderful, and just a short stroll to a fantastic beach," she replied. "My dear mother happily takes care of our son, allowing us this opportunity." She held Sidney's hand. "My husband really needed a vacation incorporated into this business trip. So that's why I came along." She smiled, then with hesitance added, "A good friend of his recently passed away."

"I'm so sorry to hear that."

Sidney swallowed hard..."Alright, let me update you on Kono. I pulled some favors from friends at Naval Intelligence. What I tell you *has to* remain between us."

"Absolutely."

"All right then. Kono admitted being coerced by some Japanese naval officers scouting for information on our battleships. He only listened to their requests because he worried that you, and his family back in Japan, might be in danger. And if Kono gets deported, he fears his life won't be worth a dime."

"We can't let that happen!" Chaplin declared.

"Please calm down, Mr. Chaplin. I believe a deal can be worked out. Kono has been temporarily placed in protective custody, and those Japanese agents have been rounded up and sent back to Japan. And as you already know, for your safety, Secret Service agents will be keeping an eye on your place for the next couple of months."

Chaplin's voiced strained. "Let's keep our fingers crossed for Kono's family." He smiled at Sidney. "I don't know how to thank you enough."

"No big deal, they didn't really have much of a case against him."

As they closed in on their destination, Chaplin said, "I should prepare you. Our host, Mr. Hearst, doesn't really want to screen my movie. His own film creation, *Gabriel Over the White House*, released back in '33, was considered so pro-fascist that he now wishes to show his willingness to give the other side's perspective, to look good for his liberal friends."

"We saw his film," Irene said. "A wild story about a fictional U.S. president who has a serious car accident and is visited by the Archangel Gabriel, who pressures him to accept that his nation's problems were due by his poor leadership!"

Sidney added, "And he swears that when he regains his health, he'll set the nation right—First he dumps his corrupt cabinet, even the men who got him elected: That part was *okay*. But then, he storms into Congress declaring a state of national emergency, and bestows upon **himself** the absolute powers of a benevolent **dictator!**"

Chaplin shook his head. "Who would have thought it would end up one of the top-grossing films of the season?! America was in the depths of an economic depression, with angry cries for political change—Even if it meant Communism! Or Socialism! *And here* was this film offering simplistic solutions: waging war against organized crime, gunning down gangsters without trial, and using strong-arm tactics to restore social order: While all the time drastically limiting individual freedoms!"

"To Hearst's creative credit," Sidney laughed, "his protagonist solved the Unemployment problem single-handedly, and brought about worldwide disarmament—Even though he used forceful intimidation, his actions were presented as justified, with him dying as a martyr!"

"Knowing Hearst as I do," Chaplin said, "it's easy to understand the appeal that would have to an all-powerful newspaper mogul!"

"So tell us about *your* latest film, Mr. Chaplin," Irene asked.

"It took several years and a huge budget out of my own pocket. I'm the director, producer, and also an actor in it. It's called *The Great Dictator*—a comedy, but more serious than anything I've done before. It's about Fascism."

Where do you find humor in Fascism? Sidney thought. "Which dictator has the starring role? Hitler, Mussolini, Franco, or perhaps Stalin?"

"Hitler gets the lead," Chaplin chuckled, "with Mussolini in a strong supporting part. However, due to America's neutrality with Germany, I've received pressure from censors who want me to neither ridicule Hitler and his Nazi Party, nor present them too seriously."

Chaplin scoffed, "As one of the owners of United Artists Studio, I'll be damned if I'll let them push me around!"

Irene pointed, "What's going on, there's a buffalo on the road ahead?"

"We're now on the estate grounds," Charles laughed, "where animals have the right of way, free to roam as they please. You might as well relax."

After the buffalo had shown who was boss, the journey continued, meandering through hundreds of acres of golden-yellow, rolling hills.

"It's like a safari!" exclaimed Irene. "Look—zebras, goats, even a giraffe."

"And there's a collection of caged animals as well," Chaplin said.

"Is that his castle in the distance?" Sidney pointed.

"Yes, His Excellency resides there."

Once they reached the mountaintop, the guards, on seeing Chaplin, swung the gates wide, and their chauffeur drove through, dropping them off.

On the way to the estate's massive entrance doors, they strolled past huge, Roman God-like marble statues and flowing fountains and pools.

"Feels like we're in Julius Caesar's palace," Sidney said. "Strange, though, even on a hot day like this, almost everyone's just sitting around the pool, feet dangling in the water, with only a couple of folks swimming."

Chaplin replied, "Most of these fancy Hollywood types don't even know how to dog paddle, but look at that man cutting through the water like a dolphin. It's Johnny Weissmuller."

"That's Tarzan! Look at those biceps, Sidney," Irene said mischievously.

"Pretty powerful, I'll admit; at least someone's enjoying the pool. Might take a dip later myself."

They passed through the impressive wooden entrance doors with knights' faces carved into them, and into the castle's expansive foyer, adorned with medieval furniture and wall tapestries.

"And now we're in the age of King Arthur," Sidney commented.

"Hearst is quite a collector," Chaplin explained. "This is more a museum than a home."

A boisterous crowd was downing drinks and socializing; familiar celebrities could be seen in all directions. A husky man in formal British hunting attire approached. "Hello, Charles. I see you've brought some new guests for your screening?"

"Let me introduce you to the Lord of the Manor, Sir William R. Hearst," Chaplin said, playfully. "Bill, welcome Irene and Sidney Mashbir."

"Charles, if you're going to throw around honorary titles, you should at least bow before you speak to me." Hearst grinned, then turned to the Mashbirs, acknowledging them with a nod.

"Make yourselves comfortable," he said, and lumbered away.

"Not very talkative," Irene said.

"He and I have a bit of a rivalry," Chaplin replied. "His Hollywood girlfriend who arranged this event was once *a friend of mine*. It irritates him. And, he knows what I think of his support for Hitler, which will go down as one of the great mistakes in American history. It was Hearst and his newspaper empire forty years ago that riled up your country to start the Spanish-American War. Pure colonialism on America's part in my opinion; Spain wasn't committing the atrocities claimed. Hearst cooked things up with jingoism and incendiary headlines. *And now,* when that demigod should be encouraging a confrontation with the Nazis, instead, his newspapers, magazines, and movie newsreels are doing everything they can in the opposite direction. None who work for him dare criticize the policies of Germany."

Chaplin shook his head in frustration.

"But—he *is* our host, and this is meant to be a festive event, so I'll stop ranting." Chaplin's attention was drawn to a piano. "Why don't you two wander about and mingle."

Moments later, a snappy jazz piece was being pounded out, as Chaplin's fingers flew across the keyboard for an appreciative crowd gathered round. He proudly acknowledged his audience, then, to their surprise, he lifted both hands—one to hold his chin while the other scratched his head questioningly—as the piano played all on its own.

"Oh, it's a *player piano*!" someone shouted, and the crowd broke out into laughter.

Nearby a commotion erupted, as the strikingly handsome Errol Flynn and his female companion were being accosted by another gorgeous, tipsy lady. Flynn was in the middle of a tug-of-war, both women pulling for all they were worth on each of his arms...Security guards rushed in to separate the ménage à trois, as the other guests smiled indulgently.

A bell rang, and everyone poured into the huge home theater, where identical, twenty-foot-tall statues of a Greek goddess lined both sides of the aisles...The room darkened as the film began—an emotional roller coaster. Chaplin played a barber by profession, who was mistaken for Hitler, whom he very much resembled. Uproarious laughter erupted as Chaplin impersonated the Dictator performing ballet while playing with an air-inflated world globe—floating it about, then bouncing it on his knee, on his head, and even on his butt, just like a toy!

Suddenly, the balloon exploded in his hands...Later on, in harsh contrast, the audience cringed as citizens' homes were broken into by *Storm Troopers*, and an innocent man was dragged into the street and summarily executed.

At the film's finale, using actual stock footage from a massive outdoor rally with hundreds of thousands of spectators, Hitler, now impersonated by Chaplin, gave an impassioned plea for reason over brutality. He begged the German nation and the world not to listen to the voices of leaders who are *heartless machine men*—whose souls are filled only with greed, cruelty, and the lust for power.

When the lights came on, Hearst was the first to stand and applaud.

"Got to hand it to you, Charles—your film is dramatic and very funny."

He walked off with a somber expression.

As Sidney and Irene were chauffeured back to their vacation cottage in Laguna that evening, Chaplin asked, "I hope you enjoyed your visit?"

"It was so exciting to experience your powerful and entertaining film—and meeting your friends," Irene replied.

"If I had known the magnitude of Hitler's cruelty at the beginning of the project," Chaplin replied. "I don't think I would have been able or willing to have attempted a slapstick, black comedy. But humor can be a powerful weapon against tyrants."

Sidney applauded.

"To my knowledge, yours is the first bold anti-Nazi statement on the American screen."

"And because of that, certain powerful individuals are now trying to have me deported, saying I'm pushing your nation into war."

"They're just idiots afraid of Free Speech."

That vacation was just what Sidney needed. In fact, when he returned to Washington, D.C., he promised himself, *someday*, he might just retire to sunny Southern California.

In the meanwhile, he was busy running the Washington Institute of Technology. His secretary entered his office, flustered. "There's a woman on the phone who says she needs to see you. Claims to be Miss Hedy Lamarr."

That afternoon, Sidney came face to face with one of the most beautiful woman he'd ever seen—such lovely eyes! And the starlet's sheer black dress with its plunging neckline took his breath away momentarily.

"How can I be of assistance?" he asked.

"I'm currently spending some time here on the East Coast. One of my friends in L.A. mentioned they'd met you at the screening event for Chaplin's film, and said you're involved in manufacturing for the military?"

She turned the full force of a dazzling smile on Sidney, and he became aware he was blushing, something he hadn't done since he was sixteen. He wasn't a movie buff, yet he still had a vivid image of Lamarr in that famous nude swimming scene, in the film *Ecstasy*.

He paused. "Yes, I do some military-related manufacturing, but it's hard to imagine why that would interest you, Miss Lamarr?"

"Call me Eva," she said. "That's my real name. Louis Mayer created that silly screen name when he brought me from Europe."

She sat.

"We need to talk about inventions, engineering, things that truly matter!"

"Oh really?" he replied, thinking this must be some sort of game.

"Do you specialize in technology for both the Army and the Navy?"

"Yes," he hesitated, "though we handle civilian projects as well."

"I understand your reluctance to speak for security reasons." She then explained how she and a friend had a new concept for a radio controlled guidance device for Navy torpedoes, making them far more accurate. She needed practical advice on how best to get it patented and assistance in getting the Navy to consider adopting it.

"I can probably help with some of that, Eva, but can you give me an idea of what makes this device a technological advancement?"

She smiled.

"It would be better for you to hear it from my friend, George Anthiel. He's a famous composer, you know, with a first-class Engineering mind as well. He's giving a small concert tomorrow night at eight. If you would be kind enough to attend, I'll introduce you."

The event was held at a warehouse that had been converted into an auditorium and gallery. Hedy and Sidney strolled about, looking at the artwork.

"What do you see in this painting, Sidney?" Hedy asked.

"Someone splattered paint and hoped for the best."

"Modern expressionism," she laughed, "unbridled by dogmatic structure."

"Okay, Eva, what do you think of this?" he asked, gesturing toward a metal sculpture composed of geometric shapes welded together haphazardly, in his opinion.

"It's sensuous, speaking to our hidden desires," she replied, feigning an innocent look.

"Is that so..." He smiled, then scanned the avant-garde crowd around him in their bright bandanas and French berets, or sporting dark sun glasses—even in the dimly lit setting. Women wore slacks and sweaters and had severe hairstyles...*I'm the only guy wearing a suit and tie,* he realized. *At least Hedy is equally overdressed in her elegant evening gown.*

"Different from your usual circuit, I imagine?" Hedy said. "They're mainly writers, artists, musicians, and poets—part of the Bohemian movement."

"Obviously a creative bunch—But excuse me, I need a bit of fresh air—I'll be right back."

Sidney stepped outside and found himself surrounded by dense smoke as some folks passed around a thick marijuana reefer.

"Want a drag?" one asked. "And I could also sell you some..."

"The occasional martini or whisky works for me just fine," he replied.

"To each his own. We all need something to handle this crazy world!"

The fellow exhaled in Sidney's direction...When he re-entered the building, second-hand smoke had begun to deliver its effect; Sidney's skin tingled, sounds were coming in distorted*

Most everyone was already seated in the auditorium as he plopped himself down next to Hedy. He overheard a woman nearby saying to her companion, "I just visited an amazing exhibit at the Museum of Modern Art in New York City. You must experience Picasso's masterpiece, *Guernica*! A nightmare come alive, with cries to the heavens against a background of destruction."

"What inspired it?" her friend asked.

"Spain was in a civil war with various groups vying for power: fascists, communists, constitutionalists, the past monarchy, even the church…Hitler and Mussolini wished to tip the balance while testing the effectiveness of aerial bomb attacks, so they demolished the city of Guernica, ending the civil war, and bringing another Fascist dictator to power, Generalissimo Franco."

This unique crowd might be more on the ball than I imagined, Sidney thought.

A short, slightly pug-nosed man standing on center stage announced, "I'm George Anthiel: Some call me the Bad Boy of music," he said with a smile. "You're about to hear one of my original pieces, *The Clash of Titans*. Hope you enjoy it."

During a blessed interval of silence between the overpowering torrents of cacophonous disharmony, Hedy leaned close and whispered, "My dear Sidney, perhaps I should have prepared you for the rather advanced music George composes?"

She's generous in her description, he thought. *It's more like a blend of owls and metal plates being put through a meat grinder.*

He managed a weak smile, hoping Anthiel's invention was better than his so-called music. Surreptitiously, he stuffed small wads of tissue paper into his ears.

When that piece had ended, Anthiel tapped his baton twice and announced, "My final work is called *Airplane Sonata.*" His seven-piece orchestra crashed into another jarring episode, accompanied by amplified recordings of engines revving up to a high pitch, then dying down, only to rev up again.

Mercifully, after ten minutes the composition came to a thunderous close, with Anthiel bowing repeatedly to applause.

As the other patrons filed out, Hedy led Sidney to the stage. Anthiel leaped nimbly down, brushing back brown hair from his perspiring forehead. "George, this is Sidney Mashbir, the man I told you about."

"So glad to meet you. What did you think about that last piece? It was to have featured the recording of actual airplane engines screaming wide open, but I couldn't locate any powerful enough to suit me. Instead, I used automobile engines with their mufflers removed— That work represents the obliteration of civilization in our time."

Hedy sneaked a mischievous look at Sidney.

Sidney wasn't taken aback—"I must admit it was powerful. If you really want airplane engine sounds, I could have my engineers record and send them to you. We test aircraft all the time at our facility."

Anthiel smiled.

"That would be wonderful. And we both really appreciate your help in getting our invention patented and considered by the Navy."

"I really don't know much about it yet," Sidney replied, sending Hedy a slight frown. "Miss Lamarr said you could better explain this device than she could."

"Of course, it's simplicity itself," he said, communicating expressively with his hands. "Once, while linking sixteen player pianos together for one of my compositions, I realized that the same principle could easily be adapted to a radio controller…"

Despite Anthiel's assurances, at the end of ten minutes of high-speed exposition, Mashbir was no closer to understanding how this invention supposedly operated.

Hedy, sensing his confusion, offered, "There are detailed drawings at my suite. I promise they'll make everything clear."

Anthiel looked at his wristwatch. "It has indeed been a pleasure making your acquaintance, Mr. Mashbir. You'll have to excuse me— I'm meeting friends for an after-performance party."

Hedy gave Anthiel a quick hug.

"George, thanks for that fine concerto," she said, then turned to Sidney. "Come on—my place is only ten minutes from here."

As Sidney drove, Hedy confided, "George is more sensible than he sounds. He lived in Europe during the horrors of the First World War, and he foresees its repetition. I was too young to remember, but recall the misery that followed. How times change."

She playfully shuffled her bare shoulders. "Now, I have every luxury. But in my youth, it was a miracle to have even enough bread!"

"With your success," Sidney glanced at her, "I would think you'd be sunbathing in the Bahamas. What motivates you to get involved in military inventions?"

"When quite young, I married a powerful member of the Nazi movement. I grew to despise him and his crowd, so when an opportunity to escape arose, I jumped at it. America's entrance into this current war is inevitable, and my new homeland needs all the advantages it can get to win."

"We're in agreement there; how'd you come to learn about guidance systems?"

"My husband ran a munitions company, and I paid attention."

"I see…A question: I've heard you've been given a hard time by the studios. Why's that?"

"Those prudes," she waved them off. "They will never forget my nude film scene. I'm not trying to be preachy—but is the human form immoral? Don't museums around the world display Greek, Roman, and Hindu statues and paintings of men *and* women exposed in all their grandeur? Far greater harm will come from the current state of American censorship limiting *free expression*."

"Do you really believe that's happening?"

She nodded.

"Just look at the American Motion Picture Production Code, which demands history, institutions, and prominent people from other nations be represented *fairly*—What they're really saying is, don't offend their fascist pig leaders! Both the president of European operations for General Motors and Henry Ford himself have been awarded Medals of Honor by the Reich, for converting their European auto facilities to the production of Jeeps and tanks. They'll claim that if they don't, Hitler will simply take over their operations. Instead, they make a pact with the devil! Other corporations supply oil, chemicals, steel, and aluminum to build the Nazi war machine, *while also* supplying the European Allies."

"Yes," Mashbir sighed, "and certain international banks make huge loans to pay Hitler's debts."

The conversation turned to lighter subjects by the time they reached her place. They took the elevator to the top floor of an eight-story building, where Hedy led him into a luxuriously furnished suite.

"Nice place," he said.

She giggled, waving her hands with an aristocratic air. "Oh, it will do..."

Her voice returned to its natural tone as she added, "I had a more formal home with servants, but I prefer this, much simpler. A cleaning lady comes by twice a week, and I usually eat out unless I have the impulse to cook for myself—or, a special guest."

With her looks, Sidney thought, *she probably doesn't have to eat many meals alone.*

He went to the drafting table, where diagrams were spread out.

"Might I summarize the process?" she asked.

Sidney smiled at the thought of an alluring actress explaining the technicalities of her invention. *She's been full of surprises so far*∗

With a professorial air, Hedy looked at her student. "Let's begin by assigning a code number to all the notes of the musical scale. Then imagine twelve player pianos, each playing a different song of the same length simultaneously...Our device reads the particular musical note being played at any moment on each of the twelve spinning scrolls, giving a constantly changing twelve-digit code number...Are you still with me, Sidney?"

"So far, so good."

"To add unpredictability to the code number generated, this device can randomly move either direction along all these scrolls."

She turned her lovely brown eyes in his direction.

"Now, if we transmit this randomly changing twelve digit code to direct a torpedo with a built-in receiver, as it moves toward its target, then enemy forces won't be able use their radio control systems to take over our weapon."

She paused.

"These are the blueprints. Look them over while I freshen up. Fix yourself a drink, if you like..."

Sidney dropped ice into a glass and filled it halfway, then took a sip while studying the diagrams. Fifteen minutes passed. He was so absorbed in the mechanics of the guidance system, he didn't realize until she touched him on the shoulder that Hedy had returned; she'd changed from her evening dress into a patterned silk dressing gown… He involuntarily smiled.

With considerable effort he redirected his thoughts. "It's a brilliant idea, Miss Lamarr. Let's hope the Navy's top brass has the imagination to appreciate the concept and aren't confused by the image of twelve player pianos strapped to a torpedo."

He looked at her.

"I must say, it's rare to find so much brainpower in one so glamorous."

"Any girl can be glamorous," she replied. "*All she has to do is stand still and look stupid*…So you really think you can influence the Navy to buy our invention?"

"I can certainly try. First thing is to get a patent for it. I can help with that."

Smiling warmly, she slipped an arm around his waist. "Good. Now on to more personal matters."

She pressed her soft, warm body against his, tilting her face upward, expecting to be kissed. Bells were going off like a three-alarm fire. Part of him wanted to gather her in his arms and taste firsthand the delights. After a sweet, but agonizing moment, he said, "Miss Lamarr—

"Please call me Eva—we agreed."

"All right, Eva, you're extremely bright, and one of the most beautiful women I've ever met. There's ten thousand guys in this town alone who would jump at the chance to make love to you, but I just can't."

"You don't like women?"

She dropped her arms and stepped back.

"No, nothing like that! It's that I'm very happily married to a wonderful woman. I messed up my first marriage by being away too much. I'm not going to ruin this one by fooling around."

"Oh, pooh, marriage!"

She moved toward him again.

"I've already had three husbands, and will undoubtedly be married at least that many times again."

She again attempted to embrace him.

"No, really!" he protested, backing toward the door, "I appreciate the opportunity, and may well hate myself tomorrow for turning it down, but I have to."

She stood quite still in the middle of the room, her head cocked to one side. A curious half-smile played across her beautiful features.

"Sidney Mashbir, you certainly are an original. I can't remember the last time a man turned me down."

He backed further toward the door.

"Hedy, I truly respect your efforts to help our nation's defense. I'll put you and Mr. Anthiel in touch with an engineer I know at Cal Tech. He can help you get the project in the form that the Patent Office requires."

He started out the door, but turned.

"It was a pleasure meeting you, Eva. I'll probably think about this evening many times in the future—you can rest assured of that."

"Goodbye, but to help you remember..."

Untying the sash of her dressing gown, it slipped off revealing a gorgeous body as bare as in her film.

"If you ever find yourself less happily married," she cajoled, "give me a call."

While riding the elevator down, he wondered, *Damn! Someday somebody's got to explain to me how come it's so hard to do the right thing!*

CHAPTER 42

Washington, D.C., November 1940

It had been a marathon six-hour read: Mashbir put down the black cloth-bound book, its spine labeled with orange-colored Japanese words. He poured a shot of whisky in his coffee, thoughtfully drank it, and then began the gauntlet, calling one publisher after another.

"Yes, I understand," he said, "the public doesn't want to read any more about the so-called Yellow Peril. But this book written in Japanese is very important, damn it! It details their actual battle plans in the Pacific, and only four guys in this whole crazy town can even read it. Fortunately, there's a Korean who has done an English translation that every politician ought to read, to say nothing of the Military Brass!"

After listening to excuses, he fumed, "All right, don't publish it, but you'll regret not doing it!" and slammed down the receiver.

"Publishers! Bahhh—bunch of sheep!" he declared. "They'll print mindless trash, but not a book that's critical to our country's survival. I feel like Paul Revere, shouting 'the Japanese are coming!' And everyone is either deaf or just doesn't care."

"Is this about that Kinoaki Matsuo book?" his secretary asked, poking her head in the door. "The one you picked up in California?"

He nodded. "That's the one. It's titled: *The Three-Power Alliance and a United States-Japanese War*—but it might as well be called *How Japan Plans to Kick Our Ass*. The author, a Japanese Naval Intelligence officer, persuades the Japanese that war is the answer to all their problems, while bragging about their superior military strength."

Sidney tapped his fingers on the book.

"It gives an amazingly accurate picture of U.S. forces: the size and location of our battleships and cruisers, you name it. Even how our officers are trained and the studies they take! And check out this quote," he said, opening to a bookmarked page and reading:

"'Even if the U.S. Fleet is fortunate enough to line up at Pearl Harbor, it will encounter an assault by a Japanese surprise-attack fleet before it is able to depart in the direction of the Western Pacific. Also, if the whole U.S. Fleet tries to come into or goes out of Pearl Harbor, measures will be taken by the Japanese Navy to inflict losses upon it by laying mines and using torpedoes in the vicinity, dealing a serious blow to the United States.'

"They boast we'll be so intimidated that we'll back down in fear, but that's not how it's going to play out!" he said, slamming the book on his desk.

"Sir, isn't there anyone else you can contact who might be of assistance in this matter?"

The following week, Sidney arrived a half-hour early at the Washington Monument, his warm breath clouding the frosty air as he paced. At precisely 1:00 P.M., the President's chief advisor, Harry Hopkins, appeared in a dark overcoat, an unlit cigarette in hand.

"Let's take a walk," he said.

"Certainly, sir. I presume this is about that book I mentioned?"

"No, it's not about that, though we can discuss it later." They walked in silence beneath leafless cherry trees, Sidney reflecting on the irony that these trees had been a peace and friendship offering from the Japanese back in 1912, and how beautiful their blossoms were in spring . . .

Hopkins continued, "I must emphasize everything we discuss today is to be treated *with complete secrecy.* Not just for now, but very possibly for the rest of your life."

He looked Sidney squarely in the eye.

"The President was very impressed by you, not only for that letter you assisted in writing to Emperor Hirohito, but by your whole demeanor. And your company's involvement in aviation will be helpful for what we're going to ask from you." He coughed. "Your phone call regarding that book came at a significant moment. We were considering who to recruit for a challenging task, which, if successful, could profoundly affect the entire Armed Forces."

"I certainly look forward to hearing how I can be of assistance."

Hopkins lit his cigarette; after a puff, he continued, "It's no secret Franklin wants to help our European allies, but he's been stymied by the strong isolationist sentiment in this country. He knows we'll inevitably be drawn into that war, and when that happens, air power is going to be critical."

"I agree wholeheartedly."

"Well, based on that realization, our President is proposing a radical realignment of the military. He wants to create a separate branch for the Air Force, headed by a cabinet officer of equal rank to the secretaries of the Army and Navy."

Mashbir stopped dead in his tracks.

"That's a great idea, but it's going to run into a lot opposition from the Military, to say nothing of the Congress—which will call it just another costly, unnecessary bureau!"

"You're right; the Army will fight it tooth and nail, probably the Navy as well. Especially if it takes money out of their budgets. That's why we need to nominate someone to that cabinet position whom they couldn't reject."

"Who do you have in mind?"

"There's only one man with that kind of status, Charles Lindbergh."

"That's a fantastic idea, and Lindbergh is the best choice for sure," Sidney replied enthusiastically. "Not only is he a fine aviator, but arguably the most popular figure in America. His ticker-tape parade down Broadway eclipsed any other, and that kidnapping and murder of his first child has opened the nation's heart to him. But sir, I hope I can speak candidly?"

"Of course!"

Hands clasped in front of him, Sidney shifted his weight side to side, wondering how best to put it.

"It wouldn't be the President also sees this as a way to silence his most prominent critic leading opposition to America's entry into the war? ... I heard Lindbergh speak with great conviction on that subject at one of his mass rallies, and in my opinion, it's going to be almost impossible to convince him to sign on."

"We're well aware of that," Hopkins replied, "but you've got to try and persuade him that it's his higher duty to country . . . FDR was disappointed and angry about all the negative things Lindbergh has been saying about him, but he's willing to overlook all that, and *hopes* Lindbergh is willing to do the same."

"But I have no official position—why would Lindbergh even listen to me? He'd think I was some kind of nut."

Hopkins smiled.

"Don't underestimate yourself. As for you getting to see him—that will be arranged at the highest levels, without him knowing why. *Your* job is to get him to consider the offer privately; the President can't publicly announce such a radical cabinet change with Lindbergh's name attached, should he reject it. And unfortunately at this time, it's Lindbergh, or no one."

Mashbir took a deep breath.

"It sure seems there's a whole lot of politics being played."

"Don't kid yourself, Mashbir: There's politics in getting *anything* done," Hopkins replied strongly. "And I believe with every fiber of my being that FDR is not only the best politician to come along in a hundred years, he's also the best statesman. And there's a hell of a difference, Colonel. I feel more comfortable calling you that, and you're to use that rank from now on during this mission, whether you're currently active service or not." Hopkins tossed his cigarette.

"So will you undertake this assignment at the personal request of the President of these United States and your Commander-in-Chief?"

Near Englewood, New Jersey

It was evening as a taxi pulled into the sweeping circular driveway. Sidney tilted his head to get a full view of the majestic two-story stone structure. "Are you sure this is the Morrow residence? Looks more like a big city library."

The driver gave him an odd look. "Of course I'm sure. There ain't but one Morrow house, and this it. Colonel Lindbergh and his family have been staying with his wife's folks since they came back from Europe. That'll be five bucks."

"Here's twelve, if you don't mind waiting to take me back to the train station? I doubt I'll be more than a half hour."

Might just be two minutes, for that matter, he thought, *if they throw me out on my ear.*

"Suit yourself, Mack. I'll be right here."

The cabbie picked up a magazine from the seat beside him and positioned it to catch the light from the imposing front porch.

Mashbir climbed the steps to the huge oak door and rang the bell. It was soon answered, not by a servant, but by Lindbergh himself. His slim build and youthful appearance belied his almost forty years.

"Colonel Mashbir? Come in, please. It's quite cold this evening; I thought we might be more comfortable in my study."

He led the way down a hallway to an open door. There, a fire was burning in a marble fireplace. Two walls were floor-to-ceiling bookcases, and there were a couple of glass-topped curio tables in the center of the room. Lindbergh indicated a pair of worn, but comfortable looking leather armchairs near the fireplace. They sat half-facing each other and the blazing fire.

"Would you care for something to eat or drink?"

"No, but thanks for the offer."

Mashbir's voice took on a serious tone.

"There is one thing I would like to request: that you promise me that whatever we speak of tonight, you will never divulge it to anyone, unless we come to an agreement."

Lindbergh looked confused, but nodded.

"All right, you have my word. I'll give instructions we're not to be disturbed."

He exited, leaving Sidney to wander about the room. The glass-topped curio tables caught his attention. They held an impressive array of medals from the United States, plus many from other countries. A large, rather gaudy one with a swastika stood out. Sidney realized this must be the one presented by Goering, head of Hitler's Air Force.

Lindbergh re-entered to see Mashbir examining the medals, but made no comment. He locked the door behind him, and they returned to their seats.

"I know you didn't ask for anything, but here's a cup of tea to warm you up."

"Thank you."

"Now what's this all about, Colonel? An old friend in Washington asked me as a personal favor to hear you out, but wouldn't tell me anything more."

Mashbir smiled. "Your friend probably didn't know. In fact, I doubt more than a half dozen people in the world know what I'm about to tell you. Please read this, but I'm afraid I can't leave it with you when I go."

Lindbergh silently examined the handwritten note, then read it aloud:

> "'Colonel Lindbergh,
>
> Please give every consideration to the proposal Colonel Mashbir is about to present to you. He speaks with my full approval and authority.
>
> Sincerely,
> Franklin Delano Roosevelt.'"

Lindbergh inspected the Presidential seal, then handed it back.

"Well, you've certainly gotten my attention."

Sidney took a deep breath, then plunged in.

"Charles, you more than anyone are aware airpower is playing an ever larger role in modern warfare. I, myself, am in the aviation industry, involved in the development of swifter planes with better navigational devices for military uses and for the advancement of civilian aircraft."

Lindbergh nodded affirmatively.

"Based on these factors, the President and his top advisors asked me to present an offer—They want to create a new cabinet post, a secretary of Air Force, to be on equal footing with the secretaries of Army and the Navy, with all Army aircraft and personnel transferring over.

And, there'd be more funding available for the development of better planes, just as you have advocated for years."

Lindbergh shot out of his chair, striding back and forth in front of the fire.

"That's a terrific proposal. So they want my advice, or maybe a public statement of approval? I'd be happy to do that!"

"That's a kind offer, but actually—they want you to be the first Secretary of the Air Force."

Lindbergh, face flushed, stopped pacing and stared at Mashbir for a long time.

"You know what's wrong with this wonderful picture? I'll tell you: I'd have to become part of Roosevelt's team. I couldn't live with that. It's been my mission to prevent him from dragging us into another terrible conflict in Europe which is likely to be called World War **Two**—and he hates my guts for it! Add to that, ever since that airmail carrier disaster, he hasn't forgiven me for speaking out against him. What did he expect, they could just take a bunch of young lieutenants straight out of flight school for mail routes over rugged mountain ranges and vast deserts?"

Sidney let him vent, then calmly replied, "Roosevelt is willing to say publicly that you were totally right, and that he should have listened to you from the start."

"Wants me that bad, does he?" Lindbergh declared. "Do you have any idea what this offer means to me? All I ever wanted was to be around planes. Saw my first when I was nine—a barnstormer, working his way through the Midwest—giving rides to kids and their folks for a few bucks. From then on, I ate, slept, and dreamt aviation."

Lindbergh calmed down. "They call me *Lucky Lindy,* because of my trans-Atlantic flight. I hated that—what I did had little to do with luck. It was years of preparation."

"I realize that," Sidney said, smiling, "and you also happened to be the best pilot around. That's why you're the right man for this job, damn it! Excuse me, Colonel, but it sticks out a mile that you could do great things, things nobody else could do as the head of the Air Force!"

Lindbergh returned his smile, but a bitter one.

"Are you familiar with scriptures, Mashbir? You're taking me to the mountaintop and tempting me; not that I'm comparing you to Satan, you understand. Though, I'm not sure I can say the same for the man who sent you; nor am I comparing myself to Christ either, but like him, I must decline."

Sidney got out of his chair and stepped forward. "I know you have grave differences of opinion with the administration, but you've got to be bigger than that. If you don't accept, there won't be an Air Force for a long while. Your country needs you more than ever!"

Lindbergh shot him a hot look. "I love this country, sir. I'm aware that life for Europeans in general right now, and for Jews in Europe in particular, is not going so well—and that's not right.... But that's **not** America's problem. I'd rather have Germany rule all Europe than have it fall to communism and the semi-Asians of Russia and the Orient!"

"You're willing to sacrifice all the democratic countries of Europe to the Nazis? This is literally a life-and-death struggle, and you could make a big difference. I know you have powerful friends whom you respect, but those words sound like theirs, not yours."

Sidney noted a slight hesitance.

Lindbergh shook his head. "No, I've told you what I believe and I'll stand by it. Go tell the men who sent you that I refuse to help them in their schemes."

"Please, think it over. You have until Thursday night to give your answer."

Lindbergh scoffed, "You want to know why Thursday night? I'll tell you: because on Friday I'm giving a national speech over the radio on behalf of *America First*, and Roosevelt would do almost anything to silence me⬜Thanks for coming, and I appreciate your position. I'll remember this offer for the rest of my life, but once and for all, I must decline!"

What else can I do? Mashbir thought.

Lindbergh showed him out, then returned to his den and stared into the glowing fireplace; a woman entered.

"Darling, you look exhausted. Who was that visitor?"

"A very dedicated and persuasive individual who offered me a kingdom."

"Really?" she replied. "One doesn't get offered a kingdom every day. Did you accept?"

"No; it was the toughest thing I've ever had to do. I'm sorry, Anne, but I can't tell you any more about it."

She tucked her arm through his and smiled.

"That's okay. I'd hate to live in some drafty old castle!"

PART THREE

CHAPTER 43

American University Park, a neighborhood of Washington, D.C. November 24, 1941

A barrier of sandbags were piled three-high outside, along with a special curtain ready to drop, sealing off the entrance from poison gas, should the need arise...Inside, Civil Defense Warden Sidney Mashbir and his three volunteer deputies, Wilson, Fred, and Captain Edward Hill, gathered round the transmitter and radio reception equipment. A hundred first-aid kits, stacks of civilian defense pamphlets, and two dozen cases of canned food lined one wall, with two fifty gallon water storage tanks nearby.

"I really want to thank you guys," Mashbir said. "It's hard to believe a couple of weeks ago this was just a car garage. But with your help, we've created the first completely equipped air-raid shelter headquarters in the Washington, D.C. area. And within a month, a half dozen more are scheduled to be built."

His companions nodded with approval.

"And even though we're no longer in active military, we couldn't just stand around doing nothing like ducks in a pond, waiting to be blasted; not after seeing all the destruction the German Luftwaffe had done to London, bombing it day and night for almost two months."

He scanned their faces. "I know you've probably had jokes thrown at you, calling us alarmists, that the war is thousands of miles away." He laughed. "Well, if those blind optimists are proven wrong, they'll find themselves running to our shelters, and we'll be the ones keeping communications open and directing aid to those in need."

Irene called from inside the house: "Sidney, I've made coffee and baked up some banana nut muffins for you and your friends."

"Thanks, almost done. We'll be in the kitchen in a few minutes!"

✳✳✳✳

Two weeks later, Sunday afternoon, December 7, 1941.

Eleven-year-old Donald and his dad, both in pajamas and robes, listened to the radio in their living room. "What do you think, Dad, can the Redskins beat the Giants, and win it all again?"

"I don't see why not. Sammy Baugh is slinging them as well as ever, and their defense is solid—though it might be tough getting by the Bears."

The radio went silent, then a new announcer's voice broke in:

"We interrupt this program to bring you this bulletin: The U.S. Naval Base at Pearl Harbor has just been attacked! The attacking aircraft appear to be Japanese. Repeat, the Naval Base at Pearl Harbor in the Hawaiian Islands has come under attack by Japanese planes, which have sunk at least two ships. Total casualties yet unknown. Stay tuned to this station for further developments."

The radio program returned to the football game. "Dad, it sounds like the sports broadcasters don't even know what was just announced." Sidney was already headed up the stairs. "What does this mean, Daddy?"

He didn't answer . . . Twenty minutes later he returned in full Army uniform.

"More ships are sinking," Donald cried out. "It sounds real bad."

Sidney placed a calming hand on his son's shoulder.

"For fifteen years I've been trying to convince these blind idiots in Washington that the Japanese were going to hit Pearl Harbor."

He softened his voice.

"When Mom gets back, please tell her I had to report to Army headquarters downtown to see where they want me to go—probably the Pacific. I'll contact you just as soon as I know something." He gave Donald a quick hug and left.

Trudging back that evening, Sidney saw his wife and son hovering around the radio. He tossed his uniform cap and jacket on a chair, then slumped onto the couch.

"Have you had anything to eat?" Irene asked, noting his gloomy expression. "I'd guess you haven't. Let me fix you something."

"I'm not hungry."

"Where are they sending you, Daddy, and when do you leave?"

"You know, I went everywhere, Army, Navy! Even offered to serve without pay, but they're all running 'round like chickens with their heads cut off. Too damn busy to even listen."

He sighed.

"And add to that, my military records are somehow sabotaging me. Problem is, everybody who can back me up is somewhere else. Witsell's in Panama, and Zach's at Pearl Harbor in command of a cruiser." *My God, he may be dead!...No, I can't think like that. He'll come through this, but you can bet his hands will be more than full for a long while.*

"Listen, Sidney," Irene exclaimed, "when they come to their senses, they'll need you! You're the best they can find when it comes to Intelligence on Japan."

The following day, America declared war on Japan...Three days later, Germany and Italy, in support of their Japanese ally, announced war against the U.S. The European war that had been raging for almost sixteen months, now became World War II!

※※※※

March 1942, Southern California

Rows of ruby-red strawberries freckled the rolling landscape. Naoki, the Japanese soldier who had once saved Mashbir's life in the Sonora Desert long ago, was now in his mid-forties. He and his eighteen-year-old son, Naokio, were both gathering fruit.

After hours of filling cardboard cartons, Naoki stretched his arms and shoulders. "It is time to take a rest, my son."

He chose a succulent fruit and took a bite.

"Is it not a glorious day?"

"Yes, Father," Naokio replied, smiling as he ate several strawberries.

"How are your night classes at the community college coming along?"

"I'm doing well, Father."

"That is good to hear, Naokio; I appreciate your help, but wish you could go full time. You have a bright mind, and should use it."

It was early that evening when Sheriff Anderson pulled his car in front of the small farmhouse. He and his two deputies approached the entrance.

"Damn Japs, it's about time we—" one deputy said.

"Shut up," Anderson ordered. "We're on official business."

He knocked on the front door. Naoki opened it.

"Your son around?" the sheriff asked.

Naoki was confused. "What is this about?"

A voice called out in Japanese, "Father, who's there?"

"Something serious," Naoki replied in Japanese.

Naokio came forward, no longer in his work overalls, looking collegiate with his metal-rimmed glasses.

"Oh, Sheriff Anderson. Nice to see you, how can we be of assistance?"

"Well, um…" the sheriff mumbled, looking at his boots. "Let me just read this to you, son."

He held up a piece of paper:

By proclamation of President Roosevelt, all people of Japanese ancestry are to be excluded from the entire Pacific coast, including California, Oregon, and Washington. These individuals are to be transported to, and then interned at, government-run Relocation Centers in other areas of the western United States.

"I'm sorry to tell you, but your family has to pack up and be ready to relocate within a week."

"Can I see that document?" Naokio asked.

After reading it carefully, he whispered to his distraught father; he then faced the sheriff. "This can't be! I was born here; I'm an American citizen. My father arrived over twenty years ago and bought this farm with savings from working as a cook for the U.S. Army."

Anderson shrugged.

"Supposedly this is for your own good, *and* our national security. Ever since Pearl Harbor there's been widespread panic, fearing the existence of vast Japanese spy networks. But even before the attack, there was lots of anger simmering toward you folks—Now it's ten times worse. Your neighbors have had rocks thrown through their windows and car tires slashed. And I'm afraid it's only going to get worse."

He looked at them earnestly.

"Personally, I like your family. You're honest, hardworking people...*And* I've been told these relocation camps aren't too uncomfortable and it's just temporary."

"But who will run my parents' farm in the meantime?"

Anderson looked away. "Sorry, Naokio, I'm not sure how it will all work out. We're at war, and our leaders are doing what they think is best." He looked into their eyes. "For what it's worth, I don't agree, but they ain't asking my opinion."

CHAPTER 44

With most of Europe defeated or under siege by the Nazis, many Southeast Asian countries that had been ruled for hundreds of years saw an opportunity to throw off their European colonial oppressors—but soon found themselves also immersed in war.

The world watched in amazement as Japan, which already controlled Korea and much of China, expanded her territory to the border of India in the west and New Guinea in the south, also conquering the British colonies of Burma and Hong Kong, all of Malaysia and Singapore, the Gilbert Islands, and the island of New Britain. *And all of this in only six months' time!*

With the consent of France's Nazi-controlled Vichy regime, Japan took over French Indochina (Vietnam, Laos, and Cambodia) and conquered all the major islands of the Dutch East Indies (Indonesia). Thailand wished neutrality and at first attempted to resist, but was pressured to align with Japan militarily.

As for U.S. losses, Guam and Wake Island, their outposts in the Eastern Pacific, had been taken—though the area of most concern to Americans was the Philippines; despite being well aware of a possible invasion, there was only a limited U.S. Army presence, a smaller force of Marines, and some Filipino troops assigned to assist them... They found themselves unprepared for the size of the assault, and were steadily pushed back.

General MacArthur, who had been in command there for five years, followed *Battle Plan Orange*, the very strategy that had been updated by Mashbir fourteen years earlier: their troops yielded ground to gain time, with the hope of at some point mounting a decisive defense...There was hard fighting, and in fact, Japanese losses were substantial, but by April 1, 1942, American forces were besieged at Bataan, a peninsula on the island of Luzon.

President Roosevelt ordered MacArthur to leave quickly to avoid being captured. With humiliation, the General gathered his family and a few of his staff, evacuating by night in PT boats...This left General Wainwright to carry on the struggle, which ended in his surrender on May 8—a bitter blow to U.S. morale; because up until Pearl Harbor, the Japanese hadn't been considered to be capable fighters.

From his headquarters in Australia, MacArthur made his famous declaration regarding the Philippines, '*I will return*'. But many Americans were doubtful of his capability to do so, while strongly supporting the overall war effort.

July 1942, Eastern Signal Corps Training Center, Fort Monmouth, New Jersey:

Mashbir visualized the events, as Zach described over the phone how he had commanded one of the cruisers escorting Lt. Colonel Jimmy Doolittle's task force for his Tokyo raid in April 1942: America's first successful bombing of the Japanese home islands after Pearl Harbor. This demonstrated that Japan was also vulnerable to air attack, thus providing a confidence boost for America.

"Sid, I know how much you want to see some real action, but at least you're now back in uniform! So what's the Army putting your talents to?"

"I'm in charge of the Statistics and Reference branch of the Signal Corps, an intelligence organization. But in truth, I'm a glorified librarian maintaining military records."

"Well, my friend, that's all going to change. Your next assignment will take you to the other end of the world."

✳✳✳✳

The dust from the airfield landing hadn't had time to settle when Sidney disembarked and found himself facing a two-man reception committee.

"Welcome to Australia, Colonel Mashbir. I'm Colonel Black," his greeter said, brushing off his uniform before offering to shake hands.

"Thanks, Colonel. It wasn't necessary for you to meet me yourself. Your driver could have taken me to my quarters."

"Wasn't my decision, *mate*," he replied, as they hopped into the Jeep. "Word came down from MacArthur himself that the local ranking Australian Liaison officer—that's me—was to bring you directly to Staff Headquarters. I'm guessing he wants to meet with you before you even get a chance to settle in…"

MacArthur hadn't changed much since he'd seen him eight years earlier, he thought, *though he must be at least sixty.*

"Lieutenant Colonel Mashbir, reporting as ordered, sir."

"Stand at ease." MacArthur shook his head. "You know it took quite a while to locate you, Colonel. Some idiot waylaid you to a glorified desk job, and you even found a way to reorganize that department. It was your Navy buddy Zacharias who finally helped connect us."

"Organizing is something of a compulsion of mine."

"That's a good thing—you'd be surprised how many senior officers can't do it. That's why we've chosen you, *that, and your language skills,* for a special assignment: You're officially listed as my chief Japanese translator, but you will be doing a whole lot more…You'll be working with Colonel Tomlen—he's young, but I've heard a most capable administrator."

MacArthur then smiled at his seated companion.

"This gentleman on my left is Baron Adolf Tscheppe-Weidenbach, but we call him General Willoughby, my Chief of Staff G-2—and my pet fascist."

Willoughby acknowledged Mashbir with a nod.

MacArthur continued, "Be prepared to work sixteen-hour days, Colonel, everybody here does. Now please wait outside. General Willoughby will further brief you as he directs you to your quarters."

Once Mashbir was gone, Willoughby commented, "You obviously have a great deal of confidence in this colonel."

"More than you can imagine," MacArthur replied, remembering

Mashbir's assistance in ridding him of his beautiful, but tempestuous lover, Isabel!

As Mashbir and Willoughby exited headquarters, he asked, "Sir, I hope you don't mind a few questions, but were you really part of the European aristocracy?"

Willoughby waved it off.

"I left that all behind when I moved to the States as a teenager."

Mashbir hesitated.

"And what about that remark calling you his pet fascist?"

"The General enjoys reminding me of my youthful enthusiasm; I was once an outspoken supporter of General Franco in his battle against the Communists in Spain—and speaking of our pasts, you don't remember me, but twenty-five years ago, I was accused of pro-German sentiments during World War One. You headed the Army counter-intelligence section that interviewed me and cleared my name."

Mashbir grinned. "And now you're one of my commanding officers."

"Life is full of surprises. I must say, Colonel, your letter of introduction from Captain Zacharias was quite impressive. It's a rare occasion when Army and Navy Intelligence both back the same project one hundred percent! You're to command a top-secret organization, ATIS, the Allied Translator and Interpreter Section, whose task is the strategic evaluation of all Japanese documents obtained from the battlefield. You and your team will also interrogate most of the Japanese prisoners of war, of which we've only gotten one so far, though many more will be coming."

"How large is ATIS?"

"It's in its early stage, staffed by less than forty men, mainly drawn from the Australian, Canadian, and British Army, Air, and Navy personnel. There are some Chinese and White Russians, and even a few East Indies Netherlanders—but up to now, only a handful of Americans, which your leadership position says to us is about to change!"

"Sounds interesting. I have one last question, out of curiosity:

There was an Army Intelligence officer, Captain Henshaw, stationed in Honolulu. Do you know what happened to him?"

Willoughby smiled.

"He'll be spending the duration of the war on the coldest, foggiest Aleutian island the Army can find."

"And his fiancée, Ruth Kuhns?"

"She's still on Oahu; as a matter of fact, she, as well as her mother, father, and half-brother, are all guests of our government—in a prison, that is...They were arrested the day after Pearl Harbor. We found evidence they'd been feeding the Japs information for a long time; their cottage overlooked the harbor, so they could keep an eye out for fleet comings and goings. They sent coded messages to enemy ships offshore, utilizing a flashing light system. We caught them as they were about to escape via a Jap sub."

"Sounds like they finally got what they deserved!"

Five months later, December 1942

Colonel Mashbir and a young Australian Army captain focused on a Japanese map that had just been retrieved after a battle in New Guinea.

"I see why this caught your attention, Caiger," Mashbir said. "Something is strange; most of their coastal military positions have generic games—this one for instance, *Hill Alpha*, and this one, *Ocean Point*...But as you mentioned, those we've circled in red have names that aren't haphazardly chosen—I wonder why?"

Caiger shrugged.

"Are you saying they might have significance for the Japanese?"

"Exactly. This one is named after a shrine to Emperor Meiji. And these others relate to battles, a couple going back to feudal times—and not necessarily winning battles either—but heroic fights against great odds while confronting invaders—Similar to American battles, such as *The Alamo*, or most recently, our bloody defeat at Bataan."

"Mentioning that last battle ought to get MacArthur's attention," Caiger ventured.

Mashbir was silent for a while. "Now what if," he began, "the Japanese strategy is to stage a 'to-the-last-man defense' at those positions? It could take us the better part of two years to move up that coast, with God knows how many casualties."

He stretched his arms upward to loosen up, and took a deep breathe…"I'm going to write a recommendation based on my interpretation, *crediting you* for bringing this map to my attention; I'll then pass it on to General Willoughby, and see where it goes."

Within thirty minutes of delivering his evaluation, Mashbir and Willoughby were outside MacArthur's office, waiting to be summoned in.

"General, I'm pretty nervous. I thought my suggestion would go up through regular channels; I didn't think I'd be explaining it personally to MacArthur so soon."

"He told me to bring you over ASAP. It's your concept, so it's your show."

An orderly opened the door for them to enter, then closed it and left.

MacArthur was seated behind his desk straightening a pile of papers, as they came to attention. When he'd finished the task, he looked up. "Stand at ease, gentlemen.

"Mashbir, I've been meaning to commend you. When you first took over ATIS, it was divided along the lines of the various military branches and nationalities, each working against one another in a petty fashion, competing to be the first to discover significant information. You've streamlined operations to handle an ever-expanding flow of material, and somehow created a team-spirit where information is shared."

"Thank you, Sir."

MacArthur fired his first question: "So explain exactly why you think the Japs are going to act in this most unusual fashion?"

Mashbir stepped forward.

"It would be clearer if we could look at a map."

MacArthur obliged by pulling down a rolled wall map and handed Mashbir a pointer.

"Here's what struck me, General, when analyzing a Japanese map we'd captured."

Mashbir tapped out the positions.

"These four are significant locations with major concentrations of Japanese forces. These other places between them also have troops, but not nearly in equal numbers. What caught my attention was that each of these four strong points had been given a name sacred or famous in Japanese military history or samurai legend: *And they were all fights-to-the-last-man!*"

Mashbir wiped his perspiring forehead. "So what I'm predicting is that they plan to fall back to these positions as we advance along the New Guinea coast, making a last-ditch defense at each of them."

Mashbir put down the pointer and looked his supreme commander in the eye.

"The Japanese very much honor the heroic actions of their ancestors. Just as an Englishman would rather fight and die at a place called Agincourt than one named Pimple Hill. Or how American troops would rather make a last stand at a site named after *The Alamo*, rather than one called Prairie Dog Gulch."

"I get the point." MacArthur, who was usually without humor, showed the hint of a smile. "The question is, what do we do about it?"

"Well, sir," Mashbir swallowed hard, "here's the uncertain part: I believe if our main troops bypass those four strong points and instead we only assign minimal token forces to keep watch on them, then—if I've read it right—the Japanese will simply dig in, expecting a future all-out assault.

"As I understand it," he went on, "our objective is to move steadily up the coast, not necessarily kill every Japanese soldier along the way. Using this method, we'd 'leapfrog' past those points, while cutting off supply lines to them...They'd either surrender, or what with starvation, malaria, and God knows what else is happening in that rotten climate, they'll wither on the vine."

MacArthur studied the map, then seated himself on the corner of his desk as he filled his corn-cob pipe, got it lit, and took a few puffs. After he was sure it was drawing satisfactorily, he ventured,

"If I did as you suggest, Mashbir, it could shorten the campaign by six months or more, with a lot less casualties. But what if," he continued, his voice rising, "and *this* is the joker in the deck—what if we bypass those points, as you suggest, and now I've got forty-thousand Japs to my rear with no guarantee they won't break out and jump me from behind, especially if they get desperate. What do you think, Willoughby?"

"It's your call, sir—Very risky, most of our staff wouldn't recommend it...But we definitely wish to avoid battles like *Buna*, with them digging in and fighting to the very last man."

MacArthur stared out the window, remembering that battle, with its heavy loss of lives . . . His pipe tobacco burned out; he tapped embers into a brass ashtray made from a cut-down artillery shell casing on his desk, then spoke:

"All right, let's put this in motion. Beg, borrow, or steal the transports we'll need for this 'Leapfrog Strategy'. Get some Australian troops assigned to me to harass the Japs at this first location." He pointed to a spot on the map where Mashbir had indicated was one of the strategically-named Japanese sites.

"We'll keep them thinking we're going in for a major assault at any time. Mashbir, you're to keep me personally informed on any new captured materials you think might have a bearing on this matter. That's all for now."

Once outside in the hallway, Willoughby turned to Mashbir.

"Well done, Colonel! Now I hope to the heavens you know what you're talking about. If you're wrong, this could be the biggest disaster since Pearl Harbor."

"Believe me, General, you don't know how hard I'm praying!"

The following month, Australia, January 1943

With a pounding headache, Mashbir looked at the ever-growing and gruesome piles of dried bloodstained and soiled documents on his desk, retrieved from the battlefront . . . He had recently managed to move ATIS to more spacious quarters in a dilapidated estate, isolated in the countryside and well-suited for their purposes, especially privacy. Similar stacks were accumulating on the desks of his translators, creating a feeling of overload as they attempted to analyze this material *and* find enough time for sleep.

Colonel Tomlen approached.

"Mashbir, have you got that last batch translated yet?"

Looking at him through bloodshot eyes, Mashbir replied, "Not quite yet."

Then, lifting a ragged fragment of a document, covered with what he guessed was human guts smeared on it, he added, "This is only a part of a troop deposition order, giving the general allocation of Japanese forces—but not the breakdown on where individual battalions and companies are positioned. That second half of this deposition may, or may not, be somewhere in this mess," pointing to mounds of similar-looking materials.

He exhaled slowly.

"Our troops are now advancing further, and are therefore retrieving plenty of potentially important documents, but we don't have enough manpower to evaluate them."

"What do you mean?" Tomlen countered. "You've got three dozen men who all came highly recommended as proficient in Japanese!"

"Yes, in the *spoken* language. Problem is, *written* Japanese is much more difficult. In English you have twenty-six characters in the alphabet; Japanese has more than five hundred, many of which can be interpreted in several ways depending on context. On top of that, there's both the printed and their cursive form, called *Sosho*."

"I don't give a damn about number of characters and all that nonsense; I need that translation!" Tomlen demanded.

With clenched fists at his sides, Mashbir forced a smile.

"Get me more translators of the written word, and I'll give you what you want faster."

Tomlen confidently replied, "Hell, we've started that language school in Colorado. And General MacArthur has put a priority request for the first fifty coming out to be assigned here."

"Well then," Mashbir clapped his hands several times, "We can expect them about this time next year. That's how long it takes to become capable to sight read the kind of documents we're dealing with.

By the way, how's my request coming along recommending we accept Nisei volunteers—you know, American-born Japanese—as translators? *They* could be here in just a few weeks."

"I threw that memo away as soon as it came across my desk— Wasn't going to let the old man think we'd gone nuts. It's crazy, proposing that a bunch of enemy aliens interned in camps be brought into the headquarters of the Supreme Commander of the Army in the Pacific. You can't trust Japs. Probably half of them are spies!"

"You did what?"

Tomlen took a step back as Sidney moved forward until he was face to face with him.

"They're not enemy aliens. Most are loyal American citizens who hate the fanatics now running the Japanese government as much as we do. *And* we urgently need their help. I'm going to resubmit my request in even stronger terms, directly to the General, and *don't you get in my way!"*

ATIS grew rapidly, again moving its headquarters into a converted elementary school gymnasium, now filled mainly with almost two hundred young Japanese Nisei, with some Caucasians among them. Most sat at desks lined up in rows, poring over documents, as Mashbir toured the facility with General MacArthur.

"Colonel, I wanted to let you know, your translators have been doing a fine job."

"Thank you, sir. I'll tell the men. By the way, I'm testing out a fresh idea. Some new arrivals are superior in Japanese skills, but their English and military phraseology are not good. For others, it's the opposite. We've assigned scores of A, B, C, or D according to their abilities, then matched them up into teams, so within each team there's proficiency in both languages, thereby covering each other's weaknesses. It's worked out well so far."

"Sounds like something a teacher might do with students, so they mentor one another. Any other tricks up your sleeve?"

Sidney handed him a small booklet.

"What's this?" MacArthur flipped through it.

"We had a problem when we brought in prisoners, which regrettably doesn't happen much, what with our men often killing them out of vengeance."

He shook his head in disgust.

"But when they did come in, our interrogators were in the dark, not knowing their rank, which regiments they were from—or even what their medals stood for."

"I see where you're going," MacArthur replied. "So you created this booklet illustrating the ranks, medals, and uniforms of all Japanese forces, and in full color, I see."

"Yep, we're also keeping records on all officers of every division in the Japanese Army, Navy, and Air Force. We find during interrogations, when we can mention their regiments and who their superior officers are, the prisoners are more willing to confide in us Eventually, we hope to know more about their troop movements and the placement of their forces *than they do themselves!*"

"Very clever." MacArthur pointed. "And what's going on with all that electronic equipment over there?"

"I've requested a sampling of all enemy communications gear we can get our hands on, to better understand how they work. We can then better circumvent or destroy them. We've even discovered some improvements we might put into our own equipment."

"I'm impressed. Is there anything I can do to further assist you?"

"Two things, sir: As I mentioned earlier, we need more prisoners. It must be made crystal clear to our troops that they're killing potential sources of vital information. *And,* a defeated soldier is no longer a threat and should be treated appropriately. There's challenge enough in obtaining prisoners, since most Japanese would rather take their own lives than be captured. You'd think their suicide was out of fear or weakness, but instead, they believe their soul can then fight on in the name of the emperor."

MacArthur appeared unsettled by the thought.

"And what's your second request?"

"That all captured documents be sent to headquarters—no more taking of souvenirs! I don't care if our troops want to impress their girlfriends back home by sending them something retrieved in battle . . . Why, one of our own soldiers was found with an enemy map in his pocket, which he had picked up a couple of days earlier. That map would have pinpointed the artillery location which ended up blowing him to bits."

The General patted Mashbir on the shoulder.

"Good ideas. I'll put out an Executive Order tomorrow for all your requests."

The following morning, a sergeant intercepted Mashbir as he arrived at his office.

"A word with you, sir. It's happened again."

"What are you talking about?"

"A bunch of soldiers caught two of our Nisei coming out of the mess hall last night. They got into a scuffle, pushing and name calling."

He looked away.

"Well, our guys got beat up. I had warned them to walk away if they could, and they tried to do just that," he said with exasperation. "This is the third time it's happened. It's gonna get real ugly if nothing is done."

He looked Mashbir in eye.

"Those Nisei volunteered for this; it's not right them being called slant eyes, and Japs, and crap like that!"

"Who's behind this," Mashbir asked, trying to contain his temper.

"That's the problem, sir—they're Tomlen's men; two were M.P.s, with their arm bands removed. I thought you ought to know—and there's something else."

"Go on."

"Some guards got rough with prisoners during an interrogation session."

"How rough?"

"I don't want to get anybody in trouble, sir."

"Spit it out!"

"They claimed they were *softening* them up. One had a couple teeth knocked out." The sergeant gnawed his thumbnail. "I know it's not right, but we've been getting reports from the front. Many of our buddies are badly injured or coming back dead."

Mashbir strode through the building until he spotted his quarry speaking to a junior officer. "Excuse me, Colonel Tomlen, we need to talk."

"What is it now, Can't you see I'm busy?"

"We'd be more comfortable taking a stroll outside." Mashbir was already moving in that direction, with Tomlen having little choice but to follow. It was a brisk pace through the door and fifty yards beyond. Tomlen abruptly stopped.

"This is far enough. What the hell do think you're playing at?"

Mashbir prodded him in the chest with a finger.

"I know you and others hate my guts because I pushed through that Nisei program. That's okay—it was the best way to get the job done, and I don't give a damn whether people like me or not. *But here are couple of things you ought to know.*

"General MacArthur and I go back a long ways and he personally requested me for this job."

He shot Tomlen a cold glare. "Just now, my sergeant reported the latest outrage your Yahoos perpetrated on my Nisei translators. These are the same men that the General just complimented for their splendid work."

His right hand clenched.

"Added to that, your men brutalized some prisoners, *and I will not tolerate this!*"

Loathing emanated from Tomlen.

Mashbir returned a steely expression.

"I'm not holier than thou; I know how you and your men feel; I'd like to vent and slug somebody too—But my goal, as should be yours, is to win this war…The way I see it: Either you post an order tomorrow, making it perfectly clear that all my staff and our prisoners are to be treated with respect, *and* that there will be *severe penalties for harassing them.* Otherwise, we go to MacArthur, tell our stories, and one of us leaves with his military career chewed to shreds—Do we have an agreement in principle?"

Tomlen pulled back a fist.

"Go on, throw the first punch," Mashbir taunted, "I'd welcome kicking your ass for what you've done to my men!"

Tomlen thought twice, then walked away.

On Mashbir's return, a Nisei waited outside his office. On hearing the approach of his commander, he stood at attention, revealing black-and-blue bruises on his cheek and chin, combined with his slightly hunched posture.

"Sir, I have a request to make."

"We'll talk in my office."

The young man shifted nervously, searching for the right words. Mashbir broke the silence.

"Are you here to make a complaint against the men who beat you up?"

"That's not the reason, sir. It's because I and the other Nisei translators feel like insignificant *paper pushers*," he blurted. "That's what some soldiers are calling us."

To lighten the atmosphere, Mashbir smiled. "I've heard they've been calling you a whole lot worse. But we both know what you're doing is very important for winning this war."

"That may be true, sir, but please hear me out. Perhaps you remember my father?"

"What's your name again?"

Mashbir examined his features.

"Naokio. My father is..."

He was hit with a flash of recognition.

"Oh, you're Naoki's son. Your dad helped save my life many years ago. How's he doing?"

"Okay," he replied in a lukewarm tone, then described how he and his family had been part of a Japanese farm community at the time of Pearl Harbor. They and their neighbors had discussed how best to support America in the war they knew would immediately follow, believing their assistance would be needed more than ever to grow food. To their surprise, they were gathered into internment camps.

"Our living conditions were often uncomfortable, but in general benign," Naokio explained. "We smiled and acted like it was nothing to fret about: Children went to school and men worked various jobs in the encampment. Some even joked how nice it was to receive food and shelter. But *inside*, there was sadness and humiliation, seeing the barbed-wire fences and armed guards."

"I understand," Mashbir replied.

Naokio flinched, straightening his posture, shoulders back as he spoke.

"I was born and raised in America, and owe her my full allegiance. I, and the other Nisei, wish to do more!"

"What do you mean?"

"We want to accompany troops to the battlefront as translators, analyzing documents as they first come in, when they have their most strategic value. And we will also be available to interrogate prisoners immediately upon their capture—"

Sidney held out his hand. "Stop and think carefully, Naokio. You'd be placing yourselves in a very dangerous situation. It's not uncommon for Japanese soldiers to *borrow* the uniforms of American soldiers killed in battle, so as to penetrate our lines. There's a good chance of you and your fellow Nisei being mistakenly killed by our own troops. Add to that, some American soldiers despise *all* Japanese, and might *intentionally* want to get you. I hate to say it, but you might find yourself dodging bullets from all directions."

Mashbir sighed heavily. "And lastly, and perhaps most important—If you're caught, you will be tortured—and retribution might be meted out to any relatives you have back in Japan. That may be too much to ask of anyone!"

Naokio stepped forward.

"I understand, but we would risk all that to regain the pride taken from our families in our new homeland."

Mashbir took a long pause.

"If you feel that strongly, I'll get it approved on a trial basis. Your idea is brilliant. How better to contribute to the war effort than by having our organization going into battle with the troops!

"This will be strictly voluntary, however, with rotating tours of duty, so that everyone gets a chance to spend time at their desks—and in the trenches!"

CHAPTER 45

Philippines, February 1943

A Japanese supply transport truck accompanied by two Jeeps sped down a dirt road bordered by dense forest. Around the bend, the truck nose-dived into a deep trench camouflaged by branches and leaves, flipping over and crashing against a tree trunk, as the Jeeps veered wildly to avoid the same fate. From the jungle, three Americans and twenty Filipino fighters rushed out, firing rounds. Stunned by the surprise, the Japanese were soon defeated as the ambushers, gathering all the supplies they could carry, headed back up into the hills.

ATIS Headquarters, Australia

General Willoughby was on the phone.

"Colonel Mashbir, we received another radio transmission from that Colonel Cushing—you remember, he'd been a mining engineer in the Philippines before the war? He claims he's leading a Guerilla Resistance Movement against the Japanese occupation and needs our support. Problem is, General MacArthur doesn't think the Filipinos are willing to put themselves on the line enough to make it worth the effort."

Without hesitation, Mashbir replied, "It isn't easy for villagers to fight against well-trained soldiers. And, you know—it's different from Europe. Way different! Why hell, resistance fighters there can blend in and probably even speak their enemies' language—but the Filipinos don't look like and don't speak Japanese. And if they openly resist, their families are endangered!

"Trust me General, I'd give Colonel Cushing whatever he wants as he fights his private war! We need all the help we can get. Let's work together to convince MacArthur to send over a submarine with supplies."

"All right, we'll give it try. But for right now, Colonel, I have an announcement for you and your team. I'll be there in an hour."

Willoughby was led by Mashbir to an elevated platform at the front of the large gymnasium, facing six hundred translators seated in rows at their individual desks. Mashbir tapped the live microphone.

"Good afternoon. General Willoughby has something important to say. Please put down your work and give him your undivided attention."

The general took the microphone.

"I'm here to congratulate you."

He scanned the sea of attentive faces.

"Yesterday morning, some of your team members translated documents detailing a so-called non-military sea convoy traveling from Rabaul to various points on the New Guinea coast—Well, in fact, those landing craft were each carrying seventy-five enemy soldiers. Your interpreted data gave the exact routes and hideouts along the coastline used for concealing their ships…Within minutes of receiving this information, Allied Air Force Headquarters was notified, and just *forty minutes later* an air strike was being prepared."

The General's voice deepened. "At 1600 hours yesterday, over three hundred of their landing barges were sunk, with casualties between twelve and fifteen thousand! *And we did not lose a single man or plane*This surprise air strike was a Pearl Harbor in reverse, and you all deserve our deepest thanks for a job well done!"

Some translators stood up and yelled, "That's kicking their butts!" and "Those bastards deserve everything they get!" Others shouted, "Hallelujah!"

Mashbir noticed the majority of Nisei translators remained somberly lost in inner thoughts. He stepped over to Willoughby, who handed him back the microphone, which he now used.

"General, we appreciate your recognition that our hard work is paying off. But I have something to add," his voice rising. He scanned his audience, looking thoughtfully at those who served under his command.

"I know how hard it must be for many of you Nisei, *probably* the greatest challenge you've ever faced. You might have friends, neighbors, even relatives in the forces we are fighting against. And, on the American home-front, you see Japanese-Americans confined to internment camps—a cruel, unfair mistake—the product of pure hysteria. And in spite of all this, you've volunteered your services to your country!"

Mashbir leaned forward on the podium.

"I have personally devoted many years attempting to avoid war between our two great nations and do *not* take pleasure in the death of my enemies.

"A day will come when you look back with pride, remembering your role in defeating the spread of Fascism with its cruel subjugation of other nations."

He took a deep breath.

"*Our organization, ATIS, is top-secret,* but I give you my solemn oath: When this war is over, I will make every effort within my power to place the true story of your great achievements before the American public. Your sacrifices will bring respect to Japanese-Americans for many generations to come."

First one by one, then in groups, the Australians, Brits, Kiwis, Canadians, and other non-Nisei American translators stood and began applauding their Nisei brothers . . .

Mashbir waited, then saluted them.

"You're all dismissed for today," he announced and walked off with Willoughby.

"You look pale, General, are you okay?"

"I've been called dramatic, Sidney," Willoughby replied, "but you hit me to the core. Made me think about the land of *my* birth, and how I long for the day when a peace-loving government returns to lead Germany—One that her people—and the world—can again look toward with admiration!"

CHAPTER 46

April 16, 1943, Headquarters of the Supreme Commander of the Pacific, Australia

The continuous handling of the bloodied relics of war was wearing Mashbir down. Some relief came from his daily strategy conferences with General MacArthur and the rest of the staff; where he felt like he was on Mt. Olympus, looking down from a vast distance, detached from the gore.

At the conclusion of that morning's gathering, Willoughby called Mashbir aside and led him to his private office.

"Colonel, I'm about to show you something beyond top secret," Willoughby said, unlocking a desk drawer and removing two sheets of paper. "Read this and its translation, then tell me if you believe the translation is accurate."

After reading them twice, he replied, "Appears authentic. It's a flight itinerary for a very high-ranking Japanese officer's inspection tour, escorted by four fighter planes."

"That's what Navy Intelligence in Honolulu who intercepted it thinks, but they want our feedback. Here's the question."

Mashbir observed as Willoughby pointed to a map of the Pacific Theater of Operations. "See this leg of the journey from Rabul to Bouganville? You know the Navy doesn't tell us everything, but what I suspect is that's where they're planning to intercept and shoot down that high-ranking officer, who might well be Admiral Yamamoto."

Mashbir drew in a sharp breath.

"Eliminating their Commander-in-Chief of the Pacific—the mastermind behind the attack on Pearl Harbor: Who less than a year ago nearly succeeded in luring our forces into a deathtrap during the Battle of Midway—*Now that would deliver a critical blow!*" he replied. "He's by far the best they have. I met him back in the Twenties: Has a first-rate mind and not afraid to gamble when he thinks he's got the edge."

"Sounds like you were playing poker?"

Mashbir nodded, remembering that evening with mixed emotions. "Hard to believe, but Yamamoto was once one of the most out-spoken military leaders *against* conflict with America. He predicted the Japanese might have their way for the first six months, but they'd inevitably be beaten."

Sidney shook his head in frustration. "Extremists forced him to abandon his better judgment. They miscalculated, anticipating a quick negotiated peace, that would deliver to them the Philippines and a portion of China, but that was not to be!"

Willoughby replied, "I respect Yamamoto and his conflicted feelings, but now granted we've guessed right, if in fact they do manage to *take him out*, here's my question, who'd replace him?"

"Probably Admiral Koga."

"What's your opinion of his abilities?"

"He has the reputation of being conservative and by-the-book, more predictable—which could be to our advantage."

"All right, that's all for now. Again, I emphasize, *not a breath of this to anyone!*"

✳✳✳✳

Several days later, Willoughby informed Mashbir that General MacArthur had received a coded message from Admiral Nimitz that morning, stating that a detachment of eighteen P-38s had shot down two Jap bombers and four Zero fighters while on a special reconnaissance flight from Guadalcanal.

"I would guess we'll shortly be hearing about a new Commander-in-Chief of the Japanese Navy," Willoughby said. Mashbir stood silent. "Obviously, you will act as surprised as everyone else when the news becomes public."

As Mashbir returned to his office, he fondly remembered Yamamoto...*You were one good poker player, Isoroku, and if it's any comfort, this wasn't a fair deal. They knew you were coming and ran a crooked deck in on you this time.*

Early 1944

A corporal looked around the doorframe.

"Excuse me, Colonel Mashbir, I have a radiogram for you: Priority delivery."

"Where do I sign?"

"Right here. Thank you, sir."

The corporal saluted and left.

Mashbir's eyes opened wide as he read:

> *Dear Colonel Mashbir,*
>
> *I need your assistance.*
>
> *I'm in the Solomons as a private subcontractor, conducting tests on the new fighter plane Lockheed has developed. The squadron is moving to New Guinea soon, and I want to go with them, but they're afraid the Japs might shoot me down or take me captive.*
>
> *If you could somehow arrange for me to see General MacArthur or his Air Chief, I'd be able to plead my case. Please reply soon: The squadron deploys at the end of the week!*
>
> *Sincerely yours, Charles Lindbergh*

There was a look of incredulity on Willoughby's face as he read the radiogram handed him... "Is this on the level? Am I to believe this was actually sent by *the* Charles Lindbergh?"

"We confirmed it came from the Solomons," Mashbir replied. "I'm sure in my own mind it's legitimate."

Willoughby grinned.

"You're an amazing individual, Colonel: First, I find out you've known MacArthur for years. Then, I learn you're on a first-name basis with half the Japanese royal family, and even played poker with Ya-mamoto✳ And now, Lindbergh is asking for your help. What's next? Are we going to hear that Dorothy Lamour and Hedy Lamarr are coming out here with romantic designs on you?"

Mashbir reflected on his last vivid memory of Hedy and smiled. "No, sir, I don't think that's very likely." His voice turned serious. "So how do I approach the General on this matter?"

"Might be best if we do it together. I want to be there when you explain this most unusual request."

"That's the trouble, sir—I can't tell anyone how this all came about."

Willoughby gave him a cold look. "Officers requesting special attention from Commanding Generals aren't in any position to withhold information," he said, then reflected, "Unless, you're under orders to an even higher commander...?"

Mashbir remained silent.

"Okay Colonel, let's go next door to see the Man. This should be interesting."

MacArthur tapped his fingers on his desk in thought, before turning to face them. "Have a seat." Before they could speak, he continued, "I've been meaning to praise you Mashbir, for your idea of sending translators and interpreters on three-month rotations to the battlefront. It has really paid off. Yes, we've lost some good men, but it was worth the sacrifice. Please send my regards to your entire ATIS team."

"Thank you, sir. They'll be proud to hear that."

"Now, what's *this* visit about?"

"Please read this, sir."

He handed him the radiogram.

MacArthur's expression turned from somber to amused.

"So your famous pilot friend wants to fly again? But why is Lindbergh asking you in particular for assistance?"

Mashbir sucked in a breath.

"Please trust me, sir. I can't fully explain it, I've made an oath."

The general's expression darkened for moment, until the implication sunk in.

"So then you're probably aware that FDR and several of his cabinet members hate Lindbergh's guts! How then, can I let this guy back into the military?"

"General, I'm not going to defend or condemn his past. Right now, he doesn't even care if he's in the military. He's offered to be a civilian giving instructions to new military pilots on the P-38. The war effort would greatly gain by his involvement."

MacArthur smiled. "If I allow him to fly in my area of command, it will have to be on the QT, **No publicity**! What the hell, they call him Lucky Lindy—maybe he'll bring *us* some good luck. Radiogram him to come plead his case with Kinney."

Two days later, Mashbir, Charles Lindbergh, and General Kinney, MacArthur's Air Commander, left General MacArthur's office. Lindbergh offered his hand to Kinney. "Thank you, General. You won't be sorry, I promise you."

"I certainly hope not. It would be a major coup if the Japs shot you down."

"I'm well aware of that, sir."

"See that you are."

Kinney strode off, leaving Mashbir and Lindbergh to walk down the hallway in the opposite direction.

"I really appreciate your arranging a meeting with the Generals. You can't know how much this means to me!"

Lindbergh's face lit up like a kid's.

"Your reputation got you back in," Mashbir replied with conviction.

"*Maybe so*—but thanks all the same. But there's something I'm curious about, Sidney: You said you also once resigned from active duty. What were your reasons?"

"Charles, I guess you could say we each did what we felt was best for our country at the time."

※※※※

Mashbir wondered: was it Divine Intervention—or just pure Chance that controls the course of History? Little had he suspected that his radio communications with Colonel Cushing and his Filipino guerilla resistance movement would lead to one of the most significant Intelligence successes in the Pacific Theater of the War!

On March 31, 1944, two Japanese patrol bombers set off from Palau in the Caroline Islands to Davao City, on the Philippine island of Mindanao.

One carried Admiral Koga, who indeed had been named Yamamoto's successor as the new Commander-in-Chief of the Japanese Combined Fleet. The other carried Koga's chief of staff, Rear Admiral Fukudome. Koga's plane ran into a strong tropical storm and crashed into the Pacific—leaving no survivors. The plane carrying Fukudome tried to skirt around the storm—but, offshore of Cebu Island, the exhausted pilot lost control of his plane and hit the water at full speed, its fuels tanks exploding, encircling the plane with flaming aviation gasoline.

Though injured, Fukudome freed himself from the sinking plane, and by clutching a seat cushion as a float, managed to paddle to safety. He was unable, however, to retrieve the important documents he was carrying.

Accompanying him to shore were twelve crew members who were so pleased that they had survived the crash that several began singing joyfully, drawing the attention of Filipino villagers living nearby. These soldiers were soon surrounded and captured, minus two who got away.

"Kill them!" some of the villagers shouted, prodding their captives with sticks and shovels, happy to see their roles reversed.

A village elder raised his hand. "No, they are more valuable as prisoners and should be interrogated," he said, and they were taken into the lush tropical jungle highlands.

Admiral Fukudome, suffering from festering wounds and fever, was carried on a stretcher for almost a week; he and his men were delivered to Cushing, whose guerilla organization was now composed of a dozen Americans and hundreds of Filipinos. There, a doctor treated Fukudome and the other injured captives.

Cushing radioed Mashbir with this unexpected turn of events, then contacted him again several days later to tell him that villagers living farther down the beach from that crash site had retrieved an object floating in the water they felt might be important. It was a slimy, oil-covered box containing a red-leather portfolio embossed with an elaborate emblem. Inside the portfolio were wet papers stamped with official seals.

They took these documents to their homes, and allowed them to dry, then delivered them to Cushing, who didn't know what to make of them.

Meanwhile, the two Japanese soldiers who had escaped from the crash site reached an Army garrison at a nearby town. Immediately an air search was launched...

While in Tokyo, the Japanese High Command was more than a little concerned over the death of Admiral Koga and the capture of Fukudome. They wondered whether the documents these high-ranking officers carried had or had not been destroyed at the crash site. Villagers were interrogated, but denied ever seeing them. Every home was searched; nothing was found.

Japanese Navy experts estimated the box could have washed ashore near the village of Perilos, so a reward was offered—but no one said a word. For what they believed was a lack of cooperation, Perilos was burned to the ground and several villagers were killed.

✳✳✳✳

Sporadic explosions overshadowed the radio transmission:

"Colonel Mashbir, this is Colonel Cushing again. Jap floatplanes are bombing the outer periphery of our encampment. They've dropped flyers promising that if we release our prisoners, they'll stop, and they won't hurt any more civilians! We're only a few hundred men, barely armed, going against thousands of soldiers hunting us down."

He paused. "I know I've been ordered by headquarters not to give up our prisoners, but..."

"How's Admiral Fukudome doing?"

"He'd be much better off in a hospital."

"Cushing, are you sure your prisoners don't know you possess those documents they were carrying?"

"They haven't brought up the topic—probably think they're lost or destroyed."

"Okay then. From your description, I believe they're extremely important—I'm sticking my neck out so *don't quote me*. I *strongly* recommend you release those prisoners. Then *at least* we'd have a chance at retrieving those papers. I'll do my best to cover for you when they find out you went against orders. Good luck, Colonel!"

The following day, Willoughby was incensed.

"What do you mean Cushing took it upon himself to release that Admiral and those prisoners!"

"Well, sir, the enemy was closing in, burning down villages and taking innocent lives," Mashbir replied, using a placating voice. "Now things will likely calm down. I know it isn't going to be easy, but we have to find a way to pick up those documents ASAP."

Japanese forces observed a three-day cease-fire, and thereafter avoided attacking civilians. The released prisoners were flown to Saipan, then to Tokyo, to be questioned. The acting Commander-in-Chief of the Japanese Combined Fleet assumed the documents had been destroyed in the crash, but just in case, they increased the reward to an impressive 50,000 pesos, about $25,000, further emphasizing to the Allies their importance. Mashbir urged that at all costs their pickup must be kept top secret or their strategic value would be lost.

A month later, using the evacuation of refugees as a cover for a submarine's real mission, forty-one Americans were picked up, along with those documents, hidden inside two empty mortar shells for safekeeping…On the return trip to Australia, the sub kept on the surface as much as possible for greater speed, but several times had to submerge when targeted by Japanese aircraft and ships, twice surviving depth-charge attacks.

When these documents—which came to be known as *The Z-Plan*—were examined by Mashbir at ATIS headquarters, they contained Naval terms whose meanings were not clear to Army men and therefore required the expertise of Naval Intelligence translators. As soon as Naval Intelligence had done their job, Mashbir completed the translation.

It revealed that the Japanese High Command had grown pessimistic about how the war was going. They pinned their remaining hopes on preparing the Japanese Combined Fleet for a major operation against the American Navy, in one great, decisive, final battle—concentrating its total sea and air power against the next American advance into the Japanese Island Defense System.

Got to get this out fast, Mashbir thought, working late into the night, hand-cranking a mimeograph machine to run off two-dozen copies of the translated twenty-two-page *Z-Plan*. The first copies were rushed to General George C. Marshall, chief of staff of the U.S. Army, and one to General Douglas MacArthur.

Next, Sidney recognized the importance of alerting Admiral Nimitz, Commander-in-Chief of the Pacific Fleet, as to the details of the strategy that would soon be directed against him. So an Army bomber was quickly dispatched that flew five thousand miles in forty-eight hours to deliver copies to Nimitz's Headquarters at Pearl Harbor. Nimitz in turn, realizing that the Japanese planned to throw everything they had against him, forwarded copies to every flag officer associated with the upcoming invasion!

Mashbir, along with Generals MacArthur and Willoughby and the rest of their staff, waited anxiously for the first battle reports to arrive . . . Had the strategy outlined in *The Z-Plan been* changed, or more frightening, were they now being lured into a trap?

The largest American amphibious assault ever to that day mounted in the Pacific, was speeding towards the Marianas: 535 ships, 15 of them aircraft carriers, conveying 900 planes and close to 130,000 troops. They had a rendezvous with destiny, facing off against what remained of the forces of the Empire of Japan.

To meet the American threat, the Japanese used their 6 aircraft carriers and some 450 airplanes, using airfields on Tinian and Guam, as well as land-based planes from Japan. An elaborate decoy operation was attempted to lure U.S. forces westward, but the Americans didn't take the bait. Based on *The Z-Plan* and related documents, they knew that if they went full tilt after the Japanese fleet some six thousand miles west of Guam, they would be opening themselves to grave danger: Enemy planes would then be able to multiply their effectiveness by using the other airfields in the Marianas for shuttle-bombing runs and could even attack the vulnerable American ships from land-based planes flying south from Japan.

Instead, U.S. forces waited for the Japanese to come to them—and they did!

The greatest Aircraft Carrier battle of the war took place on June 19–20, 1944, in the Philippine Sea, west of the Marianas. The American fleet dealt the Japanese a major defeat, the so-called *Marianas Turkey Shoot*, shooting down 476 Japanese planes and forcing their fleet to retreat westward.

MacArthur spoke privately to Mashbir.

"I'm not sure when this war's finally going to end," he said, "but I have to tell you, you and your ATIS team have done a *splendid* job. For security reasons, we can't publicly acknowledge how important those *Z-Plan* documents were. But you and I know that this is one of the greatest single Intelligence feats of the War in the Southwest Pacific!"

Later that year, on Oct. 20, 1944, MacArthur's forces invaded the Philippines. The Japanese sent most of their remaining naval strength, their battleships and cruisers, toward the invading fleet. Again the U.S. anticipated their strategy, partially based on information from the *Z-Plan*, resulting in the Battle of the Philippine Sea, in which almost all Japanese ships were sunk or crippled.

CHAPTER 47

Early December 1944

Two buses roared through the front gates of ATIS Headquarters, kicking up dust as they came to an abrupt stop. Several dozen men gathered, smiling with anticipation, ready to welcome the new secretarial staff. As the first female passengers stepped out: WACs {The Women's Army Corps}, typists and stenographers, all in uniform— The smiles faded as the men realized these women were First Sergeants, Master Sergeants, and T-3s—all senior to every one of them in the translator corps.

How did they get all those promotions? they wondered. The disgruntled men dispersed, returning to work.

A Private approached Mashbir, "Sir that was a real disappointment. Even the ladies felt odd about it."

Mashbir nodded.

"Our men have gone through ten dangerous tours at the front lines, yet not one translator has been promoted, in spite of promises made to them at the Language School. Being a new secret organization, there are no vacancies to be promoted into, and nobody seems to care much about it at the War Department."

Later that day, a Nisei entered his office. "Excuse me, sir, this was just translated. It was recovered after a skirmish near Bagio."

Probably just one more of the hundreds of personal letters streaming in, Mashbir thought, as he unfolded the flimsy, bloodstained paper and began to read:

Honored wife,

I hope this finds you and little Hideki well. We have recently been moved from our encampment where we were stationed for the past year. The American prisoners were taken away two weeks ago, shipped to Osaka to work on roads and in the fields. I cannot tell you how much I wish I could have been on that same ship. It has been more than three years since we parted. Things are getting worse. We are on reduced daily rations, one medium ball of rice and weak tea. We haven't had meat for months and eat worms instead. As difficult as it is, our prisoners had it worse, receiving two-thirds of our daily ration, often becoming sickly with little medicine for them, and now, there is none left for our men either.

Often these prisoners were beaten if they complained or were too weak to work. My sergeant says they deserved such treatment because they surrendered rather than fighting to the death, as honorable warriors should. I would not quarrel with him, but it seemed they were not so different from us. I was on burial detail, and almost always in their possession would be a picture of a young woman and sometimes small children.

Many in our company have fallen to malaria and dysentery. Corporal Sudoki from our village died last week. His final request was that I inform his parents he gave his life in the service of the Emperor.

We have not received mail for weeks now, so I don't know when I will be able to send this, but please know I think of you and our home at all times. Kiss our precious Hideki for me, and tell him his father will see him soon.

All love to you both,

T. Kaotima, Private, 101st company

Mashbir leaned back into his chair and muttered, "Poor devils on both sides!" He checked his calendar. *Only a week before Christmas.*

Some holiday season this is, he thought, staring at the stacks of documents strewn across his desk. *An endless supply of testimonials of torture and death pouring in from the battlefront. Enough to numb the senses of any sane person.*

He poured a glass of Scotch and downed it—*I'm Death's Gatekeeper—the River Styx flows through my office carrying the memories of thousands to the underworld.*

He shuddered.

From a desk drawer, he withdrew his own personal letters bound with twine. It had been two-and-a-half years since he'd been home. He held them, trying to feel their inner warmth❋ Taking out a pad, he began to write:

> *Dear Irene and Donald,*
>
> *I miss you both so much. The war drags on and feels like it will never end. Yet at other times, I get the feeling peace may be just around the corner; no more than a year away at most. I wish I could talk more about my routine, but I can't.*
>
> *Donald, I'm impressed by how well you're doing at school. I bet you'll make a fine architect or businessman someday. Maybe build libraries, schools, and museums, who knows? You might even design rocket-ships like you talked about when you were young. And thanks for keeping me posted about your brother Forrester's promotion to Army captain in Europe. I know he doesn't much want to hear from me, but I'd appreciate you sending him my congratulations.*
>
> *Please remember your letters are the high point of my day.*
>
> *All my love, Sidney*

He sealed the envelope and wondered: *In spite of recent Allied victories, will the Japanese ever surrender?* Outside his office he heard the shuffling step of newly-arrived prisoners. Opening his door, he watched them pass in the corridor—handcuffed, with heads down, as they were escorted to their waiting cells.

Both those guards and their prisoners are probably as miserably homesick as I am, he thought, *and I'll bet there are lots of other folks around here feeling the same.*

He called over his aides.

"We need to boost morale around here; how about researching who has some musical talent around here? I want to put together a small band. Also, go to town and get a hundred bottles of wine, lots of fruit punch, and whatever can pass for appetizers."

"Sounds like a party, sir."

"About time—we haven't had one in a couple of years. You're to print up flyers saying the following—Write this down:"

Season's Celebration

All faiths and denominations welcome! To be held December 24, 7:00 P.M. Beverages, music, and snacks provided. Please wear civilian dress, and for those wishing, put on your dancing shoes.

"One last thing," Mashbir said, "all prisoners are to be given a special dinner that evening. They're humans and also need something to feel good about."

"Yes, sir, we'll get right on it."

When the holiday party had at last arrived, Mashbir blasted out some jazzy tunes on his trumpet, accompanied by several of his musically talented ATIS translators, who had borrowed instruments from local Australians. There was a drummer, a couple of guitarists, and a harmonica player, all jamming together while a female officer sang.

It's great to play again, Sidney thought, as he watched the crowd boogie across the Gymnasium floor, which had been cleared of desks for the celebration. There was lots of laughter, bringing back distant, pleasant memories of him earning a few extra bucks performing musical gigs at college frat and sorority parties. *Where have the years gone?*

A Kiwi translator approached him and smiled. "That was a fine idea, Colonel. With no uniforms, the men are less intimidated asking the

ladies to dance, in spite of them being their superior officers, and that
has certainly livened things up!"

The following afternoon, a corporal knocked on Mashbir's door and
entered. "Sir, I speak for many—Thanks for that celebration. Boy, did
we need it!" he hesitated. "But, the thing is, Sir: I'm here on something else you should know about."

"What's that?"

"Best you see for yourself, sir."

They arrived at the Prisoner Interrogation Holding Area, where
they were met by two guards and a member of the Interrogation team.
The Corporal turned to the Interrogator. "Please tell the colonel what
happened."

"It's like this: You know how some prisoners go through a trans-
formation; can't believe they were actually captured alive, so they take
on a new persona. Some become cooperative, others remain tough as
nails—Well, those two prisoners," he said, pointing to a cell, "have
been silent for months, until they got that special dinner the other
night—Suddenly, they burst out in tears, apologizing for their country's treatment of captured Allied prisoners. One admitted he was a
draftsman at a naval shipyard and voluntarily offered to draw from
memory detailed designs of every type of ship he'd worked on, even
an aircraft-carrying submarine—And his cell-mate described torpedoes of a size and range we had never heard of, although several of
our ships might have been sunk by them."

Mashbir was taken aback. "Really?...They're probably as sick and
tired of this war as we are, sensing it's a lost cause, and they want to
help us end it."

"There's one last thing, Colonel. Another prisoner, who had been
stationed in the Indonesian islands, saw those soldiers cooperating
and berated them, bragging that the Japanese would still win the war
because of something called *Tonari Gumi*."

"But that's just some kind of neighborhood association," Mashbir
replied.

"Not according to him. I sense he's holding back something that
might be important!"

Mashbir left, then returned, carrying an attaché case.

"You won't get much out of that arrogant bastard," a guard said, rippling his baton against the cell's bars. "I wish I could beat him to a pulp."

"Understood," Mashbir replied, his voice tensing. "But I'll never tolerate such comments from you again. Have I made myself clear?"

"Yes, sir."

The prisoner sat rigidly, viewing Mashbir's entry into the interrogation cell with angry suspicion. Wearing a dark-blue shirt and pants, the man looked like a mechanic.

Bowing, and then speaking in Japanese, Mashbir addressed him. "Might you want some tea, or perhaps something to eat before we speak?"

The man shrugged away the offer.

"I've heard you are wise and know the workings of your country."

A puzzled expression appeared upon the man's face, wondering what to make of this strange American officer.

Mashbir continued, "I personally know that Your Emperor would appreciate your giving us useful information about Indonesia's Tonari Gumi societies, so we can finally end this senseless war."

This statement evoked greater confusion.

"Yes, I have befriended both Emperor Hirohito and his Minister Prince Iyesato Tokugawa, and *we* are in fact allies," he said, displaying photos of himself with the royal family.

"Do you recognize Prince Tokugawa, the leader of your congress for three decades?"

The prisoner's weathered face looked distressed.

"Now let me show you this letter of friendship sent to me by one of your own generals, Kenji Matsumoto. We have known each other for many years." He handed him a copy of the letter. The prisoner silently read, his hands shaking.

"I now respectfully offer you this last item to examine. It is an official invitation to me and my wife to the Enthronement celebration of your Emperor, given by your embassy and the Royal family."

Mashbir waited, giving the man time to re-examine all the items carefully. Then he continued: "Your Emperor strongly desires to end this long, unnecessary war that has no honor to it. But his true voice has been silenced by certain traitors in your government and military."

He looked the prisoner in the eye.

"Emperor Hirohito wishes to put down this treason and move toward peace, and it is the highest duty of his people to assist him in this pursuit. *Do you understand?*"

The man nodded.

"So what is the secret you alluded to that might help us end this conflict earlier?"

The man stood and bowed. "I am Lieutenant Onaka," he said calmly, his face transformed from its prior ferocity. "When this war began, a program was instituted in Japan demanding everyone's support of the war effort. This system is called *Hoko* or *Tonari Gumi*, where entire communities are held responsible for the actions of any member of their group. If anyone disobeys, a representative is chosen from the most revered individuals of that region and they receive harsh punishment—Spies are everywhere, many recruited from society's criminal underclass, making sure the public cooperates—This allows a military governor or chief of police to coerce the obedience of five thousand by threatening a single person."

"I appreciate your cooperation. But you hinted there was a secret strategy beyond that...?" Mashbir said, urging him on.

The prisoner closed his eyes in thought, before answering. "We have used the same *Hoko system* in Indonesia, where villages are being assembled into military units to fight alongside Japanese soldiers. If they refuse, members of their families or leaders of their community are tortured or killed. So if you attempt a landing on those islands, you'll face Japanese forces supported by thousands of native conscripts." He took a long pause.

"And should all else fail, our general public has been convinced the Americans plan to destroy our homeland, to rape and pillage, and desecrate our culture. Civilians have been ordered to prepare knives and pitchforks, and to fight to the death when the Allies land on our shores!"

Mashbir thanked him and bowed before leaving, then immediately sent off a memo describing what he'd just learned. It didn't take long before he was requested to meet with General MacArthur.

"All right, Colonel," MacArthur said, "I've forwarded your recent report to my Military Secretary and Head of Psychological Warfare, General Bonner Fellers, and he extols your new insights—but I want to hear the details from you directly."

"Yes, sir. I've been in touch with professors of Asian Studies at the University of Melbourne, regarding that *spy-hostage Hoko System:* It originated in China around 1100 B.C.E., and was introduced into Japan around 700 A.D., where it became significant during the transition between Tokugawa and Meiji rule. The Tokugawa Shoguns and their feudal Daimyo lords were pushed aside, and their Samurai enforcers who had maintained order amongst the populace, had their titles and lands taken from them, and *instead* they were pressured to find jobs in farming, construction, and Sword making...It was a challenging time for these warrior overseers to adapt." Mashbir took a glance at his notes, then continued.

"Criminals, however, saw it as a wonderful opportunity. Emperor Meiji and his advisors soon realized the need to create a policing system to handle the rampant crime. They enlisted the most capable and enlightened Samurai to become their police and military, living by the highest standards of Bushido. The Hoko/Tonari Gumi System allowed them to control both the criminals and the general public. Everyone was responsible for the behavior of their family members and their neighbors, and could be punished—Want more details, General?"

"Tell it all, Colonel."

"Yes, sir—Vigilantes went so far as to capture *potential* criminals, warning these culprits they'd be hunted down if they misbehaved... This system expanded to control almost every aspect of economic and social life: bars, restaurants, and even brothels were licensed by overseers. Health, sanitation, religion, agriculture, the building trades, and forestry were regulated; it even oversaw labor union disputes; and travel was restricted between cities."

Mashbir scratched his head. "Imagine—even the smallest things, such as the rules for keeping one's home clean, were dictated for the good of the people."

"Talk about a controlling government!" MacArthur blurted.

Mashbir nodded. "Fortunately, during most of this past half century, this system evolved into more typical police departments and social service agencies, combined with neighborhood watch associations keeping an eye on each other's property to defend against criminals. And, when fires and disasters struck, these neighborhood associations would work communally, helping to rebuild destroyed homes."

"Sounds like a Good Neighbor policy."

"Yes, it worked well. Problem is, this system was perverted during the war years to coerce the Japanese on the home front, pressuring them to refuse surrender and to fight to the death, even if it was suicidal…We may well find ourselves confronting a major guerilla insurgency once U.S. forces attempt to occupy Japan."

"I see…"

MacArthur stroked his clean-shaven chin as he considered.

"Then one of the first things we'll have to do when this war ends is eliminate that system."

"That was my first reaction, sir, but I wonder if there are other options available."

MacArthur smiled.

"You mean somehow use it to our advantage?"

Mashbir smiled. "Historically it was used for law and order. Perhaps we can return it to its original function."

MacArthur looked at him appraisingly, recalling that it was Mashbir who had come up with the *New Guinea Leapfrog Strategy*, rather than fighting every foot of the way.

"According to Willoughby, Colonel, your leadership of ATIS has shortened the war by two years and saved countless lives! Never in military history has an Army known so much about its enemy prior to engagements."

MacArthur put a firm hand on Sidney's shoulder.

"When this war comes to an end, I'm recommending you for a promotion. How does Brigadier General Mashbir sound?"

That evening, Mashbir was on the edge of his seat, writing:

Dearest Irene,

It's unbelievable. For so long I doubted I'd ever be allowed back into the military, but you always said I'd have my day. Even with that being said, this will probably be as much of a surprise to you as it was to me. I'm being recommended for promotion to brigadier general, by one of the men I most respect in the world, General MacArthur.

Sending all my love to you and Donald,

Sidney

CHAPTER 48

June 1945, Philippines

Mashbir looked proudly over the past few years, being part of the team that assisted MacArthur in making good on his promise, *"I Shall Return!"* U.S. Army Supreme Commander Headquarters were once again established in Manila, with most of the Philippines now under control, and U.S. and other Allied forces advancing on all other fronts in the Pacific.

While in Europe, General Eisenhower, in spite of his limited prior experience in commanding large numbers of troops, rose to the occasion and did a fine job as commander of all U.S. forces, while diplomatically guiding Allied forces to work together for victory.

But in spite of Germany's accepting unconditional surrender on May 8, 1945, V-E Day, the Japanese still refused to quit*

Mashbir had a frightening premonition that he had to act upon, as he entered Willoughby's office. "Good morning, sir." He hesitated. "I've heard rumors from Naval Intelligence that we might be close to testing a new, extremely powerful weapon…"

"If it existed, it would certainly be used," Willoughby replied. "Washington is fed up with the Pacific war dragging on."

"But the Japanese can't last much longer—I'm sure of it," Mashbir implored. "I've even come up with a plan for ending it sooner."

"Oh really? And *what* might that be?"

"I believe that if I could represent General MacArthur's authority while transmitting radio broadcasts directly to both the Japanese people and their leaders to surrender, they'd listen."

"MacArthur isn't on the best terms with Washington's policymakers; I'm not sure they'd allow you to do that. Besides, there have already been broadcasts into Japanese airspace in the name of our president, imploring them to surrender. It hasn't worked yet."

"But the way I see it, sir," Mashbir said, moving his hands to express himself, "Japan is currently a military state which doesn't respect *our* representative government—However, if their commanders heard a voice representing a fellow warrior, MacArthur, who actually defeated them in battle, they might listen."

"Sounds reasonable, I suppose." Willoughby said.

Mashbir relaxed a bit. "I don't think the masses know how badly they're losing. The thousands who opposed the war were arrested—I hope to open the eyes of their more enlightened leaders that they can get more through diplomacy than by fighting to the bitter end."

July 6, 1945

With fingers crossed, Mashbir entered Willoughby's office.

"I did as you asked...This is all top secret," the general said. "You'll get most of what you want: a series of broadcasts to convince the Japanese to come out with their hands up. Your buddy, Captain Zacharias, also helped by putting in a good word for you...Some top brass believe Zacharias's broadcasts into Germany influenced them to some degree not to fight us to the very last ditch. But his broadcasts into Japan haven't succeeded, *so now*, it's your turn to convince them."

"I don't know how to thank you enough, sir. And please pass on my regards to General MacArthur."

"Don't thank us till you've heard it all. The top politicos have no problem with you getting persuasive, but you have to be vague when you speak of new weaponry that we *might or might not* possess."

"Dang it, that takes the teeth out of it, sir."

"There's another side to that coin; if the Japs knew too much, they'd find a way to sabotage or shoot down our weapon delivery planes... Hopefully, they'll have the sense to understand the implied threat."

Radio station in Manila, Philippines, July 19, 1945

Two government agents sat next to Mashbir, all three with copies of the evening's presentation on the table in front of them.

"Hey, Colonel, good luck with your first broadcast. Would you like a stick of gum?"

Sidney was in a trance, focused, staring at the microphone. The agent waved him off, then turned to his partner.

"Élan, check out what I found," displaying a thick wad. "These Japanese pesos *were* supposed to be the new currency for the Philippines."

He chuckled.

"Now they're worthless. I'll give you a few."

"Thanks, but how about this," his companion said, reaching under the table and withdrawing an eighteen-inch blade from its sheath, the smell of anti-rust oil lubricant filling the air. "It's a bayonet that doubles as a short sword."

His companion nodded approvingly.

"Lots of souvenirs and dead Japs everywhere, that's for sure!"

Mashbir silently reflected:

Our flyboys risked their lives dropping tons of leaflets that I helped design, warning the Japanese we were going to hit 'em hard. They were beaten, and they knew it. We even offered them Manila as an open city, so their troops could safely leave. But they refused, forcing a door-to-door battle. Where's the sense in that?

He looked at the wall clock, then began:

"Good evening, my friends in Japan. This broadcast is the first of a series of weekly discussions on the challenges confronting the Japanese people. My name is Colonel Sidney Mashbir, speaking to you from General MacArthur's headquarters in Manila...

"I've spent several years in your country and have come to know your people well. Tonight, it is my privilege and pleasure to once again talk to you...Though the fortunes of war have currently made me your enemy, I have had numerous wonderful friendships in Japan, and many of you have known me for almost twenty-five years as a man who gave his most strenuous efforts to preserve the peace and amity between our two nations...

"I will purposely not mention any of my Japanese friends whom I consider the highest true patriots of your Nation—So that in this hysteria of war, no harm might befall them because of their efforts to preserve the peace and prevent the ruin they foresaw. *We* anticipated the frightful destruction your militarists would bring upon your beautiful country as they advanced their own selfish ambitions...

"In all my many dealings with the distinguished statesmen of your nation, including Prince Tokugawa, who is now deceased, I adhered strictly to your own samurai code, living by the proverb: *Samurai Ni Wa, Ni Gon Nashi*—Never expressing one false thing in our discussions...I will continue to live by this code in my weekly reports to you." His voice heightened. "You may not like what I will tell you. You may disbelieve at first, but as time goes on you will find what I say is the truth." Sidney sipped some water.

"The bulk of your Navy lies at the bottom of the ocean, with the American fleet sailing unchallenged in Japan's home waters. The great armies that overran New Guinea and the Philippines have now been reduced to small, isolated bands roaming the mountains in search of food, facing slow starvation, or annihilation by our armed forces.

"In the Philippines alone, there have been more than 399,000 Japanese casualties. Must these needless deaths continue?

"And in your homeland there are ceaseless attacks from the air. One by one, Japanese industrial cities and factories are being reduced to smoke and ash, with your Air Force powerless to prevent it. The Allied blockade of Japan itself is almost complete."

He paused.

"You have fought courageously: Your efforts in Okinawa were heroic in the best traditions of Japan's military history. But even there you were defeated.

"The great German military machine has been shattered! Now Japan no longer has any allies, *and* Russia has now branded her an aggressor . . . *Please hear me,* there is no longer the slightest possibility of your nation winning the war. Two courses are open to the leaders of Japan: They can sue for peace, or they can continue a hopeless war and bring upon Japan the most frightful destruction that has ever been visited upon any country in the history of mankind!

"If they choose the latter course, the responsibility for this great devastation will be entirely theirs. They will stand condemned not only in the eyes of the outside world, but in the eyes of their own people for generations to come!"

His voice now softened.

"The acceptance of defeat does not mean the subjugation of the Japanese people or the desecration of your culture, as your militant leaders would mislead you to believe. America's record of justice and fair play in her dealings with other defeated countries is well known. Please recall our generosity in assisting the stricken people of Japan during the Great Kanto Earthquake. Many Americans, including myself, worked day and night at great personal risk, rescuing the Japanese.

"Our President Truman has clarified the meaning of unconditional surrender, saying, *'With Peace, the Japanese people will be free to begin reconstruction, preparing themselves to once again join the Family of Nations . . . '*

"In the coming weeks, I will comment on other important issues confronting Japan today, and I hope my Japanese friends will give serious thought to my words❋ So until next week at this time, this is Sidney Mashbir bidding you good night. *Samurai Ni Wa, Ni Gon Nashi*—the Samurai's word is final!"

❋❋❋❋

In his private quarters, Hirohito turned off the radio.

What should I do? He wondered. Over the past years haven't my military leaders led me and my people to believe they had conquered not only the Philippines, the Netherlands East Indies, New Guinea, and the Solomons, but also Australia, the Hawaiian Islands, and the West Coast of America?

They even claimed several Asian nations offered little resistance, appreciating being liberated from European colonial rule and being made part of the Co-Posterity Asian Alliance.

I assumed there was some exaggeration, but now realize they were mainly lies—and now my friend, Colonel Mashbir's words emphasize a far greater destruction may well be in store for Japan, if this war continues . . .

CHAPTER 49

Tokyo Military Headquarters

Dangling from General Anami's hand was a small piece of rope in the shape of a hangman's noose. He pulled it tight around his pinkie finger as he stared at Herr Reichmann. "Your Invincible Fatherland has been crushed," he laughed. "How fortunate you are to be our guest! Otherwise, you might well be facing a war crimes tribunal."

"Regrettably true, my friend. What was a glorious start has come to a dismal finale," Reichmann replied, doing his best to exude calmness.

Anami flipped on a tape-playing machine. Reichmann jerked his head closer to listen.

"Why, that's that damn Admiral Zacharias!" Reichmann shouted. "His radio broadcasts contributed to undermining our morale. Why play are you playing it—do you wish to rub salt in my wounds?"

Anami turned off the tape-player and stared at Reichmann. "Do you remember six years ago, that thorn in our side, Colonel Mashbir?"

"Of course, we had him blackballed out of the military. I wonder what became of him."

"Wonder no more. He's doing the same thing as Zacharias, but now with broadcasts into Asia." Anami slammed his fist on his desk. "You were right. I should have had him assassinated!"

"He now attempts to convince Japan to end a war that we can still win, *even* without Germany's support," he sneered.

"Wouldn't it be nice to somehow get even with this Colonel?" Anami said. "In appreciation of your continued safety here, Can you take care of this matter Reichmann?"

"It is as good as done."

Several days later, F.B.I. Headquarters, Washington, D.C.

In amazement, the now Assistant Deputy Director Adams examined the transcript of the radio broadcast. An hour later, Agent Martinez arrived. "I got here as fast as I could."

"Read this," Adams said, passing over the transcript.

"What? This has got to be a mistake. We shadowed that guy for months for being a foreign agent, and now he's representing General MacArthur and broadcasting U.S. government announcements to the Japanese as a colonel again?"

Martinez drove as Adams silently stared out the car window. "No fun eating crow, is it?" Martinez remarked.

"At least Mrs. Mashbir and her son can accept our apologies; and eventually pass them on to her husband."

Inside the Mashbir residence, fifteen-year-old Donald sat at the kitchen table.

"Just as you like it," his mother said. "Ketchup and lots of pickles!"

"Yummy, burger and fries, my favorite! Thanks."

Irene began cleaning the dishes.

"I can wash those," Donald offered.

"Enjoy your lunch. You can help after dinner."

"It's such a nice day, Mother. How about us going to the park later?"

Out of habit, he glanced at his two arm-supported canes, leaning against the wall. His upper body was strong, his legs on the weak side.

"Great idea, son."

Outside the Mashbir residence, Unger sat in his car, calculating. *Let's see, with the ten thousand dollars I'll receive for this job, I can take off to Central America and not return to the States for years* . . . He exited his car and came around the side house. Through a kitchen window he could see Irene at the sink. He steadied his gun, targeting her, but just before the trigger was pulled, she bent to the right, reaching for a dirty plate on the counter. On hearing the shattered glass and the gunshot, Irene jerked upright staring into her assassin's eyes. She turned to run as another shot was fired; there was a burning sensation in her back as she dropped to the ground.

"Mom!" Donald shouted.

She just lay there. He sensed an ominous presence outside, and raised his head slightly to peer out the window into Unger's smirking face.

Adams and Martinez had just parked their car and were approaching the Mashbir residence, when they heard Donald's shout. Both men ran around to that side of the house. Unger heard their footsteps and immediately turned and fired, putting a bullet into Martinez's chest. Adams froze, staring into a gun barrel.

"Raise your hands," Unger said, enjoying as he watched Adams's growing fear.

From inside the house, Donald witnessed in horror as Adams was shot in his right leg and struggled to remain on his feet.

Unger was laughing as he aimed again, just as an iron skillet came flying through the fractured kitchen window. He instinctively blocked his head with both arms as the skillet and shards of glass came at him.

When he turned to face Adams again, the agent's revolver was out. Several shots were fired. Both men fell.

That evening, Walter Reed Hospital, Washington, D.C.

Several G-men stood on guard outside the room. Inside, Irene was regaining consciousness, bandages wrapped around her shoulder and back with some I.V. tubes connected to her arms.

"Mrs. Mashbir," the doctor said, "we've loaded you up with pain medication, so you're going to be groggy."

"Where's my son—is he okay?" she said softly.

"He's doing fine."

"Was I dreaming, hearing something about two injured F.B.I. agents...How are they?"

The doctor sighed.

"One's dead; the other's lost a lot of blood, but he'll pull through. Now you get some rest."

In the hospital waiting room, Donald sat with an agent. "How are you doing, son?"

"Just heard great news. My mom's going to be okay, but I'm so sorry about what happened to your men."

"Comes with the job," he replied, his stomach tightening.

"When Agent Adams comes to, please thank him," Donald said. "And," he faltered, "Please send our condolences to the Martinez family. I have a question, though: why were they visiting our home?"

"They were going to apologize for questioning your dad's patriotism a few years back. It appears he's now involved in radio broadcasts to the Japanese, trying to convince them to surrender and end the war."

"Has he given any broadcasts yet?" Donald asked.

"Only the first of four or five, I believe."

Same day, Manila, Philippines

The phone receiver trembled in Sidney's hand.

"Colonel Mashbir, I'm sorry to have been the bearer of this bad news, but at least your wife is now in stable condition, and your son is doing fine. He's a brave and resourceful young gentleman. Probably saved his and your wife's life, as well as one of our agents."

"Are they safe?"

"It's a military hospital with lots of security, and their attacker is dead."

"I'd like to speak to them, if possible."

"Hang on…"

A nurse held the phone as Irene struggled to get the words out. "Donald and I are fine. How are you, Sidney?"

"I wish I were by your side."

"Donald informed me what you're doing is very important. Don't focus on us—we're okay."

"Irene, I love you. I don't know what I'd do without you."

"I love you too. Donald's here."

"Dad, I'll take good care of Mom, don't worry; and the F.B.I. and the hospital staff are looking out for us."

"I'm so proud of you, son…"

With eyes moistened, Sidney put down the phone and declared, "I've got a job to finish!"

CHAPTER 50

July 27, 1945, Military Headquarters, Tokyo

Major General Matsumoto, General Anami, and Commander Akano of the Japanese Air Force sat around a low table sipping warm sake as servants presented their dinner.

"Those foolish Americans!" Anami shouted with a disparaging wave of his hand. "Their President Truman offers us a worthless document demanding unconditional surrender—*and* they drop leaflets from the sky trying to frighten us, hoping we will simply give up. Never!"

"They're weak cowards," the air commander replied. "We'll fight on and prevail."

Are these men insane, Matsumoto wondered, *I remember identical conversations years ago, but now we're losing the war on all fronts—yet they remain so blind?*

The following afternoon, Matsumoto, adorned in full dress uniform, arrived at the palace reception room. Empress Nagako and Emperor Hirohito greeted him.

"It is so good to see you again, General," Hirohito said. "We've been meaning to tell you how much we appreciate the fine job you've done in maintaining Japan's homeland security."

"Thank you, Your Majesty."

"So what brings you here today?" Nagako asked, noting Matsumoto's look of distress.

"My loyalties are torn regarding certain military and political matters."

"Dear General," Hirohito replied, "am I not the one you are most bound by honor to serve?"

"Of course, please forgive me; I'll tell you all I know. Several of our top military commanders spoke of a Potsdam Proclamation, an offer from the Allies to end the war. They boasted how they would misrepresent it to the Japanese people, to fool them into fighting to the death as the only way to retain their Emperor. And that is why I am here."

The Empress bowed to Matsumoto.

"We so appreciate you coming to us to discuss this important matter…Your bravery and loyalty will long be remembered!"

✳✳✳✳

With inner sadness, Nagako poured her guest a cup of steaming green tea. *How he has aged,* she thought, *hair grayed and his body emaciated.* "Prince Konoe," she said, "it has been too long since we've gotten together. You look a bit tired."

"The ever-observant Nagako, caring for all those around her." Konoe laughed. "I prided myself a diplomat, but I'm afraid I did not measure up to the task. Pretending to walk the path of war, while secretly trying to maintain peace, can age a man."

"Certain tasks are impossible," she replied. "But, Dear Konoe, there may still be time to make things right."

He shrugged. "I have little influence with the generals now; they see me as a relic of the past—and I'm sorry to say, that is the same way they view the Emperor."

"And that is why I've asked you here."

"So what magic have you up your sleeve, Your Majesty?" he replied bemusedly.

"Hirohito greatly respects you, as do I. You must convince him that the time is right to take back the reins of leadership."

In a strained voice she added, "We've heard radio broadcasts given by our past ally, Colonel Mashbir, pleading with us to end this deplorable war before it's too late."

"The actions you speak of Nagako, might so anger the military, all our lives could be in danger."

"Do not worry, we still have strong supporters," she replied confidently.

Konoe's inner voice said, Run, leave all this madness behind, but instead, he replied, "If you're certain of your safety and that of the Emperor, only then, will I do as you request."

Deep in the innards of the Imperial Palace, Hirohito sat reading. His butler entered the underground bomb shelter and announced, "The all-clear siren has sounded, Your Majesty. Shall I request lunch be served in the small dining room?"

"Yes, and I wish the empress to join me there in half an hour. Please inform her."

The butler hesitated.

"Is something the matter?"

"I'm not sure, Your Excellency. I went to speak to her earlier, but neither she nor her attendants were to be found."

Suddenly, there was a thunderous crash, the ground shook and dust sifted down from the ceiling. "Great heavens!" Hirohito exclaimed, "A bomb must have landed just outside!" They quickly exited through the steel escape door leading to the gardens. There they saw the Empress supported by her aides, stumbling toward them.

"Nagako," Hirohito called, running towards her. "Are you hurt? Why were you outside?"

"After being cooped up for so long," she said softly, "I needed to walk amongst the flowers, out in the fresh air. I heard a whistling sound, such as a crane might make, then an explosion that knocked us off our feet. Dirt and leaves flew up like a giant fountain...some got on my kimono," she said, brushing off the debris.

"Your forearm is bleeding. Quickly come inside—It must be attended to immediately."

"It's not serious. I was foolish to be outside."

"It wasn't your fault. The plane probably missed its primary target and had instructions to jettison its bomb before returning. Lord knows, enough of them have fallen on our poor country."

Imperial Palace, August 2, 1945

While admiring his beautiful seashell collection, *nature's artistry*, Hirohito remembered cherished moments gathering them, with Nagako and the children during past vacations...The arrival of Foreign Minister Togo jolted him from his reverie. After ceremonial bows and greetings, the Emperor lifted a document from his desk and gripping it tightly, said, "We must discuss the Potsdam Declaration." The minister appeared flustered. "I need clarification," Hirohito continued, "regarding one main point. This document guarantees the Japanese people freedom of speech, religion, and thought, but asks for the unconditional surrender of all armed forces. But there is no mention of the civil government or of the role of the Emperor."

The minister remained silent.

"Let's not waste time, my dear friend and wise advisor—We must work together. Come, come, have a seat near my desk."

Hirohito pointed to a particular passage. "It urges the Japanese people to reject the militarists and follow the path of reason, and warns that noncompliance will result in prompt and utter destruction. It concludes by stating, '*These are our terms. We will not deviate from them. There are no alternatives . . .*' It is signed by President Truman, British Prime Minister Attlee, and representing China, Chiang Kai-shek."

"Yes, Your Majesty, those are their words."

"Is there any reason to question the veracity of this offer?"

Togo spoke obsequiously, "In truth, though demanding as these terms seem, I believe it is the most we can ask for."

"I thought as much, and should never have listened to General Anami and those other fanatics with their rantings of strategic withdrawals and new military offensives. You are to call the heads of the armed forces together to meet me here tomorrow."

"Are you sure? There are those who border on treason."

Hirohito looked into his counselor's eyes, "I know this will be a gargantuan responsibility, assisting the Prime Minister and me to navigate through our government to accept the Potsdam Declaration and end the war. But if anyone can do it, it is you."

The next day, his military and political advisors gathered around the long conference table. All rose and bowed at Hirohito's entrance, then sat and waited silently for the emperor to speak.

"We're here to discuss the Potsdam Proclamation," he announced. "Each of you has a copy on the table in front of you. I have carefully considered their offer, and although it is not in the spirit of the diplomacy we would wish, I believe we should accept."

Red-faced, General Anami stood.

"Your Majesty, with deepest respect I offer my humble opinion. This document is a humiliation. We still have great resources, enormous reserves of manpower not yet committed. Would you have our enemies seize all Japan's leaders, including yourself, and treat us as war criminals? Currently, they are preparing such trials for the German leaders." He stamped his boot down. "We must not let that happen! Our people will rise up in bloody revolt!"

Hirohito replied with a measured tone, "There has already been enough wholesale slaughter. And there is no clear indication they will treat me or others in such a fashion. In either case, I'm prepared to endure whatever is required to end this bloodshed."

The Emperor's voice rose with anger. "You," he ordered, pointing at them all, "must be prepared to do no less!"

"But Your Majesty," one of Anami's top aides replied, "Please reconsider. There is no Russian signatory to this proclamation. Until now, they have refrained from attacking us, but even if we agree to these terms, there is nothing to stop the Russians from taking our northern islands and Korea, which they've long coveted. Let us not respond until we know their intentions."

"Yes," Anami said. "Instead, we should begin moving our troops now stationed in China to the Russian border, to be prepared for such an attack."

"You make it sound like we have all the time in world," Hirohito replied, "but fail to mention the dire warnings of eminent total destruction."

"A mere trick to frighten us," Anami countered.

"Enough bravado." Hirohito's gaze circled the table for further comment. "Very well, we'll wait a bit longer, as our ambassador ascertains from the Russians their position. If they'll mediate as part of our surrender terms, we'll immediately accept. As soon as they've replied, we will gather again."

Philippines, August 3, 1945

Willoughby spoke privately to Mashbir. "I heard your third broadcast earlier this evening. Clever how you pointed out battles they'd claimed to be victories, but were actually defeats. You outright called some of their officers deceitful cowards, and encouraged the general populace and military rank-and-file to rise up in rebellion to take them down." He sighed. "But in spite of your best efforts, I'm afraid what you've been trying to prevent is likely to happen."

Mashbir's face darkened and his arms dropped to his sides. "I've heard rumors of an atomic test in New Mexico a couple of weeks ago, where steel towers were vaporized, accompanied by a blinding flash many times as brilliant as the midday sun, and a cloud boiling forty thousand feet into the sky!"

He peered into Willoughby's eyes. "So you believe they'll use it soon?"

A long silence passed before the general answered.

"A fortune was probably spent in its development, and the men up top will be curious to test it out in battle, both to see if it speeds up the Japanese surrender *and* to show the Russians we're the top honcho around. *So when this war is over*, the U.S. will have more leverage when it comes to Eastern European and Asian affairs."

"Isn't this also about revenge?" Mashbir asked.

"There's probably a fair amount of that as well. You never totally know what's in the mind of a politician, Sidney. They think in five directions."

"So be it," Mashbir said resignedly, "at least, there's next week's broadcast to get them to come to their senses."

Manila, Philippines, August 6, 1945

Surrounded by crumbling stone fountains and caved-in storefronts, their remnants jutting upward like tombstones in the moonlight, Mashbir reflected, *This must have been a charming outdoor plaza in its day . . .* Finding a flat open area, he began his *Tai Chi movements*, focusing on the sounds of crickets in the nearby fields and the wind passing through trees, while hoping to settle his rattled nerves.

An hour later, he was again at his typewriter pounding out ideas.

"Damn it," he shouted, pulling out the page and crumpling it. He steadied himself, grasping the edge of his desk, then removed a photo of Prince Tokugawa from a drawer. "Dear friend, I have failed you. You devoted your life to preventing war between our nations, and I was honored to have had a chance to assist you...A great tragedy now unfolds, unless I can move the hearts of the leaders of Japan!

"*I so wish you were still alive.* Together, I'm sure we would succeed." He heaved a deep sigh. "I have to finish writing the next broadcast, but I'm so tired." His eyelids grew heavy...

The smell of burnt flesh and torrents of fire surrounded him. Wailing cries from charred, dismembered soldiers—Men, women, and children grasping at him beseechingly* . .*

"Let me go!" Sweat streaming, Sidney strained to escape, his heart pounding—

Suddenly, everything changed; he wept with joy seeing Prince Tokugawa dressed in flowing robes...The Prince looked deeply into his eyes. "These are the darkest of times, Sidney-san. Remember, you've done your best—You must not bear this tragedy upon your shoulders, my son, for in the future, you will play an integral part so our two countries will once again walk the path of friendship . . ."

All dissolved into a gentle yellow glow.

His secretary stuck her head into his office the following morning and saw Mashbir hunched over his desk. *Pulling another all-nighter,* she thought. *He's been real grouchy recently; maybe some extra sleep will help.* Tiptoeing in, she turned off the lights, closed the shades, and shut the door. In the outer office she brewed coffee, then sat at her desk doing paperwork, *listening to the radio music at a low volume, until the program was interrupted:*

> *"A major announcement was given by the White House and War Department at 10:30 A.M. An atomic bomb was dropped on Japan today. This new weapon possesses more power than twenty thousand tons of TNT, with a destructive force equal to two thousand B-29 bombers, and has two thousand times the blast power of what previously was the world's most devastating bomb! There are estimates of between one and two hundred thousand lives lost...With utmost solemnity, President Truman has stated, 'One of the scientific landmarks of the century has been achieved, the 'Age of Atomic Energy,' which can be a tremendous force for the advancement of civilization, or for its destruction.' Truman has warned the Japanese of a further rain of ruin if they do not surrender."*

When Sidney opened his eyes, running fingers through sweat-matted hair, he noticed the lights had been turned off and shades drawn against the sunlight, and smiled. The smell of coffee drew him into his outer office.

"Thanks for not waking me, Kathy." She was looking out the window and not responding.

"I really should apologize," he went on. "Of late, I've been kind of a—" She turned, revealing mascara running down her face.

"Colonel, I now understand what you've been trying to prevent..."

Almost in a daze, Mashbir entered Willoughby's office.

"I know how you feel, Sidney," the general said. "But at least you have a couple more broadcasts."

"What difference does it make now, sir?"

"It could make a big difference, because there's likely another one coming real soon."

"We've only just hit Hiroshima—the Japanese need time." Mashbir's voice strained. "Remember the Great Kanto Earthquake? The populace initially stumbled around for over a week in total disbelief and denial."

Willoughby looked into his eyes. "Do you realize our fire-bombing of cities throughout Japan hasn't gotten them to quit? The Japs on Okinawa and Iwo Jima knew their positions were hopeless, yet died virtually to the last man, their only purpose to inflict as many casualties on the Americans as possible."

He threw his arms upward. "Our first bomb targeted the Imperial Army in Hiroshima, and though civilian casualties were quite large, they were sadly unavoidable. You of all people know that the fanatics have so indoctrinated the populace to fight to the death that we have to hit them with an overwhelming force. *And that might not be enough!*"

Willoughby sighed. "Who knows? It may well also require the Russians declaring war against them to end this conflict . . . The Ruskies lost millions of lives against the Nazis, and won't come into the Pacific battlefront unless they feel we've hit the Japanese as hard as we can."

"But, sir, a little time might save a hundred thousand lives or more!"

"Sidney, you're aware the Japanese are pulling four million troops from China to defend their homeland islands for one last sacred battle to the death! With MacArthur is preparing for that possible scenario with the movement of two million of our troops. This could result in the largest battle to conquer an island nation in the history of the world: The death toll of that bloodbath would be in the millions!"

"Alright, sir. I'll have my final broadcasts present a positive vision of what peace will ultimately bring the Japanese."

On August 9, 1945, the city of Nagasaki, the great industrial war plant center, was targeted by a mighty atomic bomb, which fell on this teeming city at noon. First reports indicated the attack was as effective as the explosion that devastated Hiroshima three days earlier. Nagasaki, the eleventh largest city in Japan, saw its buildings crushed like matchboxes and almost every living thing in its range killed!

The next day, banner newspaper headlines around the world announced:

RUSSIA DECLARES WAR ON JAPAN!

✳✳✳✳

That evening, Mashbir, with dark shadows under his eyes, was again at his microphone:

"My friends in Japan, this is my fourth radio broadcast. In previous ones I've spoken of the gross blunders committed by your top generals. Since then, there have been further instances of incompetence. People of Kanto, Sendai, and Kyoto: how many of your men in the armed forces have returned from their battles in Burma? The answer is none! All were annihilated. In addition, your First, Sixteenth, and Twenty-sixth Divisions became the victims of General MacArthur's victorious return to the Philippines.

Finally, some of your own top military leaders admit that they cannot possibly win the war. The Japanese fleet has been completely destroyed and Allied aircraft darken your skies night and day, bombing at an unprecedented scale: They are even using sensational new weapons which are the epitome of modern science.

The Allied proclamation states that the time has come for Japan to decide whether she will continue to be controlled by militarists whose unintelligent calculations have brought the empire of Japan to the threshold of annihilation, or will she follow the path of reason and justice?

I strongly believe the Emperor wishes peace. Years past, Emperor Meiji, in the Charter Oath of Five Articles, wisely ordered that meetings should be held on state affairs and decided in the light of public opinion.

Your Greater Japan Political Society is the one representative in-stitution left to the Japanese people. Recently, Lieutenant General Ishiwara and Prime Minister Admiral Suzuki, himself, have agreed that this organization should be a means through which the people can express their feelings.

Follow these leaders' wise advice and work with the Greater Ja-pan Political Society and neighborhood associations to demand the prompt acceptance of the fair terms the Allies are offering...The war-rior's word is final!"

✳✳✳✳

Two days later, the Imperial Palace, August 13, 1945

Hirohito and Nagako sat side by side holding hands, as they listened to a familiar voice on the radio:

"My dear friends in Japan, good evening.

This is Colonel Sidney Mashbir, once again speaking to you from the heart. This is the last of my broadcasts, so please listen carefully.

Certain of your leaders have desecrated your glorious tra-ditions, which might well lead to the ultimate extinction of Ja-pan. Their so-called sacred war has only one true goal, and that is to increase these men's own political and financial power.

However, a war based on avarice and ambition cannot re-ceive the blessings of the ancestral gods. They dared to make false presentations to the Emperor, while deceptively demand-ing the people's cooperation in his name. They recklessly chal-lenged the world, and are traitors to their country and enemies of mankind!

Please open your eyes to the fact that the Japanese Impe-rial Army is falling apart, yet these militants desire One last Glorious Battle, and in so doing prolong cruel and senseless hostilities.

America, England, and China—out of consideration for

the good of humanity have repeatedly made peace overtures, which have been rejected, forcing Allied planes to bomb Japan day and night.

You are probably aware of the Russian declaration of war against Japan made last week. It states that with Germany's collapse, the only country seeking to continue this savage struggle is Japan.

Because Germany long rejected the path of surrender, it brought upon itself national ruin. Unless Japan immediately suspends war, it will meet with a similar fate.

It is with deep regret that the Allies, after patiently trying to bring about peace, have had to use atomic bombs, which derive their energy from the Sun.

Now, even the gods of the Land of the Sun have joined to punish Japan's treacherous military clique.

You must accept the Allied terms, which are based on the principles of human justice and will lead to the restoration of peace and enlightenment. The Samurai's word is final!"

Hirohito turned to his wife. "Dear Nagako, I can no longer rule from within a cage. Yesterday, I toured Tokyo to see for myself the world outside our walls. Everywhere I went, there was nothing but death and ruin. It was a nightmare reminiscent of the Great Kanto Earthquake, but instead of a natural disaster, this catastrophe was based on human stupidity."

"Dear husband, *we supported our people during that crisis, we must protect them now!* No more should die in this senseless war!"

Their eyes met.

"Remember my love, if my confrontation with the militants should lead to my death Nagako, you must remain strong for our family and especially our son, Akihito, guiding him for whatever leadership role destiny has in store for him."

CHAPTER **51**

Air raid shelter beneath the Imperial Palace, the following day
Prime Minister Suzuki, Foreign Minister Togo, General Anami, and several other military leaders gathered for the hastily arranged meeting. It was ten a.m. when Hirohito entered the room and spoke.

"Though I resisted the war for many years, I finally gave in to pressure and then delusions of conquest based on early victories. Those dreams have turned to nightmares!"

He looked into the eyes of each of them.

"While things went well, the generals and admirals ignored me; when losses mounted, they turned to me as a symbol, convincing young soldiers that to die in my name was a great honor. I'm ashamed I let myself be used!"

He clenched his fists, struggling to control his anger.

"A month ago, a peace proposal from the Allies was offered: *at first*, it was withheld from me, and then, misrepresented…Recent radio broadcasts have since clarified their terms and carried warnings of future attacks on a scale unimaginable."

He glared at Anami.

"You mocked these threats as lies, urging me to delay acceptance until we knew the Russians' position—Well, now we know!" He slapped his hand down, shaking the table.

"They've declared war on us, and during this delay, not only have the bombing attacks increased, but two of our major cities have been incinerated. And unless we surrender, the Americans threaten to attack our homeland with millions of Allied troops, now aided by the Russians."

He took a deep breath. "Based on this, the Japanese Empire, as of today, will fight no more!"

General Anami stood. "Your Excellency, we have more than four million troops who can repel any invasion they might mount. We should fight on until we have a fully negotiated settlement, not *unconditional surrender.*"

"My sacred ancestors remind me of the masses who have perished, and of the still greater multitudes at risk!"

"I beg you hear me out," Anami continued. "We still have pilots who can defend the islands and inflict such heavy strategic attacks—"

"Silence!" the Emperor replied. "The Allies now produce in a one month as many planes as we have shot down during this entire war— Tomorrow, I shall announce in a radio broadcast with *my own voice* to *Our people,* that this war is over and they are to embrace the peace which follows."

"Your Excellency, I agree with your position," Prime Minister Suzuki said. Anami shot him a furious look, which the prime minister ignored and continued. "But Your Divine status makes it impossible for *You* to speak to *Your people* directly. If *You're* set on this course, I can prepare an address, which I will deliver, conveying *Your* wishes—"

Hirohito gently cut him off.

"Thank you, Minister. You have long given sound counsel, but I must make this point clear: The nation that emerges from this war will no longer be the old Japan. We live in a new world, where leaders directly address their people. Please leave, you are all dismissed."

Outside, in the corridor, Anami turned to several of his fellow officers, and spoke with a sympathetic voice. "The Emperor is suffering mental fatigue. It is our responsibility to protect him from caving in to the Allies. Let us further discuss this matter at my headquarters . . .

"When they arrived, Major General Matsumoto was surprised to see Reichmann had been invited as well.

Anami promptly began. "Our primary goal is to prevent the Emperor's acceptance of this peace agreement. *If unsuccessful,* we bide our time until our enemy's leaders are near our shores for the signing ceremony. *Then we strike!* Without the head, the serpent dies, and we fight on and win!"

He looked at General Matsumoto. "I have a most important assignment for you. One last sacrifice for the glory of our nation." He handed him a sheet of paper. "Here is the location of a hangar containing a surprise gift for the Allies—six dozen planes armed and ready."

"Yes, sir, I understand," Matsumoto replied. "But what happens, if in spite of our best efforts this mission is unsuccessful?"

"Not only will we succeed, but we will intimidate them into allowing us to keep more of our territorial gains."

"Most assuredly!" Reichmann interjected. "The Allies are crossing their fingers that you accept their terms."

How freely our Nazi friend offers our homeland to invasion, Matsumoto thought.

In his office, later that day, General Matsumoto analyzed the Allies' reconquest of Manila, fighting door-to-door...Even the city hall with its impregnable concrete walls fell to phosphorous bombs thrown through its small window openings...*Is this what the future holds for Japan, a punishment for our arrogance?* He remembered bragging to his American friend, Sidney Mashbir, years earlier, how the Japanese planned to burn the Russians out of their concrete bunkers with incendiaries; only to have these horrific weapons turned against his own troops—And now, the Russians' hot breath was upon their shores, waiting to see if the Japanese were even greater fools, willing to fight on toward annihilation.

A lieutenant entered.

"What is it?"

"Sir, I have a drunken prisoner outside, perhaps crazy, admitting crimes that you should know of."

"This sounds like a police matter."

"Trust me, sir, it is best that you hear what he has to say."

The man entered, handcuffed, his clothing tattered, with knife slashes across his arms and chest, and dried blood on much of his body.

"Did you do this to him, Lieutenant?" Matsumoto shouted.

"No, he said he did this himself."

Matsumoto lifted the man's chin and stared into anguished eyes. "What is your name?"

"Gunji."

"What brought you to self-inflict such pain?"

Gunji looked away. "I murdered a great leader, and our country has suffered for the evil deed."

"Who was it?"

In spite of the handcuffs, Gunji's nails clawed at his arm as he spoke. "It was the esteemed Prince Tokugawa."

"How could a low-life such as yourself have accomplished this?"

"The Prince had routines, dining at favorite restaurants on certain days of the week," he whimpered. "We arranged for a car explosion one block away; when fire trucks arrived, sirens blaring, patrons in the restaurant were in a state of distraction, creating an opportunity to poison his tea."

The serene face of his dear mentor, Prince Tokugawa, flashed in Matsumoto's mind; he grasped the handle of his sword and longed to cut this demon in two. Instead, he spoke softly. "Who bid you to do this crime?"

"I was paid a great deal of money by a foreign diplomat named Reichmann."

"Was anyone else involved?"

"He claimed it was an order from his leaders. They wanted the poison to take effect gradually, so none would suspect." He began trembling. "I've done many wicked things, but this was different. There has not been a day that I did not regret my part...I would have already taken my own life, but wished first to confess."

Matsumoto stared at Gunji with disgust.

"For coming forward, I will allow you the dignity of *seppuku*, releasing your damned soul."

He turned to his lieutenant. "Tell no one of his confession. Now take him out of my sight!"

Imperial Palace, the following evening

Hirohito and Nagako had much on their minds; their bomb-shelter had been converted into a medical room, where their oldest daughter was now being attended to as she went through the pangs of the birthing of her first child. And while that was going on, they anxiously waited for the following morning to arrive, when the Emperor's voice would be radio broadcasted directly to their people. Accompanying them as they ate dinner, was Major Fujimo.

"Thank you, Major, for escorting me to make that recording today," Hirohito said.

Nagako sighed. "Major, when you deliver that recording to the radio station tomorrow, this nightmare will finally be over."

"I'm honored to be of service, Your Majesty."

"I would have had you take it there tonight," Hirohito said, "but feared the radio station might be destroyed in yet another bombing raid."

Nagako spoke wistfully. "The future of our people is so uncertain. Our own precious Terunomiya lies in a windowless concrete room below us, soon to bring forth to our first grandchild. What sort of world will that child inherit?"

Before Hirohito could respond, gunfire and shouting was heard from the hallway. The door burst open and soldiers brandishing rifles rushed in.

"What's the meaning of this!" Hirohito yelled. Major Fujimo confronted the intruders.

A young army captain aimed a pistol.

"Don't interfere! We've already killed the colonel commanding your Palace Guard and many of his troops. Do not force us to kill you Major."

"Have you lost your mind?" Fujimo said. "This is your Emperor. Put down your weapons at once and consider yourselves under arrest!"

"On the contrary," the captain countered, "you are the one under arrest. We mean no harm to His Majesty. He and the household staff are simply in protective custody."

"I'm your superior officer, and again in the name of the Emperor, I'm ordering you to immediately lay down your arms and cease this treason."

"My orders come from officers far higher in rank than you."

Fujimo grabbed for the captain's pistol, but he jerked it out of reach and swung it at the major's head, knocking him down. As he attempted to rise, Hirohito stepped between the two.

"No, Fujimo. Let us see what this mad dog intends!" he said, looking straight at the captain. "Now's your opportunity to kill Your Emperor," he challenged, as Nagako knelt down and cradled Fujimo's bloody head.

The other soldiers murmured amongst themselves. Beads of sweat oozed from the captain's brow.

More soldiers entered, led by another captain and a lieutenant with pistols drawn. The newly arrived older captain demanded, "What's happening here? Our orders are only to retrieve that recording."

"The major tried to take my weapon," the younger captain replied. "Where are the rest of the servants? We want everyone gathered here."

"They're being rounded up," the lieutenant replied. "This place is a regular rabbit warren of rooms and passages. Have you found what we are looking for?"

"No, not yet."

The older captain turned to the Emperor.

"Pardon the intrusion and my fellow officer's roughness, Your Majesty. This is a matter of national security. I must ask you to hand over the recording you made this afternoon. It is of the utmost importance that I retrieve it."

"I refuse. There is no pardon possible for this insult. That is my final word, except to remind you that this foolhardy plot is doomed. Within hours, if I do not communicate with my ministers and military commanders, they will storm the palace—and those of your men who die in the fight will be the fortunate ones."

Hirohito's fierce expression swept the room, looking from soldier to soldier, most of whom were ashamed to meet his gaze.

"You bring dishonor on yourselves and your families for all time!"

The captain who had knocked Fujimo down, snarled, "Very well.

We'll see how silent everyone remains as I put a bullet into the major's head." As he attempted to get around the Emperor and toward Fujimo, Nagako's ladies-in-waiting and Hirohito's butler, as well as the kitchen staff and two nurses, were herded into the room by soldiers wielding rifles with bayonets. A sergeant announced, "That's all of them, sir. We searched every room. This maid," he said, dragging her by the arm, "was hiding in a closet."

The young woman began crying hysterically. The sergeant whirled toward her with an upraised hand, but before he could strike, the butler stepped in front of her and slapped both her cheeks gently but rapidly, while demanding, "Pull yourself together. You're not helping by behaving like this."

The surprised girl's cries subsided in a series of hiccups, as she buried her face on the shoulder of another maid.

"Threatening Major Fujimo will get you nowhere," Hirohito shouted. "He knows nothing of the recording! Search if you wish, I don't know where it is myself."

"Lieutenant, take several men," the older captain ordered, "and check everywhere…"

On their return, the Lieutenant announced, "We can't find it. The only other people not present here are a pregnant woman on a table, and her doctor, both in the bomb shelter."

Hirohito suddenly realized the presence of the nurses. "What! My daughter may at any moment give birth, and you dare to remove her attending staff? You barbarians are a disgrace to the uniforms you wear."

The older captain jerked his head at the sergeant. "Take the nurses back immediately," then turned to the emperor. "Again, I apologize for any discourtesy, but it is vital that we have that recording."

Hirohito remained silent.

A blast from outside made it impossible to hear. Another followed. Anti-aircraft guns located throughout the city began firing continuously. Additional explosions, each louder than the last, announced a string of bombs hitting closer and closer. The soldiers abandoned all effort to stand at attention and were cowering along the walls, looking fearfully toward the trembling ceiling.

During a pause, Hirohito declared, "There is so little left unde-
stroyed, they are now targeting the palace itself."

The soldiers edged toward the exit.

"Where do you think you're going?" the young captain shouted.
"Get back here."

An even louder explosion drowned out any possibility of speech.
The room trembled, plaster dust sifting down as the lights flickered,
then went out.

When the lights came back on, more than half the soldiers were
gone. The captains hesitated, but when another series of explosions
began, they ran out the door, followed by the rest of their men.

The bombing finally ceased.

The butler ventured out into the hallway, then returned. "They're
gone, Your Majesty, every one of them."

"I'm going to our daughter," Nagako announced, running out of
the room accompanied by her handmaidens.

With some difficulty, Fujimo got to his feet. "I'll get my men and
follow those traitors, Your Majesty."

"That can be dealt with later," Hirohito replied. "I'm so sorry you
were hurt, Fujimo—I honestly have no idea what happened to the recording. I left it on a counter. We must make another—time is critical."

"Excuse me, Your Excellency," the Emperor's aide, Yoshihiro, interjected as he entered the room. "That may not be necessary. Is it a
large black metal disk they were looking for?"

"Do you know what happened to it?"

Yoshihiro smiled. "When those villains broke in, I hid it in one of
the rice bags in the pantry."

"Well done!" Hirohito embraced the man. "I never thought I'd be
grateful for a bombing raid, but this one came at a propitious moment...Someday, I will tell our grandchild how he or she came into
the world, between the last day of war and the first day of peace."

PART FOUR

Mashbir entered MacArthur's office to find him not his usual reserved self, but instead, overflowing with exuberance as he handed Mashbir a cigar.

"Colonel, the day has arrived," he declared, "and you're one of the first I'm notifying that the Japs have given up! But keep it under your hat—we're awaiting the official announcement. And Sidney, you'll be in charge of all the details related to the Surrender Signing Ceremony."

That afternoon, the sound of rifles blasting into the air, mixed with shouts of exhilaration, as two privates rushed into Mashbir's office at ATIS Headquarters.

"Sir, we just got this newswire from the States!"

The words *PEACE AT LAST!* were plastered across the top.

"Follow me," Mashbir ordered.

Once in the main operations room, with microphone in hand, he spoke loudly, gaining the attention of the over one thousand ATIS translators present; while several thousands of their team members were still serving at the front lines.

"Everyone, stop what you're doing. As you probably guessed from the noise outside, the moment has arrived that we've worked long and hard for!

I've a news announcement to read:

"'Last night, on August 14, 1945, in Washington, D.C., President Truman announced that the Japanese government has accepted the

Allies' terms. General Douglas MacArthur, as Supreme Commander, has been chosen to receive their surrender.

The other Allies in the Pacific war, Great Britain, Australia, Russia, Canada, and China, will also be represented at the signing by their high-ranking officers.

All Allied armed forces have been ordered to suspend offensive operations. And Emperor Hirohito has ordered all military, naval, and air authorities of Japan and all forces under their control, wherever located, to cease operations, and to surrender arms, as may be required by the Supreme Commander.

Surrender ceremonies will take place aboard the battleship, the U.S.S. Missouri.

In recognition of this important moment in history, President Truman has declared a two-day holiday for all Federal employees throughout the country." Sidney paused to let the good news sink in ... "And that includes all of you!" he said with a smile.

They came to their feet, cheering and applauding. As Mashbir watched them stream out of the room to celebrate, he thought, There were times I doubted we'd ever see this day. Now to figure out the best logistics for formally bringing this war to an end!

✳✳✳✳

The Manila Surrender Planning Conference was held in MacArthur's Headquarters in the Philippines. The temperature was close to one hundred degrees without the slightest hint of a breeze. MacArthur sat at the head of the table, along with Mashbir and six more senior officers. The meeting had been going on for some time. All the senior officers had been given the opportunity to speak in order of rank, as Mashbir listened with growing impatience.

MacArthur took a sip of water..."All right," he said, "we've settled how the Japanese emissaries get here on a single plane. Now we need to decide the mechanics of how they are to be received."

A brigadier general stood. "How we treat these *jokers* when they get here sets the tone for everything that follows! We *dictate* terms and treat these guys like any other prisoners of war. And when we put them back on their plane to Japan, they need to know for damn sure they're on parole, released only to carry back the surrender documents."

Several officers nodded in agreement.

MacArthur looked around the table. "Anyone else have some ideas?"

This isn't a popularity contest, Mashbir thought, *so I'll speak my mind. It's now or never.* "Well, sir, with all due respect, while I wholeheartedly concur that this meeting will set the tone for future relations, I can't agree with the proposal just given. To treat them in such a way would be a grave mistake."

He loosened his tie. "Instead, we should meet them in a welcoming fashion. Their cooperation is essential; they're carrying back our request to their Emperor that he sign an authorization allowing delegates from the *Imperial Japanese Civilian Government* and the *Imperial General Military Headquarters* to act as signatories at the final surrender signing ceremony.

"And to further engender goodwill, these emissaries should be given time to confer among themselves as they review these documents, while *we emphasize* there is no negotiation going on."

"Bullshit!" another general broke in. "These guys violated every accepted rule of warfare. They have no right to expect to be treated like diplomats."

"I'm sure you're correct, sir," Mashbir replied. "They probably don't expect to be treated with any courtesy. To me, that's all the more reason we should. In their culture, to receive respect obligates them to return respect. They're whipped, and they know it. These are the same people we're going to have to live amongst for years to come."

Arms spread wide, raising his palms upward, he bowed slightly as he calmly added, "That's my advice, based on having lived among them, and having studied their culture for over two decades."

Mashbir's voice now hardened, "One last important consideration: Several of these representatives' colleagues have already committed suicide, rather than be part of this surrender. And, there have even been threats they might be shot down on their way here, by fanatical members of their own military. If we don't put a positive spin on this, the general populace might respond in a hysterical way, violently resisting our occupation, or taking their own lives en masse."

Several of the more hardline generals stared angrily at Mashbir. MacArthur allowed anyone else to voice their view; no one did. He stood and straightened to his full height.

"I thank you all for the opinions rendered today," he said, "but I've decided to go with Mashbir's plan. As a matter of fact, Colonel Mashbir is going to be standing on the tarmac when their plane lands. He'll take charge and will act as liaison as necessary with General Willoughby."

MacArthur turned to the general who had voiced the most heated objections.

"Jim, I'm counting on you to make sure they know the plane transporting those Japanese diplomats must have the right markings: painted white with several green crosses. When they clear the South China Sea, two of our P-38s will escort them the rest of the way. And they'd better give the correct code word when they come up on our radio frequency, or they'll be shot out of the sky—You can see we're ready for any threat and taking no nonsense!"

MacArthur smiled coldly as he looked at them.

"I understand the anger you feel. The code word they'll use is *Bataan*—To remind them we haven't forgotten their treatment of our captured soldiers during those death marches…All right, gentlemen, a big day tomorrow. Dismissed."

Turning to Sidney, he added, "Could you remain a moment?"

Once the others had gone, MacArthur threw Mashbir a rigid look. "As you're well aware, there are some strong feelings that we demand the emperor step down immediately. Matter of fact, several of my staff believe he could be put on trial for war crimes—I don't go that far, but I'd like your input."

Mashbir nibbled his lower lip. *I've been waiting for this moment for a long time and here it is*, he thought. *Hope I don't get tongue-tied, or anger the general.*

"Well, sir, I strongly recommend he retain the honorary title. The vast majority of the Japanese revere him, and it would go a long way toward pacifying the more militant elements. As far as a war criminal, there's no way to justify that. I knew him as a young man through my friend, his uncle, Prince Tokugawa, who has since passed on▯

"Hirohito was never in favor of the war. Since the early thirties, Japan has pretty much been under the control of militant factions. Honestly, I doubt the Emperor was even kept fully informed of events after the earliest Japanese victories."

MacArthur put up a hand to slow Mashbir down.

"Okay, Sidney, I'm convinced. But there's one more issue. You've got to remember, the guys they're sending may know you, at least some of them. The last thing I need is a photo splashed on the cover of every newspaper with those Japanese reps grinning as they shake your hand. You must be all business. No hint of friendship. That's firm, no exception!"

Moments later, Sidney proceeded down the hall mumbling to himself, "Right you are, sir. Don't shake hands, but don't insult them. Be cordial, businesslike, but no friendliness. How come senior officers think it's easy to do contradictory things at the same time?"

That evening in his room, Mashbir stood at various angles in front of his mirror, employing unconventional hand movements, while thinking how best to greet the Japanese emissaries as they deplaned. *If they try to shake my hand, I'll swing mine upward and over my right shoulder with the thumb out, indicating they are to proceed to the building behind me...Hopefully, they'll understand why I'm acting this way and won't get pissed off.*

August 16, 1945, the Philippines

The plane touched down hard, rolled, and then came to a complete stop at the end of the landing strip. From behind the roped barriers lining the runway, crowds of curious soldiers watched...Two Japanese admirals, a general, a colonel, and a military aide, all in uniform, exited the plane. Accompanying them were several civilians; among them was Foreign Minister Okazaki in a white suit, representing the Japanese civilian government.

All approached Mashbir, some with friendly expressions of recognition. Nearby, photographers representing major magazines and news services were ready, their cameras clicking or motion picture cameras rolling to capture the historic moment: the first diplomatic contact between the Allies and the Japanese after four war-filled years*

Just what I need, Mashbir thought, *them calling me Sidney-san and suggesting we go out for a drink later. And there's that* Life *magazine photographer, with me in his sights, capturing this awkward moment.*

Mashbir subtly redirected the emissaries' view toward some of his commanding officers at the sideline, all of them scowling. *I sure hope they understand the pressure I'm under . . .* A couple of the emissaries gave a nod of acknowledgment, but when one held out his hand, Sidney flawlessly carried out his well-practiced maneuver to avoid shaking it, with a thumb over the shoulder, directing the representatives to nearby waiting cars that would take them to their assigned housing at MacArthur's headquarters.

In spite of orders to keep quiet, there were hoots of "*Banzai*," coming from some GIs, and "*Baka*," meaning "fool," shouted by angry Filipinos.

As they drove to headquarters escorted by MPs in Jeeps, Mashbir realized that the peace process was still skating on thin ice when he heard the Japanese military leaders referring to the civilian emissaries accompanying them in a highly derogatory fashion; going so far as to describe them as 'unwelcome guests!'

Minister Okazaki whispered to Mashbir: "Let them talk. It won't be long before Japan returns to a civilian-ruled government."

Over the next day, conferences were held with the Japanese representatives of the Army, Navy, and Air Force, arranging the disarmament of their remaining millions of troops. Mashbir recognized the courage of both the military and civilian representatives, who expressed serious concerns that their plane might be shot down by their own militants when they flew back to Japan. For that reason, they emphatically requested they return in two planes, to double the odds that at least one might make it back with the peace documents for the Emperor to sign.

It seemed as if things were going smoothly, but when Mashbir visited the emissaries waiting to board their planes for their return he sensed something was very wrong. Several were sweating and fidgeting, with looks of despair in their eyes... Mashbir spoke to Okazaki, "My friend, what's the matter?"

Okazaki handed him a copy of the documents they'd been given and pointed to a section.

"This isn't what I wrote," Mashbir declared. "Oh man, did it get fouled up!" He told the emissaries to delay their departure until he returned, then took off at a good clip and was soon facing MacArthur.

"I'm sorry, General, it's imperative we speak."

"What's so important?"

"This word, sir, referring to Hirohito," he pointed. "It's *terribly* insulting. It could be used to mean a common laborer, or even a bum, but it would never be used to refer to the Emperor!"

"What are you talking about? You gave us that document in English and one of our translators turned it into Japanese. I figured you were busy with lots of other details, but it's your wording."

Mashbir forced a smile. "Sir, you know those moments that you look back on years in the future and laugh, but today feel earth-shattering in importance?"

"Go on..."

"This is that kind of day. Those emissaries are probably contemplating whether to commit suicide before or after they'd delivered that document . . . And, if it gets into the hands of militants, it might incite the masses to rise up to fight, rather than see their spiritual leader treated in that way."

"Then get it fixed, Mashbir—and fast. Glad you caught it!"

Not long after, Sidney was placing the revised documents into their hands. After reading the new wording, the emissaries repeatedly bowed in gratitude, with Generals MacArthur and Willoughby observing with satisfaction.

"Now you make sure, Willoughby," MacArthur said, "that Mashbir is put in charge of *all* details of the formal signing ceremony. And that includes assisting me with my closing remarks."

Willoughby later pulled Mashbir aside.

"Don't let it go to your head, Colonel, but it looks like we don't know what we'd do without you."

Just outside of Tokyo, early morning

Armed guards in front of the structure snapped to attention on seeing General Matsumoto. "Open the doors," he ordered. "These mechanics will inspect the planes to make sure they are in good flying condition. Be alert, we are not to be disturbed."

Matsumoto, accompanied by several soldiers, escorted a dozen men dressed in gray denim overalls into the cavernous aircraft hangar; the doors were then shut—Two hours passed, and when they reopened, the mechanics were stained with grease as they returned to their waiting vehicles.

Later that day, a long double-line of pilots marched into the hangar as several generals and a lieutenant stood outside, watching with pride. "Those arrogant Westerners!" General Anami said. "I wish I could see their shocked faces as our planes explode on their decks."

"Yes," another general responded, "but isn't it a pity that our assassination attempts against Prime Minister Suzuki and the President of the Privy Council were unsuccessful?"

"At least those traitors' homes were burned to the ground for allowing the surrender to move forward," Anami gloated. Nearby, General Matsumoto remained seated in his Jeep, deep in thought.

The pilots climbed into cockpits and turned their ignition switches, but nothing happened...Shouts rang out from all directions. "Something's wrong! Check the fuel gauges and engines." Maintenance crews unlatched and opened the engine covers. Confusion reigned as the mechanics discovered that all the ignition spark plugs had been removed, and many electrical wires severed. Until lengthy repairs could be made, these planes would go nowhere.

General Anami looked questioningly at his lieutenant, and then with anger toward Matsumoto.

"What's going on, General? You were in charge!" he shouted.

Just then, three military convoy trucks pulled up, and nearly a hundred soldiers jumped out.

Matsumoto exited his Jeep, and holding up a document, he approached Anami and the other officers.

"By this Decree of the Emperor himself," he announced, "I have been given seniority and final say over all military matters here."

He turned to his troops. "You are to disarm and arrest General Anami and his associates."

All eyes focused on General Anami, whose face had turned ashen: Would he challenge the emperor's command?

With reluctance, Anami relinquished his sword and pistol and was marched away.

"Soldiers," Matsumoto called out. "Go into the hangar and inform the pilots and mechanics this mission has been aborted by order of the Emperor!"

German Consulate in Tokyo, the following day, Reichmann's shirt was drenched with sweat as he frantically tossed stacks of papers into a blazing fireplace, unaware of Matsumoto's arrival.

"Herr Reichmann, how curious—the temperature is quite warm, yet you need a fire?" Reichmann jerked his head around.

"Destroying the evidence of your dealings in Japan, perhaps?" Matsumoto added with a smile.

Reichmann's pockmarked face turned molten red. "I've been informed of your treason against General Anami. You will pay!" he yelled.

"Perhaps, but speaking of payments due, I have heard of your murderous treachery."

Turning slightly, Reichmann slipped his hand into his pocket.

"Yes," Matsumoto continued, "your assassin, Gunji, speaks highly of you."

Despite his bulk, Reichmann moved with agility, pulling out his Luger, as Matsumoto unsheathed his sword. Shots were fired, and in almost the same instant a hand was severed, its index finger still hooked around the trigger. With another swipe of razor-sharp steel across the throat of the astonished Reichmann, his huge torso toppled over.

Wheezing as he left, Matsumoto pressed a hand against his bloody chest as he staggered into the hallway and out of the building.

※※※※

The wardroom aboard the battleship U.S.S. Missouri, Tokyo Bay

Mashbir looked at the gathering of U.S. Generals, Admirals, and their staffs, and thought, *How ironic, here we are on the battleship that fought at Iwo Jima and Okinawa, but now it's the stage for peace agreements . . .*

"Gentlemen, I trust I've made all the details clear regarding the surrender ceremony? After everyone signs, General MacArthur will declare the proceedings closed. I'll then escort the Japanese back. I must emphasize; please instruct your men there are to be no fireworks, loud celebrations or gun salutes."

MacArthur spoke supportively, "No sense rubbing their noses in it. Firing off guns might make the Japanese think we're bombarding them."

"One last thing," Mashbir added. "The Asian mind places a great deal of value on formal ceremony. Some of the delegation may be wearing full military dress uniform, including a ceremonial sword."

"No swords!" an Admiral shouted. "Our side's not wearing 'em, and I'm damned if I'm letting some Japs come on board one of my ships with them!"

Mashbir turned to MacArthur. The general shook his head in the negative.

Another senior officer spoke. "That's right. We don't know how desperate these guys are, and remember those *banzai* charges. What if one whips out his sword and starts hacking at the general?"

Mashbir looked at him. "We've already agreed they'll be searched for weapons. And these are only ceremonial swords, duller than seventh-grade arithmetic."

He turned to MacArthur and continued, "When I was growing up in Arizona, your father was a legend in West, winning the Medal of Honor serving under General Grant during the Civil War. At the risk of being presumptuous, might I remind you of the surrender at Appomattox? General Lee *would have* given up his sword to General Grant, but Grant refused it, saying a defeated enemy deserved respect if one hoped to make a friend of him in the future...I think if Grant or your father were here today, they'd counsel you to do the same."

"You've made your point," MacArthur replied, shaking his head. "I swear, Mashbir, you sure can be persuasive. However, I stand firm: No swords during the signing. Okay, gentlemen, you can all leave, except for Colonel Mashbir."

Once alone, to Mashbir's surprise, MacArthur's stern expression turned into a smile, as he put a friendly arm over Mashbir's shoulder like he was one of his buddies.

"Sidney, we'll soon be leaving for Japan to establish our headquarters there and to pick up those Japanese representatives." He looked him eye to eye. "I just wanted to let you know how much I appreciate all you've done so far in putting together this signing ceremony— Henceforth, you're to be my personal translator and specialist on all things Japanese." He saluted him. "And, you'll be honored by being the first American non-prisoner to set foot on Japan since the war started."

"Why, why, thank you, sir!" Sidney said, fumbling for words.

"Don't thank me too fast—We haven't yet formally signed a peace treaty . . . *We're* about to go on one of the greatest adventures in military history: entering the enemy's country with only a handful of troops, while looking down the throats of nineteen fully armed divisions and seventy-million potential fanatics. One false move, and the Alamo will look like a Sunday-school picnic!"

CHAPTER 53

This would be the crowning travesty, Sidney thought, *to live through the war, only to die on a pleasant, sunny day, while bringing back a peace delegation* . . . Mashbir, along with General MacArthur and a dozen others spearheading the Army of Occupation, were flying to Japan from Manila, protected by an escort of fighter planes. They'd been preparing for over a week, then were delayed by a typhoon over the islands—But now, on August 30, 1945, they were en route to the Atsugi airport, where at 2:14 PM Tokyo time, their landing gear would make contact with Japanese soil.

The Japanese authorities who met them there weren't sure themselves how the general public would react to their visit. The only transportation they could offer were the most battered vehicles they'd ever seen, available nowhere else but in war-torn Japan. Motors sputtered and hissed, while leaky radiators steamed, as they drove to the Yokohama Grand Hotel, where General MacArthur was to stay.

The surrounding villages they passed through gave them little attention. The destruction along the way re-ignited Mashbir's memories of the Great Kanto Earthquake.

Crowds in Yokohama were emaciated, having lived on food rations for so long, almost starving. They, too, looked at them with minimal curiosity and without hostility.

Once MacArthur had settled into his room at the Grand Hotel, he called Mashbir in. "You're to go to Tokyo," he said, "and check the overall situation there. Inspect the embassy: See whether or not it can be used as my long-term personal living quarters. I'd also like you to inspect the Imperial Hotel, and decide if it will make suitable accommodation for our staff..."

It really looks like I'm going to be the first American officer to enter Tokyo, Mashbir realized, as he was driven along the bumpy road followed by a car with a couple of fellow officers. Halfway there, their path was blocked by an entire armed Japanese division filling a train station and overflowing into the surrounding area, waiting to be evacuated from the city.

"Wow! What do we do now, sir?" Mashbir's driver asked.

"Just act like we won the war," he replied. "Honk them, and move on."

Everyone loosened the flaps to their holsters and held their breath as they proceeded slowly, cutting a lane through the mass of soldiers who simply moved aside while staring blankly at them.

Upon their arrival at the American Embassy, Mashbir discovered it had miraculously sustained minimal damage.

The next stop was the Imperial Hotel, where only the right wing section had been destroyed by a fire.

September 2, 1945

After two days of arranging accommodations in Japan, General MacArthur and the rest of his staff departed to the U.S.S. *Missouri* for the signing ceremony, leaving Mashbir and another officer to accompany the Japanese delegates from the Yokohama pier.

While Mashbir and the Japanese delegates were onboard the ship conveying them to the *Missouri*, Minister Okazaki asked him, "Colonel, do you recommend we salute, bow, shake hands, or simply smile, when we meet the Ally representatives?"

Mashbir thought a moment.

"I'd suggest your military officers keep their hats on, and the civilians amongst you take them off—And please remember to put on a *no-emotion face*, in recognition of the historic significance of this event."

As their ship neared the *Missouri*, a problem arose. Looking up at the Naval Lieutenant on deck, Mashbir shouted, "You're telling me that the Japanese delegates have to climb down a rope ladder to get to the gangplank of the U.S.S. *Missouri*? There's got to be another way—one of them, Mr. Oka, has a wooden leg!"

"I'm so sorry, sir; but I believe your ship has a boatswain's chair that could be rigged up for your crippled Jap."

"Alright, if there's no other alternative. But remember, Lieutenant, stop using the word *Jap*, this is a senior diplomat arriving for the signing of an international peace treaty! General MacArthur wants them treated with the same respect as any other foreign officials when they come aboard!"

Soon Mr. Oka was strapped into a chair suspended precariously from a crane device swung out over the side of the ship, and was hoisted down. Seeing the elderly gentleman so awkwardly treated caused Okazaki to ask, "Colonel Mashbir, I humbly request the photographers not take photos of this humiliation."

"I'll do my best."

As Mashbir led the Japanese procession up the U.S.S. *Missouri*'s gangplank, they were honored by being piped aboard, with the blowing of the bosun's ceremonial whistle.

That's the second time in my life that's happened, Mashbir thought bemusedly. *Last time was my visit to Vladivostok, a million years ago...*

The massive deck of the *Missouri* was packed with the ship's crew perched everywhere on all levels, watching events unfold. A throng of war correspondents accompanied by their photographers closed in, taking hundreds of photos from all vantage points.

The event went like clockwork, with Mashbir overseeing the entire process. Ceremonies began with the representatives of the Allies: the Americans, the Australians, the British, the Canadians, the French, the Chinese, and the Russians each coming up to the signing table, leaning over, and affixing their signatures to the document.

This was to be followed by the signing of the Japanese.

By now, there was lots of festive small talk from the observers, with only the occasional glance at what was actually occurring with the delegates. "Ah, dang it," Mashbir said under his breath. *One of the*

Allies is tipsy, probably celebrated a bit early and signed on the wrong line. This brought the whole process to a halt.

A Japanese delegate asked, "Colonel Mashbir, is this delay meant shame us?"

"Of course not," he replied calmly, "just a minor correction is needed." Then, turning to General Sutherland, Mashbir whispered, "Our slightly inebriated Ally friend screwed things up. How about we just change the printed names to match the signatures later?"

Sutherland nodded, and the signing moved forward to completion.

A respectful hush came over the crowd as MacArthur walked to the microphone to give his parting remarks:

> *"We are gathered here, as representatives of the major warring powers, to conclude a solemn agreement whereby peace may be restored. The issues, involving divergent ideals and ideologies, have been determined on the battlefields of the world, and hence are not for our discussion or debate. Nor is it for us here to meet, representing as we do a majority of the people of the earth, in a spirit of distrust, malice, or hatred. But rather, it is for us, both victors and vanquished, to rise to that higher dignity which alone befits the sacred purposes we are about to serve, committing all our people unreservedly to faithful compliance with the understanding they are here formally to assume.*
>
> *It is my earnest hope, and indeed the hope of all mankind, that from this solemn occasion a better world shall emerge out of the blood and carnage of the past—a world dedicated to the dignity of man and the fulfillment of his most cherished wish for freedom, tolerance, and justice."*

Attention was then proudly drawn upward by the roar of a vast squadron of U.S. aircraft passing overhead, as a tribute to the occasion. Once they were out of sight, the assembled officers and onlookers began to drift away.

Heaving a deep sigh, Mashbir remembered General Pershing

thanking him for his successes in counter-espionage on the American home front, and then poignantly describing the signing ceremony in Europe that ended World War I.

How he had longed to have been there...And now, twenty-six years later, he had the honor of orchestrating the closure of World War II!

"Oh, thank God," he whispered. "Now to get these Japanese gentlemen back to their homes."

Sidney smiled. *Could have been worse—at least nobody fell overboard!*

CHAPTER **54**

Accompanied by hundreds of soldiers, MacArthur and his staff arrived in Japan, using the Yokohama Customs House as their military headquarters and the U.S. Embassy in Tokyo as their home base; it was at these comfortable quarters that evening that MacArthur, Willoughby, and Mashbir gathered over glasses of sherry.

MacArthur grasped his chin in thought. "If we're going to run an occupation government, we must freely move among the people."

"That might be easier said than done," Willoughby replied. "There are still plenty of fanatics running around."

"We'll have some help," Mashbir said. "I've recruited a good number of our ATIS team to stay on, assisting as translators during the transition."

"A fine idea," MacArthur said.

Mashbir continued: "Do you remember our discussions about the Hoko—that system for controlling the masses before and during the war?"

Both generals nodded.

"Well, *now* would be a good time to use it for our own purposes: to eliminate the people's fear of reprisals from the militants in their midst for cooperating with us. It might also circumvent a guerilla movement using terrorism against our occupation forces."

"I strongly support your idea," Willoughby said. "Japan is a disaster zone, with an urgent need for stability."

"We're counting on you, Sidney, to put this plan into action," MacArthur said emphatically.

The following day, Minister Okazaki and a Japanese general visited, paying their respects and conversing with MacArthur, as Mashbir facilitated...Okazaki, using fluent English, announced he had been chosen as head of the Liaison Office dealing with the American occupation.

After the meeting, Okazaki remained, wishing to speak further with Mashbir, alone.

"I, and the Emperor, wish to thank you for so ably overseeing the surrender ceremony, and for correcting the document which the Emperor signed."

"I appreciate the acknowledgment," Mashbir replied. "I hope the Emperor is comfortable with MacArthur's request that the Emperor visit him in the near future, instead of the other way around?"

Okazaki smiled. "Not only is the Emperor comfortable with that request, but my visit today will soon be followed by the Prime Minister and then by Admiral Suita, the Grand Chamberlain, who will make the final arrangements for the Emperor's unprecedented visit..." Okazaki hesitated before handing Mashbir a document. "Colonel, I hope you will not take offense—this is a list of infractions committed by *your* troops in the four days since they've landed: an alleged rape, the pilfering of a truck, and several American soldiers stopping Japanese civilians on the street, asking the time, then snatching their watches—Other soldiers pushed around some Japanese police and robbed their swords."

"I assure you, Minister, General MacArthur will see this list and I'll encourage him to make an announcement applauding our GIs' soldierly conduct in battle, while reminding them to maintain that same respect for their uniforms in the face of their defeated enemy. *And we'll emphasize* that *any* inappropriate behavior on their part will be sternly and swiftly punished, thereby gaining the respect of the Japanese people."

Mashbir felt he had to add, "But please be aware, with the exception of the alleged rape, your complaints are somewhat *trivial* compared to charges against the Japanese Army in its occupations and campaigns."

The magnitude of Okazaki's surprise made Mashbir believe the minister really didn't know the extent of what was being alluded to.

"Are you aware," Mashbir continued, "that the *Fourteenth Area Japanese Army Order* was captured in Manila?" From out of a desk drawer,

Mashbir displayed photographs and presented several atrocity reports for Okazaki to read, with related Japanese documents attached.

After reviewing them, Okazaki's breathing was labored and his face turned a ghastly white, as if he were going to faint.

"Please, let us not discuss this matter anymore today—I can't stand it! I'll come back tomorrow—If it were not you who told me this, I would not believe that some of our people could do such things."

Mashbir was amazed by the shock and revulsion so apparent in this very sincere man. Although Okazaki had been operating on a very high governmental level throughout the war, no word of the frightful brutalities committed by certain Japanese forces had ever been leaked to him.

"Do you have the names of those leaders who committed these crimes?" Okazaki asked.

"Damn right!" Mashbir replied. "And soon you'll be called upon to turn them over to us for punishment."

"Just give us their names, and we'll gladly punish them ourselves. The existence of such criminals is a disgrace, not only to the Japanese, but to all mankind!"

That evening, the Emperor sat rigidly listening, as Okazaki described what he had heard. "This is deplorable!" Hirohito said. "Colonel Mashbir actually showed you the documentation related to these war crimes?"

"Yes, Your Majesty; it is quite convincing."

"Oh, God!" The Emperor looked down in despair.

"Please leave. I need time to consider what you've told me."

Once Okazaki had gone, Hirohito wept.

※※※※

Passing Japanese soldiers and civilians, Mashbir's Jeep rolled through Tokyo. His driver, a sergeant, turned to him, and commented with his raspy voice, "They look almost in a daze."

Mashbir nodded. "For years they've been ordered where to go, what to eat, and where to sleep—It's now our job to get this country back on track. You'll see, they'll soon adapt to their greater freedoms."

The first stop was the Imperial Hotel lobby, where Mr. Ito, the hotel manager, ran to Mashbir, bowed, and then hugged him.

"Sidney-san, I heard of your arrival," he declared. "It's wonderful to see you once again!"

"The feeling is mutual, my dear friend." *He must be close to ninety,* Sidney calculated, *and still has a mind as sharp as a tack.* "I bring gratitude from General MacArthur to you and your staff, for supplying our officers with accommodations."

"It is a pleasure to be of service. The nightmare is over: It's time to rebuild! *And* we appreciate your assistance."

"Mr. Ito, do you know the whereabouts of General Matsumoto? The last time we met, it was here at your hotel eight years ago."

Ito whispered, "I suggest you not ask too many questions about your Japanese friends. There are still members of the Black Dragon who might take revenge. As for your enquiry specifically about General Matsumoto," Ito looked away, "I regret to inform you that he died recently."

Ito observed Sidney's stunned expression of despair.

"Do you know that for sure?"

Ito supportively put his hand on Mashbir's shoulder.

"It is said, he was killed while showing loyalty to the Emperor and bringing back our country's rightful government: *a noble death.*"

Sidney's fists clenched, nails digging into his palms, as a montage of memories flowed through his mind: climbing Mt. Fuji with Kenji, visiting one another's homes during Kenji and Jinne's time in America, and laughing over golfing mishaps✻ . .

Damn it, he thought, eyes moistening, *he almost made it.*

✳✳✳✳

The Imperial Hotel, one month later, October, 1945

Persistent tapping woke him. Outside Sidney's door stood the servant, Shige, who bowed. "Colonel Mashbir, please excuse the early hour. I come with an important request from the Empress."

That afternoon, Nagako, accompanied by Mashbir, strolled a garden. "Please give us some privacy," the Empress ordered, waving her entourage of aides and guards to follow at a good distance behind.

"Dear Colonel," she faltered, "my husband is emotionally distraught. So many disheartening revelations have come to his attention, on a scale beyond any one man's ability to cope."

She whimpered. "He feels personally responsible for the millions of lives lost both in Japan and throughout the world."

She braced herself, putting a fist between her teeth.

"I'm so sorry," Mashbir said. "What is it you wish me to do, Your Majesty?"

She looked deeply into his eyes.

"Last week, Prince Konoe committed suicide, fearing he might be convicted by a war crimes tribunal. He was a wonderful man, who to the end wished to maintain peace, but whom destiny trapped beyond his control...My husband so looked up to him as an older cousin and confidante."

She sighed.

"And now, Hirohito remains in his room with all the window shades drawn, trying to shut out the world, and speaks only a few words to me or the children during the entire day." She trembled. "I fear he might also wish to end it all."

Sidney froze.

"Your Majesty, please forward my condolences to your husband on the passing of Prince Konoe—He was a fine man, and I greatly regretted his death, but knew nothing of your husband's reaction... Though, I noticed several of our invitations for the Emperor to attend meetings with General MacArthur were postponed."

"I'm at my wits' end. Dear Sidney-san, won't you please help us," she implored.

The following evening, dressed in a civilian suit and tie, Mashbir entered the Imperial quarters. Nagako, her face pale and wringing her hands, whispered, "He wishes to speak to you privately; he hasn't eaten all day."

Mashbir entered the adjacent room.

A hoarse voice emanated from a dark alcove, "Hello, Colonel, so kind of you to visit." Only his shadow was visible.

"Nice to be with you again, Your Majesty. I hope all is well?"

There was nervous laughter.

"You've spoken to Nagako and know the answer. What difference does it make anyway? Japan is desolate, the smell of death everywhere!"

"I understand your feelings, Your Majesty, but your wife and your children—As well as millions of your subjects are still alive, awaiting your guidance."

With sudden anger, Hirohito replied, "I have strong doubts that I am capable to direct anyone!"

Sidney moved through the darkness to come face-to-face.

"I'll make you a promise, Your Majesty: If you give your cooperation to the Allies, respect will be given to you and your nation. No other living person can do the good that you can at this time."

Hirohito listened.

"Once in a dream, your Uncle Tokugawa came to me and foretold how *you and I* would work together to rebuild your nation—That time has come."

There was a long silence. "So your General MacArthur is a man of honor?"

"Yes, Your Majesty. He realizes Japan and America, as well as the rest of the world, have suffered enough! Now is the time to bury hatred and move toward a brighter future."

The frail Emperor, in black robes, rose slowly and proceeded out of the room, followed by Sidney. Nagako welled up with tears at the sight of them, and began ordering servants to bring food, as they all sat around a small table . . . Hirohito held Nagako's hand, and with his other he grasped Sidney's. Looking at one another, their strained faces turning into smiles.

※※※※

Inside the U.S. Ambassador's Residence, Mashbir was finishing up his briefing with MacArthur.

"Sir, I'm sure you're doing the right thing not taking a hard line with the Emperor."

"You believe he'll fully cooperate?"

Mashbir nodded confidently. "In spite of his status as a god to his people, his willingness to come to you—*versus* you coming to him, is a true sign he wishes to work with us."

MacArthur gritted his teeth. "So remember, Sidney, if you catch me losing my temper, please step in and cool things down. I want this meeting to go well."

A maroon-colored pre-war Imperial limousine with scratches and assorted dents, pulled onto the grounds of the consulate. The Emperor emerged—and was met by an escort of Marines.

Moments later, in total privacy, three men stood in silent anticipation.

I'll break the ice, Sidney thought. "General MacArthur is honored by your visit, Your Majesty."

"And I am likewise honored to meet with him."

They shook hands, bowed low to each other, and then seated themselves.

Sidney continued, "The General, and I, who am acting as both his liaison and translator, are here today not to place blame but to move forward toward the restoration of Japan as a democratic society. Have you anything you wish to express, Your Majesty?"

Hirohito placed his hand on his heart.

"I am ready to accept total blame for the actions of my nation and will resign from all authority if you wish."

The General gave him a hard stare…"That's not what we desire. We feel you're the *only one* who can inspire your people during the rebuilding of Japan."

The Emperor nodded solemnly.

"The General wishes you to speak freely," Sidney explained. "Nothing said here will ever see the light of day, as long as we live. Do you understand?"

Before he could reply, MacArthur added, "There may be times,

Your Majesty, when what we ask you to do will go against your traditional role as Emperor."

Hirohito displayed a half-smile.

"You mean to say that I shall no longer be seen as a deity by my people?"

"That's part of it."

"I've already come to that decision on my own, General, because I believe it is the best course."

"Japan is fortunate to have such a wise leader," MacArthur replied. "Colonel Mashbir and I believe a series of a dozen or so private meetings between the three of us are needed to iron out the details for the reconstruction of your nation."

※※※※

The Imperial Palace was but a shadow of its former opulence, having been heavily bombed. *It's hard to imagine*, Sidney thought, *this was one of the great wonders of the world.*

"Are you ready, Your Majesty?" Sidney asked.

"Yes, although a bit nervous," Hirohito replied. "How do you like my attire?"

"Your suit, striped trousers, and fedora hat make you look like one of the people."

Hirohito smiled.

Mashbir hesitated. "Your Majesty, while we travel together, I hope you won't mind if I take the occasional photograph?"

"Feel free to do so, Sidney. If I'm going to be a public figure, it's something I'll need to get used to."

Their chauffeured limousine drove through the palace's black iron-barred *Sakashita gate* and across the granite stone bridge, passing over the moat where graceful swans once floated . . . Escorted by U.S. and Japanese security vehicles, they entered shattered Tokyo, where mile after mile of crumbled and burnt-out buildings surrounded them.

Their silent journey took them into the countryside, arriving at a farm cooperative.

"I'm not sure I'm ready for this," Hirohito said.

"Just look how excited your subjects are to see you." Mashbir pointed at the large gathering. "Isn't there a sense of freedom at being able to intimately see your people?"

Hirohito smiled. "Your words rekindle pleasant memories of Uncle Tokugawa urging me to visit England twenty-five years ago, where joyous crowds greeted me."

"Well, then, this is an encore!" And with a flowing gesture of his hand, he quipped: "Your public awaits, Your Majesty!"

From a distance, camera in hand, trying not to get in the way of the photojournalists, Sidney followed the Emperor.

As Hirohito approached the workers, most remained bowed or prostrated. After a couple of throat-clearing coughs, he announced, "Please rise, and straighten yourselves. I appreciate your respect, but henceforth, you need not fear looking directly upon your Emperor."

With arms outstretched, he added, "I wish to come closer to my people, sharing in your times of joy, and of sorrow…Dear farm laborers, I thank you for your hard work, feeding our country. Come, line up—Let me shake your hands."

The workers had cleaned up for the occasion, but one, upon examining his callused hands with their ground-in dirt, frantically tried to wipe them clean on his pants.

"Don't worry," Hirohito said, smiling as he extended his own hand. "After all we've been through, a little dirt won't hurt me," which brought laughter from the crowd.

※※※※

The following week, Hirohito stood at the front of an elementary school play yard filled with animated kindergarten, first, and second-grade students, giggling and bobbing about, barely able to contain their excitement; with their teachers overseeing them from the sidelines…"Precious students, as your Emperor, it is my honor to speak to you today. But before I give my presentation, your teachers have told me it is time for your calisthenics exercises, and suggested I lead you in that activity!"

He playfully guided the youngsters in stretching and reaching to the sky numerous times.

"Now pretend you are trees blowing in the wind," he called out. "And teachers, you're welcome to join in the fun."

And they did, everyone twisting and swinging their bodies and arms to either side.

A junior high school was their next stop, with students ranging from twelve to fourteen years of age. Sidney noted the boys had their hair shaved quite short and wore identical school uniforms: black woolen jackets adorned with shiny brass buttons. The girls wore navy-blue blouses with white bands circling their collars, giving them a nautical look; their hair had a straight level cut across their foreheads, with bangs on the sides.

One young girl appeared frightened, as the Emperor neared her and her classmates. Hirohito spoke gently to her, as if no one else in the world existed.

"What is your name?"

"Miyako," she answered timidly.

"What courses are you taking?"

"Math, Science, Geography, Reading, and Writing." She hesitated. "Are you really? ... The Emperor?"

"Yes."

"Why, then, would you visit us?"

"Young people are the future of Japan. I wish to know your feelings and hear your words of advice, so I and your other leaders can better serve you."

The twelve-year-old looked upward in thought, then asked, "I do not understand, why has there been so much sadness and death during much of my life?"

I can barely answer that for myself, the Emperor thought, as he stared at her sweet innocence.

"You show wisdom in asking such a question, Miyako."

He sighed.

"Life can sometimes be very hard, but you will be all the stronger from having endured it, and will be able to help and lead others as you grow older."

He bowed, then smiled.

"It has been a pleasure meeting you."

Sidney stood in wonder at the intimacy, as the Emperor moved up the line, showing warmth and understanding, giving the students time to introduce themselves and their interests.

"This will be an afternoon long remembered by those children," Sidney commented as they drove away.

✳✳✳✳

On their next trip, the Emperor brought along some of his own children, giving Mashbir an opportunity to see this loving family. Their vehicle came to a stop on a lush countryside road. "We've arrived my *Dear children*, thank you for coming with me on this special visit." Then, turning to Sidney, he added, "And I very much appreciate your companionship as well."

"I'm privileged to be included, Your Majesty."

"It's so beautiful," Suganomiya said, looking at the gently winding, tree-lined trail.

"And the morning mist makes the air so refreshing," Hisanomiya added.

The Emperor, took a deep breath. "Let us begin our pilgrimage." With solemn expressions, the family walked the earthen path.

Sidney, along with an entourage of officials, security police, and guards, followed respectfully behind, heads tipped downward to show humility.

As they neared the large Shinto shrine, Hirohito gestured to Mashbir that he might accompany them as they walked through the tall, black and orange, wood-beamed *torii gates* and onto the sacred pastoral grounds.

At the building's entrance, they stopped at a gray stone fountain.

"This is a Purification Ritual, Sidney," Hirohito explained. "You're welcome to observe or participate as you wish. It is a tradition going back twenty-five hundred years."

Both men ladled water to wash their hands, then poured water into their mouths and rinsed, after which, as was customary, they spit it out onto the grass. Next, they took off their footwear, placing it on a shelf in the entrance area and proceeded to the shrine's offering hall.

His subjects watched as the Emperor and his children put paper currency and coins into a donation box. Sidney looked to Hirohito for approval, as he also brought forth a donation.

"Now, we will take a moment for silent meditation..."

Hirohito placed incense upon a bronze holding stand and lit it. After watching it burn a short while, he began waving a hand quickly over it to put out the flame, then fanned the rising smoke toward himself and his children, motioning to Sidney to do the same.

"This encourages the healing of the body and the mind," he explained.

From there, they entered a spacious, wood-paneled main hall, where Hirohito signaled Sidney move to the sidelines with the many other onlookers.

The Emperor, with his children, went to the front, where a circular brass gong stood. Hirohito gestured toward the attending Shinto priest, who, using a wooden striking rod, firmly hit the gong, which emitted a deep, resonant sound.

He viewed his subjects as they stood in awe at seeing their ruler. Once the gong's strong vibration had run its course, he bowed to the assemblage.

"When you wish to pray," he said, "you're welcome to do so in this holy shrine." His voice rose. "But, no longer to see me as anything more than your leader—a man of flesh and blood, a husband, and a father!"

He pulled his children close to him.

"Instead of *me* being seen as the God, *let us all pray for Divine guidance from above* ... My sincerest hope is that my actions and words will be pure, and that Japan can once again become a great nation!"

Many in the crowd were moved to tears.

✳✳✳✳

The following month, sparks flew and steam fumed as molten metal gushed through furnaces…The Emperor in military uniform adorned with medals, wore a safety helmet and face-shield as he and his entourage mingled among the metalworkers.

"Your Majesty, we're already producing a hundred tons of steel daily," the factory tour guide proudly stated.

Nearby, one of the workers said to his companion, "I always respected our Emperor, but to see him visiting our workplace makes me hope he will always continue as the father of our nation."

Sidney noted these words' effect on Hirohito.

When the tour was over, they re-entered their vehicles for their next appointment.

"You didn't comment on my military uniform, Sidney."

"You must have your reasons. However, your prior wearing of civilian clothing showed your great humility and your connection to the general populace."

Hirohito nodded. "And Now I wish to show respect to my war veterans for their sacrifices…I was urged I wear a uniform to give the message that Japan is still a mighty nation with self-confidence."

"You show great wisdom, Your Majesty—Especially, if it calms the situation during this difficult transition, so be it."

Soon the Emperor was surrounded by a large audience of ranking military officers anxious to greet him. They lined up in formation in the expansive courtyard, as Hirohito strode among their ranks doing an inspection, with an occasional greeting to a familiar face.

Once done, he went to the front and spoke:

"I truly wish this war had never happened, but I very much respect your bravery and the many sacrifices you have made during it. You've honestly and courageously given your best for your country…" The Emperor thought to himself, *but this was a not a war fought for me, but for others who used my name falsely! To prevent such misuse of power in the future, I will become more familiar with the current events of our nation, and will lead through firsthand involvement.*

As the evening's reddish-orange sun neared the horizon, Sidney and the Emperor were chauffeured back to the palace. "You're a natural-born politician," Sidney declared, speaking in Japanese.

"You flatter me. Truly, I've tended to be shy and reserved, but in spite of that, I hope my message is understood."

"It's being heard *loud and clear, Your Majesty.*"

Hirohito searched Mashbir's eyes, *He is so comfortable with our culture, I have to remind myself he is not one of my own subjects✻✻.* "Thank you so much for your support, Sidney-san."

After a light meal followed by plum wine, the Emperor asked, "Do you have any more suggestions where we might go next, Colonel?"

"You look exhausted, Your Majesty. Let's talk next week and plan something special," he replied.

As Mashbir left, he thought, *the Emperor has been pushing himself two hundred percent for the sake of his people…*He further reflected on this unique time in history, accompanying the Emperor during the past two months—*Here I am, a mere commoner from the West. It's hard to imagine that in the not-too-distant past, his subjects could have been harshly punished for the impudence of even looking directly upon this once-sacred king!*

CHAPTER 55

"General, we're in for a hell of a lot of trouble," Mashbir announced as he entered MacArthur's office.

"What are you talking about? Things have been going well with the Emperor's appearances, haven't they?"

"You're right, and that's why the Commies are teaming up with militant factions, taking advantage of Japan's new, more liberal, rights of freedom of speech. They'd love to wreck the economy, making us look incompetent; then throw out the Emperor and the newly elected Diet, replacing it with a Maoist dictatorship!

"We didn't see this coming, sir. A lot of Japanese ex-prisoners of war who had been detained in China, are now returning home—problem is, many have indoctrinated to act as Communist provocateurs, staging demonstrations to shut down the newly-opened manufacturing plants. They describe themselves as *Workers United to Overthrow Imperialism* and post signs slanderous against the Emperor."

"How widespread is this?"

"Currently limited to worker strikes, but I've heard they plan to instigate massive student protests as well. Our troops, accompanied by Japanese police, are standing by doing nothing, uncertain how to tackle the situation without inciting it further."

MacArthur lit and inhaled on his pipe, aromatic smoke filling the air. "So how do you suggest we keep Communism out of Japan, Sidney, without being seen as dictators ourselves?"

"The way I see it, during major transitions you need more latitude. It's a slippery slope, but we can't stand by and do nothing, though, it would be preferable if we aren't seen as initiating the solution ourselves." He quietly considered... "General, really only a few of these POWs are hard-core agitators; the vast majority were forcefully indoctrinated. We must however recognize that some of what the communists are saying has truth to it. In the past, Japanese laborers were often oppressed: most had no opportunity to vote, worked for ridiculously low wages, and were subject to harassment. For those reasons, back in the 1920s, I promoted modern methods in agriculture and business in Japan—and I strongly believe that that approach is what is needed now more than ever. The fact that most of their heavy industry has been destroyed could be a unique opportunity, because when they rebuild, they can utilize the latest technology.

"And, if these *new* industrialists treat their workers right, Japan could again become an economic powerhouse."

"But what about the current instability?" MacArthur asked.

"We've got to move forward on those development meetings for a new Constitution with the Japanese—*ASAP*...Once they have a few years of Democracy under their belt, the communists can shout all the slogans they want, and people won't give them the time of day."

"It's strange," MacArthur replied. "We prevent the Japanese from taking other nations' territories, and now these communist countries become the aggressors, pushing their doctrines upon a downtrodden Japan."

✳✳✳✳

Japanese Diet

Warm lights reflected upon Hirohito, as he stood on a raised platform, behind a dark, ornately carved wooden table. He began, "It is my honor to address you, my esteemed congressional members. There is a dire need for a new constitution, similar to the more liberal Democracies of the West, yet fashioned to meet the unique cultural requirements of our nation."

As his presentation continued, Mashbir, seated in the back row, watched the Emperor struggling to contain his temper as he was repeatedly disrupted. It was obvious, that though they'd lost the war, many Diet members did not wish to abandon or modernize their current institutions.

A member called out, "Why choose Democracy? The masses are not to be trusted."

While several socialists and communists claimed they best protected the rights of workers.

"Perhaps a coalition government is the answer," Hirohito suggested, to which a Diet member replied, "Coalition governments are constantly maneuvering to satisfy everyone, accomplishing nothing."

The large assembly room broke into many private debates.

"Distinguished representatives," Hirohito said, raising a hand. "Silence, please. I've heard your opinions and I need time to deliberate. This session is over!" As he walked off the stage, he shot a discouraged glance toward Sidney.

On his visit that evening, Mashbir smiled, seeing the Emperor and Prince Akihito seated side by side on a couch, reading in the Imperial Library.

"So good of you to respond to my invitation," Hirohito said. "I hope you don't mind if my son remains?"

"I welcome his company."

"Thank you," Akihito said. "I won't disturb your conversation."

Hirohito opened a cabinet. "Here, Sidney-san, I have a gift Prince Tokugawa once asked me to give to you. It was taken during your visit back in 1937, during a Tokyo Pan Pacific Club luncheon, hosted by the Prince."

"Yes, I remember…" Mashbir's heart warmed upon seeing his departed friend in the center of a group photograph, with himself seated adjacent to the Prince. "I will always treasure it."

"Colonel, I'm aware my uncle often conferred with you on political matters."

"It was my honor to do so. He possessed great wisdom, strength, and kindness."

"Well," Hirohito smiled, "I, too, now need your advice," he said emphatically. "My son and I have been studying your Democracy *and* economic system, based on the philosophies of Locke and Rousseau, who challenged prior social, religious, and political doctrines. They went so far as to assert that a government's very legitimacy was *de-*

pendent on the consent of those governed!" Hirohito paused. "This was quite different from the long standing monarchies based on Divine lineage.

"And your citizens are given *inalienable* rights, to Life, to certain freedoms, to the ownership of property, and to gain economically from the fruits of their labors."

"That about covers it, Your Majesty. In principle, our government is responsible for passing just laws, which the people obey for the common good," Sidney replied.

"But," Hirohito waved a pointer finger for emphasis, "if a government becomes *criminal* in its behavior," his voice rising, "its citizens have the right—even the obligation, to institute new leadership!"

Sidney bemusedly replied, "This sounds like a class in Civics, but no one but a fool thinks any system is perfect, though Democracy and Capitalism are most satisfactory to me.

"And to preserve these rights, and as a method of checks and balances," Mashbir continued, "our Constitution divides power between Executive, Legislative, and Judicial branches, and, our policy of *Separation of Church and State* prevents the majority religion from forcing its beliefs down the throats of others.

"*And we're not naive*, we outlaw groups whose goal is the destruction of our country! And if our leaders screw up, the next election is likely to throw them out!

"*As its highest goal*, Democracy is respectful of the diversity of races, cultures, and religions, rather than using them as an excuse for discord."

Hirohito reflected. "Japan does not have a long tradition of personal freedoms: It *needs* a new Constitution to better protect my subjects." He nervously laughed. "However, there is much opposition to change." He stared at his guest. "Sidney-san, can you please assist me in this project?"

"I very much support your aspirations, Your Majesty, but it won't be long before I return to the States. My family hasn't seen me for years. What I can promise you is, that until I leave, I'll do all I can."

In a depressed voice, Hirohito said, "You saw what happened at our Congress, today. Things could not have gone worse."

"You had a tough crowd to please," Sidney replied with mirth.

"If I'm to be compared to an entertainer, how might you suggest I improve my performance?"

Mashbir looked at the photo he'd been gifted.

"Your Majesty, Prince Tokugawa once told me a story concerning his father, Yoshinobu, the last powerful Shogun, who worked with Commodore Perry to create a trade treaty opening Japan to the outside world. Did he share that tale with you as well?"

"Yes, I remember it."

"Do you recall how Yoshinobu won over his political opposition?"

The Emperor stroked his chin.

"Hmm, yes. He *claimed* Perry along with his mighty ships' cannons pressured him to accept the terms, *even though, Yoshinobu himself wanted to sign the treaty for the good of our country.*"

Mashbir remained silent.

"How clever," Hirohito remarked. "But creating a constitution is a lengthy process that could be stalled forever in uncooperative committee meetings."

With a sparkle in his eye, Mashbir replied, "That's why I suggest it be done secretly—Our American Constitution was mainly created behind closed doors and only *then* offered up to scrutiny."

"Ahhhh." Hirohito smiled. "So when it's finished, I could say I was pressured to accept it so as to move forward more expediently in the rebuilding of our country."

"Exactly—you might also mention that representatives of the Diet would have ample opportunity to give suggestions for its improvement, prior to final ratification."

Hirohito sighed with relief.

"My friend, I wonder if you realize how important your support has been during these trying times, as I strive to bring back a sense of dignity to my people."

"You're a fine leader, and your generous words mean a great deal to me."

Hirohito turned to his son.

"And what do you think of this plan, Akihito?"

With a knowing expression, he replied, "Father, it looks like History is repeating itself."

Tokyo, late December 1945

It was early evening as passengers disembarked the U.S. Army Air transport. Among them was an attractive twenty-two-year-old, with curly black hair framing her fair complexion. She, and her eighteen male fellow passengers, climbed into a civilian bus that was commandeered for Army use.

A young officer stood up front, smiling as they entered.

"I'm Lieutenant Gordon," he said, gallantly doffing his hat to the lady. "What's your name?"

"Beate."

"Nice meeting you."

Once the passengers had taken their seats, the lieutenant announced, "Welcome to Tokyo, the future home of fancy restaurants and luxurious hotels—But that's ten years down the road. In the meantime, you'll be assigned housing and eat at U.S. Army Headquarters. Please hold your questions until tomorrow's briefing, because I don't know why you're here."

The following day, Beate and her male colleagues assembled in a conference room, sipping coffee and tea as General MacArthur began his address. "Good morning, *gentlemen,* and our *one lady*; you're probably wondering why you're here. This mystery will be answered by Colonel Mashbir," who stepped up to the podium.

"The war has been won," Mashbir said, "but to win the peace, we urgently need to instill in the Japanese a sense of social and political fairness.

"We hope to avoid repeating prior mistakes, such as our lack involvement in the rebuilding of Europe after World War One, where the seeds of our recent war were first planted."

He scanned the audience.

"Today, we have a unique opportunity to design a democratic foundation for Japan, similar, to that of America in 1787.

"Using your diverse backgrounds, we're going to draft a Constitution for their consideration. I now welcome your questions."

A gentleman stood.

"I'm a retired professor of Political Science. The Japanese culture is so different from ours. How can we craft a constitution that truly recognizes that, yet embodies Western democratic principles?"

Mashbir nodded. "That will be a challenge," he replied, "but my staff and I will provide guidance based on our familiarity with their culture. It won't be easy, but it can be done."

Another raised his hand. "My name's Brad Williamson—PhD, Psychology. To what extent are we going to work with the Japanese on this?"

Mashbir smiled, remembering the recent strident debate at the Diet.

"Frankly, after much consideration, it has been decided by certain high-ranking Japanese officials that it would be best to bring this project as close to completion as possible, and only then, present it to the Japanese people—the process of negotiation and compromise would at that point begin—our main concern is, if this document is given too much outside scrutiny early on, it might never get done."

The only woman in the room raised her hand.

"My name is Beate Sirota. I'm a journalist." She hesitated. "I can't resist asking, what happens if after all of our best efforts, the Japanese outright reject this Constitution?"

Mashbir, in an upbeat voice replied, *"My hope is,* that by utilizing this group's impressive talents in Political Science, International Studies, Psychology, and Law, we will make it so good, they *won't* reject it! And remember, Japan has been a Fascist regime for many years without any representative government. We need to fill this void as quickly as possible.

"You'll be split into groups of three, each tackling a different constitutional section." He smiled. "Now let's break for lunch, and reassemble at 1300 hours: that's one o'clock."

As the room emptied, Mashbir spoke to Miss Sirota.

"You probably don't remember me, Beate. You were a teenager when I met you and your father before the war. You accompanied him when he performed classical music for the royal family. Even then, you spoke perfect Japanese."

"Of course, now I recall!"

She shook his hand.

"I'm still at a loss, Colonel, as to why I was chosen, what with all these distinguished professors."

"I reviewed your résumé and remembered your language skills."

Looking at her inquisitively, he asked, "In your past positions at radio stations and newspaper services, how did you become knowledgeable on the news topics you were involved in writing about?"

"Research and more research," Beate replied, rolling her eyes upward.

"Well then, how would you handle this project?"

Beate considered.

"I'd obtain copies of democratic constitutions from as many countries as I could lay my hands on, and then incorporate some of their best elements into our creation."

"Now you're talking! So which section would you like to tackle?"

She smiled. "While growing up in Japan, I appreciated much of the culture, the music and dance, their reverence for nature."

Her voice tightened. "There were, however, parts I didn't like. Not to say America hasn't any flaws—But in Japan, women have almost no rights or academic freedom to select their careers. They subserviently walk behind their husbands, can't get divorced or own property, and have *no say* in the choosing of their country's leaders."

Beate smiled.

"What I'd really love to work on is Women's Rights. It might sound strange, but I believe greater gender equality will advance peace and stability for Japan, and perhaps the world."

"Really, in what way?"

She straightened her posture.

"With equal rights and the ability to vote, women could better confront abusive militaristic regimes—You see, based on our innate maternal instincts, we usually don't want wars."

She stepped back.

"Excuse me, Colonel Mashbir, I hope I'm not speaking out of turn?"

"Quite the contrary, Beate; I appreciate your enthusiasm. A woman's viewpoint on Women's Rights is just what we need."

✳✳✳✳

Two months later, a cavalcade of police and military vehicles accompanied the Imperial Limousine as it drove into the center of the massive sports stadium, where tens of thousands of spectators rose from their seats.

"The day has finally come," Hirohito said, turning to Sidney. "I hope I'm up to the task."

"You're more than ready! And see how thrilled they are to see you, Your Majesty!"

Hirohito ascended onto a stage platform decorated with flags and banners, where two standing microphones waited. Mashbir inconspicuously located himself to the side of the stage, his camera ready.

After taking several long, sweeping gazes at the attentive multitudes, and drawing in a deep breath, Hirohito began:

"As your Emperor, I am here to tell you many things. First, I wish to apologize to you, my people, and to the outside world, for the destruction wrought by this past terrible war. I hold myself in a large part responsible for allowing a group of militarists to take over our nation in pursuit of an empire built on cruel domination."

He held out his arms beseechingly. "I challenge current and future world leaders to reject that course of action! Instead, when difficult domestic issues arise, we must avoid blaming others, and instead find ways to resolve them through our own internal solutions and peaceful international alliances.

"It has been a hard lesson."

He paused, straining to contain his emotions.

"I want our children to grow up in a world liberated from the stupidity of war, in a stable country that is based on Freedom and Democracy."

His voice heightened as he concluded:

"With the support of all of you, we will once again become a successful nation, an example of compassion and coexistence with our Asian neighbors and the Western world!"

The audience came to their feet with a thunderous ovation . . . When it finally ended, the Emperor introduced the various ministers in his cabinet, who described the new domestic policies that would be enacted over the coming years to rebuild the nation.

As Hirohito was driven away at the conclusion of the event, he turned to his companion.

"So how did I do, Sidney? Was the applause simply given due to my title?"

"Not at all, you truly earned it."

There was silence, as Sidney's mind drifted to an observation made many years earlier, describing the promising potential of a young Crown Prince . . .

"Your Uncle Tokugawa would be very proud if he were here to see you today."

Hirohito smiled.

"He would be proud of both of us."

POSTSCRIPT

One year later, Washington, D.C., 1947

Noting that the envelope from Japan was sent by Beate Sirota brought a smile. Sidney opened it and withdrew its contents, settled into an armchair in his living room and began to read:

> *Dear Colonel Sidney Mashbir:*
> *I hope you and your family are well!*
> *We so much appreciate all the support you gave us during our early efforts. As you recommended, we kept the project under wraps, but to our surprise, the Emperor and Empress visited us and graciously thanked us for our involvement, with Empress Nagako encouraging me to push hard for Women's Rights!*
> *The Emperor described how much his family had enjoyed my father's piano performances and even remembered how I, as a teenager, along with my classmates, once gave a dance recital at the palace! We both joked that artists, dancers, and musicians may well be the best emissaries of peace and understanding. When I return to the States, I hope to get involved in the exchange of the Performing Arts between the U.S. and other nations.*
> *As for the Japanese Constitution, when the Diet representatives reviewed our final draft, they took offense when it appeared that I, as a woman, was one of the framers of the document. General MacArthur deftly pretended I was mainly a translator. He privately apologized later, explaining that for*

the greater good, I should play along. He turned out to be one hundred percent right.

The elder Japanese statesmen soon became my friends, treating me respectfully. The great irony came when almost every article of the Constitution was modified to varying degrees, but when it came to Women's Rights, MacArthur explained to the Japanese representatives, "Don't worry—you will retain much influence. Certainly your wives and daughters will ask your advice before making significant decisions. Please, as a gift to our young translator, Beate, let us leave this article unchanged."

To my astonishment, they agreed in a most chivalrous way.

The Japanese delegates and our team are very proud of the final results. Just today, the Diet and the Emperor approved it!

Women now have the vote, hooray! Some of my colleagues have playfully called me "The Mother of Women's Rights in Japan."

Enclosed is a copy of the constitution for your review.

Sidney read the Preamble:

We, the Japanese people, acting through our elected representatives in the National Diet, shall secure for ourselves and our posterity the fruits of peaceful cooperation with all nations, and the blessings of liberty all over this land. Never again shall we be visited with the horrors of war through the action of government. And we do proclaim that sovereign power resides with the people and do firmly establish this Constitution.

Government is a sacred trust of the people, the authority for which is derived from the people, the powers of which are exercised by the representatives of the people, and the benefits of which are enjoyed by the people. This is a universal principle of mankind upon which this Constitution is founded...

We desire to occupy an honored place in an international society, striving for the preservation of peace, and the banishment of tyranny, slavery, oppression and intolerance for all time from the earth. We recognize that all peoples of the world have the right to live in peace, and free from fear and want. We believe that no nation is responsible to itself alone, but that the laws of political morality are universal; and that obedience to such laws is incumbent upon all nations.

Sidney considered what he had read, then examined the thirty articles composing the balance of the Constitution. Once done, he again picked up Beate's letter:

God bless you and your family, Colonel! The General sends warm regards and says he misses having you on his staff.
                                        Sincerely,
                                        Beate Sirota

P.S. I, and the now "Captain" Gordon who greeted me when I first arrived in Japan a year ago, are engaged. A photo is enclosed. Wish you could be here for our wedding, but we'll include you in our celebration toasts!

Sidney heard footsteps.

"Hi, my love, how are things going?" Irene asked.

"Fine, darling. You remember that gutsy young lady I told you about, Beate Sirota, who was part of the team assisting the Japanese in creating their constitution?"

She nodded.

"Well, they've created a noble document."

"I see..." Irene smiled. "And it appears she's also getting married," she said, admiring the photo of the future bride next to her handsome Captain.

"Don't they just look like kids," she said sweetly. "That was us twenty-plus years ago."

He came close.

"What do you mean? We're still young," he said, and nibbled her ear.

"Why Sidney," she purred, melting into his arms.

Washington, D.C., 1948

A tall, lanky man with his chin down and collar turned up, made his way to the rear of the café and slid into the booth opposite Sidney.

"Hello, Charles, good to see you again!"

"Likewise, Colonel Mashbir," Lindbergh replied. "Thanks for coming. I'm trying to avoid reporters, hence this silly cloak-and-dagger routine. I know it's been years—but I was in town, and I haven't forgotten your help out there in the Pacific. Those two years of flying with a purpose made all the difference to me."

"Ah, heck, I just passed your message along to the Top Brass. Your reputation did the rest."

"You're modest. You were one of the key guys for MacArthur."

Mashbir shrugged.

"Congratulations on your latest book, Charles! I'm glad to see your war record is now in print. Fifty combat missions! You even taught a bunch of P-38 Lightning pilots some fancy flying techniques."

"Thanks, it's what I do best."

"So Charles, with your permission, I'm burning to ask you—Are you here in D.C. as part of the effort to establish a Department of the Air Force that I hear Congress is now considering? Something we talked about years ago."

"No, but my sources tell me it's a done deal, and it's about time. Actually, I'm now concerned with two even bigger issues—but I won't bore you."

"Try me."

Lindbergh heaved a deep sigh.

"You know, you get a different view of the Earth when you're flying. More and more it struck me, this planet of ours is a pretty small place, and getting smaller all the time. I saw factories and mines springing up all over, thoughtlessly spewing filthy smoke into the air and fouling pristine rivers and streams....It both saddened and frightened me, so I've decided to do something about it, using my reputation to raise awareness."

"A very good cause, though it's probably an uphill battle. Most people, having scraped through the Depression and survived the war, just want to enjoy the good things that technology brings, without thinking too much about the negative effects. But hopefully, one day, we'll find a way to minimize our impact and achieve a sense of balance. You mentioned two issues?"

"Oh yes, it's about those more isolated, simpler cultures I've seen around the world. The ease of travel is pushing the Twentieth Century on them, whether they want it or not." With a wave of his hand he added, "You probably think I'm nuts, but we need to deal with these issues, before it's too late!"

He looked at his watch.

"Glad I got a chance to thank you again for all you did, Sidney, but I've got to run."

After Lindbergh left, Mashbir shook his head.

I don't think I'll ever fully understand that guy. Blind in some ways, an idealistic visionary in others!

✳✳✳✳

Washington, D.C., December 1949

Cold morning mist blanketed the ground as Mashbir raised an American flag. That evening it would be lowered, a cycle repeated daily—rain or shine, whether sick or healthy—for the past few years.

He saluted the Flag, then re-entered his quiet home.

It's good Donald's has already left for school and Irene is busy with errands, Sidney reflected, *I prefer to be by myself right now.* He rattled his head, *I sure hope today's Congressional hearings are worth all the effort✳*

With time on his hands, he reread a letter from the British Consulate he'd recently received:

Dear Sidney,

I hope this communication finds you in good spirits. I'd long been meaning to get in touch with you, and here it is all of ten years since last we met.

Some documents came across my desk that I felt you'd be interested in, so I tracked you down.

You remember that courageous German, Elser, who we recruited to make a play on Hitler's life? It appears he spent most of the war years in isolation at a concentration camp. As the Allies were closing in, the Nazis ordered him executed, rather than let him survive to be a hero.

There's some light, however; recently, a concert hall in Munich has been renamed the Georg Elser Halle, where his spirit and his love of music will live on.

The memorial plaque is inscribed with his words:

I wanted through my deed to prevent even greater bloodshed.

The plaque also states:

In Remembrance of Johann Georg Elser, who on the 8th of November 1939, attempted to thwart genocide with his assassination attempt on Hitler.

Well, enough serious talk, my friend. If your future travels take you to Europe, I've enclosed my contact information. It would be a pleasure to give you a tour of the rebuilt sights of London.

Warm regards,
David

This letter guided Sidney's thoughts to the recent United Nations ratification for the recognition of the State of Israel, a memorial to six-million murdered Jews. He recalled that when Eisenhower and Patton liberated those remaining concentration camp survivors *with their death numbers tattooed on their emaciated arms,* the Generals wanted to set a precedent:

"Get it all on record, photographed, and get testimonies from witnesses," they ordered. "Because somewhere down the road of History, some bastard will get up and say this never happened!"

A ringing phone grabbed his attention.

Mashbir's somber expression turned into a smile as he heard, *"Moshi, moshi."*

"Zach, I really appreciate all your support. Think we have a chance this time?"

"It's worth a try!"

Soon, Sidney was parking in front of a colonial-style home in Georgetown. Zach was in his front yard, already lifting himself with difficulty out of a patio chair. Cane in hand, he made his way down the walkway.

He got out of the car to help his friend into the passenger seat. "Looks like you're doing better," he said, as they drove off. "I knew that heart attack wouldn't keep you down for too long. So what have you been up to?"

"Recuperation takes time, but I've kept busy: I may just have another manuscript in me…"

Sidney smiled. "Your *'Secret Missions,'* didn't do too badly—for a *first book*," he joked. "Not only a good read, it ended up making you a radio celebrity!"

"Thanks." Zach looked at him. "Why don't *you* write a book titled: *Colonel Mashbir—Soldier, Statesman, and Spy.* You've lots of secrets and adventures up your sleeve."

"That's not going to happen. After decades of only doing technical writing, my literary style isn't flowery enough. Though, I did get a good review from a friend of mine, who said that General MacArthur told him, and I quote, *'I am Mashbir's most avid reader. In fact, I imagine I have read every word of every report and manual he has ever written!'*"

"You may be better than you think: He's one tough critic."

Sidney shrugged.

"But I'd leave *Statesman* out of the title. I've pissed off too many people for that."

Both men laughed.

"So, Sid, how's the family?"

"Doing fine. And your sons?"

"Very proud of them…And your job, I hope it's going well?"

"To tell the truth, Zach, this damn new Administration treats me like a dinosaur, pressuring me out of my advisory position." He shook his head in annoyance. "Republicans and Democrats play musical chairs, reorganizing security agencies as if the outside world were suddenly so different because a donkey or an elephant runs the country. It's a waste of taxpayer dollars."

"You know you're closing in on sixty; what are you going to do with your retirement? Get a rocking chair?" Zach grinned.

"No way! Probably do some private consulting. And I'm active in Rotary, improving living conditions on Indian reservations* We're also bringing Polio vaccinations to poor countries."

"That's the spirit!"

U.S. Senate Hearing Room, that afternoon

A tall, dignified man stood and faced the committee of six men and one woman.

"Honorable members of Congress, my name is Jessie Powell; I'm a veteran of fifty years of federal service, thirty of those as a civilian advisor to a number of adjutant generals. I'm here today to represent Colonel Mashbir."

He glanced toward his client, seated in the front row, facing the panel.

"Accompanying my client, are several other high-ranking military officers who will give testimonials as to Colonel Mashbir's almost half-century of fine service to our country."

His voice rose. "Our objectives are to have all of Colonel Mashbir's previous military service credited, so he can be reappointed to the *Regular Army*. *Secondly*, we wish to clear his military record of inappropriate and inaccurate remarks. Once these things are done, we request his deserved promotion to the rank of Brigadier General be given."

Major General Witsell stepped forward, introduced himself, then read from a prepared statement:

"Distinguished congressional members, I'm about to give you a short summary of the accomplishments of Colonel Mashbir; his being an Intelligence agent, most of this material is classified...

"I personally swear and will give indisputable evidence which proves Colonel Mashbir intended to resign only temporarily from the Regular Army while in Tokyo in 1923, at the suggestion of the military attaché—He did so in order to set up *at his own expense,* an Espionage system to supply information in time of war—because no government funds were available.

"However, he was denied reinstatement due to an administrative ruling unknown to him and unpublished to the Army at large...When the need to serve his country again arose in 1926 through 1927, Mashbir was granted a temporary return to active duty, which he accepted, to revise *Plan Orange*—which became the U.S. Battle Plan in the Pacific during World War II." he paused.

"I've personally and professionally known Colonel Mashbir for twenty-nine years. In spite of technicalities closing the door to his re-entry into the Army, instead of bitterly walking away, he went into the private sector to display an almost epic, unswerving devotion, guiding American industrial companies to undertake research to meet the military needs of a country moving toward war—And when those companies' facilities were not sufficiently advanced, he used his own private electronic laboratories and factories to accomplish highly important secret projects, leading to twenty-five major scientific developments that were utilized during World War II, resulting in an incalculable saving of human lives and millions of taxpayer dollars!"

Witsell took a sip of water.

"Interspersed during this period, Mashbir carried out secret missions for Naval Intelligence at a considerable risk to himself." Witsell's voice rose, "Then, when *Pearl Harbor* was hit, he offered his services without pay to the War Department, and became Chief of the Intelligence Branch, Signal Corps...

"Soon after, he was ordered to Australia, where his new assignment demanded the full use of his mastery of the Japanese language and psychology, as well as his genius for organizing. There, he developed and led a top-secret organization known as ATIS, which grew to the strength of six-hundred officers and four-thousand men, drawn from all the armed services, including Allied and American.

"From within that organization he established forty-five advanced echelons trained for front-line interrogation and translation on the battlefront...Three-hundred-and-twenty-five of his men were eventually decorated or cited.

"ATIS also handled the vast majority of Japanese prisoners, interrogating fourteen-thousand in all, and analyzing more than a million documents retrieved from the Pacific battlefront."

Witsell looked up from the prepared statement, toward the Congressional members..."So important was this continuous flow of enemy intelligence, that it not only influenced day-to-day Pacific operations, *it also significantly shaped strategy for major battles*. Without it, MacArthur's brilliant and almost bloodless landing operations would have been impossible!

"Based on these accomplishments, Colonel Sidney Mashbir has *five times* been recommended for promotion to the grade of Brigadier General by General MacArthur himself!"

Witsell returned to his seat.

"This is going to be harder than we planned, Robinson," a Congressman whispered to his colleague."

"Don't worry, keep things moving. We'll deal with it in closed session."

"Thank you, General Witsell," Robinson said. "Your remarks are duly noted."

Rear Admiral Ellis Zacharias spoke next.

"Esteemed committee members, until recent poor health slowed me down, I was the Deputy Chief of Naval Intelligence...For many years, I've also worked with Colonel Mashbir. On reviewing his military records, I can understand that you as outsiders, viewing what is currently contained, would have questions. Several very positive documents attesting to his accomplishments have been removed, and certain inappropriate ones cast a dark shadow."

He shifted his weight, supporting himself with his cane.

"But all that should have been cleared up in past hearings," he said, his voice intensifying. "To give you an idea how much our country owes this man, it is my strong belief that Colonel Mashbir took a *unique central role* in providing and sharing vital intelligence, bridging the various branches of the U.S. military and the Allies in general...And further, without his radio broadcasts to Japan and his influence in incorporating the Emperor into the peace process, the war might well have continued, necessitating the invasion of the Japanese mainland, which could have cost an additional half-million American soldiers' lives! And who knows how many millions of Japanese civilians?"

Zacharias pointed at the panel.

"How can you not correct this obvious injustice to a *True Patriot*?"

Attorney Powell came forward, pulling a letter from his brief case.

"This is from General Pershing," he declared, *"the Commander of the entire Armed forces in World War One!*

"I would like to read it to you." He began:

> *"'I do swear to the loyalty and dedication to service that Colonel Mashbir displayed during his years as my aide in Mexico, where he went on assorted dangerous reconnaissance missions.*
>
> *As supervisor of our counter-intelligence branch, Colonel Mashbir uncovered the largest domestic German spy ring prior to and during World War One.*
>
> *This man has had an injustice against him, preventing his reinstatement into the Regular Army, which would allow his promotion to Brigadier General.*
>
> *Sincerely, General John J. Pershing.'"*

Senator Robinson loosened his tie and undid his top shirt button.

"Please give us that letter, so we can pass it around." Sweat flowed down Robinson's forehead as he conferred with his colleagues.

Another congressman spoke. "I understand Mashbir will be retiring soon. We've been told that millions of dollars went through his company paying for military-related projects. If he gets back into the Regular Army, let alone gets promoted, he'll receive full military retirement benefits, when he's probably made a fortune already."

"I'll answer that remark myself," Mashbir said, coming to his feet.

"You're right, a lot money flowed through my company, *but we were in a battle for our survival!* President Franklin Roosevelt said he didn't want to see this conflict create a single war millionaire. I, for one, couldn't stomach making excessive profits. As a matter of fact, by the time the war ended, *I was in the hole,* my company deep in debt. I paid those debts from my own personal savings. I'm managing now, but I am by no means wealthy."

Powell stood. "You've now heard oral and written testimony from three generals and an admiral. *What else do you need, a sign from the Almighty above to remedy this injustice?"*

Robinson's jaw tightened. "We appreciate your statements, and will adjourn until 1:00 P.M. this afternoon."

In a private Congressional meeting room, Robinson put the matter before his colleagues:

"The fact is, General MacArthur is practically ruling Japan and is more popular than ever in America. He'd like to run for President in '52. And while it's possible he could get elected, his autocratic style would be a disaster for our nation!

"We're finally at peace. And while people admire military heroes, the public doesn't want another war in Asia, *but now* against the Communists."

He flung out his arms dramatically. "I'm keeping partisan politics out of this matter."

His voice softened. "Now, General Eisenhower is a different proposition. He can go either Democratic or Republican, *and he'd win!"*

He slapped the table in front of him.

"It's our responsibility that MacArthur and his top staff get the clear message that Congress wants no part of them."

"That isn't fair," another replied.

"I agree with Congresswoman McKenna," an older Congressmen

declared. "I was in the Great War serving under Pershing. If he says this man deserves his due, I, for one, want that to happen."

"We need to think about the big picture, Congressman Milano," Robinson countered. "What's best for the country!"

"So we just pretend this man never did the things his colleagues have sworn to?"

Robinson smiled. "Okay, here's the compromise. We won't stand in the way of his being reassigned to the Regular Army, *but* only after additional hearings. He'll probably just give up on the whole thing."

"That's a compromise?" the Congresswoman said. "We've got to clear his name, at the very least."

"All right, I wish it were otherwise," Robinson replied, "but the benefits gained under Eisenhower are far more important than the giving of a *single promotion*, regardless of past services."

The members, one at a time, all transmitted their acceptance with a nod.

Senate Hearing Room, 1:00 P.M. that same day

Robinson spoke without looking at Mashbir.

"After much deliberation, we've decided not to stand in the way of Colonel Mashbir's reinstatement."

A wave of relief washed over Sidney and his supporters.

"However," the congressman continued, "that process will require additional hearings."

"What!?" Powell shot upright.

Robinson held up a restraining hand. "More immediately, we're instructing all federal agencies to remove from the Colonel's records any inappropriate and unfounded remarks. And, we commend the Colonel for his long and distinguished career."

Robinson slammed his gavel down.

"This hearing is now closed."

"This is ridiculous!" Powell yelled.

Sidney turned to him. "It's time to move on," he said.

"But what about your promotion?" Zach said.

Sidney shrugged, while looking away, then turned to his companions.

"Gentlemen, I thank you for all your efforts on my behalf."

As Mashbir and Zacharias moved toward the exit, the Congresswoman and the World War I veteran intercepted them.

As *she* searched for words, Sidney smiled, "I understand, it's more than just about me. It's probably part of some bigger political agenda, and I'm just collateral damage—I'm a soldier, and I can handle it."

Her voice wavered. "Colonel, the members of this committee give our heartfelt appreciation for all you've done, and apologize for having you go through this grilling—*Someday*, when the political winds change, you'll get your deserved promotion, I'm sure of it!"

"Thanks, Ma'am. But I was warned by a good friend of mine thirty years ago," he turned to Zach, "that if I chose a career in Espionage, many of my accomplishments wouldn't be known about to back me up if I got into trouble—*Or* if I were being considered for promotion . . . *And in spite of that, I'd do it all again.*"

"Good luck," she replied.

The veteran stepped forward.

"It would be an honor to shake your hand, Colonel."

This was followed by a solemn salute, which was returned.

When he arrived back at his home, Sidney avoided Donald and Irene's gaze.

"How'd it go, Dad?"

Struggling to contain bitterness welling up, he replied, "The good news is, my military records will be cleaned up. As for that promotion to General, I can kiss that good-bye.

"But never mind," he said, regaining a positive tone. "Donald, I have something I've been meaning to give you."

Donald admired the gold pocket watch and examined the small photograph inside.

"Those are your grandparents, and me at age four with my younger brother, Michael, who passed on...Your grandfather and I, didn't get along too well, but I'm sure he'd be glad to know I passed his gift on to you." He tried to hold back tears. "Donald, I've often wished I'd been a better father to you."

"Yes, father, there were times when you were hard and cold, so busy and distant. But one day, Admiral Zacharias took me aside and gave me an idea how much you sacrificed and accomplished. I truly respect you—Please wait here, I have something to show you."

Donald rushed back with a leaf of age-yellowed paper. "Forrester gave me this letter you wrote him before going on a dangerous mission, from which you might not return. He thought it might help me to better understand you."

He handed it to his father, who read it silently:

> *Dear Forrester,*
>
> *I'm writing even though I know you're too young at this moment to understand. I've been away much of your life. It wasn't an easy choice. My parents raised me with certain values: Never give up in a struggle if you feel it's significant and a devotion to our country; America is a great nation, its democratic freedoms are to be treasured.*
>
> *Your grandfather said patriots fight wars for their country, but emphasized it was also patriotic to prevent the outbreak of unnecessary wars. And to better do that, one has to understand the language and culture of other countries, so as to see their perspectives. I have devoted much of my life to that pursuit.*
>
> *I hope you'll understand these ideas someday. I love you more than you can imagine. Please give a kiss to your mother.*
>
> *Sincerely, Your Daddy*

When his father was done reading, Donald said, "After the divorce, Forrester told me, he'd sworn to his mother to cut all ties, but he really cares for you. You inspired him to reach the rank of Army Captain."

Irene stroked her husband's hair. "Do you know *what I love about you*? In spite of all you've seen and gone through, you've kept your humanity when dealing with the Japanese! You've guided our country to treat them as compassionately as possible, so that they would become—and remain our good ally with a Democracy at their helm."

Sidney hugged them.

"I'm so lucky to have you both in my life!"

They remained silent for a long moment—each appreciating the other two and feeling close and safe.

"Thank you so much," Sidney said. "I'm going to my office for a while—I've some things on my mind."

Once in his quiet retreat, he looked around; his attention was drawn to a small stone carving of two dragons intertwined.

Oh, it's that gift from Lee's grandfather, from when I rescued those Chinese councilmen in Vladivostok, back in 1923. They did say it brought good luck. In spite of assorted aches and pains—he rubbed his side—*I'm still around.*

He laughed.

A brown-tinted, miniature photo snapshot next caught his eye. It was of him and his American relief team in front of the Imperial Hotel, proudly lined up in camaraderie, after toiling for months assisting the Japanese following the Great Kanto Earthquake.

He surveyed assorted photos adorning the walls, some of Emperor Hirohito and General MacArthur; others of the Signing Ceremony aboard the *U.S.S. Missouri.*

A group photo, with Prince Tokugawa with Sidney seated at his side, stirred his emotions . . .

My dear friend, I wish I could fully reveal your great deeds as one of the Fathers of Modern Japan, whose values went beyond national borders, Bridging East and West!

You and your compatriots have my deepest respect for putting your lives on the line, struggling to hold your country together while promoting Peace, Democracy, and International arms limitations!

I wonder, Prince Tokugawa, if you'll ever receive your deserved recognition? Perhaps a holiday commemorating your birthday, July 11th, 1863, accompanied by an international essay-writing contest in schools—just like those you created in Japan in the 1920s, honoring Abraham Lincoln's significant accomplishments and values.

But this time, they'd be honoring you, with the winning students receiving a commemorative coin with your likeness stamped upon it.

Sidney smiled.

Iyesato, you rascal! By working masterfully behind the scenes you achieved so much more, but your world influence has never fully been acknowledged. Had you only lived a few years longer, your guiding presence would have kept Japan from joining the Axis Powers!

And who would have imagined that by using your influence as President of the Japanese Red Cross to create Safe Zones in Japanese-controlled areas of China, such as Shanghai, prior to World War II, would help save a half million Chinese civilian lives!

And in spite of Hitler's pressure on Japan to expel its resident Jews and those living in those Safe Zones to European concentration camps, Japan refused and instead allowed them to remain in those Safe Zones, thus saving tens of thousands of Jewish refugees, with the resident Chinese populace supportive of this process.

Sitting at his desk, he took a deep breath and pondered…

Maybe Zach's suggestion that I write my memoirs is a good idea, with the goal of encouraging America's Intelligence organizations and the general public to stay ever vigilant against those who would trample our Democracy.

Confronting his typewriter, he stared at the blank page.

Where do I start?

I've sworn to General MacArthur, a man I so respect, not to discuss my personal dealings with the Emperor in my future writings. He emphasized that the priority of reestablishing America and Japan as allies required leaving much of the past behind and moving forward…So, if I exclude what I've personally sworn not to talk about, combined with all that's classified or top secret . . .

He tapped his desk.

By golly, a spy writing his memoirs isn't going to be easy.

Plenty of reading between the lines.

I'll give it my best: At the very least, I ought to come up with a title. Something catchy❋

A ray of light appeared as he typed:

I Was an American Spy

EPILOGUE

During his retirement, Colonel Mashbir continued his active membership in **Rotary,** and also gave U.S.-Japan cultural goodwill presentations to various other organizations.

However, if an international crisis arose linked to his expertise, Mashbir would offer his strategic advice to the highest level members of the diplomatic, military, and intelligence community.

Mashbir died in 1973 at the age of 82, and was buried at Fort Rosecrans National Cemetery in Point Loma, San Diego County, California. He was posthumously honored by being inducted into the *Military Intelligence Corps Hall of Fame* in 1988. Despite this recognition, *little until now* has been written about him or those who served under his leadership because of the highly classified nature of their significant contributions.

Finally, sixty-five years after the end of WWII, those serving under Mashbir's command in ATIS, were recognized, receiving the United States' highest civilian honor for bravery and heroism.

In 2010, *President Barack Obama* **signed a bill awarding the** *Congressional Gold Medal* to the Japanese-Americans in Military Intelligence Service (MIS) who had served under Colonel Mashbir in the Pacific. This medal was also awarded to the 100th/442nd Army units, who served in Europe; known by their gutsy "Go for Broke" motto, for its size, it was one of the most decorated U.S. Army units composed mostly of Japanese-Americans who fought in France and Italy.

A ceremony was to be held outside at the *National World War II Memorial on the National Mall,* but due to cold weather the organizers worried about the health of the elderly veterans attending. Instead, it took place at *Emancipation Hall* in the U.S. Capitol. A gala dinner event was held that evening with three thousand attendees, including five U.S. Senators, honoring those who had served their country so long ago.

As revealed in this novel, the thousands of ATIS members were acknowledged for translating and interpreting strategic documents, interrogating Japanese POWs, deciphering enemy radio messages, and working as undercover agents. They also accompanied troops to the battlefront, dramatically affecting the course of the war. Many ATIS translators actively engaged in the important subsequent peaceful occupation and reconstruction of Japan.

Colonel Mashbir was quoted in a news release after the war, stating:

"America owes a debt to these men and to their families, which it can never fully repay."

The Congressional Gold Medal they received declared the following:

"The United States remains forever indebted to the bravery, valor and dedication to country of these men, while fighting a two-fronted battle of discrimination at home and fascism abroad. Their commitment and sacrifice demonstrates a highly uncommon and commendable sense of patriotism and honor."

Those serving under Colonel Mashbir's command finally received their long-deserved recognition. *Perhaps, the time is right for Colonel Mashbir to be reconsidered for that promotion to Brigadier General that he so richly earned*—though posthumous, that recognition of his sacrifices and contributions to our victory in the Pacific would go a long ways towards setting the record straight.

In 2017, based on historical materials sent by the author to the ROTC programs at the *University of Arizona* and *Syracuse University*, *they both* nominated Colonel Mashbir to be considered for inclusion into the national ROTC Hall of Fame, for his contributions to our national security preparedness.

Important Historical note linked to **Chapter 54:**

-*The Emperor and the Spy* presents Colonel Mashbir working closely with **Japanese Foreign Minister Okazaki,** just after the end of WWII. The novel's portrayal was factually **based upon** *Colonel Mashbir's autobiography I Was an American Spy,* published 1953. Colonel Mashbir describes Minister Okazaki as a sincere person who fully cooperated with the Allies in arranging the *Surrender Signing Ceremony,* thus officially bringing the war to a close. Minister Okazaki also anticipated and fully assisted in arranging for Emperor Hirohito to voluntarily make eleven unprecedented visits to General Douglas MacArthur at the general's headquarters, so that these two leaders could *together* plan the future of Japan...In his autobiography, Mashbir emphasized that Minister Okazaki responded truly shocked and unaware of the war crimes committed by certain Japanese leaders during WWII. Mashbir stated that when Minister Okazaki heard about those crimes, Okazaki strongly desired that Japan prosecute those who had committed such assaults against humanity, even if the Allies did not wish to do so themselves. Based on this, Mashbir believed that if someone in as high a political position throughout the war as Minister Okazaki wasn't aware of these crimes, then it was likely that much of Japan's leadership were also not aware or involved.

****

Following the publication of the Print and EBook editions of *The Emperor and the Spy*, a dramatically engaging **Audio book** presentation of the novel was created which is available online on Amazon.

In 2018, Colonel Mashbir's 1953 autobiography *I Was an American Spy* was republished as an eBook on its 65th Anniversary. It is accessible through the Amazon website by entering the title: *I Was an American Spy* by Colonel Mashbir. If a general Google search is done, only the 1953 out-of-print edition results, with very few copies available.

To honor the memory of Colonel Mashbir and his allies, the author has given presentations to a large veterans' group; to soldiers at *Camp Pendleton Marine Base*; to *Rotary chapters in the cities of Del Mar and Oceanside, California*; at city libraries in *Carlsbad*, Vista, and Fallbrook; also to Book Club gatherings, and a presentation for a hospital fundraiser.

In recognition of *Veterans Day Weekend*, the novel was selected by *Barnes & Noble for a book signing event*.

A presentation was also given to several high school classes at Canyon Crest Academy in Carmel Valley, California.

On June 22nd, 2016 the *Office of the Prime Minister of Japan* sent a diplomatic/educational delegation to the *Joan Kroc Peace and Justice Center* on the campus of the **University of San Diego**. A book signing for *The Emperor and the Spy* was included at this event. The Japanese representatives and the San Diego World Affairs Council that hosted the event, both appreciated that this novel honors past leaders of their nations, who heroically attempted to prevent war. *TheEmperorAndTheSpy.com* website offers a link to this goodwill event.

As for **Emperor Hirohito and Empress Nagako**, they lived long lives, bringing prosperity and healing to their nation. Emperor Hirohito's rule continued until 1989, and was followed by his son, Emperor Akihito and his son's wife, the Empress Michiko, whose reign continued into the twenty-first century. They, and their family were ambassadors of peace and understanding around the world... During 2019, the oldest son of Emperor Akihito and Empress Michiko, Crown Prince Naruhito and his wife Crown Princess Masako, will become the next Emperor and Empress of Japan.

Regarding **Prince Iyesato Tokugawa**, little had been written about him for many decades, until 2010, when a Princeton publication by Marcia R. Ristaino was released, titled, *The Jacquinot Safe Zone, Wartime Refugees in Shanghai*. The author only briefly mentions

Prince Tokugawa's role as *President of the Japanese Red Cross*, and him allying with the *President of the Chinese Red Cross* and a Jesuit priest, **Jacquinot**, to create *Safe Zones* that helped save the lives of a half-million Chinese civilians and tens of thousands of Jewish refugees fleeing the Holocaust in Europe during the years leading up to, and during, WWII—Prince Tokugawa courageously stood up against militant fascists, while shielding these innocent lives. To bring recognition to Prince Iyesato Tokugawa's many accomplishments, the author of this novel has completed an **illustrated biography** about Prince Tokugawa, which further details his impressive life. The book is titled:

THE ART OF PEACE: Prince Tokugawa Heir to the Last Shogun of Japan. This biography is available as a 'general reader' edition or in an *'expanded'* edition with an additional 100 pages of historical notes and a comprehensive index to aid in historical research. Both share a majority of the same hundreds of illustrations, many significant and never-before-available.

An application in Prince Tokugawa's name is being made for him to be considered as one of the **Righteous Among the Nations**, an official title awarded by the memorial organization **Yad Vashem** on behalf of the State of Israel and the Jewish people. It is given to non-Jews who risked their lives to save Jews during the Holocaust.

A commemorative bronze statue or plaque honoring Prince Tokugawa and his ally Sidney Mashbir is also under consideration. One possible location where it could be seen by visitors from around the world, is at the *Japanese Tea Garden in San Diego's Balboa Park*. The commemorative design might be inspired by a photo of them seated together, in recognition of their efforts to bridge the U.S. and Japan in friendship. Similar commemoratives might be placed in other cities in the U.S. and in Japan. It would express appreciation for their courageous partnership and might positively influence how we treat one another in a world that technological advances have shrunk to a dimension that would have astounded both Colonel Mashbir and Prince Tokugawa.

Prince Iyesato Tokugawa and Baron Eiichi Shibusawa were lifelong friends and allies who strove to maintain international goodwill, while encouraging higher ethics in business, politics, and social welfare. Plans are underway to gift *The Shibusawa Eiichi Memorial Foundation and Shibusawa Memorial Museum* in Tokyo, with historically significant photos that were discovered by the author while researching for this novel and the Prince Tokugawa biography. These photos are linked to Baron Shibusawa and Prince Tokugawa diplomatic efforts.

As for novel's character **Beate Sirota**, who was involved in the creation of the Japanese Constitution: she became known as the *Mother of Women's Rights in Japan*. In her later years, Beate wrote an autobiography titled, *The Only Woman in the Room.*

TheEmperorAndTheSpy.com website offers an illustrated time-line that displays a selection of Colonel Mashbir's photos and written documents. This *time capsule* reveals some of the material that inspired the book.

It is hoped the combination of **The Emperor and the Spy** novel along with the Prince Tokugawa illustrated biography **The Art of Peace**, will find their way into academic curriculum to encourage gratitude for Democratic principles and an greater appreciation for cultural diversity, while promoting the art of diplomacy in the pursuit of peace.

Acknowledgment goes out for the very helpful editorial suggestions given by Mike Sirota, Thorn Sully, Sheila Shabaz, and Hilliard Harper. Special thanks go to Kazuo Kodama, former Japanese Ambassador to the United Nations and current Japanese Ambassador to the European Union, for his many thoughtful insights which influenced the novel and the website linked to it.

Deep appreciation goes to friends, neighbors, and family members who offered constructive feedback on the evolving manuscript.

Karla Olson, President/Founder of Publishers and Writers of San Diego, organized many informative conferences on book publishing. Thanks go to Judy Bernstein (author of *They Poured Fire on Us From the Sky: The True Story of Three Lost Boys from Sudan*) for her literary comments on the novel early in its progress. Thanks go to Barbara Villaseñor, for her publishing suggestions. Recognition goes to Charles Wyatt, former lieutenant, U.S. Navy, for sharing his many insights on American military history.

For several years, literary agent and intellectual property specialist, Ellen Stiefler, represented and graciously supported the project.

Appreciation is given to brick-and-mortar bookstores, new and used, which offer a hands-on connection to reading and research.

Thanks go to: Attorney Valerie Ann Nemeth; to proofreader Lisa Wolf; proofreader David Cohen; and to book-formatter Tim Brittain.

To better understand the *inner* workings of current events, for many years I've been member of the *San Diego World Affairs Council, which is part of the World Affairs Councils of America, a national organization.* Through this fine educational group, I've attended many fascinating presentations given by ambassadors, consul generals, and other political, academic, business, and military representatives from around the globe. I've also enjoyed the camaraderie of the general membership of this organization, many of whom have engaged in cultural and governmental activities as a volunteer or as a career. Special recognition goes to David Edick Jr., former President of the San Diego Chapter of this organization and to Rita Lim-Wilby, Chairman of Programming, for their support of the novel.

Questions and Topics for Classroom Discussion and Book Club Reading Groups

1. How does the current world of Intelligence gathering compare to that of Colonel Mashbir's time? What are some of the similarities? What are some differences?

2. Colonel Mashbir and those under his command in ATIS, oversaw the treatment and interrogation of the majority of *Japanese Prisoners of War* during WWII. How does that situation compare to what we face today in the war against terrorism?

3. Were there any insights gained from *The Emperor and the Spy* related to Japanese-American history that surprised you?

4. Can you think of other novels or biographies you've read that present spies in a similar or different fashion?

5. **TheEmperorAndTheSpy.com** presents an *Illustrated Timeline* displaying an assortment of items from Mashbir's personal collection. Do you believe this novel could have been written without access to these documents, photos and personal keepsakes of this master spy?

6. Imagine you're describing the novel's main protagonists to a friend. How would you do so?

7. Which of the novel's characters would you wish to meet if you could? Are there any questions you'd ask of them?

8. What would it have been like to have lived during that period? How does it compare to the world of today?

9. Are you motivated to read other books on this period of history? While reading, did you research any of the topics in this novel to confirm the details depicted or to get further insights?